THE HEART
OF WAR

JEN KINGSFORD

The Heart of War

First published in Australia by Jen Kingsford 2023

*A catalogue record for this
book is available from the
National Library of Australia*

ISBN: 978-0-6486042-0-4 (pbk)
ISBN: 978-0-6486042-1-1 (ebk)

Cover photography by Kochneva Tetya (shutterstock) © 2023

Typesetting and design by Publicious Book Publishing
Published with the assistance of Publicious Book Publishing
www.publicious.com.au

This novel is dedicated to the military men in my family, to all who have served, and their families.

Firstly, as this novel was inspired by his service on the Western Front, in which he made the ultimate sacrifice, I offer a special tribute to my great, great uncle, Bernard Ambrose Coyte of the Australian Imperial Force- World War I. To my grandfather, Ignatius John Coyte, who served in the Australian Military Forces- World War II, and Dad, Alan James Coyte O.A.M who served in the Royal Australian Air Force and United Nations forces, much love and gratitude.

Thank you for keeping us safe.

PROLOGUE

Leura, Australia 1908

The book slammed shut on her fingers. Rose nursed them in her lap and kept her head down.

'What have I told you about taking my medical books? They are not suitable reading for a young lady.' Her father took the tome from the dining room table. He then noticed her rag doll, needle and thread. 'Stop torturing your poor dolls. Sewing stitches into real flesh is much harder than playing dolls. Go and help your mother with the darning.'

'What is all of the fuss going on in here?' Maman asked. She took in the scene and sighed, her beautiful eyes conveying concern and sympathy. 'Oh, Rose. Not again.'

Her younger brother stuck his tongue out at her from the doorway.

Rose tucked her pout back in and grabbed her tattered doll. 'I wanted to know how to—'

Her father's thunderous frown swallowed her words. The mantle clock ticked until she could stand it no more.

'Fine, I am sorry.' She shoved past her lanky brother.

'She'll never find a good husband and settle with that attitude.' Her father's words echoed as she stomped away from the weatherboard mountains cottage into the garden. She settled under her favourite gum tree. She let the blend of eucalyptus and wood smoke sooth her. A magpie gave her a baleful look from above.

'It's not fair,' she told the bird. 'I don't want to sew socks for some silly husband. I want to be a doctor.'

The magpie cocked its head as if it was interested in her plight, so she kept talking. 'But no, it will be my horrid brother who gets to do that. Maybe if I showed him I could stitch someone, he'd take me more seriously.'

The magpie warbled its agreement. She set her jaw. That's what she'd do.

She crept into her father's clinic room at the front of the house and opened cupboards and drawers looking for what she needed.

'Hey, we're not allowed in here,' Eddie said.

Putting a hand to her already thudding heart, she turned and frowned at him. 'Get out.'

He started poking around too. 'What are you doing?'

Rose resumed her search. 'I need that sharp knife thing that Father uses to cut people with. I'm going to cut my leg then stitch it up to show him I could make a good doctor.'

He grimaced. 'Won't that hurt?'

'Probably.'

He shrugged and opened a glass cabinet door. 'I don't know why you'd want to be a doctor anyway. Seeing blood makes me want to vomit.'

Rose rolled her eyes. Some legacy he was going to be.

Before she could scour among the medicine bottles, her brother yelled in triumph, 'I found it.'

She turned.

Rose blinked as a spray of blood splattered her face. Her open mouth caught some, but she barely noticed the metallic taste as she watched the fountain pooling at her feet. Her eyes connected with the wild roll of her younger brother's.

She suppressed a rising scream and willed her frozen limbs to move. Grabbing wildly at anything, she tried to stem the flow. Eddie's cheeks became waxy and his hand floppy.

'No, no, no,' she chanted, getting louder with each word.

The door slammed open and her father's usually florid face paled.

'What have you done?' he whispered as he shoved her aside.

She landed in the blood, sliding along the wood, feeling it seep into her skirt and onto her trembling legs.

She watched the flurry of her father's hands finally still.

'I tried to save him,' she whispered.

Her father rounded on her. 'He's dead.'

PART ONE:

AUSTRALIA (1915-1916)

Chapter One

Leo's legs burned as he scrambled through the spindly scrub. He could hear the puff of breath and thud of feet right behind him. Adrenalin fired through him as he slid down a dusty embankment. His dry lips sucked in hot air that seared, leaving him gasping. He plunged into the olive-green water of Borenore Creek.

A hand gripped Leo's head, shoving him under. Muddy water filled his nose. He had no time to draw a breath. His throat clamped. He thrashed about until he found the strong arm holding him and squeezed it hard—twice. The pressure was released instantly.

Bursting to the surface with a splutter, Leo finally caught his breath.

'Hell's bells! Let me get over the race first before you try and drown me,' Leo gasped. 'I didn't even have time to get my gear off.'

'Awww, you sound just like a girl,' his younger brother, Oskar, said, patting him on the head.

Leo shook his brown mop. 'No, really. You're getting a bit carried away lately ... always got the shits.'

'I know. Things are getting a bit ... look, it's not that easy with the war and all.' What was Oskar going on about? Things were fine.

'Nothing much has changed for us,' Leo said.

'We'll talk about it later.' Oskar swam a couple of strokes then floated on his back.

Leo said nothing.

Before they could get into it more, his best mate, Harry, arrived. He stripped off and with a wild yell, divebombed them.

After a long day working the vineyards with Pa, they were in no hurry to leave the cool waters of the creek, staying in until their fingers puckered like prunes. Reluctantly, they got out and trudged in companionable silence along a cart track carved between the scribbly gums. Leo and Oskar squelched along in their wet boots, knowing their ma was going to be less than impressed when they showed. Leo paused to pluck an orchid growing in a grassy rut.

'Would that be for Miss Abigail?' Oskar asked with a wide grin.

Leo sighed and smacked Oskar's arm. It was for his Ma. He was tired of Oskar having a go about him being shy around the girls.

The light was fading fast, but Leo could see the dim outline of their corrugated iron homestead. Wafts of rabbit stew mingled with the scent of the lemon myrtle that grew nearby. He breathed deeply.

Harry's eyes narrowed. 'What's the police buggy doing here?'

They all bolted for the house.

Constable Peterson was slurping a cup of tea in the parlour, reclining with a gentle sway to and fro in Pa's favourite cedar rocking chair. His feet were stretched out lazily towards the amber glow of the fire. Pa and Ma sat stiffly on mahogany rail back chairs.

'I was just admiring your ma's handiwork. She's talented, isn't she?' Peterson waved a hand towards the newly stencilled wallpaper. Ma had expertly painted a detailed frieze of gum leaves and flannel flowers surrounding a waratah centrepiece.

Leo nodded to Peterson then exchanged a nervous glance with Oskar. He moved to the fire and warmed his hands with barely a glance to Peterson, then leaned against the piano. The policeman hoisted himself up and handed Ma his teacup and saucer. It clattered as her hands shook. His ma's eyes were red rimmed and Pa's weathered face was pale and drawn. Leo's ten-year-old sister, Dot, hovered near the door. Leo gave a slight nod and Harry led her away.

Peterson casually scratched his bulbous nose. 'I need to take you in for further questioning.'

'I've already registered as an alien. I don't understand.' Pa's usually resonant voice was barely a whisper.

Peterson smirked. 'Yes, you are an alien, being of German and therefore enemy origin, and there have been some serious allegations against this family for expressing anti-British sentiments. Mr Diemant,

Demandt, Dymond or whatever it is you lot call yourself these days, I have to take these allegations seriously.'

'That's a load of—' Leo faltered as he noted the terrified look on his ma's face.

'What will happen if you believe these allegations?' Oskar asked.

Leo noticed the gleam of Pa's wedding ring as he twisted it in circles.

'If I am satisfied these allegations are indeed true then your Pa will be sent to an internment camp—probably Holsworthy—or perhaps deported back to Germany.'

Ma stifled a gasp and dropped the teacup and saucer, sending china scattering over the floorboards. The fire spat and Leo jumped, smacking his back on the piano.

Pa narrowed his eyes and he pulled himself up to full height.

'I've been here for thirty-five years. I bloomin' well fought in the Boer War for this country,' Pa said as he grabbed the fire poker.

Leo's heart froze. He wouldn't. Peterson's eyes widened and he rocked his chair so far back it nearly tipped.

'Kasper!' Ma was at her husband's elbow before Leo could blink.

His pa's jaw clenched as his hand tightened on the poker. He took a deep breath and threw a log on, poking it into place with a shower of sparks.

Ma patted his hand once the poker was stashed back in place. Leo had rarely seen his pa's temper get the better of him.

Peterson grunted as he launched himself up. 'None of that matters. Germany's our enemy now. Let's get going.'

Pa's hand shook as he laid a hand on Ma's shoulders. 'I'll be fine, love, it's all a mistake. It'll be cleared up in no time. Don't you worry; I'll be back in time for pudding.' Ma nodded but tears trickled down her pale cheeks.

Leo's mind whirled. What rotten mongrel would have told the police such lies?

Dot burst into the room and latched onto Pa as he took his hat from the hook behind the front door.

'It's okay, Dottie. I'll be back soon. Let go, now.' Pa stroked her head and gave a weak smile to Leo, who tried to pry her loose. Her screams pierced Leo's ears.

'Now, now, Miss. That's no way to behave.' Peterson waggled a finger at her and Dot turned away, burying her head in Leo's chest. He hugged her tight and breathed in hard against the burn of his tears.

Peterson glared at Dot then Leo. 'That army recruitment march is coming through soon. Might be a good idea to prove what side your bread is buttered before I have to come back and round the lot of you up.'

Pa tipped his hat and walked out into the night. Leo held Dot, trying to sooth her, but her keening continued to vibrate through his every fibre. He stared into the space that had once held Pa. Leo unclenched his hand and the forgotten orchid for Ma dropped to the floor.

Chapter Two

October 1915
Orange, Australia

'They're coming!' Dot squeezed Leo's hand so tight his fingertips were the colour of beetroot. Leo had secured them a good spot on a verandah right near the town hall. The *rump-pump-pump* of Orange's town band led the men from Gilgandra up Summer Street.

Despite being caught in an earlier downpour, the bedraggled army recruits had ear-wide grins. Flags flapped from every building, buggy and hand. Harry nearly blasted Leo's ear off with a whistle and then both he and Harry cupped their hands and cried out 'Coo-ee!' The column of over a hundred men responded in rowdy unison before coming to a halt.

A couple of the Coo-ee marchers looked at the packed verandah. They were two of the stockiest blokes Leo had ever seen.

'Hey, coves. Why don't you come and join us?' one of them called out to Harry and Leo. Leo flushed. Did he have what it takes to go to war?

'Blood oath!' Harry called. 'I'll be joining up quicker than ol' Mad Dog Morgan can steal a horse.' He sounded so confident.

The sunburnt recruits grinned, tipped their sodden hats and turned their attention to the mayor of Orange, Alderman McNeilly, who had begun his welcome speech.

'Better get comfortable, Dot.' Leo settled against a wooden pole.

'Ah, there you are. Can you believe this crowd?' Oskar pushed his way through to them. He pointed to the soldiers from Sydney that had come to form a guard of honour for the new recruits from the bush. 'Look at those flash army uniforms. I'm sure that mob will do a grand job over there.'

The men looked strong and almost regal—big Aussie blokes ready to sacrifice it all. Peterson had sent his pa off to an internment camp that was hours away. Leo knew what he had to do.

A cry went up for Captain Hitchen.

'Why's everyone so excited? Who's that?' Dot leapt up and craned her neck.

'Captain Hitchen got worried that the blokes over in Gallipoli need a bit more of a hand, so he's started what they call a snowball march to get some more recruits for the army,' Leo answered. Dot didn't need to know that it had more to do with people knowing more about the bloodbath of Gallipoli and not being so keen to join up.

'A march to throw snowballs? I don't think that'll help much.' Dot frowned and Leo laughed.

'No, silly billy. It means that the numbers will grow like a snowball, collecting more men in each town as they go.'

Dot nodded but Leo doubted she really understood.

Bill Hitchen barely greeted them before introducing the army chaplain and recruitment speaker, John Lee. Lee was a slender man with boyish looks, but his voice was strong and fired with passion.

'I thank you all for being here and for such a welcome. We might only be boys from Gilgandra, but we are going on the greatest and most glorious march. We will be remembered as the boys who answered the call from those brave chaps in the trenches who have gone before us. The soldiers in the Dardanelles need our help if we are to subvert the enemies of righteousness. God is in His heaven, and all is right in the world. We will join them and right and truth will prevail. We will win this war!'

The crowd erupted into a deafening roar. Leo's heart swelled. He was going to prove he was a good Aussie. Lee's eyes bored into the crowd and Leo felt their fiery intensity.

'The boys need our help. The odds are against them. All of you fine, young men are needed so step forward and be counted. Come! Come! Come!' Lee encouraged.

The chant was taken up by the recruits then the crowd.

'I'll come!' Harry stepped out. He straightened his shoulders and puffed out his chest. The Gilgandra Coo-ees clapped and cheered while the crowd waved their flags madly. Leo pushed forward. 'I'm in too'.

Oskar stepped up as well. The Coo-ees cheered and gave them sharp salutes. Only a few other men joined the ranks and Leo thought it was a bit of a poor show considering the number of strapping young blokes in the crowd.

He looked behind and saw Dot's peaked face. Her mouth was open, but she wasn't saying a word. Leo motioned for the mother of Dot's best friend, Mrs Nonnenmacher, to take care of her.

Mrs Nonnenmacher poked a finger in Leo's chest and shook her head at Oskar. 'Your ma won't like this. Come on, Dot. I've got an apple strudel at home that has your name on it.'

Leo nodded his thanks and ignored the flash of guilt. Ma and Dot would be fine. Surely, after everything that happened with Pa, she'd understand this was the best way. He had to join the army. Excitement and fear collided, leaving a fizz in his belly. The men of the march were dismissed and headed off to a banquet under the pavilion at Wade Park while Leo followed the newest recruits to the town hall.

Oskar hesitated at the enormous, panelled door.

'Come on Oskar, you can't back out now.' Leo nudged him into the cavernous hall foyer. 'You stood up in front of the whole town; they'll call you a shirker forever.'

Harry gave Oskar a wink. 'What are you waiting for? It'll be great. We'll see the world, shoot a few Fritzes and be on our way home to Aus with a swag of medals. We'll be heroes.'

'Okay, but maybe I should stay home and help Ma. They'll know I'm not old enough.' Oskar shuffled his feet from side to side; his face drained of all colour.

'Lie. Leo and me are going to,' Harry reassured him. The other boys were inside being lined up. A lanky man with a greying moustache and spectacles that kept sliding to the tip of his nose looked at them expectantly.

'Are you coming in or not? I'd like to get these medicals done before my meal gets cold.' The medical officer waved an arm directing them to enter. Oskar gave a panicked hiccup but followed them in. They made their way down a marble hallway into the Council Chambers.

'We might not get in anyway.' Leo's voice echoed as they entered a green room that smelled of leather. Maybe it would be better if Oskar stayed behind.

'I need to check everyone is in tip-top shape and mark down scars and such, so please remove your clothing and form a line around the walls for inspection,' the medical officer ordered.

'*All* of our clothes?' Oskar asked.

The MO sighed. 'Yes, all of them. And be quick about it.'

The room had a large, polished table in the centre surrounded by armchairs. Leo stripped off his clothes, taking his place against the wall. He tried to ignore the chill of the air. He wiggled his toes into the plush carpet and kept his eyes straight ahead.

A large, elaborately framed painting of King George was directly across the room. It was as if the king himself was scrutinising every one of Leo's farm-worked muscles. With a shiver, he turned to Oskar to make a comment, but he looked so glum Leo closed his mouth.

Harry poked Oskar. 'Cheer up, Oskar; you've got a face longer than the Murrumbidgee. I tell you I'd rather be a soldier than a doctor having to grab that.' Harry nodded down the line.

Leo noticed the MO was examining one of the lad's testicles. Fair go, wasn't that being a bit too thorough? 'Too right,' agreed Leo, 'I don't think that has much to do with whether we can shoot down Fritzes.'

Alfred Fanshaw piped up near them. 'You'd better get used to it. I hear the army checks for dirty buggers all the time. Apparently, some soldiers just can't help themselves and go sticking it in every girl they see.' He looked pointedly at Harry, who blushed.

Leo gave Alfred's shrivelled appendage a dismissive glance 'At least he likes girls. Baaaaaaaaaaaaaaaaaaa.' He was sure that Alfred and his snotty mother had more than a hand in his father being rounded up. They might own the grocery store and the pub in Orange, but it didn't mean they were better than anyone else.

Oskar stifled a laugh.

'You're disgusting,' Alfred hissed at Leo then turned his eyes to the front as the MO drew closer. It was hard for anyone to look dignified without a stitch of clothing on.

When the medical was finally over, Leo tucked his shirt in and tried to blot the sensation of the MO's invasive inspection from his mind. He stood before Captain King and tried to make sense of the Attestation Paper of Persons Enlisted for Services Abroad questions.

His brow soon furrowed as he answered the questions. No, he hadn't been convicted by a civil power or discharged from the forces, with ignominy (what?), or as incorrigible ... best answer no to that lot. Leo's head hurt. Thank the Lord that he only needed to fire a rifle at the enemy; he wouldn't get far if the war was won on paperwork.

He was told to put his hand on his heart and repeat the oath after Captain King.

'I, Leopold Dymond, swear that I will well and truly serve our Sovereign Lord the King in the Australian Imperial Force from the second of October 1915 until the end of the war, and a further period of four months thereafter unless lawfully discharged, dismissed or removed therefrom; and that I will resist His Majesty's enemies ...'

Ice needled his heart. How could anyone see his pa as an enemy?

The captain frowned, his bushy brows knitting into one as if he had two moustaches aligned on his stern face. 'Are you alright there, son?' he asked, finger paused midway through the oath on Leo's form.

'Yes, sir.' Leo sucked in his breath. He had to pay attention. If he stuffed this up, there'd be no way to help Pa. 'His Majesty's enemies?'

The captain gave him a doubtful look but continued and Leo tried to follow—'... and cause His Majesty's peace to be kept and maintained; and that I will in all matters apper ... apper ...'

'—appertaining to my service, faithfully discharge my duty according to law. So help me, God.' The captain prompted him then tapped his pen impatiently.

Leo's voice quivered. '... so help me, God.'

'Sign here and you're done. You will be with B Company of the 13th Battalion.' Captain King handed him the pen and Leo pressed so hard he nearly broke the nib.

There, he'd done it. The captain shook his hand and Leo exited the room, waiting for Oskar and Harry on the portico outside. He didn't have to wait long.

'We're in! How fast was that? On Monday we start the march to Sydney as soldiers.' Harry's eyes were wild as he smacked at one of the huge entrance columns of the town hall.

'Yep, fair dinkum ANZACs,' Leo agreed.

Oskar wasn't so sure. 'How are we going to face Ma? She'll be heartbroken when we tell her we're marching off to war.'

'You're not marching anywhere, sunshine.'

Oskar winced as Captain King's meaty hand clamped down on his shoulder.

'About face. Let's go sort these papers out and you can tell me your real age.'

Blood rushed into Leo's cheeks. How did the captain know? Would he catch him and Harry too?

The captain cuffed Leo's ear. 'You should know better than to let your brother sign up underage and without permission.' Oskar was tugged back through the door.

Alfred was coming from the opposite direction. 'Oh, did they reject you, Oskar?' His lip curled. 'The Australian Imperial Force only recruits men, not boys.'

'Then how did you get in?' Leo said as Alfred took off down the stairs. Leo stood rubbing his aching ear. Ma was going to string him up once she found out.

Harry laughed and shrugged. 'Some people just don't know how to respect a king's soldier, now do they?'

Chapter Three

October 1915
Borenore, Australia

Leo sat on the edge of the verandah and gazed at the field rippling in the twilight breeze. Blimey, what a day! He'd started off watching a parade of new recruits come into town and now he was one of them. Had he done the right thing?

Dot plonked herself beside him and they swung their legs in time. Dot slapped a mossie on her leg then looked up at the sky.

'There it is,' she whispered.

A lone star twinkled in the wash of gold and rose. She screwed her eyes hard and silently moved her lips.

'What did you wish for?' Leo asked.

'You know I can't tell you or it won't come true. Think you can guess anyway.' Her legs stopped swinging. 'Do you really have to go?'

What would it do to her, him leaving? Without Pa, he was supposed to be the man of the family and look out for her. She was the baby. Always left watching everyone move on. He pulled her in for a hug, breathing in Pears soap and country sunlight.

'You'll be fine. Before you know it, this war'll be over, and I'll be back with heaps of presents for you.'

Dot snuggled into him, her small hand resting on his leg. 'But who's going to stop Oskar teasing me or dunking me in the creek? Who's going to read *Dot and the Kangaroo* with me?'

He tucked his left hand into his pocket and felt the knobbly piece of cedar he'd spent hours whittling for Dot's upcoming birthday. He'd be gone by then.

'I was saving this for your birthday, but I think you should have it now.' He placed the carving into her small hand. Dot's fingers travelled over the bumps of scalloped wings to its belly.

'Ooooh. A kookaburra. He's great, thanks.'

'You know how kookaburras call out to their families if there's any trouble? Well, this bloke here is extra special. He'll listen to anything you've got to tell me and then I'll hear it all the way over there.'

A tear straggled over Dot's cheek. Dot might whinge louder than a squeaky wagon wheel, but she rarely cried. She hiccupped and broke into full sob. 'Don't go. Please don't go, don't. What if I never see you again?' Her shoulders shook against him and he gripped her to his chest.

Leo squeezed Dot hard. 'Hey, Dottie,' he whispered into her hair. 'I promise I'll make it back.'

She clung tighter.

He missed her already.

***

25 October 1915

Leo shifted his weight from one leg to the other. He had formed up with the other recruits near the soldier's monument at the top of the main street in Orange. The town folk were waving flags and fluttering hankies to see them off. Leo shrugged further down into the scratchy wool warmth of his new army-issue overcoat.

As they finally began to march away, Leo took one last look at his family.

Oskar had jammed his hat so far down his head, Leo couldn't see his eyes. Dot's face was hidden in the folds of their mother's coat, but even from a distance he could see her little shoulders heaving. Ma was absently stroking her back with one hand, but the other was held at her heart. She had barely spoken to him since he'd told her he'd joined up; she had only pressed a rabbit's foot into his hand for luck. His mother's face was distorted in the effort of maintaining a dignified mask. He met her eyes and almost drowned in the pools of grief. If only his Pa was there beside her.

Oskar raised an arm in a sharp salute and Leo's lip quivered as he gave them one last wave. An icy blast whipped his face. He didn't dare look at Harry. The town band's jaunty tune grated in his ears.

Alfred was marching just ahead with great gusto. His back was ram rod straight and when he turned his head, Leo could see Alfred's pointy chin jutting out, nose in the air. Leo had to keep going. If he scuttled back home, he would be marked a coward and friend of the enemy. Ethel Fanshaw would have him whipped into an internment camp with Pa before he could gulp down a long colonial beer.

'Look at Mr Fancy Pants over there done up like a sore toe. Where in the blazes does he think he's off to?' Harry said as he surveyed Alfred's Sunday clobber.

'Bloody King's School toff. Maybe Alf thinks King George himself will thank us when we hit Sydney,' Leo said.

Harry laughed. 'Must admit, I was hoping we'd get a full uniform. I want to impress some of the girls when we pass through.' He looked down at his patched moleskins with a sigh.

Leo regarded his own shabby farm clothes under the overcoat and shrugged.

They marched in time to the military drum pounding at the front of the pack, their boots kicking up dust. A biting wind was whistling down from Mount Canobolas and Leo pumped his arms to warm up. The small cottages gave way to open road and rolling, wheat coloured fields. Leo was getting further and further away from his family. He'd barely been beyond Borenore or Orange before. Dot's tear-stained face haunted him. He needed to think about something else.

He watched a lamb bounce along and then kick his back legs up, butting right into his mother. The lamb's exuberant burst of hopping and running was at odds with the sombre mood of the men marching past. Guess he wasn't the only sad sack in the wagon.

'I wonder if all of the smiles and carry on when they marched in was just for show to get us in the army,' he commented to Harry.

'Yeah, they're as lively as a dog in front of the fire. Hey, Bull, what's up with the Gil mob?' Harry called out to a Goliath of a man ahead of them. Standing at over six feet four and as solid as a mallee bull, it was easy to see how Tom McGory had been given his nickname.

'Didn't you hear? Young bloke, Bill Hunter, got a letter from his mum last night. His two older brothers that left with the 18ᵗʰ were both killed at Gallipoli. He was pretty cut up about it but he's a brave little battler, he's still marching on,' Bull said as he fell back in step with them.

'What rotten news.' Leo's neck knotted. What would he do if he lost Oskar? It had seemed so right to join the army.

A thought buzzed like a mosquito in the still of the night.

What if he didn't make it back home?

Chapter Four

5 November 1915
Katoomba, Australia

Rose watched Elise sashay across the room looking pleased with herself. She sighed. What drama was she about to share? She gave Adelaide a poke and rolled her eyes.

'You're not going to believe this, girls.' Elise paused for effect but Rose and Adelaide continued sorting packages for the Red Cross comfort stand. The Coo-ee marchers would be arriving at the town hall at any moment. Seeing she wasn't going to get much more than a cursory interest, Elise continued.

'I've joined the army.'

Adelaide dropped the socks she was holding, and Rose gasped. Elise blushed with pleasure. 'I thought it was only right to do my bit. Why should my brothers get all the glory?'

'Well, that's very ... patriotic of you,' Rose said.

'Yes, very brave.' Adelaide stooped to pick up the socks and gave Rose a warning look. They hadn't told anyone that they'd joined the army too and both knew that while Elise had some wonderful qualities, she was a terrible gossip.

Elise's green eyes shone with pride. 'I hope I get to go over and help those poor boys stuck in the Dardanelles. Although, it could be a bit dangerous on those hospital ships. Did you hear about those poor nurses from New Zealand?'

Rose and Adelaide stopped working and Elsie's voice lowered. 'They were escorting some men back and their ship, the *SS Marquette*, got torpedoed! Apparently, the ship listed so bad, they couldn't get all off the lifeboats and down in time and they lost ten nurses. Now, you'd think you were safe once you were on a lifeboat, but they lowered another boat right on top of some of the nurses and smashed their limbs. Killed them instantly. Terrible, isn't it?'

Elise barely looked at them or drew breath before she continued, 'My mother received a letter from her friend, Sister Richmond, who's just come in on that hospital ship, *Kyarra*, and she said they'd shot right at them while on deck at Gallipoli …'

They shot at the hospital ships? How awful. Rose hadn't heard that before. Adelaide was frozen, staring at Elise.

'Nurses have *died*? Oh my,' Adelaide squeaked. Rose glared at Elise and fanned Adelaide.

'Goodness, I'm sorry Addie. I'll go and get her some tea.' Elise patted Adelaide's arm.

'I didn't realise we could be shot or torpedoed. I thought …' Adelaide's voice trailed off and she stared at her nails.

What had she done? If it wasn't for her, Adelaide would not have signed up. Rose already had the stain of one death on her hands.

'Maybe we could see if it's possible for you to get out of the army. If they found out your real age—' Adelaide raised a hand to cut her off. She straightened her back.

'No. We joined together; we stay together. I'll be right as rain once I have that tea. You look—'

'Yes, I'm not feeling the best. I think I'll get some fresh air. I'll be back in a minute.' Rose left to the squawks and sputters of the band warming up. She felt drained and the night had not even yet begun. She sank onto a bench outside of the hall, content to sit in the shadows. Rose wished Elise would be more discreet in sharing her news but then she wasn't to know that they'd signed up.

Elise was a few years older and had been rather miffed to see them training at the RPA Hospital with her and often getting better marks in exams, but she was generous enough to understand Rose's position. Elise had been truly kind when her mama had taken ill.

Some of the recruits were approaching the hall.

One of them tugged his hat down and shoved his hand in his pocket, looking very reluctant to enter while his friend gave him a nudge.

'C'mon, Leo. You can't skip this dance too. You might miss out on meeting the dame of your dreams, the sheila of your sausage, the lass of your lusty loins, the filly—'

Rose stifled a giggle. Such boys.

'Go jump in the lake, mate. You're randier than a mallee bull.'

'Did someone call me?' said a giant of a man. 'Randy? Forget the girls. It's all about the dinner for me and what fine food they've turned on for us here.'

'I've got too many blisters, I stink like metho.'

'No excuses, Leo. Besides, I won the blister comp today. In you go.'

Rose felt sorry for the poor fellow. It was time for her to go back in and begin handing out all the knitted socks for the boys. She slipped through the back door. There must be enough socks in there to clothe the rest of the British Army as well.

It wasn't long before Rose heard the same cheeky bloke again.

'I've changed my mind, forget the blonde. I'm going for the dark-haired one in the middle with the—' the soldier curved his hands around imaginary breasts. Rose frowned and continued to stack socks.

'Good evening, ladies. I'm Harry Fuller, this is Leo Dymond and that's Bull McGory. We just wanted to come over and offer a dance to thank you lovely Red Cross ladies for the hard work you've been doing knitting all of these socks.' Harry offered his arm to Rose. The other girls giggled and twittered. Bull smiled but gave a small wave before heading to the supper table.

'That's very flattering, but I can't take credit for any of the work as I'm not with the Red Cross so perhaps you'd better share your thanks with Daphne. She's knitted the most socks of all.' Rose placed Daphne's hand on Harry's arm. The gangly girl with bushy eyebrows looked horrified.

'No, you dance with Rose.' Daphne stuttered but Rose gave them a firm push towards the dance floor and Harry gracefully accepted defeat. Leo grinned.

Rose smiled too. 'That's more like it, you look much better with a smile on your face.' Oh, Lord. She'd made him turn the shade of strawberries. 'Hi, my name is Rose Shipley, and this is Adelaide ...' Goodness, he really was shy; he didn't seem to be listening and was studying the exit door. 'Oh dear, was that too many names?'

'What?'

'You're frowning. I'll try again. This is Adelaide Clements and Elise Gardiner.' Leo just nodded, still looking at the exit door.

'I thought I saw Alfred Fanshaw earlier. Our families often have dinners together. Do you know him?' Elise asked. Now he was paying attention, but he didn't look very happy.

'You do, don't you? Isn't he dull?' Elise said.

Rose gasped and poked her. 'Be kind, Ellie.'

Adelaide looked up from sorting sock packages. 'Imagine how terrible it must be to go to war with the expectations his parents have for him. His mother is awfully demanding.'

Elise tried to look apologetic, 'I'm sorry, that was a bit wicked. When we last had dinner, Mrs Fanshaw was bragging about what a wonderful son Alfred was and that she fully expected that he would make her proud by coming back with no less than a Victoria Cross. Alfred looked about as mortified as he did that time Rose refused to have him as a partner at the Nurse's Ball—'

Rose gripped Elise's arm tightly and she finally closed her mouth. Leo shrugged and Rose felt terrible. What if Alfred was a friend of his?

He gave Elise an understanding smile. 'No, no Elise. I know exactly what you mean. Alfred is full of … um … hot air,' Leo agreed.

Oh no. The poor boy didn't know what he'd just done. He would be Elise's captive for the night. Rose went to hand Leo his comfort package, but Elise turned to come between them. Rose saw him gulp as Elise took his arm.

'Why, the last time we had dinner, Alfred was going on about how he would rise quickly in the ranks and he'd do his best to weed out those German spies. Isn't that just ridiculous?'

Rose saw his jaw tighten but he said, 'Yes, sure is. I tell you that Alfred's as popular as a fart in a swag with our lot.'

Rose noticed his stiff stance did not at all match his light tone and gave an inward groan as Elise glanced around her and leaned closer. 'Still, I do feel a bit sorry for him. Thomas looks just like his father. So dashing and so clever. His father was apparently the darling of Sydney. Nothing like Mr Fans—'

'Leo, I'd love to hear about the march you've been on. I heard you had to go all the way up Victoria Pass when those bushfires were burning,' Rose interrupted.

Leo gave an eager nod. 'Yeah, that was a bit of a hard slog.'

Elise shot Rose a dagger and turned her attention to Harry trying to waltz with his less than graceful partner.

The band started another tune and Rose tapped her foot in time.

'Perhaps I can tell you more about it while we—' Leo started.

'May I please have the pleasure of this dance, Miss?' Harry asked.

Rose looked at Harry. Despite his dimpled grin, he looked less certain than the first time he'd asked. Even though she thought he was a bit of a rogue, Rose agreed. She giggled as he twirled her around before joining the other couples gliding around the hall.

Rose felt the warmth of Harry's hand and smile, relaxing into his hold.

'That lavender is very becoming of you,' Harry began but as they turned, she saw a face set harder than marble. Her father was obviously furious.

'What do you think you are doing, Rose?' Spittle beaded her father's handlebar moustache. He gripped her wrist so tight that Rose flinched.

'Father, let go. I was dancing with Private Fuller,' Rose said sharply. How dare her father embarrass her.

'Excuse us, Mr Fuller, I need to speak to my daughter.'

Harry stood, dumbfounded.

'Right now, Rose.'

Rose steeled herself. This was not going to be pretty.

Chapter Five

Once outside the hall, Rose yanked her arm away from her father's grip. 'How could you do that?'

'How could *I* do that! How could *you* go and join the army? What on Earth were you thinking? Fancy not telling me. Were you planning to send a postcard from the front? And how could you abandon your mother like this?' Her father's boots squeaked as he paced.

'Perhaps we should discuss this at home,' Rose said, rubbing her arm and stepping back towards her bench in the shadows.

'There's nothing to discuss. I forbid you to stay in the army.'

Rose felt a rush of heat ripple through her body. She wanted to yell so many things at her father but instead she unclenched her jaw and spoke very calmly. 'For once, I don't think you can arrange that. I'm staying in it.'

'We'll see about that. I'm sure once they know your age, they'll change their tune and you'll be out on your ... er, they'll discharge you.'

'Then they'll be wondering how on Earth I got my qualifications at such a young age too,' Rose countered. She felt the knot in her shoulders tighten. She was ready for round two. But in the lamplight, Rose saw his shoulders slump. Guilt tied a noose, and she couldn't talk. She touched his hand, but it felt cold. He gave a slight squeeze and let go.

'You know, I agreed to you training to be a nurse so you could get your mother out of that place.'

'I know ... it's just I want more ... maybe to even become a doctor one day. Please, Father.' She hated the pleading tone in her voice but even more the startled look of disbelief on her father's sagging face.

'All of those hours we spent looking at my textbooks where you peppered me with questions and helped me at my practice ... I was so proud of your curiosity and understanding but to be honest I didn't know what else to do with you. It wasn't meant that I wanted you to follow in my footsteps. It's not a life for a woman.'

A flame flickered through Rose. 'I can't believe you would think that. I don't want to have learned all that I have to become chained to my mother's side ... that is not a life for a woman. This is about more than our family. I want to be of use to our country. I want to keep learning.' Her father was gazing up at the moon. Was he even listening? 'I can't explain it. I want to be more—'

He raised a hand. 'All I hear is *I want*. I thought you'd want to help your mother. Bring her home and bring her back to us.'

'I think it would only make her worse. She blames me.' Rose narrowed her eyes as she noticed the stone in her father's expression. 'Is that what this is? You want to punish me? You blame me too and think this is the least I could do for bringing Maman into such a state?'

'How could you say that? I had no idea allowing you to train to be a nurse would lead to such ambition. I don't know who you are anymore, Rose.' His nostrils flared. 'You are no daughter of mine. Go, serve but don't bother to contact me. I'm done with you.' He strode into the shadows.

Rose collapsed onto the bench, sucked in the cool air, and stared above her. In the moonlight, the stringy strands of bark from a gum hung like a broken cobweb.

Why had she behaved so impulsively, joining the army without talking to her father first? She didn't know who she was anymore either.

'No, I am no daughter of yours. All you wanted was a son,' she whispered.

'Excuse me, Rose. Are you alright?'

'Oh, ah, I'm fine,' she sniffed. Leo had found her.

'Are you sure?'

'No ... I mean ... how embarrassing, I don't usually carry on like this.' She wiped her eyes and gestured for him to join her.

She took a breath. 'I suppose you heard that awful row with my father. No doubt the whole of Katoomba did. He found out I joined the army as a nurse. He's a doctor and I thought he'd understand!' Her voice wobbled. 'Maybe I shouldn't have joined up without discussing it with him first.'

Strains of music and chatter floated in the air, filling the silence. Leo cleared his throat.

'My ma wasn't very happy about me joining either but sometimes you've got to trust yourself and do what you have to do. Besides, it would be a shame to waste all of that training when we need good nurses.'

'Really? So, you don't think I was being selfish?' she asked

'I think you should do what you feel is right.'

'That's just it. I don't know if I was right.' She rubbed her temple and sighed.

'I often feel better if I sit and look at the stars. Makes me all quiet inside,' Leo said, looking up.

Rose followed his gaze to the sky and took a deep breath. He was right, it helped.

Leo inhaled too. He didn't try to fill the silence and just sat with her. A strange feeling washed over her, like she had known him for years.

'Thank you, I feel so much better.' Rose dabbed her face. Footsteps crunched on the gravel towards them.

'Would you like to—' Leo said.

'Rose? Are you out here?' Harry called into the night.

'Over here.'

'What are you doing in the dark?' Harry went to sit down and stopped short. 'Oh. Hi Leo. Sorry to interrupt, but Miss Shipley, I believe we still have a dance to finish.'

Rose didn't feel like dancing but felt she should make it up to Harry.

'Yes, we do. I am sorry about my father's carry on. He usually has better manners. Do you mind, Leo?'

Leo nodded. 'No, you go ahead.'

'Thanks.' Harry slapped Leo on the back and took Rose's arm. As Rose and Harry entered the hall light, Rose turned to Leo outside and flashed a grateful smile. A grin flickered but his eyes burned with something Rose could not read. Her heart unfurled.

No, she wasn't thinking straight, seeing things that weren't there. Harry tugged her forward and into the swirl of dancing couples.

As handsome as Harry was, why did she want to kiss Leo?

Chapter Six

Friday 12 November 1915
Sydney, Australia

'**B**limey! I don't think we're ever going to get through. This is even worse than yesterday's mob,' Leo had to yell over the din of the bagpipes playing 'Minstrel Boy'.

Harry nodded and then swore as his boots got tangled in a white streamer. Streamers and bunting decorated every surface, banners calling men to enlist hung from sandstone arches and straw hats bobbed like fishing floats on a creek's surface. Thousands of people lined Sydney's George Street. Men cheered and women waved miniature flags so fast they blurred into a streak of royal blue.

Leo's throat was raw from too many Coo-ee calls to the crowd and his cheeks ached from smiling. Bubbles of excitement popped in his stomach. So many people, yet they were still dwarfed by the majestic Queen Victoria Market Buildings.

'Strike me red, white and blue! The whole of Aus must be here,' Bull said.

Leo waved the flag thrust into his hand and responded to the call: 'What do we want?'

'Men, more men and still more men,' he managed to rasp out.

What did he really want? Some peace and quiet and maybe a good, cold beer.

The crowd's tumultuous greeting dropped to an eerie silence and Leo looked at the crowd in confusion. He saw many were looking at a group of men packed tightly onto the verandahs of the Royal Hotel. Some still sported bandages or were leaning on crutches. The returned soldiers of the Dardanelles were having none of that respectful silence.

'You blokes are fair dinkum! Good on you!' Calls of encouragement were shouted. 'When you get back, I'll shout you all a drink at The Soldiers' Club 'ere!'

'Hey, what about a beer for every Fritzy you hit? Hey big fella, do you reckon you could shoot a Hun in the bum for me?'

'Is the Pope a Catholic? You'll owe me a few beers when I'm done!' Bull yelled back.

The soldiers gave a rousing cheer, then in military precision stood to attention and saluted them. Leo straightened and returned the salute, just like the men around him. One of them on the bottom verandah had the saddest eyes Leo had ever seen. Pools of melancholy in a mask of weathered skin.

He seemed to be looking right through him. As the soldier on the verandah turned away, Leo noticed the man's sleeve was tucked up.

A woman bowed her head, her shoulders began to shake, and a cluster of violets and rosemary came loose from her straw hat. Her fingers twisted a gold chain and then clutched at a crucifix. Just like Ma did. Leo shoved past Harry towards her. He plucked a rose from his pocket and handed it to her, causing her to smile and sob at the same time.

'You take care now,' she said. 'I'll be praying for you.'

He squeezed her hand and slipped back in line. Lord, he did not want to lose a limb or have his ma sobbing like that at a parade. He swallowed hard. The shine of finally making it to the city was fading. John Lee, their recruitment speaker, began to sing 'Onward, Christian Soldiers' but Leo didn't have the heart to join in. He trudged into Martin Place to the most jubilant welcome yet.

People were packed tighter than the rims of their large hats would allow, crushing them into all manner of skewed angles.

The din of the cheers vibrated right through him, only drowned out at midday by the enormous bells of the General Post Office clock from high above them.

They were cheered all the way to the Domain. Leo shook his head; they were heroes already and they hadn't even fired a shot at a German. Returned soldiers held up a stunning arbour of fifty arches bedecked with blood-red roses. It felt wrong. He wanted to hold the rose arches for them.

They had finally made it. The Gilgandra Coo-ees had completed their three-hundred-and-twenty-mile march. Leo sank with relief onto the spongy grass of the Domain.

Later, Leo listened to Bill Hitchen greet the crowds in front of the long colonnade of the GPO.

'I like you very much, and I like your cheering.' Leo had to cover his ears from the cacophony of the enormous crowd. Bill Hitchen smiled and motioned for the noise to die down.

'But I'll like you more if a lot of the men in this great crowd come forward to swell our ranks and help us fill the gaps in the firing line. There is a voice calling to us. It is the call of our brave soldiers—won't you come and help us?'

Leo had never felt particularly brave about going to war. He didn't know what to feel but as far as he knew, this was the only way to help his family.

The march was finally over, and he cast an eye over the mass of white canvas hats and dusty dungarees. No more Coo-ees.

***

The Special Army train chugged out of Central Station in a cloud of coal dust and fluttering farewell hankies. Leo and the others plonked down on the hard wooden seats as the train inched out of the station and moved along the tightly packed terrace houses that backed onto the line.

'I have to say, I am glad that's all over. I was getting pretty jack of those crowds. I thought we'd never get on the train.' Frosty put his hat on the rack above them and wiped his sweaty brow. He raised his hand in a salute to the ragamuffin children who were clinging to back fences, arms flapping to the train as it passed.

They'd met Frosty along the way to Sydney. One minute he was a swagman looking for work, the next a new recruit swayed by the promise of steady money and the chance to be a hero. Once his ragged beard and hair had been shorn to army regulation, Leo had been shocked at how young he looked. Leo had immediately liked his open smile and easy-going nature.

Harry whistled to the girls, blowing kisses and smiling as they giggled under the shade of their laced verandah.

'I'm sure sad it's over. I ain't looking forward to more of that muck the army calls food. How do they expect anyone to go off to war on that?' Bull said as he fidgeted against the hard wood. 'Who in their right mind could look forward to the lumpy porridge, meatless stew or toast and marmalade?'

Leo laughed as Bull pulled out a stash of crumbled cake and biscuits he'd stuffed into his pockets earlier and made short work of them. Bull licked his fingers and collected up every last morsel that had landed on his sweaty denim tunic, then his eyes misted. 'That was a fine meal Sargents put on for us but my all-time favourite was the roast turkey and the trifle we had after helping fight those fires at Springwood.'

'Close your mouth mate or we'll be covered in your drool,' Harry said as he flicked a couple of crumbs that landed on his leg. People crowding a train platform at Strathfield burst into ear splitting cheers as the train rumbled past. 'The Germans can probably hear we're coming. How can we lose with the whole of Aussie backing us up?'

A shower of half pennies pinged through the window, scattering over the aisle and landing among their boots. Frosty grabbed one and smiled as he unglued the address of the girl who had thrown it. Harry immediately made a beeline for the remaining coins.

He thrust one into Leo's hands and looked miffed when Leo flipped it to Frosty.

'What's your problem? You've barely looked at a girl the whole march.' Harry's eyes narrowed and he flicked Leo's head.

Leo's cheeks flushed as he thought of Rose. She'd agreed to write to Harry, not him.

'There doesn't seem much point starting anything up when we're going off to war soon,' Leo muttered.

'Bah, that's the best time to start something up. Girls like a good time as much as a bloke these days. A good meal, a dance and a big kiss with a soldier boy.' Harry made smooching noises at him.

Leo gave him a shove. Thank God the carriage was full of noisy blokes or someone might get the wrong idea.

'Fair go. I'll find a girl when I'm good and ready,' Leo kept his tone light but followed it with a warning jab in Harry's ribs.

'I know Rose Shipley is pretty and all, but I still want to see what the girls are like over there. I hope there are plenty of good sorts for us all. Maybe you'll find a nice Pommy girl, Bull. Hey, looks like we're here.' Harry stood up first, impatient as ever.

Leo was last out. His limbs were lead. Forget romance; forget Rose. It was time for him to get on with it.

Colonel Kirkland and Captain Brosnan marched them into the dust bowl of Liverpool Camp and dismissed them after a quick inspection.

Soldiers milled around the camp of large shiny galvanised iron huts. 'Hey, Marmalades! You'll be sorry!' they cat called.

'Don't worry, fellas, that's what they say to all the new recruits.' Bull just gave the jeering soldiers a hearty wave.

Leo gazed at their worn canvas army bell tents that dotted the grass like sheep. Were the soldiers right? Would he be sorry?

Chapter Seven

December 1915
Liverpool Military Training Camp

Leo stepped into line for general parade. It was only eight o'clock, but the sun's heat already had a bite to it. Being ordered to stand to attention for inspection was all fine and good but it was bloomin' hard to stay stock still with a swarm of insects buzzing all over you. Leo blew an upwards puff of air and managed to dislodge all but one of the flies crawling over his face. The little bugger's wings vibrated inside his nostril. Grabbing a handkerchief, Leo honked hard enough and catapulted the culprit into the grubby cotton folds. Got him.

'Is there a problem here, Private?'

How did he do that? There were thousands of men standing to attention. Lieutenant Colonel Jackson must have eyes in the back of his head.

'No, sir.' Leo dipped his chin and stared at Jackson's shiny boots.

'You can't afford to let anything distract you, Private. With the enemy in sight, you need to have the discipline to focus and aim true. It doesn't matter whether a fly is up your nose, or a rat is chewing off your foot.'

Leo's head jerked up. A rat chewing his foot? 'Yes, sir.' His ears were burning and a trickle of sweat dripped a salty trail down his forehead.

Jackson's stern gaze flickered, and the corner of his generous lips twitched. He continued his inspection.

A low grumble rippled through the ranks as they formed up for the morning's march. Fourteen miles. Just great. The cicadas seemed to be singing a song, 'It's, it's, it's, it's so hoooot'. It buzzed through his head as they set off.

Leo couldn't believe how desolate the camp was with its tattered tents and shimmering iron huts. A swirl of camp dust enveloped him, caking his tongue. He spat and gagged.

The rough road they marched along was treeless with bare dusty paddocks either side. With the swing of each arm, his new tunic made a sucking sound, releasing the uniform from his sweat-pasted back. Stomping boots and cicadas echoed around him. No songs, joking or grumbling. March—one, two, and one two, one ... what the hell had he done? This place was a bloody nightmare.

As the line of men marched beyond the camp, Bull pointed to some rows of barbed wire fencing over the flat, dry paddock. 'That's Holsworthy Camp, where they're keeping the Germans and other aliens.'

Leo's neck tingled. That's where his pa was.

Through the wire he saw row upon row of long, narrow, iron-roofed wooden huts with canvas walls rolled up or set out as a droopy awning. Men wilted in the heat at roughly made tables and stools while others were unloading hessian sacks from a truck. Apart from the guards at the truck and a couple dotted around the barbed wire fence, there were few soldiers to be seen. A large cobra of a watchtower reared over the dismal camp waiting to spit venomous bullets at any man that attempted to escape.

Someone was whistling the 'Ride of the Valkyries' as they unloaded the sacks. Leo's heart jumped. Was that Pa? He moved out of formation and stepped closer until he spotted the source of the tune. No. That man was long and lanky.

Pa didn't belong in a place like that.

'No, you don't. I know that look,' Harry said, grabbing his arm.

The picket entrance gates looked deserted. Leo shook his hand off. 'But I'm so close, I can just sneak in. It'll be easy.'

'Yeah,' snorted Bull. 'As easy as putting butter up an echidna's bum with a knitting needle. Why in the hell would you want to go near the place?'

'You'll get shot or wind up in there,' Harry warned.

'Harry's right, chum. I've heard the bloke running that show is a real mongrel, he'd shoot you quick as look at you.' Bull wiped his brow and squinted at the camp.

Leo's shoulders slumped and he dragged his feet. He knew they were right, and he'd be no good to anyone if he managed to get himself locked up too.

'Go ahead, Dymond. I'm sure you'll fit right in,' Alfred slowed his marching pace and dropped back. 'You know all about swilling with German pigs, don't you?'

Leo's exhausted muscles fired at once and Harry gripped his arm so tight his nails seemed to pierce through Leo's bicep.

'You'll probably all end up in there anyway. I'm sure your father's having a wonderful time as an honoured guest of Holsworthy.' Alfred gave the camp a lofty wave then narrowed his eyes. 'Maybe your ma and Dorothy would prefer the more luxurious surrounds of Bourke.'

Leo's brain and body froze.

'Why don't you make like a tree, Alf?' Harry spoke in a tone mothers seem to reserve for their children after a tiresome day.

Alfred gave a dismissive nod and swaggered ahead, picking up a large stick to trail in the dust behind him. Leo stopped grinding his teeth and felt his jaw pop in release.

'Geez, that bloke has his head so far up his arse, if he farted, he would whistle,' Bull muttered. When Leo failed to raise a smile, Bull's eyes clouded in concern. 'What's he on about then?'

'Forget it. What's at Bourke?' Leo held his breath.

'Oh. Terrible business that. Can you believe they are locking up some families at the old Bourke Gaol? Women and little kids. I mean, what harm could they do?' Bull shook his head. 'C'mon, we'd better get movin'. Leo was rooted to the spot. Harry gave him a sympathetic nod.

'Come out, you German bastards!' Alfred dragged his stick along the fence, jangling it as he raced along while his mates rattled the fence and called to a couple of internees slumped in the closest hut.

'Stop that malarkey back there and get on with it or you'll be marching all bloody night,' Captain Binstead called from ahead.

Alfred waited until Binstead moved further up before moving closer to the fence.

'Hey, you! Yeah, you sausage-eating Huns. Come over here and we'll show you what us Aussies will do to your lot when we get over there,' Alfred taunted. His mates laughed and jeered him on. The young intern flushed red while the other man tugged his cap down and turned away.

'Bunch of cowards,' Alfred called. His mouth gave a twist as he thrust out his chest. He threw the stick at them and it landed with a clang against the third row of wire. The skinny intern flinched and Alfred to broke into raucous laughter.

Enough was enough. Leo charged like a hissing goose.

'Leave them alone.' He grabbed the back of Alfred's collar and whipped him around.

'German scum should be shipped back to where they belong, not breathing good Australian air. Take your filthy Hun hands off me.'

Leo gripped him tighter.

Alfred's spittle flecked Leo's cheeks as he spoke. 'My father said it wouldn't be long and you'd be kicked out of the army and I'll be watching. If you get kicked out, you'll be booted straight over that fence.'

Leo frowned. Alfred's eyes flared with a fevered hatred.

'Jesus, Alf. What the hell has any German ever done to you?'

Alfred pulled free; the whites of his eyes gleaming against his mottled skin. Pain exploded in Leo's head and he reeled back. Harry and Bull caught him as he stumbled. That crazy bastard had punched him. Warm blood spurted and Leo clutched his nose. Captain Binstead was heading their way.

Stuffing Bull's offered handkerchief under his nose, Leo wiped the tears that squeezed out and shuffled on. Alfred turned back to him and his reptilian eyes warmed at the sight of Leo's blood-stained uniform.

'I'll tell you what those German bastards did to me, Bernhard,' Alfred hissed. 'They've taken my brother prisoner.'

Chapter Eight

December 1915
Callan Park Mental Hospital, Lilyfield

Rose touched the wrought iron entrance gate to the mental hospital for good luck. She hoped for a good visit with her mother this time. Matron Dawson had written to tell her that her mother had improved so much lately that she had been moved from the ward to a convalescent cottage. Maybe that meant Maman would get better on her own and Father would forgive her.

At first glance, the Kirkbridge Block of the hospital looked like a huge rectangle, but it was three large blocks joined by breezeways. Father might call this an 'awful place', but Rose thought the sandstone buildings with their pretty facades and slate roofs were lovely. They were surrounded by a variety of shrubs and trees. It was a far cry from the horrors of places like the old Bedlam in London.

Rose entered the cool of the administration building and signed the visitors book.

'I'm here to see Mrs Shipley, please.' Rose smoothed down her new scarlet cape.

The receptionist smiled and checked a list on her desk. 'You'll be in a different visitors room than usual. The convalescent cottages have their own. It's just down by the kitchen. Do you know where that is?'

Rose nodded and put her bag over her shoulder.

'Miss Shipley! What are you doing in uniform?' Matron Dawson came out of an office and greeted her.

'Oh, yes. I joined up last month. I thought I'd show Maman my uniform.' Rose tried to hold her head up but stared at the wooden floor instead.

'I think that's a wonderful idea,' Matron said. Rose's head snapped up and she saw only kindness in the matron's eyes.

Rose felt a wash of relief. The matron knew of her father's plan for Rose to attend to her mother as soon as she was fully qualified.

Matron glanced at the receptionist. 'I'm off to Ward B but I'll just guide Miss Shipley to the visitors room first.'

Rose followed the matron along a box-hedged path.

'I'm glad I've caught you. I was just discussing your mother's case with Nurse White. We're a bit puzzled as to what to do with her. In the last month she was sewing, talking and washing her hair, but now she has returned to her usual melancholic state. If it continues, I'll have to return her to the ward. I had rather hoped she was on the mend.'

Rose moved out of the summer sun and stood in the shade of a cypress. Matron Dawson stood quietly with her, waiting for Rose to collect her thoughts.

'Christmas is always hard. I will be just down the road at Broughton House next year so maybe I can visit more regularly.' Rose paused. 'Although, I'm not sure if that will be helpful or make things worse.'

Matron Dawson gave her arm a quick pat. 'Come now, Rose. I'm sure extra visits from her daughter will be most appreciated.'

Rose nodded. 'I'll admit I do find these visits exceedingly difficult. I don't know what to say or do when she just sits and stares. I wonder if she even knows I'm there much of the time. I don't have any trouble understanding diseases of the body, but this ...'

'Don't give up on her. Sometimes when tragedy strikes, people can go into a dark little cocoon. With time and patience, many come good.'

Yes, her mother had gone into a cocoon of grief, her father had escaped into his work, and Rose ... how had she reacted? Crying into her pillow at night at first then ... she wasn't sure how else she'd managed.

They continued down the path. 'It is a shame they've done away with giving nurses psychiatric training. I've found it most helpful and Callan Park is rather progressive if I don't say so myself. If you're going to be at Broughton House, such training would have been useful to you,' Matron said.

Rose's breath caught. 'Why?'

Matron Dawson paused and looked at her. 'Oh, you don't know? I've been in consultation with the army and it seems Broughton House is being set aside mostly for soldiers with neurasthenia.'

'Oh.' Rose's mouth went dry.

'Now, weakness of the nerves is nothing to be too concerned about in general but I'm quite curious how it will be for men coming home from battle. You'll be sure to come and talk to me about how you're getting on, won't you? Ah, here we are.' Matron waved at a cottage. 'I'll leave you to your visit.'

Rose barely had time to say goodbye before the matron strode away.

From the kitchen block next door to the cottages, Rose could hear plenty of clanging and banging but her nose wrinkled at the smell of cabbage soup. Rose entered the visitors room. Rather than the lofty, airy wards this room was comfortable and cosy. Her mother sat in plump lounge chair, staring out the windows to the distant Blue Mountains.

A nurse was taking wilted flowers from a vase. She took in Rose's scarlet cape and grey army uniform with wide eyes. 'Good morning. I feel like I should salute or curtsy. I'm Sister Tucker. I've thought about joining up myself. How do you find it? Do you think if I joined now I'd see some action overseas or do you think the war might end before that? It's definitely not going to end this Christmas though now, is it?' Deep red petals flew everywhere as she waved her hands about.

Rose laughed at the nurse's rapid-fire approach. Sister Tucker finally drew breath and noticed the mess she'd made. 'Oh, dear. Matron Dawson won't be pleased.' Rose helped her pick up the dahlia petals.

'I can't answer how I'm finding it as I've only just joined up and am to start at Broughton Hall just over the hill. I'm hoping to go overseas and by the way, I'm Rose Shipley. I'm here to visit my mother.'

Sister Tucker looked at the drawn woman with stringy hair at the window and gave her a nod. 'Well, don't let me be a bother to you. I've got a couple of housekeeping things to do and I'll be out of your way.'

The cane chair gave a loud screech like fingernails on a slate as Rose scraped it on the floor. She put her bag down, gave Sister Tucker an apologetic smile and picked up the chair. Her mother hadn't even flinched at the noise.

'Good morning, Mama. It's me, Rose. I've come to give you your Christmas present.'

Rose placed a small box into her mother's limp hands.

'I've joined the army nurses, Mama. I might even get to go and visit your homeland if I'm lucky.' Her mother remained silent. Rose leaned down. 'Look at my lovely uniform. I especially like these little badges. See it says ...' Rose trailed off. Why had she bothered to come?

She lifted the lid on the box and placed a tortoise shell hair clip in the shape of a butterfly into her mother's hands.

'You've always had such beautiful hair. Remember when Eddie and I would brush it and play with it for hours until it shone? He would pull it across the top of his lip and say he had the longest moustache ever.'

Her mother blinked.

'Let me put it in for you.' Rose started to comb through the matted hair with her fingers.

Her mother snatched her hand and squeezed so hard that Rose cried out. Sister Tucker rushed to help.

'Let go of Rose, Mrs Shipley. You're hurting her.' Rose was released instantly. She rubbed her wrist, knowing there'd be finger shaped bruises there tomorrow.

'Rose? I have a lovely little girl called Rose and my Edward, he's so clever.'

They both froze. She was talking. In a strange sing-song voice but she was still talking.

'Mama. It's Rose. I'm right here.' Rose kneeled in front of her mother's chair and touched her hand. Then, like clouds clearing, her mother's vacant stare changed. But it revealed a searing sun.

'Go away! Leave me alone.'

Rose dropped her hand and stood. Her mother looked up at her and when Rose did not move, she gave Rose a small shove.

'*Edouard est mort et c'est votre faute.*'

Even though her French was rusty, the words slapped Rose hard. Her mother had not forgotten at all and she certainly hadn't forgiven her.

'Are you alright? What did she say?' Sister Tucker took Rose's elbow and led her outside. Rose squinted in the sun and tried to catch her breath, desperate not to cry.

'She said Edward was dead and it was my fault.'

Sister Tucker squeezed Rose's arm. 'I read in her file that she lost a child and had lost her senses while grieving but it was an accident.'

Rose shook her head. 'No, she's right. It was my fault. It's probably best I leave her alone for a while.' She took off before the nurse could make any further attempts to reassure her.

There was nothing anyone could say that would make her feel better about losing her little brother. There was nothing that could ease the guilt. Her father had been wrong.

Rose could never nurse her mother back to health. The fact she lived at all would always remind her of the precious boy she'd lost. It would be better if she left—got as far away as possible.

Chapter Nine

March 1916
Sydney, Australia

Leo checked the face of the enormous clock that hung at Central Station. He made his way through the pea soup of soldiers to the platform just as a locomotive pulled in. Oskar was coming in to see him off to war. When the rush of coal-flecked cloud melted away, Leo spotted him.

He crept up behind his bewildered brother and with a leap had him in a headlock. After a bit of a scuffle, Oskar gave in but then squeezed Leo in a bear hug.

'Easy, you'll crack me ribs,' Leo managed to groan out.

'Struth, I thought I'd never find you. You blokes all look the same.' Oskar stared at all the soldiers on embarkation leave milling around the station, but Leo was staring at him. In just a few short months since he'd been left behind, Oskar seemed to have grown a foot taller and filled out. He looked like a front-row forward for the Orange footy team.

'How was the trip in?' Leo asked.

Oskar beamed. 'Brilliant. You're not going to believe this, but I was talking to these two nurses that got on at Katoomba and it turns out they know you and Harry. Rose and Adelaide. If they are anything like the rest of the nurses, it's worth signing up. Adelaide is so pretty *and* ... hold on to your hat ... she said I could write her, just like Rose is writing Harry.'

Leo swallowed the sour taste and pasted on a grin. 'That's ... um ... great.'

Leo was tired of Harry swanning around with Rose's latest letter or hearing about their dates. What he wouldn't give to be in Harry's place.

'Wakey-wakey. Did you hear me?' Oskar was dancing about the platform like a like a school kid waiting for the home bell.

'Sorry, mate. What?' Leo said.

'I said … I'm coming over too! The Duffy and Ford boys were giving Ma a hand and saw what a misery guts I was, so they convinced her to let me join up. Ma agreed if ol' Will came to look after me. Billy's joined up too,' Oskar babbled on as they walked out of the station. 'We'll have a bonza time, all be heroes together in the victory march. Billy reckons it'll be a stroll in the park.'

Leo's heart was in his boots. 'I'm not sure it was such a good idea to sign up after all, Oskar,' Leo began.

Oskar gave an impatient toss of his head. 'Too late for that, I'm going to do my bit too. C'mon ol' boy, cheer up. I'm here to see you off, not go to a funeral.'

***

The next day the barracks buzzed with men putting on their uniforms. Leo held his throbbing head then fumbled with his puttees. Blasted things, he still couldn't wind them around his legs nice and tight. He shouldn't have gone to the pub. Boarding a boat was the last thing he wanted to be doing.

'Buck up, cove. You are such a two-pot screamer. This is it. We're finally going to war!' Harry hooted and shoulder barged him.

Nausea rolled over him. Was it because he was still drunk? Scared? Leo didn't know. 'Leave me be. I've got a mouth like the bottom of a cocky's cage.'

'Time to form up you lot,' Captain Hunter bellowed.

After another celebratory march through flag-fluttering streets, they were soon walking up the gangway in military order while the silent crowd waited. Once on deck, the troops quickly broke loose.

Leo threw his gear down and scrambled to secure a good vantage point on deck. He scanned the masses that surged through the gate. Pals cock-a-doodle-doed to their mates, and dads waved and stood proud. Among the hiatus, a solemn black figure clung to a sprig of rosemary, shook her head and turned away. A young girl turned to sob on her friend's shoulder. Images of Leo's ma and Dot bubbled up and he swallowed hard. Then he spotted Oskar flapping about like a galah and couldn't help grinning back at him.

Streamers unravelled from all directions. One lad threw a blue streamer to his mate and the soldiers grabbed the other end. Blokes on shore clutched the streamer in a row and they began a mock challenge of tug of war with the soldiers. Another streamer hit Leo square on the head. He caught it and followed its scarlet trail to the dock. Rose held up the other end. Her eyes widened in recognition and her whole face glowed when he waved to her. A bolt of heat streaked through him. It wasn't the first time he wished he'd asked Rose to dance before Harry had stepped in. He sighed. It didn't matter. They were off to war.

His gut clenched. Had he made a mistake thinking that joining the army would save them from internment, save the vineyard and protect his family's future? He couldn't let his pa down but maybe he was going about it the wrong way. Maybe it would have been easier to break him out of Holsworthy.

The gangways dropped with a clatter and the great ropes were removed. The enormous ship, *Star of England,* shuddered under him and rolled forward. He felt the streamer grow taut and he clung on for grim life, leaning so far over the rails that Harry gripped his belt and yanked him back.

'Oi, you can't go back now, mate.' Harry said, 'Although I must say I wish I could jump off and give Rose one last kiss for the road.'

Bugger it! Why should Harry have all the luck? If Leo ever saw Rose again, he was going to try a hell of a lot harder to get to know her.

The streamer snapped and joined the cobweb threads of others that hung forlornly from the transport ship, no longer part of life on shore. He carefully folded the streamer into his pocket then waved frantically until Rose and Oskar became tiny specks in the distance.

He dropped his arms as they headed away from the Heads out to open sea. Silence fell as Sydney faded in the distance. Leo avoided Harry's face and gulped the briny air. He tried to remember he'd chosen this.

'Now that the Dardanelles are empty and Fritz is having a go at Verdun, do you reckon we'll end up in France?' Harry thrust his head into the breeze.

Leo shrugged and stared out at the vast ocean.

'I 'spose that stunt could be over by the time we get there. As long as the whole shebang isn't done. I want to get one shot off at least. Some blokes reckon we might end up at Lemnos or Belgium. What do you think?' Harry asked.

'I dunno. It doesn't matter much. Wherever it is, there's no turning back now.'

Chapter Ten

March 1916
No. 13 Australian Army Hospital
Broughton Hall, Lilyfield

The bedroom door banged open and Adelaide tumbled inside. Rose finished smoothing down the sheet on the bed she was making, took some fresh linen from the nightstand and handed it to Adelaide.

'You're late, Nurse Clements.' Rose tweaked Adelaide's nose.

'I'm sorry. I just couldn't stop thinking about what a wonderful lunch I had with Oskar. He took me to …'

Rose had stopped listening and watched Adelaide flit around the room, babbling away one minute then sighing dreamily the next. Rose was used to Adelaide's romantic ways; she was quite besotted with thoughts of finding her own Mr Darcy. Adelaide got plenty of attention at dances and loved going to balls but her flights of fancy rarely lasted more than a few weeks. But there was no melodramatic swooning this time. Something was different. Adelaide was sparkling, fizzing like Champagne.

The tiny crack in their friendship was widening and Rose felt it. She frowned and then it hit her. Adelaide didn't want to become a doctor. She wanted to get married.

'There aren't many beds in this room, are there? I wonder—Rose, what's wrong? Oh, here I am going on about Oskar, and Harry's just sailed off to war.' Adelaide put a hand on Rose's shoulder and Rose felt a twinge of guilt. She hadn't had time to think about Harry since he had left … or she hadn't made any time.

'No, it's not that. I'll miss Leo, of course, but I've just—'

Adelaide stopped fluffing the pillows. 'Did you just say Leo?'

Rose turned and smoothed the blankets. 'Uh, I'll miss them both. I wonder how they are going or even where they are going?'

Adelaide raised an eyebrow and sat on one of the beds ignoring Rose's frown. 'Mmm, you rarely talk about Harry. You don't even keep his letters. Silly me, I put it down to nursing being important to you. So, Leo huh?'

Rose flicked out a sheet and made up the last bed, trying to avoid Adelaide's eye.

'Fine, Harry's taken me on some lovely outings and I'm quite fond of him and I think Leo's a nice fellow, but as you said, nursing is much more important to me. I'm fairly certain Harry has no plans to settle down any time soon either. At least this way I can ward off any interest from other men and the other nurses thinking I am odd if I don't have a beau.'

She sat next to Adelaide. 'On the other hand, I believe a certain Oskar has won your heart.'

Adelaide's eyes widened. 'I've never felt like this before and I barely know him.' She shook her head. 'Don't worry. I'm not going anywhere soon. Oskar is so excited to be in the army so I doubt anything will come of it. I should be more like you—focus on work. Forget about love.'

Rose took Adelaide's hand. 'Don't be so sad, Addie. Oskar's got his work to do and so do we but when the war's over, I'm sure things will be different for you. I won't say no to love but for now, I love nursing. I still want to become a doctor and that seems to be all I have room for right now.'

Adelaide lifted her head. 'Me too.'

Rose looked at her. 'Really? Are you sure that's what you want?'

Adelaide flushed and fidgeted with her apron.

'Rose, you've been my best friend since you stuck Abigail Carter's plaits in an inkpot for teasing me on my first day at Ascham and I've followed you everywhere since ... but ... while I like nursing ... I don't really want to be a doctor and I really hope we stay safe at home while we are in the army.'

Rose groaned. 'Why didn't you just tell me? I feel awful that you joined up because of me.'

'No, no, no. I didn't want to be left behind. Don't feel awful because I wanted to stay with you.'

'That's a terrible reason to join the army.'

'No, it's not. That's what all of the men are doing.' Adelaide got up and started sweeping the floor with vigour. 'Joining up with their friends. We'd better get this done or Sister will have our he—'

'What on Earth is taking so long in here?' Sister Atwood demanded. She swooped in and plonked a jug of water on the dresser then surveyed the finished room.

'Just done now, Sister.' Rose replied with heat in her cheeks.

'Good, the new patients are due here any minute. I must warn you, unlike many of the others here, these men have sustained some horrific injuries. Their nerves are still intact, but it may take them a while to mentally adjust.'

'Here we are, Private Ferguson,' Sister Rees said.

They all turned to the door and Rose heard Adelaide gasp. Rose quickly pulled her face into a pleasant smile.

'Hi, nurseys. Don't let this ugly mug scare you now,' Private Ferguson said. His voice sounded slightly slurred.

Rose widened her smile at his cheery tone, but her brain sparked. The man's chin resembled a large sausage. He'd obviously had many operations but what could have caused such damage?

'Welcome, Private Ferguson. I'm Nurse Shipley and this is Nurse Clements. We'll let you settle in and then I'll pop back in with some tea, shall I?'

'That'd be right grand of you.'

Rose took Adelaide's arm, bustled her out of the room then led her to a chair in the hallway. 'You're a terrible colour. Sit down for a minute.'

The sisters nodded their heads on their way past but for once Sister Atwood did not mutter a word.

'That poor man,' Adelaide mumbled.

Rose yanked up one of the double sashed windows. 'You'll feel better with this fresh air. Come, you should know better by now. He won't be wanting your sympathy.'

Adelaide pulled her shoulders back. 'You're right. I was caught off guard. At least in a ward I can steel myself before I go in.'

'It caught me a bit too. Let's go see about that tea for him.'

As they made their way down the manor's grand staircase, Rose thought back to the day before. She had spotted Leo on the ship before she'd even realised she'd been looking for him. When she'd hit him with her streamer, he'd looked a bit stunned. She was then immersed in his warm gaze, tingling just like she'd gotten into a hot bath.

Something deep within ached. Would she ever see him again?

Chapter Eleven

August 1916
No. 13 Australian Army Hospital
Broughton Hall, Lilyfield

The winter sun was surprisingly warm, and Rose's tired limbs soaked it in. She sat sipping her tea in the peace of Broughton's beautiful gardens, watching snowdrops dance in the light breeze.

She turned to see Adelaide and Private Ferguson approaching her.

'Sorry to disturb you, Nurse Shipley. Would you mind keeping Private Ferguson company while I dig us up a hot brew?'

Rose smiled and patted the bench next to her. Private Ferguson sat down, facing away from them. Adelaide whispered that his home visit hadn't gone well and left them in silence. Rose looked at his hunched back but didn't have a clue what to say.

'Bugger the bloody tea. What I'd really like is a beer to drown my sorrows.'

'Things didn't go well at home?'

'You can say that again. Me wife's visited enough to have gotten used to the way I look but when I got home the youngest, Frank, ran screaming and wouldn't come out of the dunny. I go inside and find the wife crying her eyes out. To top it off, the bloke who'd offered me a job came over, clapped eyes on me and said I'd scare the customers off. He hadn't been told much about what I looked like; just thought he was doing the right thing by a returned soldier. To think, I used to run my own store before the war.'

Rose touched his shoulder but when he flinched, she let her hand drop into her lap. She was at a loss. Tom Ferguson had been doing so well. He was one of her favourites, always with a joke and no trouble at all.

'Could be worse, I 'spose. I could be like ol' Charlie over there.'

She followed where his finger pointed and saw a man's spindly legs slowing, making their way across the lawn with the support of a nurse. The awkward Charlie Chaplin gait and claw-like hands were now a familiar sight to Rose. Many men had come back from the war where something in their brains had snapped and the body now refused to cooperate.

'Everyone has their own battles, Tom. Pain is pain, no worse or better. I'm sorry things went so poorly.'

Tom Ferguson bent down and picked up an autumn leaf. It was still a muted shade of orange. He crushed it and let it crumble to the ground.

'I've had my time, I'm no use to anyone anymore.'

Panic flooded her brain. What could she say? How could she make things seem less bleak? Tom finally turned and looked at her.

'Thanks for listening and for not even trying to make me keep me chin up. Nothin' worse than some good egg telling me to stay strong. Sometimes you just need to be a misery guts for a while. I might head in, can you let Nurse Clements know?'

Rose nodded and watched him go.

Adelaide returned and Rose relayed the conversation.

'Thanks Rose, I didn't know what to do with him. You are so good with the men here.'

Rose shook her head. 'I sat there like a stunned mullet. I didn't know what to say. I can handle nightmares when they are mute or learning to walk again. But when they lose hope ...'

Adelaide nodded. 'It's so sad, isn't it?' She looked away for a moment. 'If you don't mind me saying, I think I'd rather go back to nursing the body rather than the mind.'

'I totally agree. I must go and tell Matron to put him on suicide watch.'

In the distance, Rose spotted Sister Atwood scanning the grounds. She saw them and came striding towards them, veil flapping.

'Oh, dear. What have we done now?' Rose said.

'There you are. You're both wanted immediately in Matron Sullivan's office.' She looked at their faces and actually laughed. 'You're not in trouble. *This time.*'

They scurried to Matron's office and were immediately ushered inside. The matron was sitting at an ornately carved desk sorting through paperwork.

'Matron, I'm genuinely concerned about Private Ferguson. His home visit did not go well at all and I'm afraid he's lost all hope. I think he should be put on suicide watch,' Rose blurted.

'I'll be sure to let Sister Atwood know.' Matron indicated for them to take a seat while she finished. Rose glanced around at the marble fireplace and beautiful bookshelves, hinting at the mansion's previous life. She tapped her fingers in time to the mantle clock ticks.

Matron finally put her dip pen back in the holder. 'My apologies to keep you waiting but I just needed to be sure everything is in order.' She collected up the papers and tapped them into a neat pile.

'I won't keep you both in suspense any longer. This is the paperwork for your transfers.'

Rose's heart dropped. The matron knew she didn't know how to handle people with mental distress. Did she want to be rid of her?

'No need to look so worried. I've been most impressed by how you've handled yourselves here, so I've nominated to send you overseas. Your skills are needed elsewhere and I'm sure you'll do me proud with the 14th Australian General Hospital. They'll be leaving next month.'

Rose waited until they were outside before whooping with delight.

'We're off! We might even get to nurse at the front.'

Rose was bubbling with excitement but stopped when she finally noticed Adelaide's stunned expression. 'Don't you want to go? I'm sure you don't have to. We could let Matron know and you could stay here.'

Adelaide snapped out of it. 'If you think I'm letting you go traipsing off overseas without me you're madder than any soldier here. Maybe we'll ride camels at the pyramids like those photos we've seen.'

They linked arms and almost skipped down the path. Rose looked over the hill at Callan Park where her mother still resided. She hadn't been back since her last visit. This was for the best. She could almost taste the freedom.

PART TWO:
THE WESTERN FRONT, FRANCE
(1916-1917)

Chapter Twelve

10 August 1916
Pozières, France

Popuelch. A cross between a pop and squelch. The sound of men's boots squashing any unfortunate frogs that had collected after last night's rain. It seemed to be taking forever for his company to wind their way in the dark through the labyrinthine network of support trenches. Leo's feet skidded as they lost traction on a jellied mass and he gripped the back of Harry's tunic to steady himself.

'For God's sake, Harry! Stop stomping on the bloody frogs,' Leo muttered.

'Can't help it, I can't see a bloody thing. What was that?' Harry asked.

Leo listened to a scrabbling sound along the parapet. 'Probably just some rats, keep moving.'

'Those things give me the—'

A flare burst above them and flooded the trench, tainting them all with a blue tinge. Everyone froze.

'Jesus! Look at that,' Harry pointed to the parapet. Staring right at Harry was the biggest rat that Leo had ever seen. Its sleek fur glowed a bluey-black in the light. Part of its left ear was missing. Harry picked up a clod of earth and pelted it at the giant rodent, but the rat didn't flinch as the clod sailed past it. It was however disturbed enough to give Harry a hiss.

Leo grabbed Harry's arm as he made to shoot the great lump.

'You can't shoot rats in the trenches!'

'What's the holdup back there? Keep moving,' the sergeant ordered, managing to sound stern even when he whispered.

The flare light faded, and Leo pushed Harry on, feeling a bit odd knowing the rat was probably still sitting there.

Harry's breath was still rapid. 'I hate rats but that one takes the cake. I tell you he knows my ticket's been issued. He's going to be sitting there like a vulture when I get knocked,' Harry muttered.

They hadn't even made it over the top yet and Harry was already thinking he was going to die. That wasn't like him.

'Don't be talking through your hat, mate. Before you know it, we'll be back home telling Dot the rats were bigger than cats over here. No rat knows whether you're going to live or die.'

A strangled screech and rush of air. Leo's heart thumped. That meant there was a she—.

'Down!' roared the sergeant and Leo landed with a grunt, flat on the boards. The shell exploded in a fiery ball behind them, so close that Leo felt the heat on his back. They were sprayed with dirt and engulfed by the cloud of phosphorus fumes. Shrapnel cut into the trench wall above their prone bodies.

'Move! On the double, boys!'

Leo saw everyone yank themselves up and race along the trench. He could hear laboured breathing and someone sobbing. He smelt the garlic stench of the shell's fumes and tasted the sweat on his cracked lips, but his body felt strangely disconnected. It was as if some part of him was trying to detach itself and escape.

A cannibal drum beat of artillery fire started to pound around them. Flames mingled with pillars of black, white and yellow smoke as shells roared and ripped into earth and men.

They took cover against the clammy side of the trench. Leo wiped mud from his eyes and watched Harry's grim face turn a kaleidoscope of colour from the Very flares—green, blue, scarlet. Booms, hisses and screams of artillery exploded in all directions above their twisting trenches.

Time dripped like honey as they made their way along into small dugouts scooped into the side of the trench.

'Get some kip, boys,' Sarg ordered. 'We'll be right here in support. Might as well get used to the racket, we'll be up the front in a couple of days.'

Was he kidding? How could anyone sleep in this? If this was being in support, Leo sure as hell wasn't in a hurry to go up the line.

Scratching his burning scalp, Leo cursed the chats that seemed to be multiplying faster than feral rabbits. No matter how many times he turned his clothes inside out, it wasn't long before the lice made their way back. Who could sleep with chats nibbling at your scalp, fat rats running across you every bloomin' minute, and the earth ready to drop on you anytime?

He turned as best he could in the crude, muddy dugout and heard an alarmed squeak beneath his bottom that was then given a sharp nip. Jesus! He leapt up, banging his head on edge of a sheet of corrugated iron, then kicked out hoping to get the offending rat.

'What the hell?'

'Sorry, Harry. I meant to kick the rat.'

Harry scrabbled around and lit a match, then the stub of a candle. There was only enough room for three of them in the hole and Bull seemed to be taking up more than his share of it.

'Where is it?'

Leo's stomach curdled as he pointed. How could that be?

Swinging on Bull's sandbag of food, suspended from the roof above his snoring bulk, was the rat. It glared at Harry, as if daring him to use his bayonet. Part of its ear was missing. Was Harry right? Was this rat following them, telling them their time was near? Waiting to nibble on their lifeless fingers?

Chapter Thirteen

12 August 1916
Pozieres, France

With an ear-splitting crash a coal box bomb burst just in front of Leo's trench. A foul-smelling smoke filled the air and he coughed so hard he nearly puked.

'It's bad enough the Germans are at us but to be bombed by our own as well,' Bull declared as he moved sideways and sucked his gut in to allow an officer past. 'Whoever trained that mob in artillery doesn't know their arse from their elbow. Wait until I get a hold of one of 'em.'

'Bloody oath. I'll join you in giving 'em a box around the ears,' Harry agreed. Harry's elbow jammed into Leo's rib.

'Ow! Keep your bony bits to yourself. There's not enough room to swing a rat around here, let alone a cat,' Leo said as he attempted to rub his rib. 'So, it's Pulling Trench we're aiming for, right?'

'Yep, right in front of us so you can't miss it. Probably just a couple of footy fields to run,' Bull answered. 'We'll be right once we get this first hop over under our belts.'

Sure, Leo thought. It might be easy to run a couple of football fields but not these fields full of snarled wire, muddy shell holes and dead bodies. Oh God.

Leo watched the night sky explode into a firework display of Very lights and bombs. He had thought it was pretty the first time he'd seen the front, but that was from a distance when he wasn't expected to run under it all. Unable to talk above the barrage, Leo stood silently with the rest of the 13th. and tugged at his collar. It was too tight, he couldn't breathe. How in the blue blazes were they supposed to find Pulling Trench in all of this?

After what seemed an eternity, they were given the signal to move into the deep forward trench. Harry glanced over at Leo as they fixed their bayonets onto their rifles and yelled above the din.

'Keep your pecker up, Leo. This is what we came here for. Time to christen the squirt.'

Leo felt like he was a kid again about to leap from a towering rock ledge into Dead Man's Waterhole below. What would it be like to stick his bayonet into another man's gut for the first time? What if he was the one stuck? He shook away the thoughts and held his rifle tighter.

A flare gave Frosty's nervous face a macabre red glow. Bull was bent over like an old woman, the trenches too shallow for his height. Would everyone come out the other end in one piece?

A whistling scream announced the arrival of another shell and Leo crouched against the wall of the trench, flinching at the hiss of shrapnel flying past. He sucked in a breath and tried to stop his hands from trembling against the cold steel of his rifle. He hitched it to attack position. Somewhere beyond the shell-torn earth of no man's land were the Germans. Had they left their trenches when the barrage first hit? Or were they braced against the chilly trench walls, bayonets waiting? Even worse, were they grey shadows creeping?

Three shrill blasts from a whistle. Holy sweet Mary and Jesus, time to go.

Harry grinned and yelled, 'Over the top and the best of luck.'

Bull legged Harry up, who rolled over the sandbags and melted into the smoke. Leo followed and was immediately rocked by a shell exploding with a vivid red flash to his right. Where did Harry go?

Shit! Shit! Shit! Leo's new war mantra filled his head, blocking out the cacophony around him.

Shells hailed down among shadowy forms. Aussies or Germans? Sparks flashed as machine gun bullets nicked the wire around him. He stumbled over a snarl of wire, tugged his pants free and moved on, trying to ignore the menacing staccato. He struggled through the churned earth and spikes of jagged shrapnel. All around him men were dropping. Leo sucked his breath in against the dust and fumes.

'Keep going, Private!' Sergeant Strachan's voice boomed behind.

Leo turned. The sergeant thudded face first into the ground.

'Sarg!' He was supposed to leave any wounded for the stretcher bearers, but he bolted to the fallen man, turning him over.

'I told you to keep moving! Now leave me and get to that damn trench. It's just a little …'

Blood poured from the sergeant's mouth and the metallic smell of blood filled Leo's nose as he scrambled for a field dressing. A slick wetness seeped from the officer's chest and into the dressing Leo pressed down on.

'Stretcher! Stretcher!' Shots cracked all around him. Time to move. He marked the position with Strachan's upended rifle and blundered on to rejoin the line.

The ping of enemy bullets and steady putter of machine gun fire was broken by the rumble of another fiery shell. Smack! Something heavy sent him sprawling into the dirt. Was he dead? A fetid smell curled into his nostrils. Smelt like one of the dead, bloated kangaroos he sometimes found back home.

Oh God. Rotten flesh. Blown up from a grave, a rotten corpse had landed right on top of him. His throat jammed with a strangled scream and he threw the man off. Fresh and rotting bodies littered the ground, some still writhing and jerking like fallen wind-up tin toys. This wasn't what he'd signed up for.

He stumbled into Pulling Trench. An Aussie sauntered past. He looked at Leo panting against the wall and said 'All good, the Germans have cleared out. Bloody living like kings over here, they are.' Leo could only manage a nod. He had no idea how long it had taken him to make it to the objective, but it felt like he'd been at it for hours.

''bout time you showed your ugly mug, Dymond. Seems the whole German Army has it in for us.' Leo's eyes pricked with tears. Thank God. It was Harry.

In a daze, Leo followed Harry down the neat timber lined trench. The dugouts were enormous, some able to hold hundreds of men. Even though they were told the trench was empty, they both paused at the entrance of a large dugout.

Neat bunks lined the walls. A candle still flickered on a desk next to a velvet chaise longue. Pilfered French ornaments littered shelves and a huge oil portrait of a beautiful woman in a gilt frame stared right at them. It was obvious to Leo that the Germans had expected to stay put in their trenches for a long time.

Harry checked around the bunks while Leo poked his bayonet at a pile of folded blankets.

'Bugger, was hoping to stick a little blighter,' Harry said, then immediately started scouring for souvenirs. He whooped when he found a Pickelhaube helmet.

'What's *Gott mit uns* mean?' Harry asked as he examined the helmet.

'God with us,' Leo said.

Harry's lip curled. 'Not bloody likely.'

He put the German dress helmet on his head and grinned. '*Guten tag, Kamerad!*'

Leo gave an involuntary shudder. 'I think our tin hat suits you more.'

'Just think. If your ma and pa hadn't come to Aus, you might have met me here wearing this thing,' Harry said as he tapped the shiny metal and then continued poking around.

'Doesn't bear thinking about,' Leo said but Harry was too busy guzzling down some Schnapps he'd found. Leo couldn't believe how muffled the barrage above was. He knew they should be moving down the trench, but his muscles ached and his head hurt. A scuffling noise jolted Leo into alertness. Shit!

Leo's breath caught as he aimed his rifle. '*Stop oder ich schießen!*' Leo ordered with his heart hammering in his ears. 'I mean it, I'll shoot.'

Harry swung around, eyes wild. The glint of metal withdrew to the shadows and Alfred stepped forward.

'You bloody idiot, Fuller. I nearly shot you. I suggest you take that stupid helmet off and keep moving.' Alfred took the bottle of Schnapps from Harry's hand and swished it around. 'I should report you for drinking on duty.'

'Ah, give your arse a chance, Alfie. We've just worked our way through the corpse factory. Just a little celebratory drink for making it to the trench.' Harry stumbled back to his rifle. 'Dingle copped one in the neck right next to me. How many of us are left?'

Alfred put the bottle on the table. 'I don't know but I reckon the Germans will want this trench back so sort yourselves out. Just you remember which side you are on, Leopold.' He shoved past him and left the bunker.

'Bloody Alfred,' Leo muttered. 'Of course, I know what bloomin' side I'm on. I just want to get out of this hell hole and back home to my own bed.'

'Too right. Either way, we're a bit luckier than a lot of those blokes tonight.

'S'pose Alf's right. We'd better get going,' Harry said, attaching the German helmet to his belt. He grabbed a couple of bottles of Schnapps and put them in his bomb pack then clinked out the entry.

'Yep, we're lucky alright,' Leo muttered. But just how long would that luck hold out?

Chapter Fourteen

13 August 1916
Pozieres, France

The poplar spears lightened from black to purple silhouettes as the grey sky transformed with the flush of dawn. Within minutes, tongues of crimson and gold were licking at the shroud of mist on the horizon.

Leo tingled with the beauty of the morning and took a deep breath. *Ugh!* For just a few minutes he'd forgotten. Forgotten he was huddled in a boggy trench so close to them. While he couldn't see them, he could smell them. Remnants of one lay matted into the woollen fibre of Leo's tunic. Hundreds of strapping young men who had once been so rowdy now lay silently rotting in no man's land.

'Would you get an eyeful of that bonza sunrise? Feels like we should be off fishing, not stuck here in this bloomin' trench. I don't like being stuck on this toothpick of a salient like this.' Bull checked through the gap in the trench wall, known as a loophole, for any movement from the Germans. 'I wonder when they'll come back at us. Boy, I'd sell me own mother for a drink right now.'

Leo narrowed his eyes. It was strange to him that Bull sounded like one of the toffy Brit COs one minute, and an Aussie bullocky the next. He couldn't work him out. He leaned against the clammy trench wall and continued to admire the changing hues of the clouds above them.

'Bloody Fritz. I wish he'd stop taking out our boys bringing up the food and water,' Harry said as he offered Bull a drink from his canteen.

He turned towards Leo. 'You're a bit on the nose, chum. Not much better than the blokes out there.'

'Yeah, got a bit grubby when I tripped last night.' Leo swallowed hard but it couldn't keep at bay a vivid flash of last night's encounter with the corpse. He questioned whether he would ever be able to erase the grotesque image. He looked through the loophole.

'Leo. Hey, wake up Australia,' Bull's voice pierced through. 'Are you alright? You've gone whiter than a saint's undies.' Leo moved aside and let Bull look.

'Too right they want it back.' Bull shook his head and made room for Frosty to look.

'Shit! There's a whole horde of 'em comin' at us,' Frosty said as he clutched his rifle closer but left his face jammed into the gap in the sandbags.

Bull nodded. 'There must be more than a company heading this way.'

'I ain't about to just hand the trench over, we worked hard for it and they can go to buggery,' said Harry, adding his two bobs' worth.

Then they heard the drone above them. Like a swarm of wasps, planes dotted the sky. Leo's whole body tingled. Bombers.

'Strike me pink! There's more than sixty of 'em.' Bull crossed his chest. 'Better make me peace with ol' Hughie upstairs.' He looked further along the trench at the rest of the men in their platoon.

'Let's get out of here!' Leo clambered up the trench wall and tumbled over the sandbags.

The bombers closed from fifty yards to only twenty yards away. They began to drop their deadly load onto Meyer Trench to their left. Leo held on tight to his rifle. Apart from crumpled blobs of khaki and field grey, the barren earth was like a tilled farm field. The din of Lewis guns and exploding shells roared around him.

The air was so pungent with the stench of the corpses and bitter explosives that he struggled to breathe. The bombers were roaring above, dropping bombs and spitting bullets at them as they ran. What bloody idiot would volunteer to come to this hell hole?

'Heads up!' Bull yelled.

A black mass was spinning towards him.

'Aw, Sweet Mary, it's a rum jar. We're done for.'

Harry sprinted away nearly tripping over Bull, who rolled into a shell hole. Leo grabbed Frosty and hit the dirt. The air behind him shuddered and the earth trembled beneath his thumping chest.

'Onward march, fellas. It missed us,' Bull called.

Leo pulled himself up to a crouch but Frosty remained on the ground, spread like a lanky huntsman spider. Leo knelt and gave him a gentle nudge, 'C'mon, Frosty. Time to go.'

Frosty raised his head. 'What's up?' Had Frosty lost his nerve? After all, the rum jar had almost smudged them. The German motor bombs were shaped just like the large earthenware jugs that their rum issue came in and packed a nasty punch.

'I don't think I'm cut out for this. If you tell anyone, I'll kill you.' Frosty's face was flushed crimson.

The bullets whizzed around them.

Leo twitched with impatience. 'Just tell me. I don't want to hang about having a yarn in no man's land.'

'I've shit me pants alright.'

Leo looked at his mortified face and remembered his own guts had turned watery when he'd seen the rum jar arcing towards him.

'Don't worry I nearly shit myself too. Just toss 'em.' He dropped and wiggled over to a fallen cobber and with some effort yanked off the corpse's pants, puttees and boots. He threw the pants to Frosty, who looked rather disgusted.

'He doesn't need 'em. Do you want to explain why you're running around no man's in the buff?'

Frosty shot him a withering look but rolled about getting the pants on, giving up on the puttees.

'Ready?'

'Thanks.'

Leo handed him his rifle. 'San Ferry Ann, cove. Let's move.' No matter. What's a bit of shit between chums? That's all Pozières smelt like anyway.

Leo and Frosty ran double time and caught up to the line where the others were squatting behind the low hedge at the side of a dirt wagon track. Most of the section had ended up there with them.

Harry signalled to Leo to come closer and whispered, 'Look at 'em, just strolling down the track like they're on a Sunday picnic. Hey! I can see their OC; he's got an iron cross hanging from his collar. I'm going to give the little Kaiser a lead breakfast.'

The German officer spotted some of the Aussies and before Harry could squeeze off a shot, the Germans launched some stick hand grenades. They were so fast! A piercing scream. The air smelt like a piss pot in the morning mixed with old cabbage.

'Sweet Jesus. He just took the sarg's leg off.' Harry started firing into the mob. Leo stared at Sergeant Brown writhing on the ground as he clutched a weeping stub. The three Partridge boys were on the ground near him, calling out to each other.

What would poor Mrs Partridge do if she lost them all in one go like that? Zip! A bullet whistled past his ear. Bugger, what would my ma do if she—.

Leo dropped lower and poked his rifle through the hedge. He took aim at the advancing steel-capped group and fired for all he was worth. Men were cut down in every direction but at least he had some cover. Leo's hands burned as the Enfield rifle became hot. It was easy to shoot the men running clumsily forward in a line.

He glimpsed a bomber spiralling to the ground behind the advancing Germans and felt a glimmer of relief that the Lewis guns were shooting down the planes like a kid at a country fair. The squalls of bullets finally became a trickle. With a whoop of triumph, everyone reclaimed the German trenches.

Hallelujah!

It was soon obvious the Germans were not happy about the failure of their raid. They were pelting down the bombs.

Yet there was something else between the booms and crashes. Melodious notes rang out in the pauses.

'Did you hear that?' Leo asked Bull. Bull gave him a quizzical look.

'Are you kidding? My ears might be ringing but I can hear the minnies going off alright,' he answered.

'Not that. The tune in between … listen,' he urged.

At first, the notes warbled then rang clear. Bull and Harry both grinned.

'It's a bird. Must be in those couple of trees left over there,' Harry said.

They listened carefully in the next break.

'There it goes again, sounds almost like a magpie,' Bull said. 'Yeah, just like a magpie … from home.'

'How can it just sit there and sing in this bloody racket? You'd think the little blighter would have taken off. Sounds right cheery.' Harry squinted at the straggly poplars. 'I can't see him yet … hang on, there he is.'

Alfred shoved Harry as he walked past in the packed trench. He froze when he heard the sweet birdsong then sneered at Bull's serene expression.

'It's just a stupid bird.'

'Shut it, Alf. It's the best thing I've heard in days.' Bull didn't even bother to look Alf's way.

Alfred gave a snort and moved further up the trench, muttering something about them being sentimental idiots. They all sat and waited for the pauses to be filled with the dulcet song of the bird. A sharp retort shattered the brief silence.

'The bird just dropped out of the tree!' Harry made to scramble over the trench walls, but Leo grabbed his arm. No, surely not even Alf would stoop so low. They stared in the direction of the rifle shot.

Alfred lowered his gun and shrugged his shoulders. 'There's nothing to bloody sing about out here,' he said flatly. He plonked himself on a fire step and in the stunned silence, he polished his rifle with a rag.

Leo's jaw clenched. When he could finally utter a word, he released Harry's arm and stood in front of Alfred. 'You cold-hearted bastard.'

Alfred's eyes widened. Harry and Bull moved next to Leo and he saw his own rage mirrored in their faces. As Leo raised his fist, a fresh storm of bullets and bombs erupted, sending them all in all directions looking for cover. Leo glared at Alfred, who flattened himself against the trench wall next to him under a piece of tin. Any bet the Germans thought shooting the bird was a miserable act too.

A bullet ricocheted from the wire and skimmed Alfred's helmet. Shame they missed. Leo's lips were pressed so tightly he tasted blood. What sort of man would shoot a poor little bird?

Chapter Fifteen

18 August 1916
Halloy-lès-Pernois, France

Leo sank down onto the tattered cushions on the old wooden chair at the table with his mates, feeling almost human after a wash and receiving a new uniform. How long would it take before he was again burning the lice away from the seams with a cigarette? The aroma of fragrant herb and potato stew wafted over from the next table.

Mmm, what to have? Stew? Eggs and chips? Or both? Thank God for the French and their little *estaminets*. The cafe was a simple affair—a motley collection of battered wooden chairs, benches and tables set up in a crumbling stone cottage.

Bull called out to the woman running the cafe. 'Bongjour, Madame, some point blank over here for my cobbers.' She nodded and glided over with a few glasses of white wine. She had doe eyes set in delicate features. Only the bruise of shadows under her eyes marred her youthful appearance.

'Vill that be all, messieurs?' she asked.

Harry gave her his best dimpled smile. '*Oui, merci*. Perhaps we could share some dinner when you have finished?'

Frosty sniggered nervously. Leo noticed her chin lift and her cheeks wiggle as she tightened her jaw. He found his hands fiddling around his pockets. Seriously, did Harry really think she would?

'Ah, such an offer to dine with a brave Australian soldier but as you can see, I have many such soldiers to comfort with my food.' Harry coloured at her emphasis on the last two words and nervously gulped his wine.

She smiled and added, 'Perhaps you should save your strength for the war.' She snatched up some fallen rose petals near the tiny vase in the centre of the table. As she crumpled them in her fist, they let off a sweet aroma.

'I think we'll need another round to get through this war then. Mercy Blow Through,' Bull said, giving Harry an elbow.

'*Je m'excuse pour ces imbéciles incultes Madame. Nous apprécierions une carafe de vin blanc veuillez,*' Alfred piped up from the next table.

Bull calmly turned towards Alfred and gently took the woman's hand in his. '*Je ne veux pas vous offenser, je faisais juste fun. Le vin est délicieux. Merci beaucoup.* Shut your mouth, Alfred, or you'll catch a fly.'

Who knew what Bull had just said? Who cared? That sure took the sunshine out of Alfred. Madame patted Bull's hand and beamed at him.

'I am glad you find the wine to your taste and no, you did not offend me at all. You speak French very well. My name is Madame Louise. I think you need more than wine. I will bring you some of my son's favourite onion soup. He's also a soldier out there somewhere.' She smoothed her chignon and bustled off to get their soup.

Harry's cigarette burned to ashes in his fingers, but he didn't seem to notice.

'Don't worry, Harry. She's a beauty. It was worth a shot,' Bull comforted him.

Harry wiped his hands on his pants and lit up another cigarette. 'What's this with all of the Froggy talk then you dark horse, Bull?'

Bull fiddled with his glass. 'It's nothin', just learnt a thing or two over the years. Boy, I can't wait 'til she brings us that soup.'

Alfred's chair scraped in Leo's ear. Alfred stood and tossed an envelope onto the table in front of Leo.

'This got mixed up with my mail.'

Leo recognised his ma's neat hand that had written an address, but it was pa's spiky script that had written his name and he felt a rush of excitement, which dropped into irritation. They'd been given a batch of mail days ago. The letter looked as if it were a century old, all tattered and worn. Leo ignored Alfred and checked the seal.

'I didn't read it, I've got no interest in the scribbles of an enemy alien,' Alfred said as he turned back to George at the table. George's eyes had a glimmer of sympathy.

Harry flicked some cigarette ash from their table to Alf's. 'Give it a rest, Fanshaw.' He grinned when it arced straight into Alfred's bowl of soup.

Alfred glared at him, but Harry was more interested in Leo's letter. 'Go on, Leo, open it.'

Leo's fingers were stiff as he clumsily pulled out the letter. He was shocked to see it was dated before he'd left for war.

> *Dear Leopold,*
>
> *I hope this letter finds you well. I have tucked it inside a parcel for your Ma in the hope my friend, Heinrich, in the censor room is able to get it to you. We are permitted two letters a week, but they are limited in words and are heavily censored. He warned me that the mailroom is a mess, and it may be a while before you receive it.*
>
> *I'll be the first to admit I was less than happy that you chose to sign up. I was hoping you'd look after everyone for me but when your Ma wrote and told me she admitted she was worried you'd end up in here with me and the money is a big help so I guess it was the right thing to do. I'm mad with those Fanshaws for landing me in here but I should've seen it coming and made a move earlier. They'd better look after your Ma or there'll be hell to pay when I get out of here.*
>
> *This place is a dusty misery pit. They've stuffed thousands of us into wooden sheds divided up so that five of us have to share a space about nine by twelve feet. We are given a sack with a bit of straw for a bed and that's it. Lucky I can knock together some wood for a bed and a chair, or I'd be stuck on the floor. Ma, Oskar, and Dot want to come visit me, but I'll put them off as long as I can. Your Ma would sob if she saw it and I'd be worried they might catch something in the cess pit. Just to give you an idea the lavs are fifteen lidless tin buckets on the ground and we have to sit on a wooden rail. It's a bit a sight to see fifteen blokes all lined up but I won't even venture to describe the stench! Mind, now that you are in the Army, you're probably more than used to such luxurious conditions.*
>
> *I can't help thinking of what needs doing around the vineyard and have no idea if things are being taken care of the way I'd like but enough of that. How are you getting on?*
>
> *I don't know what to say about how to handle yourself in war. I wish I had some pearls of wisdom that would help get you*

*through beyond keep your head down and make it back in one
piece. It does damage to see the darkest parts of man, but you can't
escape seeing that when you're out there. No one who hasn't been
in that place could ever understand that. I am pained to think of
where war will take you, but I'll be here when you get back. I'm
glad Harry is with you as it can help to have a good mate at your
side when things get rough. No doubt you've both made some new
chums too, but you and Harry look out for each other.*

*I'm not sure when I'll get to write a letter like this again but
know you are both in my thoughts.*

Your loving Pa.

'Was it from your pa?' Harry asked. Leo nodded and handed the letter
to him. He watched Harry's face flush and his Adam's apple bob up and
down once he'd read the letter. He handed it back to Leo and lit another
cigarette without a word. He made out the smoke irritated his eyes but
while it seemed he fooled no one at the table, neither did they draw
attention to his teetering tears.

Madame Louise presented them with large bowls of fragrant soup,
transporting Leo back even more so to Borenore, slurping up his
mother's delicious fare. He'd barely had two mouthfuls when Bull's
spoon dropped into his empty bowl with a clatter. With a sigh of
contentment, Bull had all but inhaled the soup.

One of the boys started banging '*Aupres de Ma Blondes*' out on the piano.

'*Dans le jardin de mon pere, les lilas sont fleuris...*' Harry began
singing along. Madame Louise frowned at the rowdy men then at Harry.

Harry smiled and continued singing.

'*Aupres de ma blonde, qu'il fait bon, fait bon, fait bon...*'

Harry stopped. 'What does that song mean, Madame Louise?'
He was the picture of innocence.

Madame rolled her eyes. 'It is not a proper song.'

Bull coughed. 'Well that sure was a proper soup. *Superb*, Madame.
Oi, Bluey. How 'bout you play us "Australia Will Be There".' The piano
man obliged.

Madame Louise beamed at Bull. '*Merci*. You are *un home tres
amiable.*' She touched his bristly cheek, smiled at Bull's flaming cheeks,

and moved off to serve another table. Leo and Frosty sniggered to each other and continued with their soup but Harry sat brooding. He blew a lazy smoke ring over Bull's head.

'That's enough out of you lot.' Bull paused to knock back the rest of his beer. 'Listen up, we'd better soak it in now because I've heard we're heading back near Pozzie. Off to Mouquet Farm. That's a hard nut to crack, that one.'

They all groaned.

Harry pushed his soup aside, 'Let's hope the 50th and the 51st are somewhere else then. Last stunt they couldn't work out where the bloody hell they were. They left us all the dirty work and we had to give up all that ground we made. As useful as tits on a bull, that mob.'

'Yeah, what a balls up. We were lucky Mad Harry knew what to do. What about those poor chaps who kept going straight into German trenches and got caught?' Leo said as he chased a sliver of onion around his bowl.

Frosty nodded sympathetically. 'Too right, we lost some good men.'

Bull scooped up Harry's discarded soup.

Madame Louise returned with an armful of baguettes. 'Come on, my brave soldiers, eat up. My daughter has made you some baguettes. We are so fortunate to still have our farm and it is due to you helping us. *Bon appétit.*'

Bull immediately grabbed one of the crunchy sticks of fresh bread and smiled in delight. He gulped it down. Leo thought he'd better give one a try before Bull devoured the lot. Heaven.

Madame's laugh tinkled in Leo's ear. 'Per'aps, I had better get more, eh?' Bull nodded his encouragement, and she went to the door and called out.

'They are delicious. Try one, Harry,' Leo encouraged.

'I'd rather have a go at that.'

Leo followed his gaze. A young woman handed Madame Louise some more freshly baked bread. Her jet black hair fell in a glossy curtain over her finely chiselled cheeks. She glanced over, locked eyes with Leo and he drowned in their warm coffee colour. A bolt of heat shot straight to his groin. With a small smile, she disappeared behind a weathered door. His fingers dug into his pockets and wound themselves around Rose's handkerchief that she'd dropped so long ago at the dance where they'd first met. No, no, no. It was Rose he really wanted. And she wanted Harry.

'Oi, I saw her first,' Harry said, blowing smoke right in Leo's face. 'It's a shame there's plenty of food around here, she's definitely worth a full loaf.'

What a pig! Leo didn't know if the rumours of French women selling their bodies for food were true or not, but hearing Harry talk like that was … well, it got him all bent out of shape. Rose was too good for the likes of Harry. He thinks he's bloody Casanova Fuller.

Leo flicked a breadcrumb at Harry. 'Settle down, Harry. It won't fall off if you give it a rest, you know.'

Harry stared at Leo then blew a smoke ring into his face. 'Just being a red-blooded bloke. I wouldn't need bread to bribe her anyway.'

He stubbed his cigarette out, swung back in his chair and rocked with his hands behind his head, sprouting his elbows out. 'Not like you, eh.' He gave Leo a sympathetic look that had him squirming.

Harry winked. 'I try to help Leo out with the ladies, but I swear if it was raining virgins he'd be locked in the dunny with a tinkle-tinkle.'

What the blazes? How dare Harry tell everyone that he thought Leo preferred blokes? His jaw locked and Harry's smirk blurred. Blood pounded in his ears like waves thumping into a dinghy. So much for Pa's request to look out for each other.

Leo glared at Harry. That was it. He didn't care if Rose was Harry's girl or not. If he ever got the chance to see her again, he'd give Harry a run for his money.

'Horse feathers, Harry. Leo's just a bit shy. You can't handle it that she was giving him the eye and not you. Besides, that's no way to be talking about the lovely ladies of France,' Frosty admonished as he folded his arms to his chest.

'Right you are there, Frosty. Here comes Madame now,' Bull gave Harry a look blacker than a railway tunnel at midnight.

Madame went to offer a fresh loaf of bread to Bull's eager hands and then seemed to think better of it, handing the loaf to Frosty. 'My daughter, Helene, might like her hard work to be shared by more than one of you.'

Harry watched as Helene returned with another loaf for Alfred's table.

'We would all like to share Helene's … bread,' Harry muttered as he lit another smoke.

Madame Louise's face grew stony as she faced Harry. 'My *fifteen-year-old* daughter is beautiful, yes. She is a talented *boulangeree* and that is *all* she will be to you.' Harry's cocky smile slipped, and he gave a contrite nod. Her nostrils flared as she continued. 'Remember you are a guest in this country. Perhaps it is time you went back to your billets.' She grabbed Helene's arm and returned to the kitchen.

'Bloody hell! Don't blow your nose, Harry, or your bloomin' head'll cave in. Damn well won't be welcome back 'ere again, now will we?' Bull drained the last of the beer and indicated for Frosty to leave the loaf on the table. 'Better make ourselves scarce.'

Alfred blocked Harry with his leg as he tried to slink past.

'Maybe you should act more like a gentleman and let your brain speak for you rather than your dick. You're a disgrace to the 13th.'

Leo pushed aside Alfred's long legs and looked him square in the eye. He was pissed off at Harry, but Alf could go to buggery before he'd let him lord it over any of his chums. 'Who asked you, Fanshaw? Maybe the 13th can do without people who freeze when Fritz comes at them with a bayonet, so no one has to save their skinny little arses.' For the second time that day Alfred's mouth formed a silent 'O'.

'I'm off to give my best to the ladies of the red lamp. Don't wait up, now,' Harry said with a casual wave. He headed to a small cluster of cottages.

'Think his brains are in his pecker. He'll end up lit up if he's not careful,' Bull said. 'Was he always like this?'

Leo scratched his head and tugged his hat on. 'He's always liked the girls but nah, not like that.'

Leo sighed. Harry's cheeky flirting had hardened. If Leo got the chance, he'd warn Rose off Harry.

Harry was like a fox in the chicken coop. Deadly.

Chapter Sixteen

29 August 1916
Mouquet Farm, France

Could a bloke get any wetter? Even a duck would get bogged in this lot. Leo huddled against the sticky trench wall. Icy rain sluiced down his mac and somehow into his great coat underneath, weighing it down. The unrelenting water trickled down his spine and even found its way up his sleeves. The ground had turned into a muddy caramel syrup. Another dozen or so salvoes poured down on to the 14th and 15th Battalions in Browning Trench on the front line just ahead of him. Poor beggars.

He surveyed the desolate French landscape. No longer fresh green hills dotted by clumps of forest. It was a churned, barren mass of fetid mud and spindly stumps. Rats darted from one bloated corpse to another. In the distance, Leo watched a salvo disappear into the soup with a puff of black smoke followed by a fountain of mud and tree limbs spiking into the slate sky. Hell wasn't fire and brimstone, it was Somme mud.

There was nowhere dry to escape the deluge. Bull was snoring against the slippery wall of the trench. How could he sleep in this? There was no way Leo could sleep so he settled for working one leg at a time out of the mud. B Company had stayed behind and done their job carrying up the rations—cold spuds, cheese, bread, and jam to add to tins of bully beef. Leo clicked his tongue. When was his section going to be allowed to move up to join the rest of the battalion? It was just Leo and his mates left now, Harry's grumbling having got them the honour of cleaning the dixies when they got back. As if things weren't bad enough already, a wailing scream sliced through the air and he dropped into the slush.

'Bloody artillery! That was one of ours. Didn't anyone train that bunch of idiots?' Bull was awake now.

'My oath.'

Finally, Frosty had completed his share of the pot scrubbing and they were off to relieve the 15th on the front line. The light was fading as they struggled through clotted fields to the forward area. At least it had stopped bucketing down. Leo tugged hard and managed to extricate one leg from the knee-deep morass, only to find his other had sunk even further. Bull yanked him out with slurping release. Most of the duckboards had been devoured by the hungry earth.

'I reckon if we keep going, we'll eventually get swallowed up and with any luck pop out the other end in Aus,' Harry said.

'Don't you mean China?' Frosty asked, yanking hard but the mud held on to his boot.

'Who bloody cares? I say the Germans are welcome to France. They've turned it into a field of stumps, mud and wire. What in the hell are the brass thinking? It's pissing down, we've been at it in this shit for hours and we'll be stuffed before the stunt. Do they expect us to flamin' mud wrestle our way to victory for Mouquet Farm? This is hell out here, I'm done.' Harry flopped onto the mud in protest.

Everyone slid down to the ground in an exhausted heap. Leo could feel the insidious liquid mud pull downward. It had the consistency of thin cream on top followed by a layer of sticky toffee then firmer chalky clay. It reeked of manure and corpses.

'Better not lay here too long, chaps, or we'll be joining the others,' Frosty warned.

Leo rolled towards him, opened an eye and froze. A mud-daubed hand, with its rat-nibbled fingers, reached out towards him.

With a gasp, he leaped into the air, tripped over a protruding boot and just managed to avoid stomping on an upturned bloated face.

'What in the hell are you doing up there? You're worse than a spooked horse. Stop that racket before you draw the crabs,' Harry grumbled.

Leo shoved him. 'Get up. We need to get moving.'

'You don't think we'll get shelled right here, do you?'

They were all upright now.

'Who bloody knows?' Leo set off.

'Spooked alright, he's off quicker than a bride's nightie.' Leo heard Harry say.

Too right. He wasn't hanging around that corpse-riddled mud a minute longer.

Leo didn't get more than another hundred yards before he found himself thigh deep in mud again. His legs were so cold, the mud soon numbed him. He stuck his rifle in the soup and tried to lever out but only managed to jam his rifle up. With a roar and a splat, a shell exploded about fifty yards to the right of him sending up a dark brown geyser of mud and shell splinters.

Leo doubled his efforts but couldn't get his legs out any further than the knees. He heard the mud squelch behind him and put his hand up for Bull to yank him out yet again.

'Swilling around in the mud where you belong, I see.' Leo groaned. Now there was an unwelcome voice. He thought Alfred had left ages ago.

'Go stick your head in a dyke,' Leo responded.

'Good evening to you too, Private Dymond.'

Leo twisted and he could see the others slopping thorough the mud towards him looking like bunyips from an Aboriginal tale.

'Are you gonna give him a hand or what, Alf?' Alfred gave Bull a doleful look, so Bull huffed and passed his rifle to Leo. Leo's hands were coated in slimy mud and it took a few goes before he was able to clamber back up to the duckboards.

'Thanks, Bull.' Leo flicked mud from his pants in Alfred's direction.

Alfred rolled his eyes. 'How mature. I don't have time for this. Haven't you noticed that we've been left behind?'

Leo saw he was right. There was only the churned earth punctuated by a few splintered oak trunks sticking out of the sea of mud like masts of a shipwreck. Not a sign of their battalion. His gut curled, sending a snake of unease up to his throat. He didn't want to be stuck out here in the dark.

Frosty and Harry caught up to them.

'What are you doing out here, Fanshaw? Thought you'd left with C,' Harry said. He flicked his cigarette butt to the duckboard.

Alf tapped his foot. 'What's it to you? Why were you lot rolling around in the mud like pigs when you should be moving forward?'

'Some of us are bloody tired from lugging up the grub while it seems others are fresh as a daisy after a rest and a beer at the local,' Bull muttered. Bull always had his finger on the pulse. Leo hadn't noticed Alf sneak off to an *estimanet* rather than carrying the rations up. Sneaky, lazy little …'

'Don't know what you're yapping on about.' Alf stopped talking as he was drowned out by the roar and plops of a few shells, each one getting closer to them.

'You're full of bullsh—, Alf. It's getting hot here, time to go.' Frosty waved them on. Leo raised his eyebrows. He'd never heard Frosty utter less than a friendly word or offer any direction to anyone.

'Nobody asked you, Winterbottom.' Alfred shoved past Frosty, sending Frosty's arms flailing as he lost his balance and tipped backwards. He landed in the mud, which sucked him in up to his arm pits. Alfred laughed and stomped away.

'You're such an arsehole, Alf. Get back here and give us a hand to pull him out,' Leo called after him.

Alfred didn't bother to turn, just gave a flick of his wrist in a mock salute.

'Let 'im go. Hopefully, he'll get stuck out there himself.' Bull lined himself up on the duckboard in front of Frosty.

'C'mon, Bull. I'm sinking,' Frosty yelled, waving an arm. He'd been lucky to have his arms raised when he'd fallen.

Bull extended his rifle and pulled hard but Frosty was firmly wedged. They tried with two rifles and two men each side but Frosty screamed in pain.

'We're going to break his back the way we're going,' Bull groaned.

'Well, we can't just leave him there.' Harry frowned and started pacing the duckboard. 'Maybe if we double it, we can catch up to the others and get some more help.'

Bull caught his breath and nodded. 'You go. We'll keep trying.'

In the distance, a few more shells exploded in a puff of black smoke and mud. Harry didn't need any more encouragement to get moving.

Bull gave a grim smile. 'Let's see if we can get you out before it gets pitch black out here.'

Leo rocked on his heels biting his thumb nail. He spotted some communication wire that had been sliced by a shell. 'What if we tied that around the tree trunk behind him?'

'Good thinking.'

They slopped through the syrup and tied the wire around a sturdy trunk and then Frosty, shifting duckboards to stay afloat as they went. Leo used his entrenching tool in the surrounding mud but couldn't break the seal of suction around Frosty. Frosty didn't utter a sound as he watched with haunted eyes.

Bull and Leo continued to dig around Frosty then heave on the wire in turns. Leo kept digging, his knees aching worse than when he knelt on the hard pew kneelers in church. His hands were raw. He felt cold fingers grip his hand.

'You have to go. Leave me,' Frosty told him.

Leo sucked in his breath and squeezed Frosty's hand hard. He couldn't look at him. He kept digging then made his way back to Bull.

'We've got to get him out on this one.' Bull nodded. With bullock strength they heaved, slipping and sliding until a release of tension landed them both on their bums in the bog.

'I'm out!'

Leo felt his muscles flop. Thank God for that.

Frosty rolled up and untangled himself from the wire then turned to face them.

Bull roared with laughter. The French mud had finally released Frosty but had kept his pants in exchange.

'It ain't funny.' Frosty investigated his vacated hole in the mud but it had already filled with water. His pants were lost.

'Sorry but you're a real sight with those chicken legs. Like one of those Frenchy girls, you look—' Bull hadn't been watching as he stumbled towards Frosty and had fallen straight into an oily shell hole. He burst from the greasy sulphur-coloured water, spluttering and swearing. Frosty convulsed with glee.

'C'mon Bull, now is no time to be playing you're a U29,' Leo teased. 'I reckon we've got five minutes of light left.'

'Shut up, you lot. Don't just stand there cackling, give me a bloody hand.' Bull wasn't making any headway trying to get out of the crumbling shell hole and his splashing dislodged a body. The grisly figure bobbed right into Bull's stomach, which promptly emptied at the sight of the mashed skull.

Frosty grimly handed Bull his rifle and they heaved him out.

'It's like being in hell out here, hey Bull?' Frosty gave Bull's shoulder a pat.

Bull emptied his helmet of tainted water and slammed it down on his solid skull.

'Thanks, fellas. I won't ever forget that.' Frosty's voice cracked.

'You're right there, Frosty. Don't go getting all sentimental.' Bull nodded his head to a couple of corpses near the tree. 'Grab some pants and we'll get moving. Gotta tell Harry before he brings the whole platoon out in this swamp.'

'Okay, not like I haven't borrowed some daks before.' He grinned at Leo and went off to scrounge some pants while Leo and Bull started making their way across the field.

'What's taking him so long? I'm getting bloody cold after my little dip.'

Leo shivered too, what little warmth the miserable day had offered was being quickly leached away. He turned and was surprised at how far they'd already travelled, the duckboards obviously keeping them above the mud rather than having to wade through it made a big difference. Frosty was just a speck in the gloom.

'Can you see him?'

'Yeah, he's just coming out now from the tree. Maybe he stopped to collect tags or something.' Leo knew Frosty liked all the boys to be accounted for so their families would know what happened. They would never be found if the mud made its final claim.

'Probably. He's a good kid but we don't have time for that now.'

The last of the grey light deepened into ebony nightfall. Bull was right to be tense. Leo heard the plops of a couple of duds land then another more ominous sound. A familiar whistle. They dropped to the ground.

Trees splintered behind them and then the most awful sound. A hellish scream of pain then nothing.

'I'm going back.' Leo struggled to get up on his jelly legs.

'Wait for me.'

They tapped along the duckboards for an eternity. When Leo sensed they were near the poplars, he flicked on his torch. Who cared if they could be seen, he had to find Frosty. He could still smell the sulphurous fumes smoking in the trees, only two trees of the clump of oaks were left. He squinted and poked around but couldn't see Frosty anywhere. He wasn't in the shell hole among the gnarled wire or mangled bodies.

'Can't see anything.' Bull scanned the earth with his torch too.

'Stop! What's that?' Leo was sure he'd seen something glint as Bull swept his torch across. He guided his torch to a set of tags hanging from the lowest branch of the oak that had assisted them earlier. Leo's fingers trembled and he swallowed back. He would not vomit.

Bull picked them off the branch and examined them. With a nod, he wiped the blood from them and tucked them into his pocket. They were Frosty's tags but, where was he?

They scoured the area around the tree, poking sticks into shell holes and tried not to fall into mud sink holes. The Germans must have improved their aim as the shells were being aimed square into the front line instead of over shooting into their field.

The horizon flickered and boomed in battle while they continued to search. Leo kept his ears tuned for the slightest murmur or groan. In the distance, he saw a flicker of light bob up and down.

'I hope that's Harry.'

Harry arrived with five of the burliest blokes Leo had ever seen.

'Rounded up these blokes from A Company to give us a hand. Where's Frosty?'

'Not sure, but think he got smudged by a rum jar.'

'Shit.'

Leo's throat felt like he had jammed a sock at the back of it and his ears ached. He refused to cry in front of these blokes he didn't even know. One of them gave his shoulder a squeeze and started rolling other corpses over that they had hadn't looked at yet, adding them to the line Leo had started. The others joined him in the grisly task as Harry inspected each one. Leo kept searching among the shell holes.

Bull gave Leo's back a gentle pat. 'I think it's time, chum. The moon's comin' up.'

Leo felt as weary as Bull sounded. He looked up at the sky. The clouds had mostly cleared and the biggest tangerine moon he'd ever seen was rising. It was as if the moon had moved its orbit to help them find Frosty. It was moving higher, behind the oak branches.

No. Leo's knees buckled, and he felt his bottom sinking into the chilly muck. He threw his helmet off and gripped his scalp. No, no, no.

'What's wrong?'

Leo pointed to the tree, hand over his mouth.

'Oh, sweet Mary.' Bull sank next to him.

Whether the borrowed pants were blown off or he hadn't yet managed to get some on, Frosty's spindly white legs were silhouetted by the moon, dangling in the oak's top branches. Only his legs.

Bull threw his torch down. 'It ain't hell here, this is stinkin' purgatory.'

Chapter Seventeen

November 1916
5th London General Hospital
St Thomas' Hospital, London

For the first time since they'd arrived in London, Rose was excited. Both Rose and Adelaide had been sorely disappointed to find themselves split off from the other Aussie nurses and added to support London's 5th General Hospital. It didn't help that the Queen Alexandra's Royal Army Nursing Corps had given them a right royal frosty reception. Even the normally cheerful Adelaide had paled in the grey of London. Rose had been convinced they'd made a grave error in coming over.

But today would be different. They were finally being given a tour of the surgical ward and she couldn't wait. It would make up for the weeks of scrubbing floors, changing bed linen and other mundane housework. Today she'd see fresh surgical cases, men not long from the front.

'Quick, Addie. We must hurry.'

Adelaide gave a yawn, gulped the last of her tea and they joined the other nurses leaving the dining hall. They met Senior Sister Plunkett at the entrance of one of the surgical wards.

'Good morning, everyone. Today, I thought it would be helpful for the Australians among us to have a look at a case of frostbite as I am fairly certain this will be an unfamiliar condition to you.' Senior Sister Plunkett waved them into the ward.

Rose shrugged to Adelaide. The sister was right; they had never seen a case. At that moment, Elise arrived, veil askew and puffing hard.

Unlike Rose and Adelaide, Elise hadn't minded joining London's 5th. Rose put it down to her having an English mother.

'Nice of you to join us, Nurse Gardiner.' Sister's tone was as icy as the morning air, but Elise just smiled her apology.

The ward was a sea of men in hospital blues and varying lengths of bandaged limbs. Rose's nose soon wrinkled at a sickly-sweet stench that only grew worse the further along the ward they walked. Senior Sister Plunkett stopped next to a bed that seemed to contain the source of the foul odour. Rose blinked her watering eyes and steeled herself. Many of the small group paled and swayed around her.

The sister told them to come closer and surround the bed. The soldier looked as if he was asleep, but Rose was certain he was alert.

Sister Plunkett yanked down the poor man's cover, revealing two bandaged limbs. One leg had been amputated just below the knee.

'Firstly, I'll show you the case of frostbite, then I'll show you what happens when the polluted soils of France have gotten in and done their work—gangrene.'

The soldier's jaw tightened and he grimaced when the sister unravelled the bandage on his left foot.

'Oh, dear,' Elise gasped while Adelaide started to sway against Rose.

'Unfortunately, trench warfare and French winters are not kind to feet,' Sister said. Rose nodded.

The soldier's foot was missing most of his toes and was a waxen colour. He was covered in fading blisters that made his foot look as if he'd dropped a pot of scalding water on it.

Sister started unbandaging the other leg. 'If you happen to be sent forward to the Casualty Clearing Stations, you'll see plenty of this. When men stand in cold, boggy trenches for hours on end, they are not getting enough blood circulating and frostbite, trench foot and trench fever can result. This condition can worsen to become completely gangrenous.' She paused and seemed to think better of taking off the bandage until she'd finished her lecture.

'The majority of cases among the soldiers is due to anaerobic infection and takes the form of gas gangrene. This soldier has already had one operation to deal with the condition, but unfortunately it seems to have spread further than first thought and he will require further attention.'

She took the bandage off and the smell was even ranker, drawing a few groans from other patients. The soldier's eyes were open now but he stared at the ceiling.

'Here, you can see the swelling and these blebs are filled with a bloody serum which, after bursting—as in here and here—leave a raw surface and a rather unpleasant odour.'

At this point, Adelaide grabbed an enamel bowl and threw up and another nurse fainted. Three other nurses bolted from the room. Sister Plunkett waved some orderlies over and asked them to attend to things. Rose then saw the horrified look on the soldier's face.

'What's your name?' she asked

'Billy. I'm real sorry about that.'

'Oh, you're Australian. It's hardly your fault. Where are you from?' Rose asked softly.

He grinned, showing one of his front teeth was missing. 'Yep, sure am. I'm from up the Blue Mountains, Blackheath.'

Rose grinned back. 'Me too. Leura. We're practically neighbours.'

'So, these are your last girls standing, Sister Plunkett,' a cheerful voice said behind Rose. She turned and saw the doctor and realised he was right. There was only Rose and Elise left next to the bed.

'Uh, yes Major Richmond. Nurse Gardiner and Nurse –' Sister looked desperately at Rose and she quickly jumped in. 'Shipley. Nice to meet you, Major Richmond.'

The doctor was tall and had an elegant, no-fuss air about him, but his smile was broad and engaging. With a touch of silver in his hair, Rose guessed him to be in his early thirties.

'Quite. I was just explaining how frostbite could quickly turn to gangrene.' Sister Plunkett tried to regain her composure, but the doctor wasn't letting her off so easily.

He waved away her offer to apply fresh bandages and did them himself. 'While I don't necessarily approve of this being a first introduction to the surgical ward, it does give one a measure of who has a cast iron stomach and may do well in surgery and who might not be so well suited. What do you think Nurse Shipley?'

Rose almost sniggered at his emphasis on her last name. 'It's certainly a difficult case. I've heard there is a crackling sensation when the skin's pressed due to gas in the tissue.'

He smiled. 'Yes, quite right. It's very unfortunate for Private Thompson here to have to go undergo another operation, which I will be doing shortly.'

'Will that mean above the knee?' Rose asked, looking at where the motley skin returned to a normal colour.

'Yes, it does.' The doctor's face reflected her solemn feeling.

'Nurse Shipley, you can remove your hand from the patient's now. I know you Australians might think this appropriate, but such behaviour is not welcome in our wards,' Sister Plunkett said primly. 'Perhaps you can tell me how you would treat frostbite at first contact.'

Rose looked down and saw she was holding Billy's hand. She flushed and dropped his hand while Elise glared at Sister Plunkett and the doctor frowned. He then stuck his head down to complete the dressing.

'I would use friction to restore circulation, massage limbs with olive oil and do daily immersions in hypertonic saline as it assists with pain relief and keeps the wounds clean. I've heard that some of our Gallipoli soldiers responded well to a treatment of dry boracic and cotton wool,' Rose rattled off. She then looked at Billy's face and her anger spiked. 'I also think a lot can be said for the power of comforting an ill soldier with a friendly word or hand squeeze.'

Sister Plunkett opened her mouth but didn't utter a word. Major Richmond beamed at her and Rose felt a glow of pleasure.

'Seems she knows her stuff, Sister. I know who I'd rather have holdin' me hand in the war,' Billy piped up.

'Too right!' echoed around the ward.

'That's quite enough from you men. I'd best leave you in Major Richmond's capable hands while I check on the other nurses.' Sister Plunkett practically flew from the ward as the men cackled after her.

'Sorry, Nurse Shipley. I've probably just made you an enemy worse than the Hun,' Billy said as Elise propped him up on his pillows.

Major Richmond looked up from filling in Billy's chart. 'Don't you worry about Nurse Shipley. She can come to me if she has any further trouble. I think that's earned you a trial entry to my surgical team. What do you say?'

Rose squealed.

'I'll take that as a yes.'

Rose nodded and Billy squeezed her hand. 'If anyone had to cut off me leg, I'd rather you be the one to keep an eye on 'im.'

'If I have my way, Billy. One day, *I'll* be the one cutting off your leg.'

Both men looked at her in surprise.

'Better watch her, Doc or you'll be outta job.'

'Don't you worry, Private.' The doctor winked at Billy. 'I've definitely got my eye on this one.'

Chapter Eighteen

December 1916
London

'For goodness sake, stop sighing and turn on the lamp,' Elise grumbled in the dark of their nurse's quarters.

'Sorry,' Rose replied. 'I'll be quiet.'

'Tell me what's bothering you and maybe we'll both get some sleep.' Rose could hear Elise fumbling in the dark and then the cave of the room that they shared with Adelaide was lit with the feeble glow of the lamp. Adelaide was on night shift. Elise propped her pillows against the wall and wrapped her shoulders in a woollen shawl she had draped at the bottom of her bed. She sat waiting expectantly.

Rose cleared her throat. 'You're right, something is bothering me, but it's not exactly a problem.'

Elise sniffed. 'You mean Adelaide's whirlwind romance with Oskar?'

Rose gasped. 'Did she tell you?'

Elise arched a brow. 'No, her mooning about every time she got a letter and finding out he's coming over wasn't very subtle. What are you worrying about?'

'That she's going to throw all of her training away and go and marry him before she gets the chance to even find out who she is.' Rose sighed.

Elise shrugged. 'Well, not much you can do.'

'She's seeing Oskar tomorrow. Hopefully, he won't be foolish enough to propose before he heads to the front.'

'She's a big girl, Rose. Maybe it's more that she'd be leaving you behind.'

Rose felt the punch of that truth. She scowled.

Elise stuck her hands up in surrender. 'Only making an observation. You'll be fine. I'm still here, I know I'm not as close to you.'

A weight settled in the pit of her stomach. Concern and irritation collided. Would Oskar ask her, and would she say yes? Maybe she should worry when there was reason to. Elise was gazing at her and the last of her words penetrated. 'Oh, yes. Thanks. Of course, we'll still be here for each other no matter what happens.'

'Let's hope they'll be sensible enough to remain sweethearts until the war is over.' Elise rummaged in a drawer next to her then offered Rose a biscuit.

Rose munched on her biscuit, enjoying the sweetness but finding it hard to swallow. She stopped eating. If she'd have known her time with Adelaide would end soon, she'd have been much more attentive. She dreamed of them ruling the RPA wards as doctors one day. That was the problem. That was her dream. She needed to let go and let Addie find her own way.

'I'm sure I'm worrying over nothing. I should let you get some sleep. Thanks, Elise.'

Rose lay quietly in the darkness. Everything would be fine. Even if Oskar proposed, it wasn't as if Adelaide would marry him in an instant and ship off back home.

***

Rose scanned the ward and was satisfied that all the men were comfortable. She was grateful for the extra time to spend with Billy.

''Ere's my favourite nurse. I was hoping to catch you before I left.' Billy pulled himself up to a seated position, took Rose's offered cup of hot cocoa and sipped it. 'Aah, that hits the spot. Not the same as a beer, but beggars can't be choosers, now can they?'

Rose sat on a chair next to him. 'No, they can't. Now, where are you off to?'

'Queen Mary's. Someone told me they have some beaut ideas for blokes like me, but with a buggered foot and an amputation above the knee, I'm not holding me breath. Can you get my Blighty bag for me?' he said, pointing to a small chest of drawers.

Rose handed him a Calico bag with a drawstring. He gave her a small box, tied with a satin ribbon.

'It's a bit late, but Merry Christmas, Nurse Shipley.'

'Billy, you're not supposed to—' He held up a hand, so Rose opened the box. She pulled out a crystal bottle of French *parfum*. 'It's beautiful … I really can't.'

'Yes, you really can.'

Rose opened the brass cap and the scent of orange blossom and sandalwood made her tingle with thoughts of summer.

'I got it from a French family I helped. They said to give it to someone special and … here you are.' Billy blushed but there was a determined glint in his eye.

Rose shook her head. 'I'm sure they meant *your* someone special.'

'Take it. You don't want to hurt an Aussie soldier's feelings, now do you?' He sipped his cocoa, but his eyes stayed fixed on her.

'Of course not. I'll treasure it.'

'Oh bugger!' In trying to shuffle up higher, Billy had spilled cocoa down the front of his gown. 'Lucky, it'd cooled down.'

'I'll get you a fresh gown.' Rose put the perfume back in its box, then in her pocket.

'I might need a sponge bath with that,' Billy called as she headed to the storage cupboard.

'Nurse, I've spilled me tea too,' a couple of soldiers piped up.

One of them was getting a temperature check from Adelaide and she slapped him on the wrist. 'Be quiet, you cheeky thing. Bit frisky tonight, aren't they?' she said to Rose.

'As always.'

'We can't help it. We've barely seen a woman for months and then we get landed in here with two of the prettiest angels on earth. A man's only human,' grumbled Adelaide's patient.

Adelaide looked up from writing her notes on his chart. 'Flattery won't help. I still have to change your dressing before you go to sleep.'

The man groaned and rolled from his side onto his belly. 'This is not how I'd prefer you to see my bum.'

Rose and Adelaide laughed. In a ward full of polite Tommies, the crude Aussie humour did not cut it with the English nurses, but they didn't mind.

Rose came alongside her. 'So, did you get it?'

Adelaide beamed. 'Yes, and it's beautiful.'

'I can't wait to see it.' Rose knew her smile was tight and tried to broaden it. It was as she feared. Adelaide had been thrilled when Oskar had arranged dinner at The Savoy and proposed to her. It seemed he wasn't the only romantic in the 54th Battalion. The men had pitched in for the fancy dinner. She planned on marrying him as soon as possible and had just managed to find a wedding dress.

An orderly handed Adelaide a telegram. She finished up her patient before ripping it open. Rose watched her expectant face drop from excitement to misery. She slowly tucked the paper away and tidied up, shooting a glance at the matron working at her desk at the other end of the ward. Rose took the hint and returned to Billy, fixing his gown.

Adelaide moved closer and whispered. 'The wedding's been cancelled.'

'What? Wait until I get a hold of that Oskar Dymond. I'll wring his bloody ne—'Adelaide shushed her. 'No, it's not like that. They're moving out, probably to France. He'll try to make it back as soon as he can.'

Rose hugged her. 'I'm sorry.'

'I'll stay on as long as I can, but I hope he doesn't take too long.'

Something about the catch in her voice made Rose suspicious. 'Why the rush? I know you love him and are happy to give up all of this glory here, but …?' Adelaide had a protective hand over her belly. '… are you?'

'Yes. I'm sorry I haven't said anything. I thought my illness coming over was just seasickness. Oskar is so happy. I don't know what we are going to do now.' Adelaide looked so wretched that Rose found she felt sorry for her rather than angry.

Covered in layers of Adelaide's uniform, there was no sign of what lay beneath, but how long could she hide it?

'Let's hope he can manage some special leave and make it back in the next few weeks.' Matron coughed and they drew apart. 'We don't want Matron finding out. We'll talk later.'

Adelaide nodded and moved to the other side of the ward.

'Sorry for listening but that's a tough break,' Billy said, jolting Rose from her thoughts.

'Yes, it is. She was really looking forward to being married on New Year's Eve,' Rose said.

Billy's face was drawn. 'Yes, that's tough, but what I meant was her bloke heading off to France.'

Despite all the time Rose had spent with Billy, he had not spoken about his time at the front and Rose had left it alone. Not many of the men liked to talk about it.

'Where were you at the front?' Rose asked.

'I was at Pozieres first. Bloomin' blood bath that was. Lost a lot of good blokes from the 13th,' Billy said, his eyes glazing over.

'The 13th? I didn't realise. I know some men in the 13th. Harry Fuller and Leo Dymond. I haven't heard from Harry in months. I guess it was hard to find the time to write and I've been so busy myself …' Rose stopped as Billy's gaze remained fixed.

'Billy. Billy, are you alright?'

He snapped back and looked at her.

'Would you like to talk about it?'

He looked around the ward of broken men.

'Pozieres was hell.'

Chapter Nineteen

1917
London

'Aaaaah,' Adelaide yawned in Rose's ear. While Rose agreed, they *had* been sitting on the hard-wooden chairs listening to Matron Robertson lecture for quite a while, and unlike Adelaide, Rose was fascinated by what the matron was sharing. She poked Adelaide's side and indicated that she should stop slouching down in her chair as it made her slightly bulging stomach more obvious. Adelaide immediately straightened and gave a cursory glance around the dining room cum lecture hall. Rose turned her attention back to the educational.

'As some of you may well head off to France once the Spring Offensive begins, it's important that you are aware of some of the treatments used on the front line. An important development in treating infection, thus minimising the need for amputations, in the last year is the Carrel Dakin treatment.' The matron pointed to an apparatus set up on one of the tables. It was a maze of glass bottles, tubes and rubber hoses. 'As you know, Dakin's solution is a careful mixture of calcium chloride, sodium borate and water that sets free hypochlorous acid gas, which is a powerful antiseptic.'

Rose ignored another yawn from Adelaide and found herself nodding. It was particularly important to get the mixture right. She watched as Matron held up a large glass container attached to a rubber tube that was then attached to a series of smaller glass tubes.

'These smaller tubes are instillation tubes. They are perforated on four sides for a few inches of their distal portion, and at the end tied with silk or linen thread. These small tubes are layered with bandages and the Dakin solution runs through them to sterilise the wound.

The size of the wound determines the number and length of tubes. This installation apparatus delivers the solution using irrigation that allows the right balance of antiseptic efficiency and minimises toxicity. Delivered every three to four hours, this treatment has been found to be most effective against infections from France's filthy soil.'

Rose shifted in her seat. She wished Billy had been lucky enough to have received such a treatment in the field. Maybe they could have saved his leg. She narrowed her eyes as Matron continued.

She would make sure she understood how to do this treatment. One day she might find herself in France and be able to save a soldier's life or limb with it.

'Oh,' Adelaide gasped next to her. Rose looked at her with irritation. Adelaide had her hand on her stomach.

'What is it? Is something wrong?' Rose whispered.

'The baby kicked.'

Rose smiled at her. How wonderful. Adelaide was sitting right next to her with a tiny baby growing in her belly. It must be awfully strange. She gave her hand a squeeze and totally lost interest in listening to the advantages of using Dakin's solution. Words like antiseptic, non-toxic and hypertonic floated around her but her brain failed to fully absorb them. A spike of worry took over. Oskar still hadn't managed to make it back to marry Adelaide. She really needed to sit her down and come up with some alternative plans. A shift in Matron's expression caught her attention.

'Before you all leave, a serious matter has been brought to my attention.' The room snapped into alertness and Matron gave a tight smile of satisfaction. 'As you are fully aware, we have a strict code of moral conduct as nurses of the Empire. I have already explained that I expect you all to abide by these rules and if you know of any woman failing to do so, I expect to be informed. Women who breach the rules or know of others doing so risk the reputation of us all.' Faces were flushing and guilty glances between friends were exchanged. Rose kept her eyes right on Matron, but her shoulders tightened. Matron looked like a schoolmarm poised with a cane.

'I will not tolerate nonsense in my hospital, and you will be dealt with firmly.' Matron looked at Adelaide for so long Rose's shoulders became a vice squeezing her so hard she could barely breath.

'I was horrified ...' Matron spat the words. '... just horrified to be told that one of you has dallied with a soldier and found herself in the family way yet has continued working here, totally flouting the army's rules.' A gasp rippled around the room and Rose's stomach dropped like a stone in a lake.

'Nurse Clements. I will see you in my office. The rest of you may go back to your wards.' The nurses obediently started filing out.

Rose finally looked at Adelaide's pasty face and every part of her wanted to protect her from the matron, but she sat numb.

Adelaide stood and robotically followed Matron from the room. Rose could hear the hallway erupt.

'What will Matron do? Do you think she'll—'

'Oh, she's such a nice girl. I never would have thought—'

'How could she expect to get away with—'

'I always thought she was too sweet to believe.'

Rose listened to the voices of those that she had barely bothered to get to know and felt a bolt of shame for Adelaide. Her closest friend deserved better than to be a target of idle gossip. Why wasn't she screaming at these vultures in Adelaide's defence? Her shame deepened. She didn't want to be tarred with the same brush. She wanted to keep her reputation as a dedicated nurse intact. Some friend she was.

She finally stood and made her way back to her ward for the day. She tried hard to focus as Nurse Appleton did her handover of the ward.

'Nurse Shipley, are you alright?' broke through the fog.

'What? Oh, not really. My friend's in a lot of trouble.' Rose put her hand on her mouth. She didn't want to go into it nor have Nurse Appleton think she was a part of Adelaide's deception.

Nurse Appleton's eyes softened in sympathy. 'I heard about Nurse Clements. I've been doing night duty with her and I think she's a wonderful girl. Very plucky, indeed. I'm going to miss her.' Rose stared at her.

'Well, I do think it's brave of her to wait here until Oskar can make it back. She didn't tell me about the baby, but I don't think she realised how much it was showing. I'm the oldest of fifteen so I could always tell when Ma was sporting another little one. Why don't I stay on here for a bit and you go and check on her?'

Rose could only nod, almost crying at such kindness. She plodded back to her quarters, searching for words of comfort or a plan of action but she was met with blankness. She gave a tentative knock then entered. Adelaide was throwing clothes into her suitcase. She was not in tears as Rose had expected. She turned to Rose, her eyes flashing.

'How could you? All of this time, I thought we were friends.'

Rose was stunned. 'But I didn't—'

Adelaide held up a hand. 'Don't you lie to me. I know how much your bloody career means to you and I was a danger to it. Well, I'm not going back on the first boat as Matron has demanded. I'm staying while there's a chance Oskar can make it back.' She slammed her suitcase shut and buckled it tight. 'And you are no longer invited to the wedding.'

'I swear it wasn't me, I'd never—' The door slammed shut and Rose crumpled onto her bed. How could Adelaide think that of her?

Elise burst through the door. 'Where is she? Is she alright? What did Matron say?'

'Gone, I don't know, and she told her to take the first ship home but she's staying in London.'

'How awful. Matron should not have humiliated her like that.'

Elise sat beside her and put an arm around her shoulder. 'Adelaide thinks it was me who told and now she's run off all on her own.' She took Elise's offered handkerchief.

'Good grief. Where would she go?'

The full horror of a pregnant Adelaide wandering London homeless hit Rose and she bolted to standing. 'We've got to go and find her—help her.'

Elise nodded and grabbed their coats.

***

Two hours later, they returned weary and worried.

'We'd better get back to it before Matron sends us onto the street too. We'll look every chance we get.' Rose agreed even though she wanted to keep looking. She thanked Nurse Appleton and told her what had happened.

They set to rolling bandages, but Rose was haunted by Adelaide's words. She should have been more supportive—talked to her about what they could do if she was showing and Oskar was still yet to show, maybe looked for a boarding house. Now Adelaide had run off thinking she didn't have a friend in the world. Rose would never forgive herself if any harm came to her.

Chapter Twenty

Senior Sister Plunkett stared at Rose with myopic eyes, magnified by her glasses. 'Well, Nurse Shipley?'

Rose adjusted her starched collar just a little higher, hoping to hide the rising colour. Weariness and frustration argued within. How dare this horrid woman demand that she special a soldier in isolation for hours beyond her usual shift, but what choice did she have?

'Of course, Sister Plunkett. What does he have?'

'That's *Senior* Sister, thank you.' Rose gritted her teeth as the sister flicked through a chart. 'He's just been moved to isolation as he has a case of diphtheria. I'll be in to check on you later.'

Rose took the chart thrust at her and hurried to her room to gather some supplies. She quickly squeezed some lemons from the kitchen into water and hoped the poor man could still swallow.

Rose found Private Morris isolated in a small side ward, lying flat on his back as pale as his sheets. A sickly, sweet odour filled the room.

'Good morning, Private. I'm Nurse Shipley, here to take care of you for a while.'

The man gave a slight nod, his breath wheezing in and out. He opened his mouth before she had a chance to ask. Peering in, Rose checked herself for her alarm not to reach her eyes. She was relieved her mask hid the rest of her face. He was in a bad way.

A leathery, dirty yellow membrane covered his posterior pharyngeal wall and extended across the palate, almost to the gums, Rose noted. She set to work, setting up a steam tent using a mix of lemon and eucalyptus oil to help him breathe more easily. She then assisted him to sip a mixture of lemon juice and the herb, slippery elm. He screwed his face in pain as he swallowed, gave her a weak smile, and dropped off to sleep. Rose was relieved that he seemed to be breathing more clearly.

The door swished open and Sister Plunkett marched in. 'What is that awful odour?'

Rose steeled herself. 'It's eucalyptus and lemon oil. My father uses it to—'

Sister raised a gloved hand. 'You might think you can take it upon yourself to offer Australian treatments in this hospital, but I assure you, I will have you removed if you continue to do so. *The chart* clearly says serum and brandy. *Not* oils.' She lifted the cup on the side table. 'This is not brandy.'

'In the children's ward at RPA, one of the nurses showed me that slippery elm soothes the throat and she had great success with lemon juice in restoring the children's health,' Rose said firmly. She noticed a vein pulsating at the sister's temple.

The sister set the cup down firmly and picked up another, gave it a sniff and handed it to Rose. 'This brandy is already measured. Next time he wakes make sure he gets the full dose and another of serum and *nothing* else.'

Not trusting her voice, Rose nodded and the sister left. Rose paced the room. What an absolutely beastly woman. Rose knew the treatment worked. Why on Earth would you give a sick man brandy? Silly English stuffiness. She finally settled and checked on her patient. His pulse was still fast, but he was breathing well.

She pulled up a chair and settled in, her thoughts soon drifting to Adelaide. Where was she? Was she fine? Would she ever find her? Would Adelaide ever talk to her again? Her head and heart ached in time.

Private Morris woke with a splutter of coughing and Rose handed him a bowl, supporting his back as he spat up vile substances from his lungs. She gave him the brandy and serum and he settled again.

Nurse Appleton stepped into the room a few hours later to take over and Rose collected up her bottles of oil.

'Why did you give him so much brandy?' Nurse Appleton asked, looking up from the chart.

'That's what Sister Plunkett said to give him. She said it was already measured.'

Rose grabbed the chart and a stone dropped in her gut. There was much too much brandy in the cup. Why hadn't she checked the chart or even noticed once she wrote down the dose that it didn't match?

Private Morris gave a whooping gasp, sat and clutched at his chest, his face rapidly turning from grey to black.

'Run! Get the doctor,' Nurse Appleton ordered.

Frozen, Rose stared at the soldier's bulging eyes.

'Now! Good Lord, I hope you haven't killed him.'

Rose's muscles finally fired, and she shot into the corridor, straight into Major Richmond. With no words, she gripped his arm and led him inside the door.

Nurse Appleton was pulling the sheet over the patient's face.

'Oh ... I killed him. I killed him,' Rose muttered. How awful for that poor man to survive the horror of the trenches only to die because of her. Maybe she wasn't fit to be a nurse let alone a doctor.

Chapter Twenty-One

4 February 1917
Stormy Trench

'Nice night for it,' Bull wryly commented as he fixed his bayonet to his rifle. They were jammed like sardines along the trench. Leo scratched his ear and felt the familiar tiny lump of a chat making its way down from his scalp. After an impatient squeeze, he flicked it away. He stomach gurgled from either nerves or hunger; he didn't know anymore. He felt like a lump of numb, not at all keen to get back into it. He shifted his sandbagged boots on the frosty ground.

Bull was still prattling on. 'I wonder if Fritz has a better menu than us. I'm fed up with Anzac macaroons, broke me tooth on one of 'em this morning. Next time, you can do me one of those carvings with the bloody things and I'll send it to me ma.'

'Sure. Those biscuits don't taste any good anyway. What time was zero again?' Leo gulped down his rum ration, barely noticing the warmth in his throat. It was bloody freezing.

'Ten. Must be getting close now. Leo, you mustn't think too hard on what happened last year, especially to ol' Frosty.'

Leo looked at Bull in surprise. 'It seems to me no one talks about anything that happens out here, let alone something like that.'

Bull's grey eyes darkened. 'That's the trouble mate. You can't keep stuff like that inside or drink it away. A little bit of a chat and a good cry can do wonders.'

Leo thought Bull was having a lend of him. He looked at Harry on the other side of Bull, but Harry was busy scraping mud from his boot, not listening to them at all. Leo couldn't imagine a big bloke like him crying but Bull's face was serious.

'I'm not sayin' turn into a sheila and make a fuss over every little thing, but it can help to empty the soul of grief now and then.'

'Prepare to advance!' Wells sloshed past them, slapping them on the back as he went. 'You ready, chaps? This is what it's all about. Forget the guns, a bit of hand to hand will tell those damn Huns we mean business. Best of luck.'

Instead of feeling inspired, Leo felt a stab of icy fear. A bit of hand to hand. He still had no urge to stick it to 'em with a bayonet.

'Don't worry Leo, we'll be right. Mad Harry's scouted ahead. He's as game as Ned Kelly, that one,' Bull said while checking his bayonet.

Leo found it hard to focus. He moved his feet to get some feeling back into them after standing in mud stew for the last hour.

'Kennel up you lot and get ready,' Harry growled.

A resounding blast of one of their own shells had everyone cheering. Like a pack of mad banshees, they erupted from the trenches in two waves, following their own barrage. Cheers soon turned into taunts and threats that were roared into the distance.

War cries of, 'Run Fritz! Stick-it-to-'em! Imshi tout-suite!' rang out. Leo kept his mouth shut, saving his energy for getting across to the other side.

Artillery smoke filled the air. *Pop!* It was like he'd stepped on a snail. Don't look down. If it was spongy underfoot, it was bound to be a body.

Oh Lord. He just had to look, didn't he? Leo had trodden on a man's skull, maybe driving his nose in to the soft cheese of his brain. A sizeable hole and grin gaped up at him. Hit by a shell. Leo's stomach churned. That jellied flesh was once a man.

'Sorry, cobber,' he stammered. Putting his head back up, Leo resumed his charge through the silver streaks of buzzing bullets until he hit the German trench. It was squirming with battling men.

The clatter of Mills bombs and tings of bayonets clashing blended with the chaotic yells of men as they struggled against each other. Some of the German soldiers were climbing out and running for their lives. Harry lined up a few. One yelped and tumbled back into the trench while another dropped with a thud onto no man's land. When he realised the man was still alive, Harry completed his mission with the swift application of the bayonet. With barely a glance, he signalled to Leo to follow him up the trench.

They rushed past the mopping-up party that was gathering prisoners and joined with the attackers up ahead.

'Out you come!' Harry's voice boomed into the inky depths of a dugout. Barely waiting for a response, he plucked two bombs from his cache and threw them down the stairs. With a rattle, they landed and exploded with a muffled retort.

'That'll take care of that then.'

They pushed on up the trench, flying past the wounded with their clutching hands and weak cries of '*Kamerad!*' With barely time to wipe the stinging sweat from his eyes, Leo continued flinging bombs into cavernous holes for all he was worth.

'Pass us another bomb, Leo,' Harry croaked, his voice hoarse from yelling. He stood ready, gripping the tattered blanket at the front of a dugout.

'It's me last one,' Leo noted with alarm.

Harry snatched the bomb and threw it in without bothering with a warning. He looked at Leo and reassured him, 'No worries, most of the yellow bellies have run for it or been caught anyway.'

'What the—' The egg-shaped bomb had been flung right back at them.

'Shit!' Leo scooped it up and tossed it over the parapet and they dropped to the ground.

'Why, that little bastard, I'll get him. Get out here, you mongrel Hun,' Harry roared. He charged into the dugout.

'*Komerad, Komerad*'.

Expecting Harry to emerge with a hulking giant, Leo tensed.

What? He was just a boy. Leo lowered his rifle. Harry had the razor-sharp point of his bayonet into the soft folds of the boy's grey coat.

'Thought you'd have a go at killing an Aussie, did you? Well I'll teach you to mess with us.'

Leo stood transfixed as Harry drew back ready to plunge the blade in. The boy's legs buckled, and he collapsed in a heap. The sour smell of urine leaked into Leo's nostrils.

'Poor beggar, he's wet himself. He's just a kid.' Leo helped the lad up.

Harry glowered at the peach-fuzzed face. 'That bloody *kid* nearly killed us both.'

Tears were streaming down the youth's filthy cheeks. Harry softened.

'Fine. We'll take him prisoner then. Let's go hand him over to the mopping-up boys.'

The boy watched them anxiously.

Leo explained that they were not going to kill him, and the boy's eyes widened in surprise at Leo's German.

As Leo explained that the boy was their prisoner, the boy spoke rapidly. '*Tut mir leid. Ich möchte nicht Ihre Gefangenen zu sterben. Ich habe gehört, dass Sie sie essen. Ich will wieder nach Hause zu meiner Familie zu gehen. Ich will nicht sterben. Helfen Sie mir, bitte. Ich bin nur vierzehn. Ich will nicht sterben.*'

The boy ended his outburst in a fresh flood of tears.

'He's only fourteen. He's terrified because he's heard we eat our prisoners and he doesn't want to die,' Leo explained.

Harry sighed. 'Fourteen. As if anyone would eat him; he's just skin and bones. What are we going to do? We can't just let him go.'

The boy thrust a photo into his Leo's grimy hand.

'*Mein Name ist Peter. Dies ist meine Familie. Meine Mutter werden so traurig, dass ihr einziger Sohn gestorben.*'

'Okay, Peter. Yes, my mother would be sad too if her only son died,' Leo responded in German. Leo's heart thumped hard in his chest. Harry was his best chum, he'd understand. He just had to try. 'How about we let Peter go? If he makes it, he does. If he doesn't, he doesn't. I can't do it to him. Not after Frosty.'

Harry looked from one to the other and sighed. 'What the hell. Turn him loose but he has to keep his trap shut about it.'

Leo told Peter he was free to go. Peter cast them a doubtful glance then a quick smile of thanks. He climbed over the top of the bags and crawled along the ground with the awkward gait of a goanna.

'Damn, I forgot to give his photo back.' He put it into his pocket, alongside Rose's hanky and streamer.

Harry wiped his grubby face and stood in front of Leo, 'Listen chum, don't go making a habit of saving the little beggars or even I'll have to wonder which side you are on.' He slapped Leo's back and then scanned the trench. Leo guessed he was hoping to redeem himself and catch another prisoner to replace Peter. Yep, he was a good mate all right.

'Thanks, Harry.'

Harry grinned, his teeth glowing green in the flare light. 'Enough yarning. There's a war on, you know. Let's go and get into it.'

Leo smiled as they resumed their charge down the trench, but the smile disappeared as they ran smack into three large Germans who were cautiously emerging from their dugout.

Harry swiftly attacked one with his gleaming bayonet. Leo's reflexes kicked in and he felt his weight pushing forward and the bayonet connect with the solid muscle of a German's stomach. With a startled grunt, the man dropped and clutched his gut as Leo yanked back the blade. The Germans lay huddled, writhing in pain.

Casting a look around for the third man, they saw him hightailing it up the trench. Harry tore after the disappearing form. Leo shadowed him but Harry had things under control and the soldier lay dead in a matter of seconds. Leo recoiled as the German's bowels released.

'This war really stinks,' Leo muttered in disgust.

'We're done here; think the boys have moved on. Let's go.'

Gritting his teeth, Leo followed Harry into the chaos of no man's land. He evaded the swarm of bullets by some miracle but watched in dismay as German reinforcements poured from the ground like an army of ants.

Leo and Harry tumbled into the next trench amid urgent calls for more bombs. Leo found himself diving again for the ground as a red flame burst above. They were soon caught in a downpour of bombs. The Germans knew exactly where to bomb their own hastily evacuated bays.

Like drunken sailors, the Anzacs continued up the trench as the earth shook beneath them, only stopping to crouch against the wall. At one point, Leo's jellied limbs wouldn't carry him upright and he crawled on all fours while he prayed not to be hit by the lead and iron that whistled around him.

His stomach knotted as he flailed along the bay. How are we going to make it out of here in one piece? Every muscle was held as tight as a wire and his mind began to fray at the edges. With a puff of air, something skimmed past his cheek.

'You're bleeding, Dymond.' Alfred's voice penetrated the haze. Leo's left cheek was stinging. He wiped the blood off.

'Lucky, just a nick,' Alfred said as he clapped his shoulder and moved along to continue to scour the gloomy trench for Germans. We must all be going crazy. Was Alfred almost being a caring human being then? Was he sorry about Frosty?

A blast sounded from up the trench. Stretcher! Stretchers! Leo found a soldier lying face down in the mud and turned him over. The man's uniform was in tatters, revealing a gash across his chest and a mangled mess of guts.

The man looked grimly at Leo and stated, 'I'm done for, cobber.'

They both knew that anything in the stomach was a death sentence.

'Will ya send a letter to me wife? She'll want to know what happened. Tell her straight. Tell her I'll miss her … and … I love her,' he grunted.

Leo nodded solemnly, 'I will.'

Content with Leo's promise, the soldier sighed and let go. A warm tingle rippled across Leo's body then there was a rush of cold air. Bugger. No tags. Leo wouldn't be able to dig through his pockets to find anything that would tell him any details as remnants of the man's belongings were strewn like confetti, tangled in his intestines.

Leo didn't remember catching up to the troops. He froze and closed his eyes as the green glow fizzled slowly down. *Plop!* That had to be a Minnie. He squinted but the Very light still blinded him. Where was it going? In the daylight he would have been able to see its tumbling trajectory but in the gloomy night he had no way of knowing where to duck for cover from the large German motor shell. The ground shuddered beneath him and he crouched with his hand on his helmet as the mud showered down.

'There she goes,' Bull observed flatly as another *plop* was heard. Leo clenched his jaw. Waiting … there, a faint whisper and then … nothing … just eerie silence. His stomach quivered. It was coming. A steadily growing shriek built to a screaming roar. With a fiery burst, the world shook around him. The fumes burnt his throat, and the sting of salty tears blurred his vision.

'Bit close, that one.' Bull was the first one up. Before Leo could even catch his breath, the putter of machine guns began and he could barely restrain his legs from taking off in an altogether different direction. He tumbled into the crater of a shell hole. Bull's heavy breath was hot in his ear. A flurry of bullets mowed down pockets of men as easily as a scythe cutting hay. How were they going to get out of this one?

'Shit! Most of the 13th is getting skittled.' Bull moaned. Leo moved his mouth, but any words clung to his throat.

The barrage broke out in full force around them and he squeezed into the sticky paste of the shell hole walls with his legs knee deep in freezing water. He might have to stay wedged between Bull and Harry for hours yet.

With the German's continual bombing from Courcelette and sweeps of machine gun fire, he didn't see how they could make a move.

He didn't want to. But Harry gave his sleeve an impatient pull and he followed Harry over the crumbling lip of the shell hole. Harry might be as game as a piss-ant, but Leo wasn't thrilled to be a moving target again.

Leo stumbled over a snarl of telephone wire, cut by razor sharp artillery fragments. Great. Bugger all communication as usual. Would the runners have made it back to tell them the stunt had gone to hell so they could fall back? This second stunt didn't seem to be going any better than his first.

The tug of a bullet swished through his gas mask. Sweet Mother Mary! Leo's heart had almost hammered through his skull.

'Come on, you lot! Advance!' Lieutenant Bentley roared. Bentley waved at Leo, yelling something about cleaning some Germans out of a sap up ahead and he strained to hear him.

'Company C has found heap of Huns, we've got to—'

In slow motion, Simpson's skull was neatly sliced in two. His body slumped to the ground. His mashed brain was bathed in a rosy glow. Leo was falling too. Strong hands gripped his torso, and he was yanked into a shell hole.

'Are you hit?' Bull's face hovered over him.

Leo flew above Bull's blurry form, above the silver streaks of bullets and fire, balls of artillery and into the inky, star-studded blackness. From above the starbursts of poppy red and orange, it was a heartbreaking view.

Men lay in lifeless clumps next to the writhing forms of those that struggled in the glutinous mud like flies in their death throes stuck on a sheet of fly paper. It was so quiet way above them, so peaceful. Maybe he would join Frosty, free of all of it. He could just float away and leave it all behind.

Chapter Twenty-Two

February 1917
France

Something was on his arm. Leo pried his gummy eyes open. Just a fly. The fat bluebottle crawled along his hand, stopping to rub its wiry legs every so often. The insect's back glowed an iridescent blue and then green as it moved in the early morning sun. It was almost pretty. What else had this fly been crawling on though? The decaying flesh of soldiers?

The previous night's events hit his brain and he bolted upright, briskly checking over his body. He sank back with relief. He was fine. Except for the fact he was stranded in the middle of no man's land. He surveyed the muddy shell hole, his back still cool from the sucking clay. His heels were just touching the yellow slime that filled the bottom of the hole. It was a fairly big depression, probably made by a few shells hitting the same spot.

A German was slumped face down next to him. With a thumping heart, Leo gave the bulky body a poke. Nothing. Phew. He released his breath. He didn't fancy spending a few hours next to a corpse, but he wasn't sure it was safe to move yet. Leo licked his cracked lips then realised he'd lost his canteen somewhere. Maybe this guy had some water left. His mind swirled with questions. How was he going to get back to his unit? Where was his battalion? Was he left for dead? Leo blew out a breath. He'd grab a swig of water, risk sticking his head up to check where he was, and then figure out what to do.

He rolled the German onto his back. Flinty blue eyes locked with his. Shit! In a flash, claw-like fingers gripped his throat. Leo managed to squeak out a weak, '*Kamerad.*'

The soldier only squeezed harder. He was no friend of Leo's. Leo turned his head to get a snatch of air and quickly rotated his hips, allowing him to thrust the soldier to the left. He'd turned the tables for a second but couldn't keep the man pinned down.

The German grabbed Leo in a crocodile death roll and pushed his head towards the fetid water. Leo held his neck taut. No way was his last breath on this earth going to be taking in that poisonous gunk. But his strength was draining, and everything started to blur as his throat was squeezed.

Stop ... let go ... He was splashing in Borenore Creek ... brother ... horsing around ... tell him to let go ...

'I give in, Oskar. Oskar, you win. Let go ... *Lass mich gehen.*' He gave their signal to stop.

Leo gasped as the pressure stopped and air flowed in. He was tossed backwards, splatting into the soft mud ...

He sucked in more air. The soldier was kneeling above him, a deep furrow in his brow.

'*Woher kennen Sie meinen Namen?*' What did he mean, how did he know his name?

Leo rolled to the side and did his best to crab crawl and get some distance from the soldier. He sat up and faced his foe. Oskar was a solid man with a strong jutting jaw, chiselled cheeks and a curious expression. He waited patiently for Leo to regain his breath.

Leo scratched his head and switched to German.

'I didn't know your name. My brother, Oskar, and I used to dunk—' Oskar looked confused, so Leo scrabbled for another word in German. 'I mean, put each other's head in the creek back home. I must have thought I was back there.'

Oskar still looked uncertain, 'Where?'

'Australia. My ma and pa are German though.'

Oskar smiled and leaned forward. 'Ah, I have some relatives in Australia. What's it like over there?'

Leo frowned. One minute this man was a ruthless soldier, the next he wanted to chat like a school chum.

'Uh, it's not like here. It's a lot hotter and drier. Some of the houses used to be made of the stuff you use in the trenches. Wattle and daub. Ours isn't stone like from here, it's corrugated iron.' Kasper nodded for him to continue. 'We don't graze sheep or grow wheat like a lot of farmers back home. We have a vineyard.' Images of home flooded Leo and he blinked rapidly. He took a breath and continued, 'In *meiner Familie gibt es in Ma und Pa, einen jüngeren Bruder, Oskar und Schwesterlein, Dot. Sie?*'

'My mother died when I was five. We were all drafted. I have … *had* my pa and three older brothers.' Oskar's jaw tightened and he looked away. 'There's just me now.'

Leo swallowed. Someone he knew could have shot Oskar's family. *He* could have. Leo gazed at the lip of the shell hole. An Aussie soldier with 13th Battalion patches on his sleeve stared vacantly back at him. A fly crawled over the corpse's cheek. Some Aussie Leo was. Sitting here feeling sorry for the enemy, chatting to him like a mate. Letting that boy, Peter, escape. Leo's solar plexus turned to stone. He didn't know what to think anymore.

'Why do you travel so many miles to fight for a country that seems to care so little? So many of you Australians slaughtered? We have watched you attack Mouquet Farm again and again. Why do the British waste you like that?' Oskar's eyes had softened to the blue of a robin's egg. Leo could see he was truly mystified by British war tactics.

Buggered if Leo understood what the top brass were thinking. 'Wish I knew.'

The dreary shell hole they were sharing was littered with silent bodies of patriots from a few countries.

'Not that we seem to do much better going time and time again at Verdun. I will be happy when it's all over.' Oskar's eyes clouded. 'With the terrible harvest from last year, and the British blockade, people back home are starving.'

The French refugees Leo had seen when he first arrived had looked so forlorn but back then they had been plumper and had animals with them. Not anymore. Their bones now protruded from tattered clothes as they trudged away from one bombed village after another. He hadn't realised the German civilians would be suffering too.

'I didn't know … I'm … that's awful.' Was he sorry? Sad? No, he was so bone weary of it all. He attempted to clean out his muddied rifle but soon threw it down in defeat.

'I'd rather be back home studying history and philosophy,' Oskar confided. 'If we had we been sitting here one hundred years ago, we would have been fighting Napoleon together.' He motioned to a mud-crusted Frenchman. 'I am sure morale for the Germans will pick up now Hindenburg has come out of retirement, but it is not good news that Romania and Italy are against us. I mean, Germany.'

Leo flushed with heat. Napoleon? He didn't know much about him. Hindenburg? Why did Oskar seem to know so much more about what was going on? For the first time, Leo wished he had more than his basic bush education.

'You are right. I am sorry to go on about the politics of it all.'

Leo gave a wry smile. He was relieved that Oskar had interpreted his silence thinking Leo was finding the conversation topics disagreeable rather than the truth of his ignorance.

Oskar's stomach rumbled. 'I'm so hungry I would even enjoy our vile turnip soup right now.' Leo curled his lip. Yuck! He'd never liked turnips. He rifled through his muddy pack, found his iron ration of bully beef, and tossed it to him. Oskar gulped down half and handed it back to Leo.

'That's better, thanks. When I get home, I can't wait for a slice of *Schwarzwaelder Kirschtorte*,' Oskar said, leaning back against the shell hole wall.

Leo got a vivid image of the cherry chocolate cake made with layers of cream that his mother made for special occasions, and he was drooling. 'My ma makes that too.'

Oskar gave him a wry smile. 'It's a shame you're on the other side.' He reached into his mud-splattered pocket. 'Here, to remember a *Kamerad.*' Oskar handed him a sketch of a town. 'This is my hometown of Ladenburg.' On the postcard was a corner tower rising above the houses, much like the circular towers on pictures of medieval castles Leo had seen. A bolt of recognition shot through him.

'*Danke.* Hey, that's where my ma and pa are from. That's the *Hexeturm* where they once kept the witches,' Leo said, poking the card. He dug into his pocket and took out a kookaburra carving that he'd just finished. He was intending to send Dot a matching one, but he was sure she wouldn't mind sharing.

'This is an Australian bird called a kookaburra. When they call out to each other, it sounds like they are having a big laugh.'

Oskar smiled and admired it. '*Danke.* You are very talented.'

While Oskar ran his fingers over the bird's sharp beak, Leo became aware that he could hear the chirp of starlings and the drone of flies. Why was it so quiet?

'Nah, my pa is the one with the real talent. Hey, do you hear that?'

'What? I don't hear anything,' Oskar stopped mid swig from his canteen.

'Exactly,' Leo said. Where in the hell was everyone? Was last night's stunt a real shambles? 'What if everyone's dead but us?'

Oskar cautiously raised a helmet stuck on top of his Mauser rifle above the edge of the shell hole. Nothing. Feeling more confident, Leo risked sitting a bit higher as Oskar elbowed his way up.

'Only bodies out there,' Oskar declared.

What should they do? Not knowing who had secured what line during the night, they both risked capture. Leo massaged the tight knot in his neck. There seemed to be acres of carcass riddled fields around them.

A shrill whistle sounded in the distance and they dropped to the ground.

'What do you think?' Oskar whispered.

'Stay here, I'll go look.' Dodging shell fragments, bodies and other war paraphernalia, Leo crept towards some dim shadows that were moving freely around no man's land. He cautiously leapfrogged from hole to hole until he was close enough to observe more clearly.

Love a duck, would you look at that!

Both Australian and German soldiers were collecting the wounded and dead. He gawked as an Aussie soldier loaded a wounded German onto a stretcher and shook hands with a German stretcher bearer. Some soldiers were chatting and swapping pictures, food and cigars. He raced back to report to Oskar.

'I have heard of this happening during the first Christmas in the trenches. We have since been told not to fraternise with the enemy,' Oskar struggled to keep his voice steady. 'It makes it too hard to shoot them.'

'Must be time to get in there and lend a hand and they'll be none the wiser,' Leo suggested. They crept together to the busy field.

'It was good to meet you,' Leo said as he offered his hand.

'*Viel Glück für Sie.*'

'Good luck to you too, Oskar.'

Leo smiled and gave Oskar's hand one last squeeze before he sauntered over to pick up one of the wounded. He glanced behind and saw Oskar wander in the opposite direction.

'Strike me pink! Leo!' Bull lumbered in from behind him and wrapped Leo into a bone crunching hug.

'Easy Bull, I think you just cracked a rib.'

'Sorry mate. I thought you'd gone west.'

Bull released him and stood grinning at him for a second then started to fill him in on the latest.

'It was a big one last night. I reckon we must've lost over two hundred good blokes, dead or wounded, to that damn trench. Thank God we've captured the bloody thing. Seems the Huns are getting out of Warlencourt Salient with us lot here.'

Bull rattled on, not even stopping for breath, as he lifted and passed a beefy, groaning soldier to the stretcher bearers. The man was holding sausage-like entrails in his trembling hands. 'We caught over seventy of the buggers last night and get this, they think the 13th are specially picked stormtroopers. They knew the Aussies were comin' at 'em since we were at 'em straight after the barrage.'

Bull glanced at Leo. 'You look a bit green around the gills, cove. Let's get you a hot tea and some grub and you can tell me what your night was like.'

Within a few minutes he was sitting in a trench slurping up rum-laced tea, enjoying the warmth that flooded through him.

Bull threw back his own tea, smacked his lips and said, 'I've been looking for you all morning in this lot. So, how'd you get on last night, Leo?'

Even though everyone was chatting to the Germans that morning, Leo decided it was probably better to keep his encounter close to the chest. He didn't want anyone accusing him of being a spy.

'Just a cold night in the hole.'

'I'm glad you came back in one piece, mate. You finish your tea while I go find the others and let 'em know you're okay.'

Leo raised his cup and watched Bull lumber down the trench. He pulled out Oskar's sketch and noticed some words scribbled on the back. He read:

Ist der Mensch lediglich ein Fehler von Gottes? Oder ist Gott bloß ein Fehler des Mannes? - Nietzsche.

Leo gripped the sketch tighter. He didn't have an answer for Oskar's philosopher. 'Is man merely a mistake of God's? Or is God merely a mistake of man's?'

He'd been trying to protect his family, but signing up for this war was the biggest mistake he had made, God or no God.

Chapter Twenty-Three

March 1917
London

Rose threw her mask and apron into the linen basket as Major Richmond did the same. He waited until the room was empty of staff then turned to her.

'What's wrong, Nurse Shipley? You've gone from almost reading my mind and giving me the right instrument before I've even asked for it to having to be asked twice. I'm beginning to question my decision to allow you onto my team.'

Rose's eyes filled with unwanted tears and she wiped them roughly. Despite his seemingly harsh words, his tone and eyes were kind. She stood mute, unable to find the words.

'Let's go and get some fresh air, shall we?'

Rose followed him out of the dark hospital hallways and into the spring sunshine. They continued to stroll silently into Archbishop's Park. Rose's mood lifted as she watched a squirrel dart up a plane tree.

'There, I can see nature has already done my work for me. You look much better. I thought once the investigation was closed things would improve.'

Rose's numbness shifted to gratitude. 'I can't thank you enough for speaking up for me during the investigation. Perhaps I deserved to be sent home though. I should have checked the chart.'

He shook his head. 'You were extremely tired and had had a terrible run in with the sister over treatment. We are human, Rose. Mistakes will be made. Was that your first death?'

Rose nodded.

'Patients die. I think we all remember our first. I've had many die now and it's sad to admit I don't remember them all anymore. What I do remember is the lesson if there is one to be learned, then I do better next time. It's not about being infallible.'

Rose slowly digested his words. Did she expect to save everyone?

'Was it that? Or is there something else?' Major Richmond asked.

Rose bit her lip. She had no idea where to start or what was appropriate to share.

'Is it something to do with Nurse Clements?' he prompted. 'I understand she was a close friend of yours.'

Like a burst riverbank, she flooded him with her woes. 'The worst part is that Adelaide believed I had betrayed her trust in favour of my career.'

Major Richmond smiled. 'You can be rather single-minded, but I wouldn't believe that of you.'

Rose sighed. 'I know, and I don't think even some of the nurses understand that I'd rather have my head stuck in my medical books than go dancing or have a gossip while we knit. But it doesn't mean I don't care for my friends.'

Major Richmond paused and looked hard at her. 'There's no shame in having such interests but be careful not to dismiss the joy of feminine pursuits. Becoming a doctor can be a very lonely process and … pardon me for saying so, even more for a woman. Having said that, I do believe you are the right candidate to become one. You have the right combination of determination, curiosity and courage.'

Rose blushed and Major Richmond coughed and resumed their walk.

'I don't mean to say these things as mere flattery. There will be times the others around you may feel left in the cold and sacrifices will have to be made. I hope Adelaide will contact you but, in the meantime, I'm asking you to regain that focus. I'm intending to put together a team to go to France soon and I'd like you to be on it.'

Rose's exhaustion lifted to a bubbling excitement.

'Knew that would cheer you up.'

Rose fired off a series of questions until Major Richmond held his hands up, laughing. 'I don't know the details yet. I just want to know I can count on you.'

Rose almost skipped along the path. 'Of course, you can.'

'Wonderful. I should head back. I'll let them know I've sent you on an errand for me. Take some time.' He left with a wave and Rose continued walking, mulling over all he had said. Even though it was cold, she soaked in the peace of the park, listening to the gentle burble of the pigeons and distant shrieks of kids at the children's playground. Rose stopped suddenly when she spotted a familiar tumble of honey curls escaping from a bonnet.

Rose stared harder at the woman reading a book against the trunk of a tree. Yes, it was definitely her, but what should she say? A flash of anger crept in. All this time worrying. She strode over.

'Adelaide Clements, what do you think you were doing walking off in a huff and not having the common decency to let me know you hadn't found yourself in a ditch or strangled by some mad man?'

Adelaide looked up in shock then started to giggle. 'You should see your face.'

When Adelaide finally got a grip on herself, she snapped her book shut and Rose saw how large her belly had grown. 'I know. I'm as big as a Zeppelin. Sit down.'

'I'm sorry,' they said in unison.

'Me first. I'm sorry I accused you of telling Matron. I never should have put you in that position in the first place. I haven't known how to—'

Rose shook her head. 'No, Addie. I should have been more supportive. I got so caught up working that I didn't give you enough time, but I promise it wasn't me.'

Adelaide's face flushed red. 'I knew you didn't. I was so scared.'

They gave each other an awkward hug.

'Where did you go? I've been at every Lyon's in London and I've been hunting everywhere for weeks.'

'Remember Martha with the baby and little girl, Bessie? Well, she found me sobbing outside of Lyon's and took me to this place in Poplar. Poplar is not my cup of tea at all but the people at the maternity cottage take good care of me.' Adelaide dropped her head. 'I was going to write.'

Rose waved it away. 'As long as you are fine. Have you let Oskar know? Have you heard from him?'

Her face fell. 'Only a brief note to tell me he's arranged for some of his pay to go to me and he could be in for his first stunt any day now.'

Rose knew Adelaide would be troubled by images of the shattered men they had nursed but could do little to console her, so she held on to a tongue full of platitudes. She certainly didn't know if Oskar was going to make it through unscathed if he would make it back soon to marry her, or even if Adelaide and the baby would survive childbirth. A needle prick of shame hit her heart. For the first time in a long time, her thoughts flitted to Harry but settled on Leo. What were they suffering through? She had forgotten what the war was doing to families everywhere.

'Bloody stupid war.'

Adelaide's eyebrows shot up. 'I think those Aussie boys are a bad influence on you Miss Shipley ... but yes, bloody stupid war.'

They sat silently. Rose watched the leaves dance as a soft breeze puffed through them, then Adelaide gave a little moan as she attempted to lever herself against the tree and stand.

'I don't know what I was thinking, sitting under a tree like this. Remember we used to do it at school all the time? It's way too cold and I'll never get up gracefully. Lucky you came along, can you give me a hoist up?' Adelaide asked. Rose groaned with the effort and they both laughed.

'How have things been with you? Have you heard from your father?' Adelaide asked as she patted away any debris on her dress.

Rose sighed. 'I've been terribly busy at the hospital so not much time for anything as usual. No, I haven't heard from my father.'

Adelaide gave her a sympathetic pat on her arm. 'Oh, I'm sorry. I probably shouldn't have pushed you to write him. I really thought he'd see sense by now.'

'It seems he hasn't. I have even written purely of the work and what I am learning here and still nothing, but who knows how reliable the mail is.' Rose wanted to believe her father still cared.

'Harry?'

Rose nodded. 'It's very strange. I mean, we barely know each other but he writes as if we have been sweethearts for years. I thought he would have forgotten me by now. I really don't want to have made any false promises, but I did not promise anymore to him than to write. As we have little to say, he keeps telling me he will get leave and come and see me. Addie, is it awful that I have no desire to see him but now feel obliged to keep his spirits up so can't dash any hope he has?'

Adelaide smiled. 'No, it's the kind thing to do while he is fighting. Once the war is over, you can set him straight. Or perhaps when you find someone you *do* like, it would only be fair to tell him.'

'I doubt that will be happening any time soon. Now that I've found you, I feel bad, I must get back. Let's meet up soon.'

As Rose left Adelaide to return to work, her shame deepened. A part of Rose loved the war. Did she need the constant flap of death's cloak for her to see how fragile life was? She had never felt so alive. A hazy image of Leo's smile filled her senses. Was he still alive?

Chapter Twenty-Four

'Isn't the show marvellous? I can't wait to see the second half,' Elise said as they made their way out to the golden Italian style foyer of Daly's Theatre. 'I'm enjoying our day off together.'

Rose smiled. She'd found the show entertaining but struggled being away from the hospital, wondering how the patients were getting on. As more people flooded out, they continued down the staircase to the entrance hall and it wasn't long before Rose found herself tapping her foot on the mosaic floor. She really wanted to get back to the wards.

'What do you think of *Maid of the Mountains* so far?' a soldier asked Elise. She gave him her most engaging smile and Rose left them to it. She wandered over to the huge American logwood stove and was soothed by the dance of the flames. Her ears pricked up at a heated discussion nearby.

'I'm telling you, BIPP is the way to go. We've had great success with this treatment.' A sigh and the volume dropped in her voice. 'I don't know why they are reluctant to accept it in the field.'

A more familiar male voice piped up. 'I think the Carrell Dakin treatment has a lot of merit. I thought we were coming here to enjoy the show, not spar like the old days in medical school.' A laugh. 'Yes, I miss those days too.'

Rose scanned the crowded hall for Major Richmond and realised he was only a few people away, but she'd failed to recognise him out of uniform. He was with a woman. He locked eyes with Rose and beckoned her over to them.

'Nurse Shipley, perhaps you can resolve this dispute so we can get on and enjoy the show. Have you heard of the BIPP treatment for gunshot wounds?'

'Yes, I've recently read an article in *The Lancet*.' Rose took an offered glass of wine from a waiter.

'So, Carrell Dakin or BIPP?'

Rose hesitated but she saw a gleam of humour in the other woman's eyes as she nodded her encouragement. 'From a nurse's point of view, I think the Carrel Dakin treatment is rather labour intensive, with constant monitoring and changing of bandages and sheets as the solution soaks through. There is also the discomfort to the patient to be changed every four hours. The strange apparatus and soaking in solution must be extremely uncomfortable for them.' Seeing them consider her words carefully, Rose continued.

'Surely it makes more sense, and is more practical, where there are shortages of staff and bandages in the field, to BIPP them. Bandages are changed every few weeks, the wounds heal and don't smell, and the patients are without pain.'

The woman gave a vigorous shake of her head. 'There, I told you it was all about common sense and this woman has it in spades. If you're not careful, Charles Richmond, I might steal her away from the 5th.'

Major Richmond gave her a look of mock horror. 'Traitor. Oh, how rude of me. Nurse Shipley, may I introduce you to the writer of that fine article, "Major Garrett Anderson, Chief Surgeon of the Endell Street Military Hospital".'

Rose gasped and Major Garrett Anderson laughed. 'That was a beastly thing to do to you, but I'm incredibly pleased to have met one convert out there. I've heard people describe Australians as backward colonials, but I tend to find them quite inventive and open to new ideas. Not even a huge fuss made about the vote for women.'

Major Richmond groaned. 'Don't get her started on the whole suffragette saga,' he said, then seeing the other major's thunderous expression, he quickly added, 'Now you know I'm very supportive of women in the workforce and so on. Nurse Shipley would very happily follow in your esteemed footsteps.'

Major Garrett Anderson's eyes narrowed in interest. 'A surgeon?'

Rose blushed then nodded. She was still in awe of being in the presence of a woman who had helped set up the only all-female staffed military hospital.

'Don't be coy about it. It's a wonderful thing for a woman to have ambition. What is it about being a surgeon that appeals to you?'

Rose pondered the question for a moment. No one had ever taken her this seriously. 'I'm not entirely sure but I find myself fascinated by the mystery of the human body. I want to be able to understand it, mend it, remove what no longer works, and alleviate a person's suffering.'

Major Garrett Anderson smiled broadly. 'Excellent answer. You'll be fine. You have that hunger. If you ever need a sponsor, come to me.'

The warning bell for the next act sounded and the major farewelled them to return to her seat.

Major Richmond shook his head. 'I should have known better than to put the two of you together. Now I shall spend the rest of the show reconsidering whether it's better to BIPP my patients.'

Rose was still glowing from Major Garrett Anderson's offer of support. 'Well, I'm sure the patients will be most grateful for it.'

He was about to leave then touched her elbow. 'Louise is not an easy woman to impress, take her offer seriously.'

Elise barrelled into her and they both started talking at once.

'I've been invited to dinner tomorrow. He was—'

'I've just met the woman who runs the all-female staffed military hospital and she said I could—'

They stopped and started again, then chatted as they made their way into the darkened theatre.

'Rose, you sound more excited at the prospect of becoming a surgeon than ever being romanced by a man. It's rather tragic if you ask me,' Elise declared.

Rose's spirit plummeted like a gull diving into the waves for its prey. From the waves, came a squawk of rage. After meeting a kindred spirit in Louise Garrett Anderson, she was tired of explaining herself to others.

'Well, I didn't ask you,' Rose snapped.

Elise's eyes widened and all humour faded. She turned to the stage, stony faced. Rose felt an immediate reflex to apologise but held her tongue. She was fed up with being considered odd for wanting something different.

As the music swelled, Elise looked at her. 'I'm sorry. I know you're a very dedicated nurse.'

Rose was grateful that Elise broke the tension first. 'I'm sorry I didn't listen to you. I want to hear all about him at tea.'

Content, they watched Jose Collins begin to sing her next sublime song. After a while, Rose's attention wandered. She left the bandit maid, Teresa, lamenting her betrayal of her love, Baldassare, in the musical and pondered her own life. Did she have the hunger to be a surgeon? Her head said yes, her heart said yes, but something at her core niggled. Leo's face flickered in her mind. NO. She was not like the other girls. This would never do.

Chapter Twenty-Five

12 March 1917
Ribemont, France

Leo threw down his pen. Even though he'd heated the ink over the brazier in their small hut, the ink had frozen on the nib on his pen before he'd written a word. Dot would just have to wait until it was warm for him to write back. He jammed his leather fingerless gloves back over his woollen ones. His hands ached. He leaned against his equipment pillow and pulled the covers up to his chin.

Harry was over in the corner, playing cards with three new recruits. He scratched his head through his woollen cap. Among Harry's jumbled gear, Leo's eye caught Harry's scrawl. *Dear Rose.*

Leo's gut tightened. They were still writing. Leo checked Harry was still playing cards and carefully plucked up the letter.

My dearest darling, Rose,

It's hard to believe it has been so long since I have kissed your sweet lips. It was a lonely Christmas over here without you. I'm sorry I have hardly written but even so it's not a happy life without you and I am hoping to get some leave and come to England to see you again soon. Just the thought of seeing you and holding you gets me through.

I am hoping you are safe. I admit I can't help worrying when you write and say you are seeing the sights without me. I know we didn't get the chance to know each other very well before I left but you have captured my heart and I worry someone else will capture yours.

How are things going at the hospital? I imagine you have some idea now of the sufferings of war and I hope you and the other

girls are looking out for each other when things get hard. There's nothing like having some good chums when times get tough.
    I hope that we meet again soon. Please wait for me, my lovely.

Yours,
Harry xx.

Who was this strange person? Harry'd barely been able to write at school and here was Mr Romance himself spinning out sweet words of honey. Was Harry serious?

Leo reread the letter until his hands were frozen claws. He wanted to crumple the paper into a tight ball and peg it straight into the fire. How could Harry be writing love letters to Rose, talking about kissing her lips, while he'd been flirting and doing God knows what with every French girl he could?

He returned the letter and sat staring at Harry. Harry's face glowed in the light from the brazier, eyes sparkling after a win in poker. He grinned at the bloke next to him, shifted on the wooden crate and fanned the cards in front of him. As if he could feel the burn of Leo's stare, Harry's eyes met Leo's. Harry frowned and his eyes darted back to his cards. Leo didn't know what his face had looked like but the tension in his neck radiated down to his shoulders in a dull ache. If Harry ever hurt Rose, he'd kill him.

His forehead tightened in a throbbing band. Leo's ruminations were interrupted by a more pressing need. His bladder was ready to burst. This wasn't going to be easy. He had two flannel shirts, a sheepskin vest and a great coat on. No doubt looking like he had all the grace of an old grizzly bear, he rolled out of his bed to jam his semi-frozen boots over his socks. His shoes refused to accommodate his five pairs of woollen socks, so he peeled a couple off and left the boots undone.

He made his way through the crowded hut and with a deep breath he steeled himself and pushed through the door.

Hell, it was cold. The icy blast with its stinging needles of rain caught him full force. He lowered his head and crunched on. The frigid air whipped around him, and he found that the urgent call of the bladder competed with his penis shrivelling and trying to retreat snail-like back into a warm cocoon. He had a disconcerting image of an icicle bridge of urine forming between him and the glinting snow, stuck there for all to see until the thaw of spring. Maybe he'd have to snap his pecker off. He completed his business and turned to go back to the cabin.

The wind whipped more glacial spikes into his face, making his eyes water. His eyelashes became stuck fast and he became a stumbling blind man. He rubbed his eyes but only put more ice into them. Damn it!

His arms flailed about seeking the solid wall of the cabin. He continued to hit air. Leo made bigger strides instead of cautious shuffles. Still nothing. Heat spiked up from his gut. What an idiot, fancy getting lost just taking a leak. Would they have found him frozen to death just a couple of paces from the cabin?

He started to stomp and kick about in the crunchy snow until a big kick too many upended him. He spat out the ice and attempted to get up. Unable to get any traction, he slid and fell again. Are you laughing at me, God? Having a jolly old time up there? With a howl, he let go and screamed and kicked for all he was worth, thrashing about like a toddler in full tantrum. Curses streamed from his mouth until a voice penetrated his foggy brain.

'You done yet? It's so cold out here even the snowmen are migrating south, no time for rolling around in the snow.'

It was Harry.

'Leave me be.'

'What's up your bum? You've barely said a word to me in weeks. Out with it.'

Leo's eyes opened enough to see a dim shadow standing over him. 'I said bugger off.'

'That's it!' Harry jumped on him and they wrestled in the snow.

'C'mon, grow some balls. Spit it out instead of stewing like some woman. I can take it.'

Leo rotated his hips and rolled so Harry was pinned. 'That's the bloody problem with you. You take what you want and don't give a shit about anyone else.'

They were eyeball to eyeball. Leo's eyes were finally unstuck.

Meaty arms yanked them both up. Bull stood between them.

'What the hell is going on with you two? What are you thinking? You could bloody freeze to death out here.' He glowered over them like a father separating brothers. 'So, hurry up. What's the problem?'

'I was just telling Harry he was a selfish shit, taking whatever he wanted whenever he wanted,' Leo said as he started to shiver violently.

'No need to get your knickers in a knot, I'll pay you back when I can,' Harry protested.

'I'm not talking about that.' A bitter taste coated Leo's tongue.

Harry's brow furrowed, 'What then?'

'Forget it.' How could he explain how he felt about Rose when it wasn't as if she was his anyway.

'Alright, seems we need to brave this and head off for a round or two. Think that ought to cheer you lot up. My shout,' Bull said as he braved the snow. 'Geez, it's colder than a grave digger's shovel out here.'

Harry shrugged. 'Don't need to ask me twice.'

Leo felt like an idiot. He pulled his hat down and followed them.

Chapter Twenty-Six

'Hey Bull, do you know where Harry's got to?' Leo asked. He'd come back from chatting to some blokes at the next table. Leo pulled on his uniform.

'He was pretty cranky we wouldn't lend him a cartwheel to check out the girls. I'm not wasting my five francs on him. You'd think he would have learnt from his last stint with the clap in Egypt.'

A scan of the Madame Aubrey's *estaminet* did not reveal Harry holed up with a bottle of red in the corner somewhere, so Leo decided to check he hadn't wandered off in his drunken state to be frozen outside.

He couldn't find him, and the cold was making him drowsy. Might be a good place to grab a kip. He wandered into a crumbling barn and climbed up to the loft, making a comfy nest in the hay. He began to reread his letters from Dot. Most men just kept the latest letter they had yet to answer as their packs were too heavy to cart any extra weight, but Leo couldn't bear to throw Dot's letters away. The creak of a door and a giggle soon disturbed him. He peeked down and spotted Harry in an amorous embrace with Madame Audrey's young daughter. Blimey, what does a bloke have to do to get any peace around here?

Leo sighed. One day some madame would catch Harry and probably do more damage to him than a German soldier. Should he let him know he was there? He peeked through a crack of the loft floor. How did Harry get those girls swooning anyway?

Harry was kissing the girl, her milky skin blushing with colour as he moved to her long neck. She gasped and allowed him to lay her down in the hay. Her eyes were closed as she returned his kisses. He released her hair and brushed her long, dark curls then ran his hand along her arm, skimming her breast. Leo felt a rush of blood harden him.

Leo pulled back. He should stop watching and lay low until they left. He heard her groan. With magnetic pull, his eyes returned to the gap. Could they hear his breath? He tried to hold it as his knees weakened.

Oh Lord! Harry had released a creamy breast and was nuzzling it. The girl playfully pushed his head away and tugged at her blouse to cover herself. He was persistent and she attempted to clutch at his hand that soon disappeared under the folds of her skirt. With a loud rip her blouse tore apart and Harry squeezed the other breast, leaving a red finger mark. He shoved a hand up her skirt, his other hand gripping her wrist. He lay on top of her. The girl was no longer kissing him back or giggling. She tried to wriggle out from under him and gasped in pain as his hands found their target. Leo couldn't move. That poor girl.

Tears were trickling down her face and Leo's gut tightened. What if Harry did this to Rose? Leo's muscles were frozen, and his eyes locked on the scene below.

The girl's eyes widened and rolled as Harry fumbled with his pants. She called out but Harry clamped a hand over her mouth. Leo was transfixed in horror as Harry plunged into the girl. With a low groan, Harry bucked at her. She twisted and turned but was pinned and it only seemed to add to his pleasure. She threw her head to the side and screamed, '*M'aider, aidez-moi veuillez!*'

Harry gave one last thrust. He rolled off her and she scuttled back into a corner.

'Don't you tell anyone, or I will come back and kill you. *Sans parler,*' Harry warned, running his finger across his throat. He straightened his clothes and left.

What had Harry done? Leo couldn't breathe. The young girl's tangled hair was matted with straw and her torn clothes were held tight. She started sobbing and it was worse than listening to the wounded in no man's land.

He should have stopped Harry. He should've yelled out when they first came in. He should've come racing down the ladder and pulled him off. He should've punched the bastard. He should've—.

God, he was a gutless wonder. A piece of hay floated down and landed on her head. She lifted her tear-stained face and their eyes met.

No! His heart crumpled. Now she knew someone had witnessed her shame and, even worse, he had not protected her. She covered her mouth and stumbled from the barn.

Leo threw up.

The sour taste of vomit wouldn't leave his mouth. He needed a drink. With wooden limbs, Leo made his way back to the café and flopped in a chair next to Bull, now sitting alone. His head ached and his guts hurt. What in the hell was wrong with Harry?

'Did you find him?' Bull asked.

'Um, no.'

'He'll be right. Don't feel bad about not giving him any money for upstairs; it'll probably save him a visit to the special hospital.'

The *estimanet* was full of soldiers. They sat sharing a yarn, joining in on a song or a bottle of wine. Were most of them like that? Would they do what Harry did to that girl? Even if they paid, did that make it okay?

'I don't get it.' Leo gulped down a beer sitting on the table, not caring who it belonged to.

'Women? Bit like the drink for some chaps. Can get 'em into a whole heap of trouble though.' Bull sighed and sipped the last of his red. 'Not sure what's going on with young Harry. He moons about after that girl, Rose, he writes to but then he's a right rogue over here. Can't blame the war for everything, ay?'

Leo's jaw clenched so tight his head throbbed. Should he ask Bull?

'What would happen if an army bloke got caught forcing a girl?'

Bull's eyes narrowed and Leo felt heat flood into his cheeks.

'I know some of the blokes think they can do what they like over here but that sort of caper would land you in front of the firing squad. Why?'

The room swayed like he was on a boat. It was too hot … too smoky … too rowdy. Someone at the next table dropped a glass and he winced as it shattered onto the flagstone floor, splattering his pants with wine.

Madame Audrey scuttled over and began picking up the shards of glass. She waved one of her daughters over and pointed to Leo's leg. The young girl drew a cloth from her waist and began dabbing the wine.

Her hand was shaking. Her dress was different, and her hair was smoothed into a bun, but it was her. She had only seen part of his face through the loft floor. Did she know it was him?

Leo went to take the cloth from her trembling fingers, and she flinched.

'I'm sorry. *Desole.*' His leaden heart couldn't find the words.

It was then she looked up at him. Her eyes bulged and she backed into the next table, bumping it so hard that a pitcher of wine toppled to the ground, where it shattered into more pieces than the wine glass. The floor looked like a blood bath.

'Lisette! Look what you've done. I am so sorry.' Madame Audrey shooed Lisette away, scooped up the clay shards and put them into the pitcher base that was still intact. The men resumed their chatting and singing, but Leo sat in silence.

She'd feared him.

He hadn't hurt her. But he hadn't helped her either.

Chapter Twenty-Seven

11 April 1917
Bullecourt, France

A sudden boom jolted through him. Adrenaline fired through Leo's veins and he began to sweat inside his woollen uniform.

'Bloody hell, can't see anything for the smoke already. Damn snow's no help either.'

Bull was right. The shells were dropping everywhere, and the haze was dense. Leo shifted his boots in the muddy bog. Those new blokes were in for it. He looked down the crowded trench. He hadn't even bothered to learn most of their names. What was the point, they'd probably be dead within the hour.

He did know the one closest to them. A young sapling Bull had nicknamed 'Stumps' after his brilliant performance in snowball cricket. Stumps was sloshing about like a dog in a tub. Was it to release tension or keep warm? A sudden retch. Definitely nerves.

'Great, Stumps. Now they'll smell me coming,' Bull complained.

'I'm sorry, Bull.'

'No worries kid, but if you need to heave, double it to somewhere other than my back. It's your job to clean this up when we get back.'

Jack, a vet from Gallipoli, and Leo laughed.

'Don't worry, Bull. You smell as sweet as a bucket of prawns left out in the sun.'

Bull growled, 'Shut up, Jack.'

Jack mimed zipping his mouth shut and Leo sniggered.

It seemed the wrath of hundreds of shells and flashing machine guns hailed down on them.

'At least we've got Mad Harry with us. Can't think of a better bloke to be leading us through this shit storm. He doesn't need a VC to prove it, but doesn't hurt to have a medal, I guess.' Bull was soon drowned out by the din.

Two minutes of ear-shattering fire calmed like a thunderstorm cooling to a tinkle of rain. The 16th rose and advanced and now it was their turn.

Leo joined in the charge, tingling in every nerve. Bodies thudded into the snow around him. He would do battle with death again. Who would win this time?

'Get to the right boys. You're swinging a bit too close. Come on, the 16th is getting hell!' Leo heard Murray yell out over the cacophony.

Very lights lit up the sky, adding to the streaks of machine gun fire and the bullets hitting the tanks in star bursts.

He pounded into something soft, soon realising he'd bumped into a bloke hung on the wire. He heard the ping as men smashed the barbed wire with rifle butts and others ripped at it with their bayonets. He dropped and wiggled under it, using the poor bloke as cover just as a machine gun aimed at them. Murray was trying to direct men to where a tank had crushed the wire, but Leo watched as many were mown down.

'Shit!' So much for the tanks or artillery damaging the wire. The men had bunched together, and Fritz was lining the parapet, shooting them down like rabbits.

'Get down, 13th, until it passes,' Murray yelled. Leo stayed close to the ground and listened to the bee drone above. The snow leeched in as he waited, wondering how the hell they'd get through the two belts of wire and get into OG 1 and 2. At least the smatter of snow had stopped, but it was almost daylight now.

Finally, there was a pause in the racket, so he charged forward, found a trench and slid in. Dead Germans littered the frozen ground. He'd missed the first hand-to-hand battle. A few soldiers were making quick work of stacking the dead to one side. OG 1 was wide and deep with earthen walls.

'Give us a hand, mate,' Harry asked as he dragged a body on top of another. Leo grabbed a boy's ankles, while Harry wrestled with his arms. Harry dropped him as if he were moving nothing more than a sandbag. Bull and Jack arrived from the left while Alfred and George came in from the right, each escorting about ten rattled Germans. Bull relieved a nearby captive of a fine German cigar.

'You should be digging in, not pilfering,' Alfred said as he pushed a German aside.

'Let's you and I worry about getting these chaps back to headquarters, shall we?' Bull emphasised the last two words by putting the cigar in Alf's pocket and giving it a firm pat. 'This stunt is a total balls-up. Have a peek over the top, Stumps, and give us the all clear, will you?'

Stumps stuck his head over the sandbags.

'Not a gander, you fool, a peek; get your arse down—'

Whizz-bang! They all ducked for cover. Stump's shredded torso slid down and plopped between them. A German screamed and another cheered. Bull pushed them both and pointed to the direction of a dugout.

'Vent a Tair, boys!' Bull roared over the din. Leo didn't need to be told twice to run at top speed. Entering a deep dugout lit with lamps, Alfred surveyed the prisoners and strutted over to the smallest one, a shivering mess that flinched every time a bomb shook the earth. The boy had bulging green eyes and large ears. Alfred's face flushed crimson and he poked him with the tip of his bayonet.

Leo turned to the others, but they were all preoccupied exploring the bunker. Only Alf's mate, George, was watching as he guarded the prisoners in the corner.

'Empty your pockets, you Hun scum. Now!'

Alfred's shrill voice grated on Leo's nerves and caught Bull and Harry's attention. The boy began to cry and seemed confused. Alfred yanked at the boy's grey pocket, tearing off its bronze button. He pulled out a photograph of the boy in uniform standing proudly next to a sleek Doberman, another with solemn family members, a crumpled letter, and a field postcard.

Harry sniggered and drawled, 'Ooooooh, I'm sure we had better rush this to HQ, this could end the war.'

'Shut up, Fuller. There's more of them than us. What if they turn on us? We should kill them all right now.'

'Steady on, Fanshaw. We'll get them all back to the cages soon enough,' Jack said. 'We really should be getting on to OG 2.'

Alfred threw aside the boy's possessions and returned to menacing him with his bayonet. Rolling his eyes like a terrified horse, the lad appealed to a stocky man. The man's neck strained as his comrades held him back. This boy was important to him and things were getting out of hand.

How could Alfred carry on like this when his own brother was at the mercy of German captors? Would he want his brother treated like this? Alfred had had enough fun; it was time to tell him to pull his head in.

'Leave him alone, Alfred,' Leo said as he picked up the lad's things and tucked them back into his pocket. He pushed Alfred's bayonet aside.

'Bloody Hun lover. Maybe I should take you in with them ...' Alfred shifted the point of his bayonet to Leo's stomach. '... as a traitor. Or will I just leave you like your little friends, to play stuck in the mud?'

A flare of fire ripped through Leo's body, blending with clammy fear. 'You rotten mongrel.'

Everyone stood frozen as Alf and Leo glared at each other. The bayonet tip was pushed in enough to feel it through his tunic but not enough to tear it. How dare that arsehole have a go at him. How dare he sound so callous about Frosty's death. It was Alfred's fault. If he hadn't shoved Frosty like that. This bloke had a lump of coal instead of a heart.

'I'd rather be a Hun lover than an Australian prick like you. You kill me and you'll be in the lock up for the rest of the war.' Leo sounded confident but his legs trembled. He had always thought Alfred was all bluster and no bite, nothing to worry about, but this war had hardened him. Alfred blinked his reptilian eyes.

'They are the army's prisoners; they don't belong to you.' Leo indicated for the boy to return to the group.

'But he's mine for now,' Alfred muttered.

Alfred struck with lightning speed, plunging his bayonet deep into the boy's back. The lad slumped to the ground face first. Blood spurted from his wound as Alfred withdrew the weapon and lifted his head with a nod of satisfaction.

Leo snapped out of shock and brought the butt of his rifle down on Alfred's skull, giving him a boot as he crumpled onto the bloodied dirt. In a flurry of activity, Harry and Bull bandaged the German boy as best they could but his waxen face gave them little hope.

George stood over the rest of the prisoners, far less confident than when he had swaggered in with them. The stocky German's face had paled but his eyes sparked when they locked with Leo's. The dying boy gasped frothy bubbles of blood.

If only he had left Alfred to his little power trip cleaning out a few pockets, the poor beggar would be a prisoner of an idiot, but he'd still be alive.

With every gurgle, Leo held his breath. He sank to the floor and touched the lad's hand. The boy sighed and released his grip. Jack gently placed a blanket over him. Alfred emitted a low groan and sat up with a slight sway.

The brawny German shrugged off the grip of his fellow captors and stepped out of the forlorn tangle of prisoners. Pushing past George's limply held rifle, he made his way to the blanketed form and flipped back the cover. He knelt next to the gaunt boy and tenderly kissed his pallid cheek. A candle flickered and went out, leaving a wisp of smoke.

The German's piercing grey eyes glared from Alfred to Leo. '*Er war mein Bruder. Sie werden beide bezahlen,*' his guttural voice echoed in Leo's head.

The German lowered his head and Leo saw a tear drop from his nose.

'What did he say?' Harry whispered.

'He said the boy was his brother. He wants to make me and Alf pay for it,' Leo whispered back.

'Bloody hell, lucky he's a POW then.'

Leo slumped onto a crate. He'd tried to help and all he'd done was got a boy killed. The German stared at him with a grief-stricken face and stony eyes. The eyes of a true enemy.

PART THREE:

ENGLAND (1917)

Chapter Twenty-Eight

May 1917
Bermondsey, England

Gentle hands touched his forehead. His eyelids were lead and his throat whistled like a desert canyon. Water trickled onto his lips. Aaaah. He sniffed. Under the acidic smell of carbolic soap was a sweeter scent of delicate flowers, a bit like the white beards from home. He frowned and even though his lungs ached, he sucked in another breath. Where was the familiar sour smell of sweaty men and the reek of manure and corpse- tainted soil? Was he dreaming?

'Leo! Hey, you lead-swinging bastard. Wake up!' someone whispered.

'I feel like hell, piss off,' he croaked. Hang on, was that his brother? 'Oskar?'

'Yeah, it's me.'

Leo opened his grainy eyes and stared at Oskar's clean-shaven face. Where was his uniform? Was he in hospital blues? Leo snapped awake and pulled himself up. A motley group of bandaged men were sleeping on hospital cots lined up in neat rows. Some groaned or called out in their sleep while others snored and farted.

'Where in the hell are we?'

'Hospital. Don't you remember?' Oskar moved from his own bed and sat with a squeak on Leo's. He smelt of carbolic soap.

Leo strained but his sticky golden syrup mind gave up nothing. No, wait. He saw Alfred plunging a bayonet … a young boy's pale, grey face … eyes blacker than coal.

'The last thing I remember is Alf killing a POW.'

Oskar widened his eyes. 'He what? Rotten mongrel. I was told that you got stuck trying to take Stormy Trench and got pneumonia. Do you remember being in that shell hole?'

Dark, velvet nothingness. No, he didn't remember.

'Well, you did. Then you got carted off to Rouen and then to old Blighty. First, you were in Lewisham Military Hospital and now we're here at the Ladywell in Bermondsey.'

Leo nodded but couldn't believe it. He was in a hospital in England and Oskar was with him. He frowned. 'Why are you here? What happened to you?'

Oskar shifted and bit his lip. 'I, uh, got shot out at Bullecourt. Felt like my whole gut was on fire.' He looked around the dim ward. 'Probably wasn't a great idea to join up, was it?'

Leo nodded. 'You can say that again.'

'Oh well. Listen, I need to have a chat with you about something.'

Leo had slid back down his pillow and he felt his eyes closing. 'It's so good to see you but I just can't … in the morning … we will. I'm really tired.'

'It's important—about Adelaide.'

Leo smiled. 'A lovely girl', he murmured.

'C'mon Leo, wake up.' He felt hands shake his shoulders but he couldn't will his leaden eyes to open.

'I'll put my stuff in your Blighty bag.'

'Mmm, 'kay.'

Leo woke with a start and looked at the cot next to him. It was vacant. Two nurses stood at the end of his bed. The younger nurse's lustrous skin glowed in the lamp light.

A tendril of auburn hair hung in a spiral curl next to her cheek until she tucked it back under her nurse's cap. A waft of sweet blossoms. Was she the one who had stroked his forehead?

'Do you need anything, Private?' the nurse next to her asked. She was another story. Even though she had slightly averted her face from the light, Leo could still see half of a large port wine birthmark that ran down from her temple to her jaw like a drunkard had slapped her. Even without the stain, her thin lips, blade-like nose and sour expression gave Leo the shivers. A heart of flint.

'No. I was just having a yarn with my brother, Oskar, earlier. Do you know where he is?' Leo waved to the empty bed.

A look passed between them.

'Mmm, hmm. Time to get some rest.' Sister Blossom and Sister Sour tucked him back in. His eyelids drooped again. Hands fumbled near his calves. Sister Blossom was tucking his Blighty bag back into a small locker between the beds.

'I'm looking after my brother's stuff too,' he mumbled.

She stroked his cheek. Her hands were so gentle. Soothing. He sank into the blackness.

'I was talking to him just this morning about his little sister, Dot. He was telling me about walking in the bush back home. He was almost poetic.' Leo listened to the gentle murmur of the nurses.

Dot grips his hand as they wander among the turpentine trees and golden orbs of wattle. Droning bees gathering nectar from yellow pea-flowers and pretty white daisies don't deter Dot collecting specimens for her pressed flower collection. *Shhhh.*

A luminous pink chick sits among cream and red-specked eggs nestled on the brown velvet of a Banksia. *Screech!* A mother honeyeater puffs her white tufts and gives them a sharp scolding. They run snorting and giggling through the bush.

Was that Dot and his ma chatting while they made supper? No. He couldn't smell any supper wood smoke or hear the rhythmic chopping of carrots.

'I think we had better send him to the 3rd Auxiliary at Dartford. They know how to handle cases like this,' he heard a prim voice say. Who was that?

'It's so sad.'

'Come and get me if he talks about his brother again.'

Leo gave the snort of a sleeping man. The scent of flowers faded as the voices moved away.

'It must be so hard on them.'

Leo's fake snore caught in his throat and an icicle pierced his core. Did they think he was having a nervous breakdown? He opened his eyes. They had moved to the other end of the ward. The bed next to him was untouched, not a crinkle on the surface. Where was Oskar?

***

May 1917
3rd Australian Auxiliary Hospital, Dartford

Leo settled back into the padded chair of the small office. A comforting number of old, vanilla-scented medical tomes lined the shelves on one wall and the other was patch worked with impressive, framed certificates. He was in good hands.

'That's it, Leo. Just relax and look at my watch ...' Dr Springthorpe's soothing voice instructed him.

Leo followed the handsome silver fob watch as it swayed from side to side, and took deep breaths. Heavy ... let go. His muscles dropped into the soft folds of the cushioned leather.

'You are safe here. Imagine the weight just dropping from your shoulders. There is nothing to worry about or concern you. Close your eyes and go to your safe place.'

Leo lay in the shade of a eucalypt and listened to the rustle of dry leaves. Bell birds tinkled in the bush around him and his bare foot twitched as a fly crawled in the crevasse between his second and third toes. If he opened his eyes, he would see the rolling sway of yellow grassed hills with Mt Canobolas rising above the blue summer haze beyond them.

He melted into the serene nothingness.

'Very slowly ... bring yourself back to this time and place,' Dr Springthorpe's voice echoed in his head.

No, not yet. Leo wanted to stay wrapped in a cocoon of sweet memories.

'Feel the weight of your body in the chair. Let the images in your head become as small as a postage stamp. Take a deep breath. You will feel calm and relaxed and this feeling of wellbeing will continue. When you are ready, slowly open your eyes.'

Leo yawned and reluctantly opened his eyes. The doctor's blue eyes were piercing. All sense of calm dissolved as Dr Springthorpe became animated. How could a bloke sound like a priest giving a sermon one minute and a stockyard auctioneer the next?

The doctor opened Leo's file. 'It was the same again. Alfred killing the POW and some legs running around an orange moon. You did mention someone called Harry this time and told him not to hurt her. Would you like to share more about that?'

Not bloomin' likely. How did that one sneak out?

'No, ah, that's okay.' Leo tried to sound casual, but his voice betrayed a pleading tone.

'We'll leave it there. Maybe a little bit of amnesia isn't such a bad thing. You've done very well. Is there anything else today?' His eyes were pools of compassion.

'Did Sister Sou—I mean the sister at Bermondsey mention where they sent my brother, Oskar? No one seems to be able to tell me anything.'

'No, I'm afraid not. I'm sure you'll hear soon enough. Is there anything else?'

Should he mention his dreams? They were bothering him. Would he sound crazy and get locked up? 'Actually, I've been having some ... uh ... dreams about large silver planes bombing London.'

'I suppose that is quite reasonable given the recent attack on Folkestone. It does make sense as a military target with the boys leaving to go to France from there, but London hasn't had any trouble save for the odd Zeppelin attack at night. You certainly aren't the only one having nightmares in this war. Perfectly normal.'

He got his stethoscope out and Leo pulled up his shirt, wincing as the cold metal touched his chest. Leo would keep his mouth shut. He didn't want the doctor to think he was some nervous ninny unable to cope with the war.

'Ah, your chest is much clearer. Mmm, your heart is still beating a bit wildly. I've seen that a lot in the men coming back from Flanders and the Somme. Nothing to worry about. We call it soldier's heart,' he said as he set the stethoscope down on the worn oak desk. Leo watched the pen nib float inky observations about him over the paper.

'I think you just need some time to be that six-bob-a-day tourist. I'm sending you on furlough to London for a couple of weeks. Make sure you pay a visit to the Tower of London.'

Leo looked at him with surprise. He would be allowed to go on leave? Just like that?

'Listen, Leo, you are in much better shape than a lot of men here, but I don't think you are ready to head back to France. Have a couple of weeks, then to Perham Down to ease back in. Now go and have some fun and forget about the war for a bit. Mind, I'm not saying get yourself in trouble with those London girls, but a bit of romance might do wonders. I've just gotten married myself. Great for the soul it is.' He closed the file and gave Leo such a warm smile that Leo wanted to give the doctor a bone-crunching bear hug.

'I'd be a fool to turn down such a good offer.' He was more than ready to leave Dartford. He hadn't seen bandaged heads or stumps at Dartford, but plenty of men who walked like gangly new colts only to collapse onto the floor with a thud. Others screamed into the night like a banshee. These bug-eyed blokes were broken on the inside.

'How do you do it, Doc?'

The doctor put Leo's file on top of a teetering pile on his desk.

'Do what?' Leo pointed out the window where men were digging with hoes in a field.

'Oh, the men. I try to give them what they need. I don't agree with the way the Brits are dealing with these men. I don't think sending them back in or punishing them harshly for being weak is what's needed here. We've had some of the bravest soldiers I've ever known become lost souls in this war. I talk to them just how I talked to you; it's called hypnosis. Some kindness and salt of the earth work in the fields seems to do them the world of good.' Leo could hear how compassionate the doctor was. Thank God for good Aussie blokes like Dr Springthorpe.

They walked to the door of the small office and shook hands. Leo towered over Dr Springthorpe, but he thought he had never met a bigger man.

'Take care of your soldier's heart. Share it with a girl and it'll come good. The war'll still be waiting when you're done.'

He tried to ignore the spider-tingle on his neck and dismiss thoughts of sparkling silver planes bombing London. He screwed his nose up at the sharp scent of carbolic disinfectant and hurried down the freshly scrubbed hallway. Maybe he could find out where Oskar was at Army Headquarters.

He was finally on leave in Blighty. Would a woman heal his heart from the disease of war? A tremor of excitement rippled through him. He was off to London. Would a girl be waiting there for him?

Chapter Twenty-Nine

June 1917
London, England

L eo dumped his kit at the Australian Headquarters on Horseferry Road and secured accommodation across the road at the War Chest Club. He'd put in that he was looking for information about Oskar and as there was nothing else he could do, he set out for this Tower of London that Dr Springthorpe had mentioned.

The streets were a muddle of people. Reserved Englishmen with top hats and tails strolled with sombre women. They somehow seemed oblivious to the ragged street urchins pleading with an outstretched hand. Men with huge baskets on wagons called out but Leo couldn't understand what they were selling, their accent strange to his ears. Scottish soldiers with swaying kilts darted among strolling Tommies holding sweethearts on their arm. Motor cars tooted and horse carts trotted by.

A girl in a lilac cotton dress detached a posy of violets from her wide purple cummerbund that encircled her waist and pressed it into his palm. What did she want? He had heard of girls trying to take advantage of the well-paid Aussie soldier, getting the unassuming clod to take her to the moving pictures and tea so he was immediately wary.

He glanced up from the wilting flowers and into her glistening blue eyes.

'I found out that I lost my Bert this morning,' she whispered. She put her head down and hurried off. Boy, he could get it wrong sometimes. That poor lass. He didn't even thank her or utter a word of comfort. Leo stood on some stairs and craned his neck to get a glimpse of her purple-ribboned hat among the bustling crowd. It was no use. He continued and felt a strange sense of familiarity with London's meandering streets, as if he had walked them many a time.

He stopped to take in the Palladian front of Mansion House with its imposing Corinthian columns and ornate facade. What a grand city. St Paul's Cathedral beckoned with its dominating dome, but he wanted to find the Tower of London. Leo wound his way along the Thames. The river was as murky looking as Bobs Creek but at times it ponged.

He spotted the small domes of the White Tower peeking above the trees and was soon at the Tower of London. He stood in front of its solid stone walls and dry moat. This could be one war in which the Tower would fall. Artillery would just blast through those thick walls as if they were made of eggshell.

He felt a tingle as he walked on worn cobblestone. He was treading on the exact same steps that medieval kings and queens of England had walked on. How amazing was that? Displays of gleaming silver armour of past soldiers of England and their weapons filled the great hall; even King Henry VIII's full battle armoury was there. The man must have been huge! He tried to imagine himself wearing armour like that and running among the trenches. No wonder they didn't wear that stuff anymore. He moved beyond the large banquet hall and descended the tiny steps of the spiral staircase that wound around and around to the point he felt quite dizzy. The metallic smell of the wire rope he held to steady was also making him queasy.

Leo made his way around and stepped down into the dank air of what appeared to be a medieval torture chamber. It was almost like an ancient cave except for the various implements hanging on the walls. He tried to imagine some of the poor sods that had been chained to the walls in the manacles, and he shivered in the cold mustiness.

How could people be so cruel to each other? What drove a man to take on the role of torturer or executioner? What stains must their souls carry? As a current soldier of the king, was Leo any better? He shook his head. It didn't do to be thinking like that. He'd made his choice and he was stuck with it.

He joined the trickle of other tourists going to the Wakefield Tower to marvel over The Crown Jewels. A whistle escaped his lips. Would you look at that! It was better than a pirate's treasure chest. As Leo admired The Sceptre with Cross with its newly fitted Star of Africa diamond, his nose twitched with a tantalising smell of lavender.

'You'd have to have the neck of a mallee bull to cart that crown around on your head, don't you think?' said a girl behind him, in an

Australian accent. His throat dried as he looked straight into Rose's violet eyes. Elise was with her.

'Sure would. Have you seen the armour they had to wear? I don't know how they went off to battle.' He felt the heat in his cheeks as he croaked the last word out.

'Private Dymond! Harry wrote that you'd taken ill and been sent to England. You look just fine now,' Rose said as she gave him a smile.

She remembered him! He wanted to bounce and leap around the room like a spring lamb. He swallowed and hoped the pounding of his pulse in his throat would slow so he could sound halfway normal.

'Please, call me Leo. I've been given a couple of weeks to play tourist and I'd rather forget I was a soldier for now.'

Elise's whole face glowed. 'Being a tourist on your own is no fun. You'll have to come and see the sights with us. Won't he, Rose?'

'Of course, you're more than welcome. Assuming you want to, that is.' Rose flushed with colour. Did she want him to? Leo nodded so hard his teeth rattled.

'Great, that's settled then,' Elise said. She looked at her watch. 'Oh bother, I had better get going. My shift starts soon.' She looked expectantly at Rose, and Leo's shoulders dropped. Was she going already?

Rose glanced at him and said, 'Since my shift doesn't start for another couple of hours, I might keep Leo company.'

Sweat was now beading on his forehead. Elise gave Rose a tight smile and nodded.

'I'll see you soon then, Leo.'

He was with Rose again. If only Harry hadn't met her at the same time. Leo cleared his throat; it was so dry, and his cheeks felt so hot.

'It's a bit warm in here, maybe we should get some fresh air,' Rose suggested.

The warder gave them a pointed stare, which only made her giggle like a naughty schoolgirl as they left the Tower.

'Are you sure you are allowed to associate with the likes of me now you nurses have rank?' Leo asked, pointing to the two stars on the shoulder straps of her Norfolk jacket.

Rose shrugged. 'Maybe, if I was one of the snooty British QAs, but us Aussie girls aren't much better than you boys in respecting the military rules. I'm still not used to the British MOs expecting sick men to stand at attention at the end of their beds. I've had to tell a few to stay put. I've been in trouble for making up the beds instead of letting the male orderlies do it, but I can't stand around idle. The Queen Anne girls are more concerned with how their ward looks and doing the paperwork than worrying about the men. I can't wait to get to an Australian unit.'

She paused in the shadow of The Bloody Tower attached to the Wakefield Tower. 'What an awful place to be held prisoner. I heard that there's an Irish rebel being held somewhere here right now. Do you think he could be up there staring down at us?'

'What? Really? I'd have thought using this place for prisoners would've ended donkey's years ago.'

They wandered around the grounds of the ancient castle and while Leo tried to listen with rapt attention as she chatted, he barely registered anything beyond her sparkling eyes and rosebud lips. They left the Tower and sat on a park bench under a London plane tree facing the sienna brown waters of the Thames.

Leo kept a respectful distance, but he wanted to reach out and touch Rose's smooth cheek, trace his fingers around her lips, stroke her petal soft skin … No! She was Harry's.

'How have things been for you?' Rose asked.

Leo nodded. Rose's laugh was both hearty and musical.

'Have I been a bore?'

'What? Oh, no. Not at all. I can't believe I've found you aga— … I mean that we've bumped into each other like this,' he stuttered. What a galah. He took a deep breath.

'I know. What are the chances? I was asking how things have been for you since you got over here.'

How could you put the last few months into words to someone who hadn't been in it? Images flashed like a disjointed moving picture and he closed his eyes. Shattered stone buildings, grey desolation, corpse-encrusted mud, flickering red and yellow blasts of explosives … Frosty's legs dangling from a tree … Alfred plunging his bayonet into that boy … Harry plunging into Lise— … oh Lord! How could he keep that from Rose? His chest felt like a horse had sat on him.

'I'm sorry, I shouldn't have asked. I imagine it's been awfully hard on you. I hear such awful things from the men when they first come in, then they stop talking about it.' Rose's eyes had darkened to the colour of aubergine.

'No, it's not that. Well it is … I don't have words for it right now.'
Slender, warm fingers closed over his. His body hummed like an electric tram.

'I didn't mean to upset you.' Rose squeezed and released his hand.

Leo blew out a breath and lifted his chin.

'You didn't upset me, Rose. Now, I've got two weeks in London, what other sights do you reckon I should take in while I'm here?'

Before she could answer, a gaggle of school children passed by and Rose smiled at them. Leo returned the salutes of some of the boys.

'I hope it will be over soon or some of them will get dragged into this mess too. I wish Oskar and the others hadn't followed me over here,' Leo said. 'I saw him at the hospital.' Her eyes popped in alarm. 'No, he's fine. Shot, but on the mend. He said he wanted to tell me something about Adelaide, but they moved him before he got the chance.'

'Oh, thank goodness he's fine. I'm sure he'll tell you soon enough.' Rose stopped tapping the bench. 'Before I forget, we're going to see Westminster Abbey in a couple of days; would you like to come along?'

Would he? Is the Pope a Catholic? A group of Aussie soldiers strolled past, tipping their hats at Leo and giving Rose an appraising eye. Rose gave them a good-natured wave.

Leo laughed when he heard one comment, 'She's a bit of eyes right, eh? Lucky bastard.'

If only he was. Harry was the lucky bastard.

'Incorrigible lot, aren't they?' she said mildly.

'Hopeless,' Leo agreed. His hand tightened on the edge of the seat until his knuckles felt like they would pierce his skin.

'I wonder how Harry is going over there, I haven't heard from him since he wrote about you.'

Leo gazed at the Tower Bridge. He didn't want to think about Harry. The massive stone and granite Victorian Gothic towers seemed to guard the entry to a mysterious dark lord's castle on the other side of the Thames. Would Sydney ever build a bridge so grand? Leo stared off into space.

Rose gave a couple of coughs. 'That's a mighty bridge, isn't it? I can't believe that it splits open for the ships, can you?'

'Does it? I thought Sydney was pretty good, but London seems to have more beaut buildings than you can poke a stick at.'

Rose touched his arm. 'It's okay if you don't want to talk about your friends. You must be missing them.'

Leo's heart fisted and he closed his eyes. He did miss them but how could he tell her that he was happy to be with her … without Harry. Rose's fingers were warm against his skin. When he opened his eyes, everything seemed so bright. He looked down and picked up one of the spiky nuts from the plane tree and rolled it around and around. Bells rang out and they sat quietly, watching the enormous bascules of the Tower Bridge yawn open to allow a pleasure steamer loaded with men in khaki to pass under the bridge. This wouldn't do. She would think he was a real misery guts. He pointed to a huge white dome in the skyline.

'What's that over there?' he asked.

'Oh, you'll have to see St Paul's Cathedral before you leave.' Rose said, 'I've got a list I've been working through and I hope to get it done before I'm off to France.'

Leo's heart gave a solid thump. 'France?'

She picked at a loose thread. 'Yes, I'm going over too. Probably one of the Casualty Clearing Stations. Apparently, I work well under pressure and it'll be a great experience in terms of what I'll learn.'

His breath caught at the thought of such a vibrant woman stuck out there in the horror and filth.

'It's a bit of a butcher's shop over there, especially in a CCS. Not a great place—,' he started. Her face crumpled like an autumn leaf.

Rose frowned. 'You sound like my father. He'd demand I return home at once if he heard I was going to France. He'd say I'll end up shot by the Germans like Edith Cavell. Father doesn't seem to understand me at all.'

Leo tried to keep his face neutral. Did Harry understand her?

'I didn't mean, uh, I guess the army life isn't for everyone and some would say especially a woman …' Leo started. He saw a storm crossing her eyes. 'But I think that's wrong of them. Some of the nurses I have seen have been tougher than the blokes. I even saw a couple of them driving an ambulance once, incredibly brave they were.'

'How wonderful, driving an ambulance! I want to do so much more to help.' Rose closed her eyes and sighed. 'When I finally got over here last September, I expected to be looking after the Aussies but instead they split us up all over the place. I've learnt so much from the London 5th nurses, but I'd just rather be helping our boys.'

What did she imagine it would be like? He gazed at her serene face, trying to imprint it in his memory. He knew she would be different after serving at a Casualty Clearing Station, but in what ways would she change?

Rose frowned. 'Why are you looking at me like that?'

Leo snapped his eyes away. 'No reason.'

'Does it sound stupid to say I can't wait to go into the fray? I hear it from blokes all of the time.'

Leo chewed his thumb. He wanted to get this right.

'I don't think you are stupid at all. I think it's very brave … but … well, people just don't look the same after they've been over there for a bit.'

'Oh, you think I'm brave.' Rose gave a satisfied sigh and relaxed against the bench. Their shoulders almost touched.

There was a sweet scent in the air that Leo couldn't place, and his wine grower's nose tingled. A blend of lavender from Rose and smoky roasted chestnuts. It smelt so much better than being on the Somme.

'What did you do before the war?' Rose asked.

'I helped my pa run a vineyard. We made chardonnay.'

Rose twisted to look at him. 'Really? I love a good chardonnay, but my favourite would have to be pinot noir. Of course, that can be hard to get. My mother's family is from France and occasionally send us a few bottles. It's just divine.' She sighed and licked her lips.

'That's amazing. I tried some that a French soldier was lugging around. He was grateful when I helped him find his way back to his section and I was grateful he spoke English when I tasted it. I couldn't believe my luck when he told me it was his family's own. The pinot grape is supposed to be a finicky grape to grow, but it sounded like his farm in Burgundy had a similar climate to home. I was thinking I might give it a go when I get some land for myself.'

Rose grinned. 'That sounds like a wonderful plan. I'll be your first customer.'

Leo restrained his arms from picking her up and twirling her around. He grinned back until his cheeks ached instead.

All too soon, Rose had to leave to return to the hospital, but he was cheered by the thought of seeing Westminster Abbey together. He whistled as he sauntered off. She might be Harry's girl and all, but he couldn't help it if Harry was somewhere in France and he was here in London, now could he? At least he might become friends with Rose. But his heart whispered another story. He wanted more.

Chapter Thirty

The deep gong of Big Ben vibrated through them. Rose hurried Elise along to Westminster Abbey.

'Good morning, Leo,' Rose and Elise said in unison then laughed at each other.

'Morning, and a beauty it is.' Leo was right. The deep hue of the sky was almost as vivid as a summer's day in Australia. She would never take the unpolluted sapphire of Australia's sky for granted again.

'Almost like home today, isn't it?' Rose agreed.

'I've been here once before, perhaps you'll let me be your guide this morning,' Elise said as she slipped her arm into Leo's. Leo stiffened and Rose felt her smile fade. Why did Elise have to come along ... no, that was what she wanted. She didn't want to be alone with Leo.

Leo glanced at her and tried to shake Elise off. 'Oh, uh thanks but I'm sure I'll be fine.'

Elise set her jaw and kept her arm in place. 'Looks like it's time to go in.'

Rose marched ahead but soon paused when they entered the Abbey. She gazed up at the ribbed arches of the Gothic vault encasing them like God's skeletal fingers. Her soul sighed with contentment.

Her boots clicked on the sand-coloured floor and she felt dips where the stone had worn away. Rose was surprised to see dark squares where people were buried or remembered, many with names that had long since been scuffed, leaving only fragments of letters or dates.

'It's amazing, isn't it?' Rose whispered.

Leo nodded and Rose noticed he was staring at her. Elise let his arm go and she disappeared through a small opening. It was the Lady Chapel. They followed and studied the marble effigy of Mary Queen of Scots's tomb under its elaborate canopy.

'I was never interested when the sisters back home used to go on about Elizabeth the First or Henry the Seventh. I mean, what did they have to do farming and all? But ... well, now I'm a king's soldier. It's all very strange.'

He held the iron railing and tried to reach through to touch the crimson Scottish lion at Mary's feet. Rose found herself drawn to his child-like wonder.

They continued to the Poets' Corner in the south transept. Rose pointed out a statue of Shakespeare leaning on a pillar. Leo said he had no idea who many of the poets and writers were until he turned and saw the name 'Charles Dickens' in gold lettering on the floor.

'My father favours the likes of Henry Lawson, but he always told us the story of Scrooge in *A Christmas Carol* every Christmas. I wonder what the ghosts of the future would show us about this war.' Leo squatted and traced the letters.

'I hope it shows the Germans turning around and going home so we can do the same,' Rose murmured.

Elise shook her head. 'Now, now Rose. If we all turn around and go home, we'd never get to see anything. Who wants to be stuck back in Katoomba keeping house for a man and wiping the snotty noses of children? I wouldn't miss this for quids.'

Rose, having been subject to many conversations discussing Elise's romantic conquests in search of a husband, yet her equal determination that a man not ruin the fun of the war with the freedom she had as a nurse, had to choke down a snort of laughter.

'No, wouldn't miss it for quids,' Rose echoed, but Leo was like a statue and Rose followed his gaze. 'What's he doing here?'

Leo paled. 'Do you mind if we leave?'

'Not at all,' Rose said but before any of them took a step, Alfred spotted them and made a beeline for them.

Elise seemed oblivious to the tension. 'Oh, it's Alfred. I wonder if they've heard from Thomas. The last I heard his mother got a Red Cross letter card from some camp called Wittenberg.'

'Poor bloke,' Leo muttered.

'I was there when they got the telegram. I felt awful for Alfred. Can you believe she turned to Alfred and said it should have been him? Not a nice woman at all,' Elise said as they watched Alfred striding towards them.

'That's terrible,' Rose said.

'What are you doing with this traitor? His parents are German you know. His pa is locked up back home,' Alfred blustered.

How dare he! Rose frowned and moved forward next to Leo while Elise shuffled awkwardly.

Leo's voice was low but firm. 'Pa wouldn't be there if it wasn't for you. Unlike some soldiers, I also don't see the need to prove my loyalty by killing young boys when they have asked for quarter just to prove themselves.'

Elise moved back warily while Rose grabbed Alfred's sleeve. 'How could you do something like that? Private Dymond is a loyal Australian, he's joined the army. Isn't that enough?'

Alfred's cheeks paled then burned red. He wrenched his arm away and drew closer until he and Leo were nearly nose to nose.

'I wouldn't defend this piece of scum, Rose. I'm not worried about you, Dymond. The only friends you are going to have left will be the Germans. While you've been out there hugging Huns, they've been busy killing your brother and cousins.'

Alfred raised his chin in triumph. Oskar? Rose's stomach dropped.

'Yes, Oskar was killed at Bullecourt,' Alfred continued, 'Bill too. Collins made it but lost his legs. Maybe next time you won't mind when I take a German out.'

Rose gasped and put her hand to her mouth. She stepped between them and shoved Alfred away. 'His brother has just sacrificed his life for Australia. I think you've said enough for now, Alfred.'

Leo's mouth opened and closed, his words stillborn.

'Come with me.' Elise grabbed Alfred by the arm and towed him away.

Rose led Leo to a pew in the Chapel of the Faithful and sat next to him, tears streaming down her cheeks. Oskar was dead. What was Adelaide going to do now? Leo wasn't moving.

'What an awful way to find out. Poor Oskar.' Rose gulped.

'I just can't believe it. Maybe Alfred's lying; he can be such a bastard.'

Rose knew he was clutching at straws.

'Come on, let's get out of here.' Rose took his hand.

They sat on a cold stone seat moulded along the walls of the cloisters.

'How are you doing?' Rose asked. 'Leo?'

'It's my fault. If I hadn't have joined up, none of them would have.'

Rose held his cold hand. 'Don't do that to yourself. It's not your fault.'

'But it is.' He sounded so exhausted. 'I was there … at Bullecourt and didn't even see him. Didn't know he was right there. I could have seen him hit, walked over him, left him in the snow.'

Rose couldn't find any words of comfort. Nothing would ease a pain like that.

On the wall in front of them she read a plaque.

Jane Lister
Dear childe
Died Oct 7th, 1688
In memorial of her brother
Michael Lister
Who died August 1676

She felt another tear leak. They had both lost a brother too.

Rose sat absently picking at the embroidered roses on the tatty handkerchief that Leo handed her. She needed to tell Adelaide.

'I don't know if this will help or just make things worse, but I really need you to come with me somewhere tomorrow. It's something I need to show you and I'd rather wait until then to talk about it.' She felt strangely vulnerable.

Leo's grim expression shifted. She knew that look. A lid now on his grief, a pot to be opened later—when he was alone.

'Sure, I'll come.'

She smiled and turned her attention to the soggy scrap of material in her hand.

'This is a bit odd, but I could swear this is my handkerchief. Where did you get it?'

Leo's face flushed hot.

'You dropped it at the dance in Katoomba, I meant to return it.'

Her lips curled in amusement. 'You're a terrible liar. Why on Earth would you keep my hanky?'

'It'll probably sound stupid, but I thought it might bring me good luck.'

'That's so sweet. It's a bit wet. I could wash it.' She blushed.

'No, that's fine. I don't mind a few extra tears on it. Might give me extra good luck.'

She handed it back to him and held his gaze. 'I hope you have all the luck in the world. I really li—'

'There you are. I'm awfully sorry about your brother. How are you doing, Leo?' Elise plonked herself next to him. 'That Alfred is just plain terrible, boy did I give him an earful.'

Rose released his hand. Was she going to say she liked him? She was just concerned for him, that was all. Elise babbled on and they all walked along the grey columns, footsteps echoing on the pitted stone.

When they reached Leo's quarters, Rose waited until Elise had turned to go and gave him a peck farewell. She prayed he would understand why she'd kept Adelaide's secret.

Chapter Thirty-One

13 June 1917
London, England

Rose had felt jittery the whole train ride but refused to discuss her secret. Neither of them seemed in the mood for any light conversation. Hard-bitten dockers unloaded sacks and cartons from the ships onto heavy goods lorries. Sailors, stevedores and drivers all ducked and weaved among crates and baskets. It was utter chaos.

She sucked in the salty air and ducked as a seagull tried to snatch a meal from the fishmonger's wares. The woman's cry of dismay was drowned by the clanging of boat chains, motor lorries, whistles, and calls from men directing the unloading. She waved a fist and continued laying out the floppy catch onto her stall table. Leo followed Rose along the docks like an obedient farm dog.

'Hello luvvy, how's yerself?' Rose ignored a burly sailor's greeting. He winked at Leo. Rose marched on. She knew Leo must be wondering why she had them traipsing through such a grubby part of London.

Soot-stained buildings squatted together, shutters peeling and askew like a drunken man's tie. Adjoining a row of small, terraced cottages that had a yard barely big enough to spit in, were a few more modern-looking shops, including a post office. The last shop had a broken window covered with an old board. Rose silently guided him down a narrow urine-soaked alley to the back of the shops. There stood the remnants of a once attractive sandstone cottage.

One of the crumbling pillars on either side of the wrought iron gate had a new plaque attached to it. '*Manor Cottage Maternity Home*'.

Leo stood back as Rose knocked on a stout entry door and had a quick whispered conversation with the sister who answered it. She explained the situation as briefly as she could. The nurse's bagged eyes flicked over Leo and she allowed them entry. Rose kept her lips firmly clamped while they waited in the foyer until Matron Robinson introduced herself and guided them along a tessellated tile hallway. She asked them to wait at the door and bustled out a couple of women with babes in arms. They didn't look happy about the disturbance, but the matron's face was set. She gave Rose a gentle touch on the arm and left them.

'What a lovely surprise. Come and meet little Arthur,' Adelaide said.

Rose cast Leo a glance and ushered him further inside where Adelaide was propped up in an old iron bed, cradling a bundle in her arms.

'Oh, sorry. I wasn't expecting company.' She offered the swaddled bundle to Rose and smoothed her caramel-coloured hair.

'Adelaide, do you remember Oskar's brother, Leo?' Rose rocked the now squirming baby. She breathed in the talc and vanilla baby smell.

'Leo! Oskar talks about you all the time. He promised he'd write you and let you know. How wonderful that you get to meet Arthur. I wish Oskar'd gotten to see him before he left. He's just like his daddy, the sweetest little thing,' Adelaide bubbled.

Rose offered him the now settled babe.

Leo appeared to be mesmerised by the cherubic face topped with downy blond hair. His tiny mouth stretched in a yawn and he briefly opened one eye before he settled back into Leo's chest. Rose's heart twinged painfully. What on Earth was wrong with her? Leo looked like he would make a wonderful father.

'I hope you're not too ashamed of us. We'd gotten engaged before he left for France and we're getting married after the war, but we couldn't wait.' Adelaide talked so fast her words melted into each other. 'You won't tell your ma yet, will you? We'd decided to keep it all quiet for now.'

Rose choked and tears glimmered in her eyes. How could she tell her? Leo then seemed to understand why she had asked him to come.

'He's beaut. No, I won't tell anyone.' Leo's eyes closed for a second. 'I can't believe that Oskar's a father. I'm an uncle.' He laid the baby in a well-worn cradle.

'Rose, didn't you tell him before you got here? He's gone quite white,' Adelaide scolded.

'No, Rose didn't tell me. She obviously wanted to surprise me—'Leo then found his tongue quite numb. 'It's just that—'

Adelaide's amber eyes darted between them and she sank into her pillows, tears beginning to form. Only Artie made a noise, sucking his tiny fingers.

'Has Oskar been hurt?' she asked quietly.

Rose sat next to Adelaide and held her hand.

'Honey,' Rose began but couldn't look her in the eye. Adelaide took one look at Leo and made a low, guttural moan.

'No! No! No! Not my Oskar.' She threw her head from side to side until Rose held her tight.

'I'm so sorry. We just found out Oskar was killed in action at Bullecourt in France at the beginning of May. I checked the lists myself. We don't know anything else.'

Adelaide sobbed as she was rocked in Rose's embrace.

'We were going to get married. What's Artie going to do without a daddy? What am I going to do? Oh God, I loved him so much.' She held her chest. 'What am I going to do?' Adelaide kept repeating this over and over. Rose held her until she'd slowed to a few gulping hiccups.

'I don't know, but we'll get you out of here and when you are strong enough, we'll send you home to your mother. She'll look after you, okay, Addie?' Rose comforted her as best she could.

Leo scooped up Artie, who had woken at the sound of his mother's sobs. The babe whimpered then resettled into the curve of his arm. Rose couldn't help but think how sad it was that Arthur would never know the refuge of his father's strong arms, or the joy of his toddler body being tossed by his father in play or be shown by Oskar how to ride a horse. So many things …

Adelaide wiped her nose on a lace handkerchief that was woefully inadequate for the task and gave him a watery smile.

'I'm sorry, I'm not one for being very stoic or keeping my chin up as they say. Thank you for coming. Look at that, he likes you.' Leo laid Artie into her outstretched arms.

'It'll be okay little bub. We'll go home to Grandma and she'll take care of us.' Adelaide's wane face softened as she held Artie. 'Maybe it would be better if we didn't tell your ma. It would be such a shock and they'll have enough to cope with, now Oskar is …'

'No, Ma just adores helping new mums at church with their babies. I'm sure she'd love little Artie, so you needn't worry. But I promise I'll wait until you are ready to tell, okay?' Leo said.

Adelaide nodded and held her baby tight, more tears spilling down her blotched cheeks.

'I can't tell you how sorry we are. I'll pop back in a couple of days.' Rose gave the baby's head a stroke and Adelaide's forehead a kiss. They closed the door and heard Adelaide's muffled sobs resume. The matron bustled up the hall and reassured them that Adelaide was in good hands.

'Poor Addie. What an awful thing to have happen. They'd sworn me to secrecy but in the end, I thought you ought to know.' Rose felt so torn.

Leo grabbed her hand. 'I'm glad you told me, but I don't think my head can handle any more. Oskar is a father. I mean … was.'

Rose left her hand in his as she dabbed her eyes. They made their way back to row of shops.

'Are you really okay about Artie?' Rose asked.

'It's the best news I've heard in a long time. I'm happy that some part of Oskar will go on. I'm just sad he couldn't be here to see him,' Leo answered.

She squeezed his hand tight. 'I'm so relieved. Thank you for telling Addie, I just wasn't up to it.' She dropped his hand and picked at her hanky. 'It just breaks my heart.'

'Mine too.'

They strolled along the docks trying to avoid the men that were bustling everywhere, unloading crates and carrying hessian bales, and the fishmongers that hawked their smelly wares among the wharf clutter.

When Rose thought of Oskar dying at the front, leaving Adelaide and Artie behind, a strange wave of panic tugged at her. When she thought of Leo dying, she was drowning.

Chapter Thirty-Two

13 June 1917
Poplar, England

Rose's stomach growled and Leo laughed.
'I didn't eat this morning and now I'm famished. Why don't we have something there?' Rose asked, pointing to a small tearoom across the narrow road. It had tatty curtains and peeling paint but appeared respectable enough.

Leo nodded and took her arm. A cold shiver fluttered across his neck and he stopped in the middle of the road. It had been so long since he'd felt a tingle or stone of dread sitting in his stomach. The urge to escape the squalid borough hurtled through every nerve of his body.

'Leo?' Rose waved a hand across his face.

'Maybe we should head back and eat in town?' The tickle of the hairs on his neck was persistent. He didn't want her to think he was crazy but what should he do?

She gave him a sympathetic pat on the arm. 'I guess it's all been a lot for you to take in, hasn't it? What's that strange noise?'

Leo's scalp prickled as if it was crawling with chats. The rumble of large aeroplanes swarming above had him searching the cloudless sky. Nothing yet.

'Aeroplanes. I think we ought to look for somewhere safe just in case.' Sweat dripped from his forehead.

Rose raised an eyebrow. 'It's probably the RAF training. London's perfectly safe in the day. We're in the East End, what would the Kaiser want with a few poor families?'

Leo wasn't sure whether she was trying to reassure him or convince herself.

He watched as a harried teacher directed a rag tag mob of children along the street. They looked to be about ten years old. A girl in pigtails skipping reminded him so much of Dot he stopped walking. One of the boys stopped picking his nose and saluted him. Dressed in worn clothes without shoes, Leo's thoughts flew back to the simple life in Borenore.

Leo grinned and answered the salute with his own, a cluster of admiring boys stopping to do the same. He waved an apology to the teacher.

Some of the people around them looked up as the drone grew louder.

'Look!' Leo saw at least a dozen glinting silver specks drawing closer.

'What's the Air Force doing over this way?' A shopkeeper said in his strange Cockney accent. Leo didn't care anymore if Rose thought he had lost his senses. He grabbed Rose's hand and pushed through the gathering crowd. The boys gave their young teacher a glance but willingly broke off from the class to follow Leo.

'C'mon kids. Everyone move, we need to get below!' he barked at a startled pub owner who pointed to the cellar.

'What's up then?' The pub owner asked.

'Planes coming. I'm not taking any chances,' Leo explained, but the ruddy cheeked man followed his couple of patrons out the door. Leo and Rose clattered down the stairs and stood, panting, in the dim light. The boys tumbled down after them and Rose directed them to hide under some tables. They huddled together, not making a whisper. The cellar smelt of musty potatoes and spilled ale. Rose gently removed her hand from his sweaty grasp.

'It must have been terrifying for you in France, but you really needn't yank my arm off. Are you sure we should have dragged the children down here; the teacher must be frantic.'

Was he carrying on like a blue-arsed fly?

'I didn't mean to. I get these odd feelings sometimes and it's saved my life plenty.' Rose was silent. 'But maybe I've got more problems with my nerves than I thought,' Leo added.

'We'll be fine,' Rose whispered as she came closer and her sweet scent drifted over him. He could just see her face in the dingy cellar and feel the gentle puff of her breath on his cheek.

'Thank you for coming with me today. I probably should have warned you, but I wasn't sure how you would take it. You were so understanding about Adelaide and Oskar.'

Leo felt a niggle of annoyance. Yes, she should have warned him, but a glow of pleasure warmed his cheeks. He was happy she trusted him. 'It was nothing. Oskar teases me about being so shy and all, he's obviously not.' Leo chuckled.

'No, I guess he wasn't,' Rose said slowly.

Leo frowned. Oh. Grief socked him in the gut. 'I mean wasn't ... shy.'

'It'll take some time.' Rose rubbed his arm.

'Yeah.' Leo's voice cracked and he held his breath.

'You're so different from other men,' Rose said. Her hand felt so warm. 'I know your Harry's best chum, but I also know he isn't serious about me or any other girl. That's suited me fine. I want to focus on my nursing but there's just something about you. The way you make me feel ... it's like I've known you forever.'

'I feel the same about you, Rose. I think you're really special and I—' Leo turned his cheek and drew closer to her lips.

'Go on then, mister. Lay one on 'er,' one of the lads called out while the others sniggered.

'Ooh, you cheeky beggar,' Rose said with a laugh as Leo stepped back.

The ground beneath them shuddered and rolled like the deck of a ship. The tinkle of splintering glass echoed above them. One of the boys gasped and another screamed.

'What on Earth was that?' Rose gripped him.

'I think we've been hit.'

'That's impossible! Stay here, boys, while we have a look.'

They scrambled up the steps but found the door jammed.

'We're done for. Ol' Fritz has got up trapped here. We're gonna starve,' a boy with freckles moaned as he tugged at his suspenders.

'What's your name?' Rose asked as she put her arm around his bony shoulders.

'Tommy,' he said as snot dribbled from his nose. Rose handed him a hanky.

'We'll be fine, there's another way out.' Rose looked at Leo and he gave up pushing against the door and started examining the cellar. Once the dust settled, he spotted a glimmer of light. One of the floorboards had splintered. He stacked some boxes on top of each other, climbed up and gave it a shove.

'There we go, chums.' He used all his muscle and kept pushing until a decent hole formed. 'Hey, anyone up there?'

A dust-stained face peered down. 'Over 'ere.' Soon, a jumble of arms was offering their help. With a groan, Leo was tugged up by the barely recognisable pub owner onto the glass strewn floor. The pub's roof had given way above the cellar.

One by one, the stunned schoolboys were pulled free. Once Rose was free, they all crunched their way outside. Moaning, bloodied people stood in shock around them. A woman in a brown coat touched the glass shards embedded in her cheek then gazed at her bloodied fingers. A man's face was covered in rivulets of crimson.

'Boys, stay together and—' Leo looked around at the chaos for an undamaged building. 'Wait for your parents over near the church there.'

'Quick! Go and tear up some sheets. The cleanest you can find,' Rose ordered to a few women who stepped out from their doors. 'You there, can you please clear somewhere to treat the wounded?' A policeman got off his bicycle and set to work.

Leo assisted Rose by tearing up hastily offered petticoats and sheets to make bandages.

'Sister, we need your help! The school's been hit!'

Rose handed her makeshift bandage to another woman and they followed the burly dockers to a three-storey building that had taken a direct hit. Sunshine streamed through a gaping hole in the shingled roof. Singed rosebud wallpaper flapped in shreds from an intact internal wall above a tangled wreck of brick and beams. High above them a fireplace was still adorned with a tiny vase of cornflowers on its simple mantelpiece. The fireplaces on the two floors below sat naked, their mantels blown off.

Rose headed towards a small group of stunned children and two smudge-faced teachers. None of them uttered a sound. Leo followed the men into the rubble. One of them informed him that eighteen students were missing, many of them from the infants' class on the bottom floor. They carefully picked their way among the smouldering ruins. It had the familiar rabbit stew smell of burnt human flesh.

Leo lugged a beam up and spotted a sooty hand underneath. Much of the little body was charred beyond recognition and Leo's heart and stomach lurched. The poor little beggar. A callused hand gave him a sheet.

A weary face met his and they gently wrapped the tiny bundle. Leo paused to remove a delicate silver bracelet from the child's wrist before he lifted the feathery weight and placed her alongside other wrapped bundles outside, taking care to put the bracelet on top.

With a gasp, a woman crumpled to the ground. Her friend paled but took the bracelet and placed it into the distraught woman's hands as she embraced her, meanwhile scanning for her own child. Another mother rushed towards him. She was in her housedress and apron. She had only one shoe on, the other clasped in her hand.

'Have you seen my little boy, Jack?' she whispered.

Leo took her arm and pointed her towards the huddle of sooty children.

'What if he's not there?' she croaked.

'Let's go and take a look.'

'Jack!' she sobbed with relief as she folded her bewildered son to her chest. Leo released a breath.

Rose's cheeks were smeared with charcoal where she'd wiped stray curls away. Her eyes darted from patient to patient before she gracefully moved to check a scrap of a boy laying among the others on the school playground. She smiled at him and stroked his hair, then gently ran her hands over his legs, chatting as she went. Leo couldn't hear what she was saying but the boy never lifted his eyes from her face. Other nurses and Red Cross workers buzzed around them, but Rose was the picture of serenity. Leo drew in a breath and set his jaw. He needed to be like Rose. Calm. If only his gut would cooperate. He went back into the wreckage.

Leo startled when a pile of rubble near him emitted a cough. He frantically sifted through the bricks and threw fragments of desk aside. A grubby face framed with flaxen plaits peeked out at him.

He carefully removed the last beam that pinned her down and did his best to reassure her. She began to give plaintive lamb cries for her mother as he carried her out to Rose.

'What's your name, sweetie?' Rose asked as she looked over the lass's tiny burnt body.

'Grace Jones. I'm five. Where's my mam?' Her saucer eyes started to look rather vacant.

'Where does it hurt, Grace?' Rose's gentle tone did not match her frantic gestures to a nearby doctor.

'I don't hurt nowhere.'

'Stay with us, Grace,' Rose moved aside as the doctor knelt next to the little girl. He shook his head and motioned to someone with a sheet.

'But she was just talking …' Leo knelt and touched the still sheet.

The doctor squeezed his shoulder and moved on to help others.

'She was too severely burnt. We're going to take some of the children to the Poplar Hospital for Accidents.' Rose said over the whistle of police. She gave an apologetic smile as she rushed off, her scarlet cape flapping.

Leo returned to the miasma of pulverised brick, splintered wood and broken bodies. The same weather-faced man that had previously helped him was picking anxiously among the debris. The man's wiry body was taut as he lifted a scorched beam.

'You over there. Give us a hand and grab the other end.'

Leo grabbed the other end; it was still warm. They worked alongside for a few minutes, holding their breath every time a charred knob or fragment looked like part of a small child.

'I don't know how we are going to find 'em all,' the man declared as he tossed aside a broken slate.

'We'll just keep going until they're all found.'

'I expect you've seen worse than this.'

Yes, Leo had seen the most horrific things happen to young men's bodies, but his throat constricted as he thought of Grace. They were just innocent kids. Just like Dot. Tears streamed unbidden down his face.

Leo tossed some seared bricks aside. 'No, I don't think I have.'

The man's pinched face crumpled.

'I can't find Alfie, me son,' he explained.

'C'mon. I'll help you.'

'I know 'em all as I'm the caretaker here.'

Oh, that smell … it clung to his throat, choking him. Stringent explosive mixed with sweet, singed flesh. Lord no, another one. The beefy man came closer to examine the remains and stiffened. He slowly crouched down and stroked a half-melted button. Leo closed his eyes and sighed. He discreetly waved over someone with a sheet. The tiny blue button was placed in a tattered pocket.

'My wife just sewed this on his trousers this morning. Alfie's a bit careless, always losing buttons and needing his clothes patched,' he croaked before cradling the charred body that was as melted as the singed button. He took him out to the playground and gently laid him among the row of crumpled figures now being loaded into ambulances to be taken to the morgue. Leo stood uselessly by.

'Ben! Ben!'

The man groaned as a petite woman shoved her way past a police officer. 'Where's Alfie? Where is he?'

She followed Ben's eyes to the tiny form being loaded into the ambulance. He couldn't speak, he just nodded his head sadly.

Her face went from white to grey as she leaned against his broad shoulders, 'My baby, not my baby, nooooooo.'

'I got you, Alice, I got you,' Ben said as she folded into his arms.

Leo turned back to the smoking ruins but was told by a solemn policeman that they'd found them all. Rose and the children had gone. Some parents remained bereft in their friend's arms or hopeful a mistake had been made and their child would still be pulled from the wreckage.

Leo numbly wandered through the unfamiliar streets until he came upon a small stone church. It vaguely reminded him of the church at home in Borenore. Inside, instead of the plain nave and pointed Gothic windows he was familiar with, he saw a barrel-vaulted floor from which thick Tuscan columns rose. He touched one of the massive oak columns before settling on a pew.

Casting his eyes heavenward, he noticed a beautiful mosaic of ships sailing across a swirling ocean. Many had knelt right where he now prayed, asking God to protect them while on long, perilous journeys for the East India Shipping Company. How would he even begin a prayer for these little children, like Grace and Alfie, attacked by German bombs? He remembered Oskar's face lit with excitement, him dancing around Central Station, announcing that he'd joined up too. He was gone too.

His fingernails dug deep into his palms. That felt good. To feel something. He clenched tighter and then thumped the pew in front of him.

'Are you alright, my son?'

Slender fingers touched his shoulder and he turned to see the kind, crinkled eyes of the priest.

'I'm sorry, Father.'

'Would you like to talk over a cup of tea?' he asked. His liver-spotted hand was like Granny Maloney's.

'They bombed them, those poor little kids …'

Leo found his throat clenched tighter than his fists. He couldn't move. The priest drew him into his arms and Leo's heart burst its salty dam of grief.

Chapter Thirty-Three

20 June 1917
London, England

The swollen crowd milled and shifted; no voice raised beyond a whisper. It was the largest crowd Leo had seen since his arrival as a Coo-ee in Sydney, but in this crowd, there were no smiling girls waving white handkerchiefs and blowing kisses.

Girls and women now raised handkerchiefs to dab at watering eyes. No flags fluttered gaily in the breeze now, they just drooped at half-mast. Folk did not lean from decorated windows and balconies cheering for soldiers. Blinds were drawn and peeling shutters remained fixed. No one was here to bid farewell to the brave and adventurous. They were here to pay their respects to innocent children.

Leo blended into the pea soup of khaki soldiers dotted with scarlet nurses' capes. He scanned for Rose and tingled when he spotted her. With Alfred. What was she doing with that low life? His brows knitted so hard it felt like someone was poking him between the eyes.

The restless crowd rippled to a standstill around him as sombre music reached their ears. A boys' band marched solemnly by. The first of many horse-drawn hearses came into view and Leo's shoulders dropped. What had happened to Oskar? There'd be no horse-drawn hearse for him. He prayed they'd at least found and buried his body. He couldn't bear to think of him lying there in the cold mud with the nibbling rats. He sucked in a breath and bit his lip.

Leo watched Rose. Her face was scrunched, and she started to cry, turning to Alfred. Leo knew Alf was a long-term friend of Rose's family but that didn't sooth him much when Alfred held her and kissed the top of her head. His face said it all. So, Alf still held a candle for her.

Leo felt fairly sure Rose didn't like Alfred. She just needed comfort. He thought back to being in the cellar with her, smelling her sweet scent and the soft puff of her breath against his cheek. How close he'd come to touching those soft lips.

He sighed. What difference would it make anyway? Leo was back into it tomorrow, off to Victoria Station to make his way to Folkestone then France. He just had to pick up his pay and make up some good excuse as to why he was a few days absent without leave. He'd gone AWOL so he could pay his respects to the kids. He hadn't been able to do the same for Oskar. Leo turned away; he'd say goodbye to Rose later.

The feather-plumed horse clopped by. A large mossy wreath in the shape of a cross studded with periwinkles and lemon primroses dominated the carpet of flowers that smothered the coffin. Was little Grace in there?

He looked down at his own simple posy of daisies, butterscotch marigolds and pansies. Their vibrant colours and simple beauty seemed so at odds with the dismal loss they acknowledged. Everything should be as grey and dismal as the front. Rain should be pouring down like God was crying streams of tears for these sweet little souls, but the sun beamed down from a clear sky. Those kids should still be playing with balls and hoops on the street.

He waited until most of the crowd had melted away before adding his meagre posy to the field of flowers at the children's mass grave. It was the most tragically beautiful burial site he had ever seen.

He decided to stop back into the church he had visited last week to thank the priest for his kindness. A few people dotted the pews, but he saw no sign of Father. He slipped on to a pew close to the only marble column among the oaks.

He gave a prayer to the children and their grieving families, especially Ben. Was God listening anyway? If he was, why did he let that happen to them in the first place? His head throbbed with unanswered questions.

Sounds of muffled sobbing came from behind him. He didn't know whether to turn or not, but it somehow sounded familiar. Trying to be discreet, he snuck a peek. It was Rose.

He moved to her pew and sat next to her. Her head nestled against his chest and he felt the warmth of her tears soak his shirt. He stroked her arm and let her cry, not uttering a word.

'You were so good with those children, Rose. 'A low moan of such grief escaped her.

'But for some there was nothing that could be done,' Rose said, sitting up and looking at him.

'You did everything you could. You're a great nurse.'

Rose's face contorted for just a moment. It was too painful; he should let her be.

He got the sense there was more to her reaction.

'Sometimes I feel so bloody helpless. I thought being a nurse might mean I could make a difference but sometimes …'

'I don't understand it all either. Why God does what He does.'

Rose looked up at the large wooden cross at the front of the church. 'I don't really think much about God's role in all of this.'

'When did you stop believing?'

Rose looked surprised at his perception. 'I guess I stopped believing years ago.'

Leo sat silently, just touching her hand.

'I can't really blame God, I guess. It was my fault, you see. I was always annoying my father, reading his medical books in his study, and fiddling with his instruments in his rooms, attached to our house. One day, I was supposed to be watching my little brother, Edward. I can't even remember why. I was bored and suggested we go and play doctor as my father wasn't working that day. I took down a doll to practise surgery on. While I was cutting into my doll (of course, I was not supposed to touch sharp instruments, but my father had once been a surgeon and I couldn't resist), I didn't notice my brother had hold of a scalpel and was imitating what I was doing, but he had cut into his wrist. He screamed and I panicked. I did not want my parents to know what I had done so I attempted to fix him myself.'

Leo held her hand tight. It was hot.

'There was blood everywhere. I grabbed bandages and tried to stop the bleeding, but he dropped to the floor and kept bleeding. I kept calling his name, but he was unconscious. Then, I can't tell you how awful I felt. I started crying like a baby.'

Rose gulped. Leo stayed as still as he could, barely taking in a breath.

'Edward was turning blue. Still, I just sat there, crying. I heard this sound behind me. Like an animal growl. My father pushed me away but, in the end, he was gone.'

Leo bit his lip. Her grief mingled with his until he didn't know how to separate them. He shook his head. 'It was an accident, Rose.'

'No, it wasn't. I was supposed to be watching him. He wouldn't have been there or done that if it wasn't for me.' Leo's heart broke as her voice did. He realised then that it was Oskar's choice to join up. The bubble of guilt popped leaving the heavy weight of pure grief. Still, it felt lighter.

Rose wiped her tears and pulled her shoulders back. 'Here I am going on about something that happened ten years ago, and you've only just lost Oskar. I'm sorry.'

'There's nothing to be sorry about. You talking about Edward has helped. I couldn't have stopped Oskar joining up if I'd have chained him up like a dog. It's nobody's fault.' He thought of the parent's faces he had seen at the mass funeral. 'I figure I'm always going to have some pain when I think about Oskar but that's the price you pay for loving someone and … I'm happy to pay it. It's sadder to think you can just get on and all.' Leo felt another shard of grief pierce him. The shards didn't just target his heart. He hurt all over.

'Mama certainly doesn't know how to get on at all though. She …' Rose faltered.

'What happened?'

'It's not something my father likes me to discuss … she's in a mental asylum. She was lost without Edward. She told me that I had ruined her life and it was my fault for being so careless and so on but now she barely speaks at all. In part she blamed my father for encouraging me in my medical interests. My father wanted me to become a nurse so I would learn how to be responsible and he could bring my mother home, but I think I only make things worse for her.' She stared at the cross as if the ghost of her mother was pinned to it.

Anger rose hot and hard. 'Forgive me for saying this but your mother sounds rather selfish. *They* chose to leave you—a young girl—to care for a boy. She *chose* to blame you and then let her grief take over. It hardly seems right to me.' Leo almost raised a fist to the ghostly woman.

Rose was lost deep in thought and like clouds clearing, her eyes became brighter.

'And I *chose* to take the blame.'

'Yes. And you can choose not to.'

Rose sighed then kissed him softly on the cheek. 'You really are special Leo Dymond.'

Why did it always feel like he was on fire when she touched him? Did she just say he was special to her?

'Special?' he asked.

'Yes, incredibly special.'

He was so light he was sure he could float and pluck a rainbow right out of the sky for Rose.

'When are you due back?' Rose asked

Thud! Back to Earth. Forget the bloody rainbows; this was like being struck with a bolt of flesh-frying lightning. He was already AWOL and had to go back to that hell hole.

'I've outstayed my welcome already. I just wanted to see the kids were buried but if I don't get back tomorrow, they'll be thinking I have, and they'll have it posted in the *Police Gazette*.'

'What a shame. I can't have you leaving until you've tried a Chelsea bun.' Rose's smile was brighter than the stained-glass window.

He loved her. It was that simple. And that complex.

Chapter Thirty-Four

Rose pulled Leo's arm as he stopped to drool over the cakes in the display window of a Lyon's Corner House. 'Come on, I really need a cup of tea.'

They gave their order and settled back into the wooden chairs of the food hall. Leo seemed overwhelmed by the enormous restaurant with no less than five floors and an orchestra playing in the corner. Rose didn't know if was due to the recent bombings, but the place was barely one quarter full and mostly soldiers filled the chairs.

'There's our Gladys coming now. I can barely wait for my Lyon's tea. I've gotten quite addicted ...' Rose said. She gave her stomach a pat, '... and to their Chelsea buns.'

'Thanks, Gladys,' Leo said, smiling at the waitress in her neat black dress covered in a starched white apron. Rose and the waitress exchanged a smile.

'You're very welcome, sir.'

'Did I say something wrong?' Leo asked when she left.

Rose didn't want him to feel bad but felt she should tell him. 'No, not at all. It was probably my fault. They call all of the waitresses, Gladys, and the girls over there behind the shop front, Sally,' Rose explained. She sipped her tea and dropped her shoulders against the chair. 'Ah, that's hit the spot.'

Leo pretended to be fascinated with the pattern of the tessellated tiles and Rose worried she'd embarrassed him.

'Have you ever noticed that once someone dies, people don't let you talk about them? It's like they think you'll just get all upset and worked up about it. Or they try not to mention them, so they don't upset you. As if you don't think about them all the time,' Leo said.

'I know. When we lost Edward, people told me it was God's will and to be happy he was in heaven. I was told to be strong for my mother. I felt so angry with them all.' Rose's spoon clattered onto her plate. 'How dare they pack up his toys and pretend he never existed.'

'I'd rather remember.' Leo sighed and felt his shoulders droop. 'But I guess you can't change how most people are. Scared of death.'

'Given we are all going to die one day, it's a strange way to carry on, isn't it? I'd rather remember and be remembered too.' She took a breath and another sip of tea. Leo sat still and silent.

Leo stared as his fingers. 'I joined up to protect my family—small town having a go at us for having German roots—and all I want to do is get back to them. But I think I've just made things a hell of a lot worse. I've seen how it can change a man and I hope I won't forget how to be a good one or if I die, be remembered as one. I'm sorry I'm being such a sad sack.'

'Don't be ridiculous. You've just lost your brother. You are a good man. Your reasons for joining are far more noble than me running away from my family. I'm grateful to have a chance to talk about Eddie. No one has ever taken the time to really listen to me talk about it. Thank you.' Rose realised when she stared into the depths of Leo's brown eyes that she felt more than gratitude. She knew that he knew, and she squirmed.

'Strange, I needed to be away from my family to realise how much I would like my own.' Leo's eyes penetrated her soul.

No, she couldn't give him what he wanted. 'I have realised how little I need mine. I feel like I know myself and my purpose far more as a nurse.' Rose released his hand and stood. 'I'd better get back to the hospital.'

'Oh, of course. Sorry.' Leo stood too. She felt a twinge of guilt, but he didn't seem to take her words as a rejection of any sort.

They walked along the road. Small orbs of light dotted the cobblestones, with much of the lamps covered over. Blinds on terrace houses hugged their Georgian windows tight, ensuring no light spilled on to the streets below. London was in black out. Rose took Leo's arm and slowed him down to a stroll along the Thames, only passing the odd person here and there. Leo didn't bother to speak so Rose remained silent.

After the bustle of the streets in the day, hearing the lap of the river and click of army boots on the stones was almost eerie. Rose stopped at St Thomas' Hospital.

'This looks more like a French chateau than a hospital,' Leo said, and Rose looked with fresh eyes. Under the wash of moonlight, she could see the decorative stone dressings and balustrade. It did look pretty.

'Oh, here I got you a new handkerchief that I embroidered,' Rose said as she plucked out a pretty lace hanky. 'That's if you still want it … for luck.' It had a bunch of grapes and swirls of leaves in each corner. 'I did grapes to remind you of home.'

'That's great. For luck, thanks,' he said taking her handkerchief. She watched him sniff it before he folded it and put it into his pocket. Rose didn't want him to leave.

'I'm going to miss you,' Rose said. Those words weren't adequate for him. Not knowing when and if she would ever lay eyes on Leo again left a chasm so deep it split right through her soul. She loved him. She stopped under a lamp and stood close to him. She licked her lips and without thinking, leaned in and kissed him. His lips were plump and warm, and her core burned hot as their kiss deepened.

'Oh, Lord. What am I doing?' Rose said as she untangled herself and straightened her nurse's veil. 'You must think I am no better than some of those awful London girls. What about Harry?'

'No, Rose. It was my fault. I'll tell him about us.'

'But he's a good friend and now I've ruined everything for you.' She charged off. This was terrible. He mustn't know how she felt.

He rushed to keep up with her.

'Slow down, it's okay. Harry and I will sort it out.' Leo grabbed her arm. 'You're too good for him anyway.'

Rose stopped and faced him, 'What?'

'I just mean you deserve someone who will always treat you right.'

She smiled. 'Yes, I do. Are you sure? It seems silly to even start something with us both going to France but—'

He silenced her with a long kiss. Her lips trembled at first then opened, yielding to the slightest touch of his tongue. She moulded closer to him. She wanted to kiss him again and again and again. Her chest was so tight she couldn't speak. She broke off, catching her breath and pulling slowly away. She shouldn't make promises she couldn't keep. She didn't want Harry to find out and Leo lose his friend.

'Come and say goodbye before you go tomorrow. If you don't, I'll understand that Harry comes first.' She pushed through the oak panelled entrance door to the hospital and was gone before he could utter a word.

Loneliness washed over her. How could she go back to the way things were now?

Chapter Thirty-Five

June/July 1917
Aldershot Military Detention Barracks, England

How was he going to say goodbye when she'd finally shown how she really felt? That last kiss was beyond amazing.

He sighed and turned straight into a granite fist.

When he regained consciousness, his head thumped like he was back in the trenches. He gingerly touched his lips. They were wet with salty blood. His ribs were bruised and his right eye swollen shut. What a mess. Leo heaved himself up off the pavement. It was deserted. Someone had knocked him out. He searched his pockets and realised he didn't have any cash left. Bloody thieving bastard. He dragged himself back to the war chest and collapsed on his bunk.

When he woke early the next morning, he felt like he'd been in for a big stunt. He sewed a torn light-blue over navy battalion colour patch back onto his sleeve. It still looked crooked but with a swollen eye, it was the best he could do. He shuffled across the road and up to the banking section of the pay office. He told the corporal that he had lost his leave pass when someone had tried to rob him the night before and slapped down his paybook saying how lucky it was that he still had it.

The corporal gave him a wan smile and Leo wiped his sweaty hands on the coarse wool of his khaki shorts. Just his luck to get such an impervious fellow. The pay orderly ran a fastidious finger over the progressive total column of the entire book then paused. His eyes narrowed and his lips pursed.

'What's this then?' he asked, giving a slight nod behind Leo.

Leo's stomach sank. The weedy little man had just signalled for the guard to come closer. He looked to where the orderly pointed. 'What?'

'There,' he said as he jabbed a bony finger at Leo's paybook. 'It seems to me that there have been some alterations made back in March. In these three entries, the 1s have been altered to 4s. So, I would be paying you £52.10 instead of the correct amount...,' He stopped to calculate. '... £31.16. This is most serious.'

Leo's stomach continued to free fall. This was much worse than being caught absent without leave.

'I don't understand. There must have been some mistake in Étaples,' he stammered. The man rolled his eyes.

'Honest! You ask anyone from my Battalion or anyone who knows me. I would never tamper with a paybook. I'm heading back today; can't you just fix it and pay me what is rightfully owed?' His desperate plea only encouraged a withering stare.

'Corporal Geaves, please escort Private Dymond to Warwick Square. Charge him with being in possession of a falsified paybook.'

The stocky guard grabbed Leo's bruised arm before he could utter a word of protest. Leo stumbled along in confusion. He'd drawn pay since March without any trouble so why a problem now? As if he'd be stupid enough to think he would get away with changing the paybook. Only a desperate man or an idiot would do something like that. How could this have happened?

Blast and bugger. He wouldn't be able to let Rose know what had happened or where he was. Rose would think he thought kissing her was a mistake. He had no idea how long it would take until his trial was heard or what would happen to him if he were found guilty. Corporal Greaves was a solid bloke who had barely spared him a glance as he tugged Leo along.

A couple of Aussie soldiers grinned at him, but Leo felt too miserable to respond. An old lady glared at him when he stepped on the hem of her skirt.

'You no good riff-raff,' she sputtered over his apology.

Shame ate holes in his stomach. He was supposed to make his ma proud. How on Earth would she feel if she found out he was locked up? Oskar dead and Leo a gaolbird. His shoulders slumped with the repetitive twang of the words rolling around his head, *I shouldn't have joined up. I haven't helped anyone. This is bloody hopeless.*

This was even worse than going back to the front. He'd failed.

***

Weeks later, Leo sat on a lumpy mattress and reread one of the only letters he'd received from his pa. The paper was so tatty now that he had to be careful not to tear it.

June 1916
Dear Leo,

I hope this letter reaches you intact. I'm not sure my friend will be in the translator/censor room for much longer so I will write as much as I can while I have the opportunity.

I can admit to you that I am finding things a bit tough here. It is the endless idleness and lack of purpose. Being stuck here trying to fill in our days among over 2,000 others is taking its toll. When I think of what I could or should be doing on the vineyard, how I miss your Ma and the rest of you…

Enough of that. I must tell you about our recent excitement. There was a bad lot in here, called themselves the 'Black Hand'. Nothing but a bunch of thugs and thieves but they were causing a lot of trouble. I almost got a good bashing myself when I refused to hand over your Ma's fruit cake (luckily some of my friends walked around the corner just in time). Anyway, you wouldn't believe it. Some sailors from the SMS Emden joined up and called themselves the 'White Hand'. Well, they rounded up the ringleaders, belted them and then threw them over the fence!

I thought the Major Sands and the soldiers would shoot the lot of us, but they stood there and watched. The Major must have gotten wind of it as he had it photographed. He just stood and smiled. He's a strange one.

How are you going? We don't hear much about how things are going in the war in here. I can usually tell if we've had a set back because the guards, who usually leave us to it, try and stir up trouble. I haven't had a letter from your Ma for a while. Do you know how she is getting on?

I'm not very happy at the thought of Oskar heading over too. I wish I had spoken to you both about what things were like in the Boer War and put you off a bit. I know you are both trying to help your Ma but having her worry herself to death isn't doing any good. Look, it's probably no use going on about it now but there's not much to occupy a man's day here and I think about it more than I ought to. I can't really explain what losing your freedom does to a man's head.

Just look out for yourself won't you.
Your Pa.

Leo returned the letter to his paybook and paced around his poky cell like a caged circus tiger. He did know what his pa meant. At that moment, he didn't give a damn if they ordered him to dig another bloomin' trench or expect him to swelter through an eighteen-mile march lugging a sixty-pound pack. Anything but staying in the poky cell.

He didn't like having so much time to think either. He would think about Oskar. Oskar writhing in pain, sinking into the mud, bleating for Ma. Oskar's green marbled face, his bloated death belly. He would think about Ma. Sitting in Pa's chair, thumbing his beloved poetry books, holding his pipe. How would she take the news of Oskar? Did she know yet? Then there was Dot. Leo couldn't swallow. He flung the chained Bible against the wall with a satisfying *thwack*.

Sometimes he thought of Alfred gloating to his chums that Leo was stuck in the clink for three months. Alfred would love telling everyone that Leo was a sneaky, no-good German, and this proved it. If he was lucky, maybe Alfred wouldn't even find out. Leo's fists clenched and unclenched, popping in time with his jaw.

Leo flopped onto his cot. Alfred's supercilious face floated in his imagination. He watched the right side of Alf's face as it dissolved in a stream of blood, spurted like a fountain from his mouth, and gushed from his blade-like nose. His uniform became soaked in a flood of crimson and his eyes bulged as he looked down to the shredded flesh that had once been his arm, hanging near the tangled sausage intestines …

Leo's cell door clanged open.

'Move it, you lot. It's not a bloomin' picnic day,' Sergeant Major Lynch growled.

Leo left his gory phantom writhing and made his way out to the iron gallery. Was he going mad in this place?

The light flooding through the enormous lantern-like roof indicated a sunny day outside. Soon he would be caught in the back-breaking rhythm of a hard day's work. British military punishment at its best. He would raise his pick and peck at the hard, dusty earth until the fury drained away for yet another day.

As he stood in formation in the centre of the parade ground, he watched Sergeant Lynch's eyes scan them all and then narrow. Leo sighed. Some new inmate had obviously farted out of turn.

Lynch's pugnacious manner was almost as irritating as Alfred's. Almost. Lynch's short stature and habit of spraying spittle into a man's face as he blustered with temper had earned him the nickname, "Squirt".

Squirt now bellowed, 'You! What's your name, Private?'

'Roy Evans, sir.' Mmm, not good. That bloke sounded pretty confident. Squirt wouldn't be having that. Leo wanted to get a gander of Squirt's latest victim but kept looking forward.

'I know about you, Evans. One of those bloody white feather mob, not willing to sacrifice his precious little body for King and Country. Damn disgrace,' he spluttered.

'Yes, I am a CO and proud member of the NCF. It's not just my life I am concerned about. I believe all human life is sacred, Sergeant.'

Nobody dared to twitch a muscle. Leo held his breath. Squirt squawked and could barely spit out his response.

'Did I ask you to speak, Private? We are in the middle of a God damned war here. So, you'd have us all stand around and watch while Germany shoots and bombs us to smithereens? You're just a bloody coward, Evans.'

Evans wouldn't let it drop. 'Perhaps that's what you think, sir. We've already lost thousands in this war. Have you been to the front yourself, sir?'

Boy, was that chap asking for it. An audible gasp rippled through the men. Everyone knew Squirt hadn't seen any action. Leo turned for a quick peek. Bugger! Squirt caught him and marched straight for him.

Squirt eyeballed Leo and bawled, 'Want to take a good look at this gutless idiot, do you? You've been to the front. He'll end up serving a stretcher bearer instead of helping you defend us against the Hun. What do you think of these so-called non-conscription people?'

Leo resisted wiping his spittle-flecked face and despite a warning gripe from his stomach, he answered honestly, 'I think stretcher bearers are very courageous, sir.'

Squirt's eyes rolled like a spooked horse. 'Bloody Australians. Fine. If they are so damn brave, you can give Evans some tips on surviving the few minutes he'll have left on this earth as a stretcher bearer in France. Private Simmons front and centre. You too, Private Evans.'

The sergeant waved over some men holding a stretcher. He handed one end of the stretcher to Evans and indicated for Simmons to lie on the stretcher. Leo stifled a groan. When was he going to learn to keep his big mouth shut?

Evans was as tall as Leo but was rather spindly, lacking Leo's broad shoulders. He had a long, narrow face with large, protruding eyes looking something like a praying mantis. Simmons, on the other hand, was built like Bull and obviously enjoyed his food just as much.

They hoisted Simmons up and he cheerfully took up the pose of a Raja waving royally to his subjects. Squirt told the laughing soldiers they were off on a ten-mile march and if there was any more cheek today, he'd be happy to make it eighteen instead. Cackles became groans.

They'd wouldn't be able to lug Simmons for one mile let alone ten. Leo gritted his teeth. Blimey. Sometimes he could land himself in more trouble than the early settlers.

The first hour of the march passed with Leo maintaining a grim silence, ignoring Simmons taking verbal pot shots at Evans. Evans kept a tenacious grip on both the stretcher and his temper. He might look like a beanpole, but he was strong enough. Leo's shoulders and neck were now knotted in pain and the webbing between his fingers and thumb was rubbed raw.

Some of the men ahead were buzzing with a low grumble. Unlike training or in the field, there was no ten-minute break after an hour of marching. There was no rest for the wicked in The Glasshouse. After another hour, Leo's throat was parched. Even Simmons had finally shut his trap and stole guilty glances at them. He broke the silence with a cough and asked Leo what it was like being at the front.

'All of the marching and training in the world won't do much against a German whizz-bang or machine gun,' Leo told him.

Simmons twisted his head around to look at Leo.

'In France, the trenches have mud so bloody sticky that men have broken their backs when mules have tried to pull 'em out.'

Leo paused to reposition the stretcher. 'A lot of the time though you're just sitting around in the freezing rain with nothing to do but pick at the chats or shoot at the rats.'

Simmons seemed to dismiss this rather dismal picture and his voice rose in intensity.

'What about the Huns? Did you get to kill heaps of 'em?'

Leo ignored the bloodlust in his voice and replied in the same droll manner.

'Sure, when they were rushing at me with bayonets raised I did. I'm not worried about having to fight the Germans one on one in the trenches. It's sitting there listening to the scream of a shell and waiting for it to burst above you, pelting everyone with stuff that'll rip a man's arm to shreds, or leave his jaw flapping where his mouth ought to be—that I hate.'

'Yeah, it all seems exciting on your first stunt ...' Leo continued, enjoying watching Simmons grow pale, '... the next morning you can smell all the bodies beginning to rot. Sometimes they make noise, and their stomachs move with gas, scares the shit out of you. All that's left of good blokes who marched, wrote letters home and shared a beer with you only the day before. Left to rot. Some might get a quick burial but most often we'll have to tread on 'em during the next night's stunt.' There, he was green now. Big, heavy lump.

Simmons rolled off the stretcher and threw up in the dust. Evans just raised an amused eyebrow.

Simmons wiped his mouth and declared, 'Think I'll walk for a spell.' He grabbed the stretcher from them and hoisted it onto his meaty shoulders. Leo was worried about Squirt catching them, but Evans only shrugged and fell in step.

'What are you in for?' Simmons asked.

'Some mongrel fiddled with my paybook, so I got done for fraud.' He kept his eyes on the dejected tangle of men ahead.

'What a bastard!'

'What about you?' Leo asked

'Well, it was a bit like this. Over at the training barracks back at Aldershot, there's a nasty piece of work, Sergeant Macky. He makes Squirt look like a bloomin' altar boy.' He paused to wipe his toothbrush moustache. 'You see, Macky didn't take too well to a few COs that got dumped into our unit.'

'We're not a popular lot with the military,' Evans interjected.

Simmons nodded in agreement, 'Ain't that the truth? Anyway, Macky had a habit of getting one of the big blokes to have a go at them to get 'em to fight back or be pummelled. One day he had this little runt by the scruff of his neck and told me to teach 'im a lesson. What can I tell ya? Me fist just kinda slipped and Macky copped it fair on the snoz. I think I broke it.' Evans and Leo laughed. Simmons winked and swapped shoulders.

'The best day I'd had since I was called up,' Simmons declared.

'So not everyone hates us. I don't mind being a stretcher bearer, although I hope all the blokes aren't as heavy as you,' Evans said, rubbing his blistered hands.

Simmons snorted, 'I hope I won't need you lugging me around out there anyway.'

A flash of intuition uncurled, and Leo knew that Simmons wouldn't make it out of the war alive. Evans fell silent. Did he feel it too? That icy tingle as death stood there with his cold finger pointed at Simmons, beckoning? Simmons glanced at their solemn faces and his cocky grin faded.

'I'm not looking forward to going over there but if I have to, I'd rather be out there trying to save lives than taking them.' Evans shrugged.

Evans was right. A door slammed in Leo's brain. He'd had enough of walking with death hovering by his side, doing his bidding ... killing men. But he couldn't desert; the shame would eat at him like a corpse rat. He was trapped in a prison far bleaker than Aldershot.

PART FOUR:

RETURN TO FRANCE (1917-18)

Chapter Thirty-Six

24 October 1917
No. 53 London General Hospital
Wimereux, France

Another amputation. Rose sighed. Having run out of other forms of anaesthesia, she was left with Novocain, which meant that the poor bloke would have a numb body but would still be conscious. A fresh nurse arrived for duty.

'Sister Shipley, would you mind seeing this one through?' Major Richmond asked. She gave a quick nod and moved up to talk to the soldier. He had a crescent-shaped scar under his lip and was painfully young.

'So, Private Wood. How about you tell me about your family back home?' Rose tried to move to block his view but when his eyes bulged, she knew he had seen the surgeon pick up the saw.

'Harold, look at me.' She caressed his cheek. 'Do you have any brothers or sisters?'

'Oh, um, yeah. I'm the oldest of ten. My brother, Will, is over here too. Then the rest are girls,' he answered.

'Goodness, eight sisters. You boys must have been kept well in line. Where do you come from? Rose hoped her eyes weren't too bloodshot. She didn't want him to think she was too tired to talk but having worked a twenty-four hour stretch, she was glad he was the last.

'From Megalong Valley in the Blue Mountains of Sydney. If you've ever been to the Hydro Majestic Hotel, it looks out over the valley.' Harold seemed oblivious to the noise of the saw as it hacked away at his leg. Rose willed herself to keep her full attention on his face.

'Yes, I had high-tea there for my birthday once. It's a very pretty valley, lots of escarpment, right? We had a lovely view until the clouds rolled in. It was a misty trip back home to Leura.' It was also the last happy memory Rose had of her family together.

Harold nodded and smiled. 'I was always watching the weather come in. Our place was on top of a hill and you could see it get dark on the mountains in the distance. I knew if it got like a grey sheet, I had about five minutes to make it to shelter or get a drenching. It'd blow a gale too, just like being here at times but the sunsets there were something real special.'

Rose was lost in the image of rolling green hills bathed in the tangerine glow of the setting sun. A movement in the corner of her eye brought her back.

Harold continued chatting about his home then looked at her more carefully. 'Why are you with the Brits?'

'It seems to be where the army wants me for now. At least I'm finally getting to help the boys here. The Australian General across the road is getting all of the Tommies.'

Harold gasped and Rose gave an inward curse. She had lost her focus for a second and he had seen the orderlies carry away his leg.

'My leg…' was all he said.

'We've got you all patched up now, Private. You'll be on the train and back to Blighty in no time,' Major Richmond said as we threw the last of the instruments into the sterilisation bucket under the table. He looked at Rose. 'We'll finish up, you go and get some rest.'

As Rose made her way along the moonlit duckboards, she saw the orderlies transferring a pile of limbs to a wagon for burial the next day. The sound of saw scraping bone echoed in her brain. Working at a base hospital in France had been far grimmer than she'd expected.

She ran her tongue along her chapped lips and realised how thirsty she was. How heavenly would a hot cocoa be before turning in? She knew she'd be asleep before she even got the primus stove in her hut lit, let alone wait for the water to boil. A hand shot out from the shadows and grabbed her shoulder. She screamed.

'Sorry, Sister. I'm Lance Corporal Townsend from the Field Ambulance. I didn't mean to scare you.' He stepped out and Rose took her hand away from her thumping chest.

'Well, you did scare me. What do you want?' Good grief, she sounded as grumpy as Senior Sister Plunkett. Rose softened her tone. 'How can I help you?'

'I know it's late and all, but I brought in a mate a few days ago ... is there any way you could find out how he's doing? Sergeant Roberts ... came in on the seventeenth with bronchitis and covered in blisters.'

It was the last thing Rose felt like doing but she couldn't leave him like this. 'Fine. Go and wait in the mess and keep warm.

'He squeezed her gloved hand. 'You're an angel, Sister ...'

'Sister Shipley.'

'Oh, and Sister Shipley, my friend might answer to Austin Lawrence. Long story.'

Rose shook her head and headed back to the wards. She finally managed to locate him and was alarmed that he was in a bad way in the moribund ward. She hadn't been in the ward for the dying before. She hesitated and wished Lance Corporal Townsend hadn't found her.

Men were laid out in cots and stretchers, some breathing with the death rattles, some groaning and others deathly still.

A nurse carrying a lamp approached her and showed her where Sergeant Roberts was. 'It won't be long now. Are you a relative?'

'No, I'm checking on him for a friend. I wonder if I should go and get him.' As Rose turned to leave, the man gave a squawking gasp. Her stomach gave a twist as the light fell on his ulcerated eyelids. She could smell that he was covered in calamine lotion.

'Perhaps you can stay and hold his hand for a minute. I like to think they can feel someone's there for them as they go,' she whispered. 'Poor bugger. Did you hear what happened?'

Rose sat on a stool and took the man's blistered hand. Did she want to remain here and watch a man die? Her curiosity won. 'No, what happened to him?'

'I won't lie, this is the saddest ward, but some get under your skin more than others. You know how cold it's been getting ... this fellow finds a great coat in the field and puts it on and goes off to sleep in the trench. Next morning, they can't wake him.'

Rose gently touched one of the blisters. 'But isn't this bullae from mustard gas?'

The nurse nodded. 'That's it, turns out the coat's full of gas. Ate into the skin, it did. Not a nice way to go, that.'

Rose was lost for words and the weariness folded into her heart.

She could feel his pulse was thready and irregular, then it seemed to fade all together with no further sound or movement. The other nurse checked his pulse too.

'Gone west as they say. No more suffering for him.' She waved a hand to an orderly collecting up sheets.

Rose found herself breathless. She almost ran from the ward then sank onto the duckboards. Eventually she became aware of the hard wood digging into her knees and she pulled herself up. How was she going to tell his mate?

When Rose entered the deserted mess hall, Lance Corporal Townsend looked up from his tea then muttered, 'Bugger.'

'I was with him when he died. He didn't wake or say anything.' Rose sat across from him.

'He was a good bloke, always had a good yarn. I met him when he was in the 13th. Should've stopped home when he had the chance.' Townsend's face reddened and he sniffed. Rose's addled brain took in the 13th. Leo was with the 13th. She didn't want to think about him. He'd never shown the next day and she'd had to swallow that his loyalty lay with Harry first.

'Austin, or Aus, as we called him, got blotto one night and some joke thought it'd be a lark to chuck 'im on a train then tell the CO that he'd deserted. If the Jacks had caught him, he'd 'ave gone straight to the cage but I found him and warned him off. He was so worried he'd get shot like the Brits do that he hightailed it home. He signed up again when he got back—under his wife's maiden name. Now look where that got 'im.'

Rose's spirits sank further. Austin had a wife. Something else started to niggle through the fog of exhaustion. Deserted? When Leo hadn't shown, Alfred had just happened to be walking past. When she'd refused his offer of morning tea, his eyes had darkened and for the first time, she'd seen a hardness to him.

'You know, I was seeing a mate off to Scotland and I'm sure I saw Dymond jump on the *Flying Scotsman* too. I thought all his leave was up.'

Rose had kept silent.

'Would hate to think that with Oskar dying and all that, Dymond's decided to give the war up and desert to Scotland. Wouldn't be the first man to do it.'

Rose hadn't even questioned that Alfred might have lied

'You look done in. I can't thank you enough, Sister. I'll write Margaret and let her know.' He was out the door before she'd connected that he'd left. She shivered as a gust of frigid air blew in. Maybe Leo had tried to come to her. Maybe he hadn't deserted. Where on Earth was he?

Chapter Thirty-Seven

1 November 1917
Boulogne, France

As soon as Rose stepped off the tram into the icy wind, she regretted her decision to come into Boulogne. She could have stayed huddled, warm in her bed all day. Still, her Christmas gift list wasn't very long—Adelaide, baby Arthur, Father and Maman. She pulled her hat down and her scarf tighter.

The scent of the ocean was much stronger in the port of Boulogne than the more desolate camp on the cliffs. Some hospital ships sat in the harbour, their Red Cross and Union Jack flags snapping in the wind. Rose noted the brewing clouds and picked up her pace, dodging French soldiers and women selling all manners of wares. She bought a couple of pancakes from a woman cooking in a small stall on a coal stove.

Her childhood and school French had allowed her ear to come in quickly and she understood most of what was being said around her. Rose spotted an elegant looking antiquity store and stepped inside.

'*Bonjour*,' she called to the equally elegant store owner. The store was a treasure trove. She'd forgotten how gazing at beautiful objects could lift her spirits. She'd taken for granted the family heirlooms her mother had always dotted around their house. A pretty vase here, a tapestry there but it looked as if the French aristocracy had abandoned all to this woman's store.

'May I help you, mademoiselle?' the owner asked, blowing some imagined dust from an amoire.

Rose answered her in French. 'I am buying Christmas presents for my father and mother, a friend and her baby.'

The woman's thin lips broke into a smile. 'Your French is exceptionally good.'

'It helps that my mother is French,' Rose replied as the woman began to search through a cabinet.

'Where is she from?'

'Figeac in the Dordogne.'

Rose admired the heart-shaped locket with a pretty *fleur-de-lys* in the centre the store owner placed on the counter in front of her then balked at the price.

'Ah, *le Perogord noir*. There are some wonderful caves there, yes?'

Rose nodded, even though she had no idea. 'This locket is beautiful, but I can't afford it.' Rose knew her mother would love it and she was shocked to find her eyes filling with tears.

'Please call me, Madame Gifford. Perhaps these will do nicely?' Madame Gifford gathered up a selection of silver teaspoons. One had grapes for a handle, which immediately brought Leo to mind. Her tears spilled down her cheeks.

'The war is hard on you,' Madame said simply. She wrapped the locket into a silk handkerchief and pressed it into her hand. 'For your mother, who must miss you dearly.'

Rose tried to give it back. 'I couldn't possibly.' Madame was already searching for the next gift. 'Perhaps your father enjoys smoking a pipe?'

'Yes, he does.'

Rose took a deep breath. This was why she dreaded having any time off. If she was busy, she didn't think of the father that sent her packages of medical supplies but no letters, of a mother trapped in the abyss of grief, the sobs she shared with Adelaide as she left to go back to Australia, and she was far too tired to remember that last soft touch of Leo's lips on hers. How safe she felt in his warm arms.

'*Mademoiselle?* Your papa, he would like this?' Yes, Rose was sure he would like the cherrywood pipe and Adelaide would adore the fine lace. She finished with a silver spoon shaped as a lion for baby Artie. She then decided that an old fancy shirt buckle in the shape of the Rod of Asclepius would be a wonderful gift for Major Richmond.

As if he had been summoned by her thoughts, Major Richmond blustered through the door.

'Bonjour, Madame Gifford. Goodness, it's blowing a gale out there. Ah, Sister Shipley, you've discovered the gem of Boulogne. The French must cry to part with such treasures but …'

'*C'est la guerre,*' they all said in unison with a solemn nod.

'I'll just be a moment. Would you mind waiting a minute, I'd like to talk to you.' Rose wasn't sure that it was good or bad news on his mind but agreed to wait. She was more than satisfied with the gifts now stowed in her pockets. They farewelled Madame Gifford and made their way along the cobbled streets as the wind buffeted against them.

Major Richmond almost had to yell against the howl of the wind. 'I just wanted to check how you were going. Madame is a tough woman, but she was treating you like a baby bird dropped out of a nest.' He gripped his hat.

'I was buying Christmas presents and I got a bit sentimental, I'm afraid. I didn't realise how much I would miss Adelaide, but I think I'm settling in to the 53rd now.'

Major Richmond gave a grim smile. 'It's important to connect to others. Gets you through a lot, even if you miss them later.'

Rose felt awful. All this time she had poured out her woes to him, she'd not realised he would have people he missed also.

Rose looked more carefully at him. 'What is it?'

He sighed. 'You'll find out soon enough. Apparently, the Australians want you back. You're heading up to the 2nd Australian Casualty Clearing Station at Trois Arbres.'

Panic and excitement duelled in her belly. Finally, a CCS.

'I'm heading back to Blighty for a bit as my father's taken ill, but remember, I'm just a letter away. I'd like to know how you're getting on.' He wiped his eyes. 'Blast this infernal wind.'

Rose nudged his shoulder. 'I'll miss you too.'

She left him at the port with the other soldiers getting ready to embark for England, slipping his present in his hand and walking away before he could open it.

Her thoughts soon wandered to working in a Casualty Clearing Station. She'd heard when things got busy that nurses sometimes used a scalpel to clear shrapnel to save the surgeon's time in surgery. How thrilling that would be. So consumed in her head, Rose failed to notice a large wave wash over the road, catching her legs in its wake.

Before the bone-chilling water had even had a chance to soak into her stockings, a French soldier whipped her off the ground and carried her to a dry spot on the cobble stones.

'*Merci beau coup, monsieur,*' Rose spluttered as his comrades cheered him on. He bowed and made a show of cleaning her boots with his scarf. When he finally stood, she was startled to note how handsome he was.

'*Vous êtes les bienvenus, ma belle dame.*' He put his scarf in his pack and offered an arm and a coffee. Rose smiled but told him she had to get back on the tram to camp before the wild weather kept her stuck in town.

He winked and told her he hoped she would be delayed.

Rose was still smiling when she sat on the bench in the tram. It had been a while since anyone had flirted with her. Most of the men around her quickly noted the focus she had on her nursing and left her to it. Leo hadn't flirted. He'd made her feel like she was the only woman worth his heart's attention. A stab of pain in her chest had Rose sucking for air. For the first time, she wondered if heartbreak was more than just an expression.

Chapter Thirty-Eight

3 November 1917
2nd ACCS, Trois Arbres

The wind swirled in as Rose opened the door to an Armstrong hut. She was shocked to see a woman about her mother's age sitting at a table now scrambling to secure a letter she'd been writing.

'Oh, I must have the wrong hut. Mine was supposed to be empty until another sister arrived.' Rose handed her a photograph that had taken flight. The nurse gave her a warm smile and screwed the lid of her ink pot closed.

'Come in, get out of those gumboots and oilskins and have a cuppa. I'm Sister McNaughton—Kit when we're off duty. Terrible out there, isn't it?'

Rose hung her oilskins on a peg. Next to the neat coat and smooth cap Kit was wearing, Rose felt like a bedraggled dog creeping in. 'I don't want to trouble you.'

'No bother, I was finished anyway. Let's get acquainted. Sister Shipley, isn't it?' Kit asked as she put a billy on a stove. Rose flushed. Here she was bursting in without so much as an introduction. 'Yes, Rose Shipley.'

'I heard you've been spending time with the Brits. I hope they haven't made you too soft. No supervising orderlies doing the hard yards here.' Kit found two mugs and made them a cocoa. Rose sniffed the sweet scent and felt instantly better.

'I'm ready to pull my weight,' Rose assured her.

Kit had a brisk and slightly stern manner about her but when she smiled, as she did now, it softened her eyes. 'I've been here since mid-August and I can tell you it takes a bit of getting used to.'

At that moment, the big guns started thumping away and Rose resisted covering her ears. Kit continued her conversation in spaces between the raucous.

'You'll get used to that. We're only about four miles from the front at Ploegsteert. One minute t's guns, then planes or trains rumbling past. Always a hullabaloo. We won't even get started about the stench.'

Rose laughed. She had gagged when she'd first gotten out of the ambulance wagon on arrival.

'It's quite a nice camp. There's a fireplace in the mess hut and hot water in the bathroom. It's rather modern too, we have x-ray and even a warm ether apparatus in the operating room. Mind …' she paused. '… you do have to put up with the occasional bombing. When we get the wind up, it's tin hats and off to Hyde Park Hotel.'

Kit sipped her cocoa while Rose absorbed her words. What did she expect being so close to the action? Of course, they might be bombed.

'Hyde Park Hotel?' Rose managed to squeak.

'Yes, our dugout. When it's a full moon, Fritz often decides to visit, and we bunk down. It's not so bad. We even have a gramophone down there so there's often a chorus or two in the night. It is hard to get on without sleep though.'

Studying Kit's worn out features, Rose worried that they were bombed quite often.

'When were you last …' she asked

'Visited? Mmm.' Kit pulled out a blue notebook and leafed through it. 'I haven't been very diligent in the last few months. I'm afraid Passchendaele kept me on the run. Here it's not about what to do but what to do *first*, or so my friend, Ida, says.'

Rose nodded. Her stomach tensed when she heard the drone of planes above. Even worse, Kit seemed to notice her tension.

'Don't worry, they're ours.' She handed Rose a toffee from a Mackintosh's Toffee tin. Rose let the sweetness soak into her mouth but tried not to bite down. She'd had her teeth stuck together more than once by toffees.

'It takes a while to get them soft these days. I hope we're not in for a winter like last year. Do you know I spilt coffee and it froze before it even touched my uniform? Let's go give you a quick tour before I go back on duty.'

Rose was sorry to leave the warmth of the hut, but she followed Kit to a high vantage point near the railway siding, overlooking the camp.

'The boys come in via ambulance and go to the receiving hut. They'll be labelled by the medical officer. Class A urgents, often abdominals, will go straight to the prep ward. Penetrating abdomen to the resus ward, and chests to acute surgical. Compound fractures and large wounds also go to resus or prep. Class B will need surgery before evac, especially scalp or face wounds. Then Class C will be minor flesh wounds and will get cleaned up but only operated on if there's time. Class D are the walking wounded and go to that tent to get dressings done then evac onto our train, the *Queen Mary*, and off to base.' Kit pointed throughout to various Nissen huts and tents.

Rose's brain struggled to keep up. How would she remember all of this?

'I'd like to tell you we get the men clean and in pyjamas and all, but I've seen a lot of men hit the operating tables still coated in mud and in their khakis. But we try our best.'

Rose noticed some men digging in a nearby field. Kit followed her gaze.

'That's the VD squad. I wasn't too fussed on the idea of men with VD working off their sins, but it's supposed to help with the mercury treatment, and they've behaved well. It can't be pleasant digging graves in the cemetery.' Kit drew in a breath. 'That place has certainly grown in the last few months.' She looked away. 'Now, we also have enough electric lights here to light up Paris, I think.' Rose merely nodded and stifled a yawn. Kit touched her arm. 'Oh dear, I think I've overwhelmed you with too much information. Let's go get you settled.'

'That would be rather nice. Thank you,' Rose said.

'You have been with the Brits a *rather* long time then, haven't you?' Kit smiled and led the way back.

Rose smiled too. She had said 'rather' instead of the usual Aussie 'quite'.

'Yes, quite long enough it seems.' Rose looked at the men digging. One of them looked familiar. Her eyes narrowed on the misty field.

Yes, she was sure of it. One of those men was Harry.

Chapter Thirty-Nine

15 November 1917
2nd ACCS, Trois Arbres

Rose folded the last of Harry's few letters and placed it with the others in her old Arnott's biscuit tin. She tapped the lid with her nails. She should have taken more notice of the changes in them as time went on. He'd gone from the rather blasé man she knew was shy of commitment, to getting very sentimental. The latest letter was quite the fantasy of a future life together. She chewed her lip. She knew from talking to many patients that this fantasy world of being safe back home with a loving woman to nurture them got many of the men through the worst of things. How bad were things getting for Harry?

Yet, she had seen him with the venereal disease crew. Did he think he could excuse such behaviour as a man having needs? Is that why Leo flushed red every time Harry's name came up?

She released a puff of air, which hung like smoke. There was nothing else for it. He couldn't deny his escapades if she caught him here being treated for VD. He would have to accept that there was no future for them. He had to know she was still committed to her dream of becoming a doctor.

Rose added her extra layers of a sheepskin vest and great coat, leaving the relative warmth of her hut, to slide along the ice-encrusted duckboards to the VD ward. Her concentration was so great she barely noticed the constant barrage going on in the distance.

She entered the ward and saw most of the men were writing letters, playing cards or reading.

'Come to give them the umbrella, have you, Nurse Shipley?'

Rose grinned at the orderly. Even she had shivered at the thought of the device used to scrape the urethra. Surely, hearing about how painful the treatment was should have put more men off, but it seemed lust had a louder voice than sense for many of them.

'No, Corporal Saddington. You can get that twinkle out of your eye, you sadist. I'm actually looking for Private Fuller.' Rose scanned the room but couldn't see Harry anywhere. Maybe she'd got it wrong and it wasn't him. She should have checked straight away but things had been flat chat for her in the first few days.

'Sorry, Sister. You missed him by a few days, he's gone back to his unit. You could write, I guess,' he suggested.

Oh well, she had tried. What harm could it do for Harry to keep his hope of a happy future just a little longer? 'No, that's fine.'

Saddington's bushy eyebrows drew together and Rose blushed. Had he thought they were promised to each other and Rose was angry at her discovery?

'He's a friend and I thought I'd—' Rose stopped as the orderly and quite a few patients in pyjamas and slippers rushed out the door. She followed, confused until she realised that the drone of an aircraft was much too close.

'No need to worry, it's one of ours,' Saddington said but he still looked concerned. 'A Sopwith Dolphin. It's going to crash by the look of it.'

Rose looked up into the milky morning air and noticed a billow of black smoke coming from the back of the aircraft. The plane circled above then puttered down to a field in front of the camp.

At first, Rose thought it was fine but as the plane scooted along the white field, the propeller scraped the ground and the whole plane tipped onto its back.

'Get a stretcher!' she called to Saddington as she ran forward. Some of the soldiers kicked off their slippers and bolted after her. The pilot crawled from the cockpit and collapsed just as Rose reached him.

'Am I in heaven?' he mumbled, his face as pale as the snow beneath him. Rose gasped. He was the spitting image of Leo.

'Should we load him up?' Saddington asked.

'Oh.' Rose snapped back into nurse mode and gave the pilot a quick assessment. 'Be careful. He's got a fractured femur, broken ribs and

I don't like the look of the laceration on his forehead. He's also in shock so add some more blankets if you could.'

In theatre, Rose stared at the pilot's face. Her head knew this man was Captain Murray, but her heart wasn't as convinced.

'No. I asked for forceps not a scalpel,' barked Major Turnbull. He snatched the forceps from her. 'What is wrong with you today? That's the third time.'

Focus Rose, she told herself. This doctor was much harder to read and work with than Major Richmond and it wouldn't do to put him in an even more foul temper than usual. Yet, despite her inner lecture, she gazed at the anaesthetised patient again. He looked so young, just a boy. Vulnerable.

'For goodness sake, Sister Shipley. Do you need someone else to take over?'

Oh dear, she hadn't heard the surgeon's request for an instrument again. She stayed on task and left before Major Turnbull could give her a dressing down.

Rose returned to her empty hut. She tossed the biscuit tin from her bed onto the floor and dropped onto the cot. She needed to impress the staff here, not annoy them. She could not afford to be distracted by anything or *anyone*. 'Damn that man,' she whispered. This was what she got for opening her heart even a crack. He was wedged right in there. Where was Leo?

Chapter Forty

17 November 1917
Agincourt, France

Leo's cheeks burned like a stoked campfire. Lieutenant Colonel Durrant had him cornered in the orderly room. How long was he going to go on? The musty air of the hut was tinged with wisps of smoke coming from a cigar propped on a tin. The cherry scented smoke caught in his throat and made his nose itch.

'Are you sure they sent you back to the correct unit, Private?' His tone was grave.

Leo shifted in his boots and offered a meek, 'Yes, sir.'

Durrant's thick eyebrows knitted together just like Pa's did when he was cross. Leo would give anything to see Pa again, cranky or not. He bit his lip and looked at Durrant's handsome face.

'You, a 13th man? A 13th? Surely not.'

Leo attempted to stand tall, but his shoulders drooped at the words. His throat bobbed with unspoken words. My oath, he was a 13th man through and through. There was no point in claiming his innocence, he had to cop this on the chin and prove himself.

'Surely you must have forgotten you belonged to the 13th when you committed fraud. We need men with honour and loyalty here, Private Dymond. Do you want me to transfer you?'

Shit! He wouldn't, would he? Leo swallowed hard and chewed on his bottom lip.

'I am deeply sorry, sir. I won't let you or the 13th down again,' Leo said with conviction.

Durrant stopped pacing and looked at him square on. Leo held his gaze until his eyes watered.

'I'm counting on it. Any more trouble and I'll send you to the Hairy Mob of Hard Cases. Lucky for you, I need all the men we can muster. We've had a rough time of it with Bullecourt and Passchendaele.' Durrant sank into a chair behind a small oak desk. It creaked as he rocked on its legs like so many schoolboys had been warned never to do.

Leo stood silently waiting to be dismissed but Durrant seemed lost in thought as thick as the smoke swirling around him.

'Off you go then,' he finally uttered.

Thank the Lord. Leo saluted and headed for the door.

'Leo.' Durrant gave him a tired smile, 'Welcome back.'

'Thanks, sir.'

Leo dumped his kit in the billet. Going up in the world. This time they were camping out in a pig sty. And from the stench still present, a recently vacated one. He trudged over to the local *estaminet*. It was a crumbling stone house with faded blue shutters. Leo froze at the door as a prickle of uncertainty needled him. What if none of his other chums were left?

'Hey, is that a bloody ghost?' Bull said as he yanked Leo inside. They slapped each other like schoolboys who'd just won a cricket final. Bull called for another vin rouge and they settled at a small table in the corner.

Bull sat staring at him, shaking his head. 'Jesus, as I live and breathe, I can't believe it's you. When I didn't hear anything, I figured you might have ended up in cold storage. What have you been up to for the last nine months?'

Bull seemed to have aged ten years while Leo was away. His voice was raspy and he raw pink spots of just healed skin on his hands and face. What in the hell had happened while he was swanning around London with Rose?

Leo shrugged. 'Nothin' too much. I was stuck in hospital for a bit, then I was at Perham Downs retraining, and now here I am. What about you? Dolly said it was pretty rough at Passchendaele.'

Bull adopted the same nonchalant tone. 'That stunt has been and went. Damn Huns and their bloody gas though. Passchendaele's nothing but a poisonous swamp now.' They all sculled down some beer.

As he scanned the hazy café, Leo barely recognised a face. Where was Harry?

'So, I heard Oskar made it over here finally. Has he written to you yet?' asked Bull.

Leo's throat ran dry and his eyes pricked with tears. He cleared his throat but found he couldn't speak.

Bull frowned, froze mid-gulp, and put his beer down. 'No, he hasn't—'

Leo nodded and started fiddling with a groove in the wine-soaked table. He looked at Bull and added, 'At Bullecourt.'

Bull let out a low whistle and muttered, 'Shit.'

A sweet-faced woman came to their table.

'Would anyone like some chips and eggs?' she asked.

'*Non, merci.*'

'*Non?* Something terrible has happened. Bull does not want my chips and eggs?' Her playful banter stopped as Bull's face remained fixed on the table. '*Mon Dieu*, I am sorry. This war is *tres* terrible, is it not?'

Bull told her Leo's news.

She nodded sympathetically and patted Leo's arm. 'I lost my all of my brothers at Verdun. I will bring more beer.'

'*Merci, Mademoiselle* Zoe,' Bull said glumly.

Soldiers ate, drank and sang around them but Leo and Bull remained like statues. Leo had imagined being back with his mates, but he hadn't pictured feeling so numb. It was as if he were a bug in a glass jar, no longer connected to his natural world.

After a few more beers and some wine for good measure, Bull broke the silence.

'Dolly was right, Passchendaele was hell. We were stuck in the stinky bog hole of Zonnebeke and our line was already thin, only sixty of us holding about six hundred yards when we heard the gas gongs. Gas shells were plopping out like horseshit. I found Sergeant Clinen.'

Bull lit a cigarette, tapped his glass then cleared his throat to continue. 'He was having some kind of fit, and his face was blacker than a native's. Some foamy jelly bubbles were coming from his mouth and then the bugger clawed at me, almost ripped me mask off. When he can't get it off, he starts tearing at his own throat, shredding it until it was covered in blood. I had to pin him down until the stretcher boys came.'

'Bloody hell.' It must have been for Bull to talk about it.

Bull stubbed his cigarette out. 'I heard he went west. I reckon it'd been kinder to shoot him and put him out of his misery. It's no way to go, I tell you.'

Flashes of the charred bodies of the children flared up in Leo's mind.

'Go on then, Leo. I didn't come down in the last rain. What happened to you? Something did.' It all came tumbling out like some stored-up Sunday confessional. He sat back purged of all his secrets (except for Rose). Bull had sat listening without interruption but as their silence continued, Leo grew uneasy. Should he have kept his trap shut? Did he think Leo did it?

Bull thumped the table so hard the glasses bobbed wildly. 'If I find out who that mongrel was that fiddled your paybook better, he'll be sorry. I'll shove a Mills bomb up his arse and kick him over to Fritz.' Bull continued to rant on with such vivid descriptions of the culprit's demise that Leo's solemn nods gave way to belly laughs.

'Can you just imagine a bloke begging Fritz to cut him down from Madonna's hold over the church in Albert? Geez, Bull, remind me to stay on your good side,' Leo said as he ran a rag over his streaming eyes.

'Yeah you better, never know what I'm capable of. Tell us, what was London like?' Bull asked.

'It's amazing. Rose and I went—' Jesus, he was hopeless.

'Rose? Not Harry's Rose?' Bull might look like a harmless joker, but he was sharp.

'Yeah, uh, actually. I'm not so sure she's still Harry's, but things were left a bit unclear once I ended up in the clink. She's over here somewhere.'

'You dark horse, you. Does Harry know?' Bull leaned back in his chair, bumping heads with the bloke behind him. The young man, looking fit for a fight, took one look at Bull and raised his glass to him. 'Sorry, mate.'

Bull waved the bloke back to his friends. 'My fault. C'mon Leo. Does Harry know?'

Leo shrugged. 'Not unless Rose wrote and told him. Where is Harry?'

'He's okay. He's doing a stint in one of the special hospitals. He was mostly steering clear of us, drinkin' and so on.' Bull stroked the whiskers on his chin then shook his head.

Leo bit his lip. So, Harry's whoring had landed him in trouble again. He felt a touch of shame that it had taken him so long to ask about him and relief that he didn't have to face him yet. The shame melted into anger.

At least he had only kissed Rose, what Harry was doing to Rose was so much worse. He would have to find her and explain what happened.

Harry didn't deserve Rose at all and when he came back, Leo would tell him so. A guilt cloud lifted, and he raised his glass to them.

'I've got some other news too. Turns out I'm not the only dark horse in the family. Oskar kept his little romance with Adelaide under his hat. I got to meet their baby, Arthur,' Leo said, enjoying the pop of Bull's eyes and his splutter of wine.

'You're kidding!' Bull said as soon as he recovered.

Leo wiped his cheek of Bull's Riesling. 'How did she take the news?'

Leo felt in his pocket. He touched the rough wood. He had begun carving a soldier in the likeness of Oskar for the baby. Poor Addie. He bit his lip.

Bull's cheeks reddened. 'Sorry, dumb question. Why would anyone sign up for this, let alone a woman? If Rose is over here, I'll see if I can track her down and you can show her the error of her ways,' Bull offered.

'Didn't know you were a romantic at heart, Bull,' teased Leo, and Bull clouted him across the ear before he could get warmed up.

Zoe returned with more beer and wine and someone began banging away at an old piano.

'Let's make a toast, boys,' Bull said over the racket, 'To our brothers gone west in this bloody war, and to love—finding it, wherever she may be.'

'*Salut*!' answered Leo. He raised his glass high. 'To love and war, may we live through them both.'

Chapter Forty-One

3 December 1917
Billets at Woincourt

L eo settled against a stable door, wrinkling his nose at the smell of stale horse urine. Most of the men had braved the cold and wandered off to the local café. Harry was playing cards with a few new recruits while some French children watched.

Harry looked at the hand he was dealt and exaggerated his face into a mock scream. '*Nonbon, nonbon!*' he cried.

A boy of about four, with dimples just like Harry's, giggled and copied his expression while the other kids laughed. With each new hand, Harry would change his features. Shock, joy, sad until all the children were all copying him. They had barely talked since Harry had come back. Leo had forgotten how good Harry was with kids. Dot had loved it when Harry mimicked the school nuns. Leo yanked out Dot's last letter and re-read it.

> *October 1917*
> *Dearest Leo,*
>
> *I hope things are going well over there and you make it home for Christmas. I miss you. I hope you like the post card. Isn't the picture of the kookaburra and homestead just like ours! What sort of birds do they have where you are?*
>
> *We finally got some letters from Pa, all different dates. He is still at the Holsworthy Camp and told us not to worry, he is doing fine. He says he is only suffering from something called barbed-wire fever. Ma said that's like me being stuck in Sunday school*

wanting to run around the fields outside. He hasn't said anything about Oskar yet so maybe our letters didn't get to him.

Ma is hoping we can get permission to go and see him for Christmas. I hope you are both home by then. Ma has spent a lot of time at church praying since we got the telegram about Oskar. She won't say it, but I know she's scared she'll get one about you. I couldn't bear it

Ma told me to keep our worries at home, but Mrs Fanshaw was so mean to her last week. She said she wouldn't sell to those who comsort consort with the enemy or are of alien blood. I thought we all had the same blood. So, we didn't get enough flour to make strudel for Sunday. I hate that we must be nice to them Fanshaws, so Pa's vineyard is okay. Even the Duffy boys that are helping Ma hate them. I wanted to punch her right on her beaky nose but saw Ma was trying not to cry. Please don't tell Ma I told you.

Did you hear that Ernie Morris died? We pray for the soldiers at school when we find out and it seems like we are praying every day for someone and their families. It makes me scared for you. Ma told me to keep my letters cheerful, but I just don't feel real cheerful. I promise I will try harder in the next one.

Your loving sister,
Dot xx

Leo rubbed the back of his neck. Tucking the letter away, he stood and began to pace around the stable. What if he was stuck over here for years waiting for the war to end? Why hadn't he thought about that? He'd joined the army until the war ended. How often his head hurt with unanswered questions since he'd joined up. He couldn't believe he'd once been so sure about his future.

He kicked a wooden bucket. Bloody Fanshaws. How dare that witch treat his ma like that. He wished Dot had given the old biddy a punch.

'Anyone want to warm up with a bout of blindfold boxing?' Bull called from the courtyard. Leo came out from the stable. Bull raised his eyebrows to Leo. 'Heard Alfred is going in the ring.'

Too right! Leo was in.

Harry came and nudged Leo. 'You've got to do it.' Harry's eyes gleamed. 'I'll run a book and we'll rake it in.'

Harry looked like his old mate again. Not the silent, broody man of late.

Leo nodded. 'No worries, I wouldn't mind belting Alfred for nix.'

Leo rushed off to find his kit and get changed into his gym gear.

When they entered a large barn with a makeshift ring set up in the centre, it was already crowded with men cheering on the first bout. A blindfolded Alfred was dancing in the ring, cocking his head as he listened to his coach, George, yell out instructions over the din. He shifted and weaved, narrowly avoiding a fist from the robust soldier shuffling towards him. Watching men blindfolded with lengths of puttee material attempt to box was usually a comical sight, but Alfred had smooth footwork and fluid motion despite the blindfold.

Alfred landed a solid punch to his opponent, who groaned as a trail of blood dribbled from a cut above his eye. Leo gingerly gave his own nose a rub. Declared the winner, Alfred removed his blindfold and raised a fist.

'Okay, who's next?' George called.

Alfred might be good, but Leo had an uncanny knack for knowing where people were in blindfold boxing. Leo climbed into the ring and the flurry of betting started. Alfred flexed his muscles and punched the air, dancing a quick step as everyone sized up him and his new opponent. Leo rolled his eyes and waited.

'I would've thought you'd have learnt the first time. When I win, you'll owe me a tin of cigars and have to clean my boots for a month,' Alfred smirked.

'When I win, you have to promise that you and your mother'll leave my family alone.'

The ref stepped up and tied Leo's blindfold on, then led him to Harry's corner.

'You'll be right, Leo. Alf's quick on his feet and we know he packs a mean punch so build him up a bit and take a couple. He'll be struttin' around like a cock, put on a good show, and then let 'im have it.'

Leo gave a nod. He had done this enough times with Harry acting as coach back home until no bloke at Borenore would take him on. No one could understand how he could avoid punches yet land some beauties of his own. Like bubbles rising in a beer, he let his nerves release with a pop.

'Time to go, boys,' the ref announced. Leo felt a tug as the ref checked his blindfold and lead him to the centre of the ring. The tang of sweat, coffee and metho filled his nostrils. A smack on the rear and he was good to go. George immediately started a loud barrage of instructions to Alfred, but Leo followed his intuition.

He could sense Alfred moving around him but in his mind's eye he could see him, as if there were no blindfold. Leo took another hit to his gut, just moving back in time to avoid the full brunt of the swing.

The crowd roared approval to Alf and encouraged him. Leo dodged the next couple of jabs and landed one in Alfred's rock-hard bicep.

Alfred sniggered. 'I think that hurt you more than me, Fritzy.'

'Just a tickle. I'll have you done like a dinner soon enough, don't want to disappoint the lads with a poor—' Leo thumped him in the gut. '… show, now do I?'

George squawked out more directions and Leo moved nimbly left as Alfred charged at him full pelt. A rush of air and then laughter. More puffs of air as Alfred's fists flailed around him. Easy as pie.

Moving back, Leo put his arm out about head height, just out of reach of Alfred's pummelling fists, and mimed holding him back while yawning, like bullies do to a small boy fighting back. More raucous laughter from the crowd. He slinked behind Alfred, tapped him on the shoulder and clocked him straight in the nose.

'Leo, that's enough fun. Time to sock it to him,' Harry called over the din.

Letting Alf land one more hit to his shoulder, Leo waited until he was in position. Using a twist of his waist to generate maximum power, he cracked his fist under Alfred's jaw. *Ooof! Thud!* It was over. The troops cheered as if he were one of their idol boxers—Darcy knocking out Clabby.

Leo pushed up his blindfold. Alfred's prone body lay at his feet. His freckles stood out like pebbles on a beach and his nose was bloody. Harry whooped in and yanked his arm upwards in a victory punch. It took a while to release himself from Harry's jig of gambling joy. He untangled himself and stood over Alfred until he'd regained consciousness.

'Looks like you have to leave my mob alone now.'

'Fat chance.' Alfred attempted to hold himself erect but, wobbly, slid to the floor. 'I wouldn't get too cocky, Dymond. That was just a preliminary bout; I'll drop you next time.' Alfred finally heaved himself up. 'At least I know how to keep an eye on my paybook.'

A black cloak descended over Leo. Bull was the only person he'd told about how he'd landed in Aldershot. Leo raised his fist again.

'Save it for the ring, mate.' Harry said.

Alfred's eyes closed and he slumped back to the floor. Arms pulled him away from Alfred's collapsed body.

Dolly thrust some money at Harry. 'Nice work, Private Dymond. I'll be sure to put my money on you next time.'

Alfred was being pulled up to a bench and stared at Leo through groggy eyes.

God, Fanshaw got under his skin worse than a bloomin' ringworm. If it wasn't for the bloody Fanshaws, he wouldn't be in this bloody mess. How was he ever going to get back home?

Chapter Forty-Two

11 January 1918
Péronne-Bailleul (with a visit to 2nd Australian CCS,
Trois Arbres, France)

The stench of old horse manure, stale sweat and Bull's latest fart had Leo tumbling with relief out of the transport truck. Whose brilliant idea was it to jam more than thirty men into railway trucks? He was so fed up with the stink of war. Thank God it wasn't summer. He grabbed a cup of cocoa from a shivering Red Cross girl and made his way out of the swarm of men, settling on the snow-crusted embankment. Bull was soon freezing his bum off next to him.

'It's colder than a mortician's mistress out here. Damn cuppa's icy already,' Bull complained as he tossed it into the mush.

'My oath. I think even me blood's frozen up too. What does it take to get warm around here?' Leo agreed.

'I know something that'll get your blood a bit warmer. I've found where Rose is.' Bull raised his cup triumphantly.

Was he serious? Leo's blood pumped in his ears.

'Well, c'mon then. Where is she?' said Leo, giving Bull a poke in his sheepskin vest.

'I was having a chat to that Bluebird over there. Happened to mention a girl just up the road at the 2nd Aussie CCS called Rose. She said she's real pretty and I figured it could be her,' Bull informed him.

'Just up the road?'

'Yep.'

'Maybe we should find out for sure Rose is there?' Leo said.

'What? Go visit?' Bull asked.

Leo hid his face in his cup of cocoa, thinking. Maybe he still had time to talk to the Bluebird. The whistle sounded for them to prepare to reboard. Damn. He was busting to see Rose and explain what happened, but he didn't want to land in hot water for going AWL. His letters to Rose had been returned and Adelaide had left for Australia. His lips tightened on the cup rim. He wasn't sure his letters had been returned on purpose or not.

He rubbed the back of his neck as he watched everyone move towards the railway car. Bugger it. He didn't want her to think he wasn't interested or have her give up on him. She was so close … just up the road. His crotch tingled as he remembered their kiss. Lord, he wanted her. He leapt to his feet and flicked the ice from his pants.

'Marks'll probably tip me out of the 13th for it, but yeah, why don't we go visit the 2nd CCS while we're here?' Leo suggested.

Bull's eyes gleamed like he'd found a stash of chocolate. 'Off on a mission of romance, count me in. Let's get behind the shed before we're rounded up.'

They peered from behind the ramshackle shed and watched the last of the stragglers load up into the wagons. Maybe he shouldn't risk going AWL. Wouldn't it be awkward for Rose with him turning up?

'Maybe we should find her later.' Leo said.

Bull shrugged. 'Too late for that, the train's pulling out.' Bull's blue eyes flashed at him. 'Come on, Leo. Let's go find your lady love.'

'For God's sake, Rose and I are just friends.'

'Yeah, that's why you are redder than a Frenchman's burgundy.'

'Shut up.'

They hopped along the frosty tracks with their heads down to the biting wind. Leo felt his brain become as numb as his fingers.

Just when he thought they would probably become victims to the elements, Bull pointed out some grey lumps out ahead. When they drew closer, he could see what appeared to be some sort of light trolley railway coming from the main track, winding its way back to the curved roof of a massive, cylindrical Nissen hut. Duckboard walkways snaked among four large Latapie huts and snow-dusted tents. For a temporary station, it looked well set up.

A man dressed fit to challenge the North Pole waddled towards them.

He called out to them, 'Are you fellas okay?'

'Yeah, we're all fine except for a bruised arse here and there,' Bull hollered back. Bull had slipped more than a few times on their expedition and he rubbed his derriere for good measure.

'G'day. I'm Peter King, an orderly here. So, have you lost your way? Off to Steenwerck?'

Leo liked his upbeat manner and cheerful grin.

Bull approached Peter and pulled him close. 'Actually, Pete. Maybe you can help us. We're on a secret mission.' Pete's grin straightened and he puffed up with the honour of being trusted.

'Oh, I see. We are so close to the front here, only a few thousand yards to Plug Street. Do you need to see Colonel Stacy?' he whispered.

One look at Pete's earnest face and Bull dissolved into laughter. 'Sorry, Pete. I'm just spinning you kangaroo feathers. It is important though. We're on a noble quest for love. Leo desperately needs to find Rose ... ah ...' Bull turned to Leo.

'Shipley,' Leo finished. Pete lost his miffed expression and smiled broadly.

'A worthy quest indeed, kind sirs.' Peter gave a sweeping bow. 'She is here. Not just a pretty face that one. Follow me.'

Bull began to whistle 'The Rose of No Man's Land' then started singing, changing the words of the popular war song as he went.

'There's a rose that grows in no man's land,

And it's wonderful to see.

Though it's bathed in tears, it will be for years,

In the garden of my memory

It's the one red rose this soldier, Leo, knows

It's the work of Bull's master plan

Mid the war's great curse

We'll find his beautiful nurse

She's the Rose of No Man's Laaaaaaaaaaaannd.'

What a galah! The whole German Army could probably hear him. Applause and laughter erupted from within a small hut nearby.

'There's the nurse's mess hut,' Pete said, pointing to the same hut. 'I'll leave you to it. *Bonne Chance.*' They waved Pete off.

'Go on there, Leo. Give the door a knock and see if Rose is in,' Bull encouraged.

What if she didn't want to see him? Leo rubbed his hands together and stamped some snow from his boots. He hesitated until Bull gave him a shove towards the door.

Leo swallowed hard and raised his knuckles. *Whack!* The door slapped him hard in the face and he stumbled back. Owwww! He clutched his throbbing nose as tears and blood trickled down his face.

'Leo! Oh, my goodness! I'm so sorry. Here let me help you. Is that really you?'

'Yeth Robse, ib's me. Thib really hurbs,' he groaned.

This wasn't at all how he'd pictured their reunion.

***

'I'm so sorry,' Rose apologised for the umpteenth time.

Leo nodded as she added more packing to his nose. She'd taken him to a supply room attached to one of the huge Nissen hut wards that looked like giant tin cans. He could hear some of the patients chatting while others hacked coughs.

'I can't believe it's really you,' Rose said.

Leo sat transfixed as she bustled about the room. Her alabaster skin was only marred by purple shadows under her eyes.

She shed her thick overcoat and checked his nose. 'I don't think it's broken.'

Now that he'd found her, what was he going to say?

'Maybe you deserve a smack in the nose anyway.' Rose's eyes darkened, 'I waited for ages. Alfred told me you'd deserted and gone on to Edinburgh. Did they catch you?'

'He said what?' Leo yanked the packing away. 'He told you what?'

Rose was suddenly flustered. 'I didn't know what to think. I didn't hear from you and I thought you didn't want to see me again.'

Were those tears in her eyes?

'I didn't desert, Rose. Someone knocked me out and then I found out someone fiddled with my paybook. I was court martialled and sent to Aldershot for a few months. How could you think I wouldn't want to see you again?'

Rose wiped a tear, 'Oh, it's so good that you are here. I didn't tell Harry. I don't know what to say about us ... I mean ... that's of course if there is an *us*.'

He held her hand and rubbed her cold fingers. 'I'd love nothing more.'

Rose hugged him and he winced as she bumped his nose.

'Gosh, I'm hopeless. Let me check I haven't made it bleed again.'

She moved in close, her eyes focused on his nose while he drank in her musky scent. Her soft lips were so close. His body throbbed with heat as he remembered their last kiss. He melted into her and she paused but then her soft lips moved against his and his hunger deepened. He kissed her until he ran out of breath.

'I thought I'd never see you again,' they said in unison.

Rose laughed then gave a solemn stare.

'What's wrong?' He didn't want to know.

'Harry is your best friend, and I don't want to hurt either of you.'

Leo felt a guilty flush. Some friend he was. He wasn't sure Harry was a friend anymore, but did that make it right? He looked at Rose's drawn face and waited. He knew there was something else bothering her.

'I'm not sure I'm being fair to you. I'm needed more here, and I won't give up being a nurse for anything.'

'I wouldn't ask you to.'

Rose smiled and moved so close he could feel her warm breath on his lips.

'I really need to stop kissing you,' she murmured. Leo's stomach flipped and his whole body tingled.

'Excuse me, Sister Shipley, I think that will be enough. You've disrupted my whole ward.' A gravelly voice said behind them.

They leapt apart sending a trolley clattering into the wall. Rose's face flushed with embarrassment.

'Awww, Matron, leave 'em be,' came a cheeky call from the ward.

Head Sister Stobo dropped her stern look. 'As long as you leave racing off with this young man until after the war. We've lost too many of our good sisters to marriage in this station already.' She straightened the skewed trolley.

'No, uh, of course not … we'll fix this up. Private Dymond, my … friend … has hurt his nose and I was just checking it, Matron. Nothing else,' Rose said as she fumbled with some instruments. Leo tried to help her.

Leo didn't know whether to shake the sister's hand or salute. His hand wobbled every which way. She laughed and he settled for a salute. She saluted him back.

'Pleased to meet such a *very good* friend of my hardest working nurse. 'Head Sister Stobo broke into a broad grin. 'I'll leave you to it.' She winked at Rose as she left.

'Phew! I thought I was in for it then.' Rose beamed and took Leo's arm. 'She must like you.'

'Aren't you done fixing Leo's nose yet?' Bull asked as he barrelled through the door.

'Yes, all done,' Rose dropped Leo's arm as if it was scalding hot.

'What do we have to do to get a drink around here? Anything stronger than cocoa would hit the spot.' Bull tapped his ample stomach.

'The girls have some schnapps and chocolate,' Rose offered.

Bull flew out the door, leaving a swirl of snow in his wake.

Leo tested his swollen nose and kissed Rose again.

'Are you sore?' Rose asked. 'You stopped kissing me.'

'I'm fine. I can't believe how lucky I am to have found you again.'

Rose smiled and hugged him close.

He squeezed her tight, almost willing her into his body so he could protect her. Was it just being back at the front or did he have a real reason to worry about Rose?

Chapter Forty-Three

January 1918
2nd ACCS, Trois Arbres

Dear Adelaide,

I hope this letter finds you both well back in Australia. I am so happy to hear that your mother welcomed you with open arms and is besotted with little Edward. You were engaged to Oskar, so I don't think it's too big a lie to call yourself a widow, as I am sure that the grief you are feeling is much the same.

I know I only met Oskar a few times but I, too, am grateful that part of him lives on. In my heart I do believe he watches over you both.

It's difficult to describe life on the front line in a CCS. I am not looking forward to the German offensive which everyone is talking about starting up. It is beyond freezing here so I can't imagine things will get started until spring but who knows? There has mostly been influenza and a bit of trench foot to attend to since the Front is quiet for now.

I had a visitor last week and I am sure my news will delight you. I have fallen in love. There I admit it. Do you remember Oskar's brother, Leo? It must run in the family as I can't resist him anymore than you could resist Oskar. He really is quite distracting. It's like looking at a beautiful sunset- that tingly yet makes you stop and feel like you are really alive feeling. For the first time I understand what you mean. Oh, how I wish we could have one of our afternoon teas at Lyons. I would chew your ear off. I miss you.

I feel so confused. I still have that ambition to become a doctor, or least continue nursing. Some of the things that are happening are quite amazing. The Thomas splints are indispensable as they can be varied and can be used for thigh, leg, arm, and forearm and allow us to dress the wounds without removing it. Wet dressings may be used, or irrigation and the patient is kept dry and… I forget this world is now well behind you but anyway I am still enthralled by it all. Then I think about Leo…

I know I can't have both worlds.

My Aunt Jeanne has been writing to me regularly since she found out I was over here, and she is desperate to meet me and have me stay with her in Paris. Wouldn't that be wonderful? To get some leave and go swanning around Paris-see the Eiffel Tower and Notre Dame and, I will stop taunting you now. If I ever get there, I will be sure to find you a lovely souvenir.

Thank you for taking the time to visit Maman for me. I had hoped she would improve so I could lay aside my guilt for coming here. Father still sends me supplies but that is all, so I have no news from home at all. I shall look forward to your letters. I won't lie and say I am not in any danger working at a CCS, but I am fine for now so please don't worry.

Sending much love from somewhere in France,
Rose.

Chapter Forty-Four

11 March 1918
2nd ACCS, Trois Arbres, St Omer

Rose watched the last of the wounded leave on the *Queen Mary* hospital train.

'Well, time to get moving ourselves,' Sister Keyes said. They both looked over the station. Rose knew it was always supposed to be a mobile camp, but she couldn't fathom how they would dismantle and move all the huts and tents.

'I hope they manage to get it all done before the Germans get here,' Rose said as they headed for the convoy of motor ambulances.

'I hope so too. They've done a lot in the past two years.' She opened the passenger door for Rose. 'I must admit, I'll miss our cosy mess hut until we get it back. I need to report to Lieutenant Colonel Stacy, so I'll see you at the 10th.' She gave Rose a warm smile and a wave.

Rose had not been sorry to see Kit McNaughton and some of the other nurses leave, but Connie Keyes was a kind, yet fearless, head sister. She seemed to prefer honey rather than vinegar in her approach to leadership and Rose welcomed the encouragement. Sister Keyes had been a very calming influence on fresh nurses facing the constant shelling around them.

'Nice day for it, wouldn't you say, Sister?' Rose agreed with her driver. She looked up to the clear blue sky then recognised the driver. 'Lance Corporal Townsend, isn't it?'

He grinned. 'Got it in one. You might want to hang on. She's a bit rough on the road.'

Rose was soon gripping her seat for dear life.

The road was more of a goat track, marred by a series of shell holes and twisted metal. There was not a tree to be seen along the side of it, just shards of blackened wood jutting from barren earth. Townsend weaved among discarded wagon wheels, the bodies of horses and snarls of wire. Rose started to keep her eyes trained on the back of the ambulance in front.

'Not a pretty sight, is it?' Townsend shouted over the rumble of the engine and the barrage starting in the distance. 'Looks like a busy morning for Fritz.'

Rose looked at the clouds of dust on her right. 'What about the men? If we're not there?' Townsend pursed his lips but remained silent. Without the 2nd in position close by, many men would probably not receive crucial treatment in time.

'Fritz must be putting the wind up for the order to move. He's a stubborn old geezer. I thought we'd be done last Christmas but now he's pushing hard for the upper hand. Poor bastards … I mean blokes … heading back into it.' Townsend shook his head.

For a moment everything faded. There was just Leo's eyes inviting her in, his lips touching hers. A flash of heat.

Boom! The ambulance skidded and rocked, then the world was tumbling and tumbling.

Chapter Forty-Five

26 March 1918
Hébuterne, France

'Now there's a good sign,' Leo commented dryly. Bull joined in with the other men calling out insults of varying degree. Nine staff officers had jammed themselves into a tiny car and were making great pace through the 13th's marching column—going in the opposite direction.

'That lot have more yella' in them than a dingo,' Bull declared.

They were marching as part of the advance party, which meant they were the first to come across a disorganised dribble of retreating Tommies, Froggies and Yanks, who all seemed to offer the same warning: 'The Bosche are close and they've got tanks galore.'

Then came the low rumble coming from clouds of dust. Leo's nose sucked in petrol fumes.

'Fritz's armoured cars coming from Souastre. There they are!' someone called out.

The puttering and clanking grew louder.

'Shit! They've been after us for miles,' Bull cried.

Officers sprang into action and gave hurried instructions, telling them to get their rifles ready to take out the men sitting on top of the tanks. Leo squinted into the dust, rifle ready. He then frowned at the odd sight as the air cleared. Were they French?

Bull obviously had doubts too. 'There aren't any French units out this way, are there?' He started to bray like a donkey.

'*Bon jour! Bon fortune!*' greetings were called out over the noise of the motors. French farmers perched on heavy motor plough tractors were waving cheerfully to them.

'Those Frogs have no idea we nearly shot them to pieces,' Leo chuckled.

'Yep.' Bull stood up and stretched. 'Can't say I'm too disappointed.'

'Yeah, I don't like the thought of tanks blasting at us,' Leo agreed.

Much like the thought of Harry's reaction to losing Rose to his best mate.

Leo chewed his lip. He couldn't do this. Have it hanging over him. It was as bad as sitting in a trench waiting for jump off, wondering what the next stunt would hold. Why was he so worried about telling Harry? It was hardly like they were good mates anymore. He sighed. For some reason, he still wanted Harry to think well of him. It was okay for him to disappoint Leo, but he'd never let Harry down. Until now. Things changed. He'd tell him tomorrow.

They marched on.

Later that afternoon, Bull and Leo and a few others, who were crack shots, were asked to join the officers on a scouting patrol. Apparently, General Brand was tired of hearing rumours and wanted to see things around Foncquevillers for himself.

'Don't get me wrong, I like Brand, but the silly old blankard's asking to be shot,' Bull said as they plodded across an open field.

'Sure is,' Leo agreed. A flicker of movement caught his eye, and he froze, rifle ready.

'What is it?' Bull whispered. Leo frowned. Was that George? What the—?

It was George and he was creeping behind a copse of trees. Alfred pushed past them and weaved up to be alongside the general.

'What are those two up to?' Leo mused.

'Go and keep an eye on George, I'm going up with Alf,' Leo said and took off after Alf while Bull tailed George. He trudged beside Alfred, who gave him an irritated frown. Leo saw Bull slip behind a large oak.

'Someone go on ahead and check that barn', Marks ordered.

Leo pushed Alfred forward. 'Fanshaw is a great scout, one of the best.'

'Go on then, Fanshaw. Quick march,' Marks nodded towards the barn.

'No, I … fine.' If looks could kill, Leo would be mutton chops.

Crack! 'Get down!' Leo barrelled in to the general, knocking him down to the chalky dirt.

'What the devil are you doing?' Brand sputtered as he retrieved his helmet and jammed it on his balding head.

A bullet kicked up dust just ahead.

'Take cover!' Leo warned.

A few more shots were pumped out, then silence. They dusted themselves off and returned fire until Marks was satisfied the 'German' sniper was long gone.

Once they were back near the windmill, where everyone was preparing for the forthcoming attack, General Brand asked Leo to stand forward. The general's hooded eyes sparkled at him. Leo turned to face the mass of soldiers. He stared at their warped reflection in the general's polished boots. What a big fuss over nothing. Brand commended Leo's brave actions and suggested there could be a medal in the works for him.

'We need more men like this if we are going to win this war,' the general proclaimed to the troops. What a joke. If only he knew Alfred had been plotting for a medal with George's help.

Leo scanned the crowd until he spotted Alfred standing at the back of the mob. Boy, he looked like steam would blast right out of his ears. Bloody idiot could have killed someone.

When Leo rejoined the ranks, Bull told him he'd grabbed George and shaken him like a pup in disgrace until he'd coughed up that he'd only wanted to prove it wasn't safe to go wandering around the field like that. Leo shared his own theory. He was sure Alfred was trying to wrangle a medal by 'saving' the general.

'I think Alf's mind has gone west. What if George had bloody shot someone?' Bull muttered

Leo agreed. 'Too right, he's as barmy as a bandicoot. That bloke needs a spell at Dartford, although Bedlam might suit him more.'

Leo felt a twist in his gut. Things with Alfred were getting out of hand. What else was he capable of?

Chapter Forty-Six

April 1918
10ᵗʰ Stationary Hospital, Saint-Omer

24 March 1918

Dearest Rose,

I hope you are being a good patient for the nurses of the 10ᵗʰ, or even better you are back on duty after your tumble in the ambulance. I'm sure the scar is not as bad as you think- at least you'll have a war wound to tell tales about later.

How is Elise? What a surprise that must have been to find her at the 10ᵗʰ. I think it's good to have a familiar face around. Friends can get you through a lot and I think, from what they are saying that you'll be very busy soon and will need a friend to lean on. I can tell you don't like her gossiping, but I don't think she does it to be mean.

I'm not sure Harry and I will be friends once I tell him about us- I admit I am still working up the courage.

Neuve Eglise is such a dreary place that I think spring has abandoned it much like its citizens. Most of it is shattered by shells and we have tried to warn the few who are determined to stay that the Germans are coming. They smile and tell us, "Eggs fini, monsieur; plus de lait, mais plentee pomme-de-terres" and continue serving us our chipped potatoes and coffee. I was having a meal and a shell hurled all sorts, smashing the last of the windows in the place and the French just nodded their heads and said, "Les sales Bosches!" and served me another coffee. Can you imagine! I guess they'll stay if they can- where else have they got to go?

We had a big Battalion sports day and I was doing pretty well in the lightweight boxing but Tossie Andrews and Private Copeland ended up in the final, going at it for 15 rounds so have to say I was happy to sit that one out. Got to watch some surprisingly good soccer matches. We moved out to Waterloo Camp the next day where we defeated the 15th in the final and won the Brigade Cup.

I was happy Major Murray has been made a Lt Col and is in command so we should be right. We've been told the Germans are making a rapid advance towards Amiens and Paris so we are heading off tomorrow and will be back in it before long. I must admit I'm not all that keen to get stuck back in. It's like watching a huge, black storm cloud heading your way when you're already drenched from the last downpour.

I miss you. I was hoping we could try and get some leave together but Fritz has other ideas so it will probably be a while before I see your beautiful smile, kiss those soft lips and hold you in my arms again.

Take care (no more ambulance rides for you).
Yours,
Leo.

Rose ran her finger along the jagged scar on her forehead. One day it would be strange telling war stories about how she got the scar. After the war, Rose was often so busy as a nurse that she barely had time to ponder life beyond the war. Would she travel back to Sydney and try to convince her father that she would make a great doctor? Would she go back to London and see if Miss Garrett Anderson was serious about helping her become a doctor? What would Leo be hoping for?

She gazed at Leo's photo. How was it that the thought of being a doctor or being with Leo filled her with the same excitement?

Elise came into the attic of the convent where Rose and a couple of other nurses from the 2nd were being billeted, and Rose quickly put Leo's letter in her pocket.

Elise rubbed her arms and sat on the cot next to Rose. 'It's freezing in here. I heard you'll be off to Hazebrouck with the 1st and the 17th, so I came to give you these.' Elise handed her a tin of toffees. 'It's been good having you here.'

Rose waved the toffees away. 'No, you keep them.'

'Please take them, Mother will send me more.'

Rose took them with a smile. Elise picked up the photograph from the floor. 'Isn't that Leo?'

Rose gave an inward groan. The cat was out of the bag now. Rose nodded. She saw Elise's face flicker with curiosity and something else. Oh, Elise liked Leo.

'I'm sorry I didn't tell you. I thought Leo had deserted and was a coward so there was nothing to tell then he found me over here and explained things and well ...'

Elise held up a hand, 'Don't tell me the rest, I can see it.'

'See what?'

'You love him.'

Rose didn't know what to say. 'Oh.'

'It doesn't matter as I'm here to be a nurse,' Rose declared.

Elise gave a disgusted snort. 'You can't be serious. Look down there.'

Rose looked out of the attic window down onto an arriving convoy of wounded. 'After everything you've seen, you would choose this over love?'

Elise was far from impressed, it seemed. She tapped Rose's scar. 'You've done more than your bit. I know you want to impress your father and maybe even earn his forgiveness, but it's too high a price. It wasn't your fault.'

Instead of feeling comforted by Elise's words, Rose felt a searing heat. She could almost imagine Elise gossiping to everyone to have gleaned such an insight. She was *not* trying to become a doctor to get her father's forgiveness. If she wanted that, she would have stayed at home and nursed her poor mother like he wanted.

Rose stood and faced Elise. 'Don't think you know what's going on with me just because you helped us after Edward died.' She pointed her finger. 'You probably gushed to half of the mountains how crazy my mother was while pretending you cared. You're nothing but a heartless gossip.'

Elise flinched as if Rose had slapped her. 'I did care.' She left the room without looking back. Rose threw the tin of toffees against the door and watched them skitter across the floor. Guilt pinched her. She shouldn't have yelled at Elise for seeing the truth. A truth that soured her stomach. Rose set her jaw. It didn't matter why she wanted to be a doctor. She was going to do it no matter what. Love would have to wait.

Chapter Forty-Seven

26 March 1918
Hébuterne, France

Leo cautiously pushed the old cellar door open. The putter of machine guns sweeping the main road of the village barely registered as he focused on creeping into the inky folds of the fusty room. His fingers crept along the rugged stone walls until the texture changed. Hessian sacks seemed to be stacked along one side. Harry bumped into him with a grunt and lit a match.

'Struth, would you look at this? I'm sure the Frogs won't mind sharing a bit.' Harry lit a lantern. He jimmied out the cork with a soft pop and started to guzzle down a bottle of wine.

Leo found another lamp and shut the door. The cellar was a French ordnance store stacked with sacks of flour, rice, beans, and tapioca. There were hundreds of neat French military uniforms and overcoats neatly folded on some shelves. Harry shed his tattered greatcoat for a new French one.

'These are a bit heavier than ours but I'm a damn sight warmer, I tell you. We'll have to get some for the boys,' Harry said as he admired his new acquisition. He threw one to Leo, who immediately got an icy chill.

'What's up? Someone walk over your grave?' Harry sat stroking the sleeve of his new tunic.

'I dunno. I think I'll stick to khaki. Something doesn't feel right about the jackets. Maybe if the Frogs spot us wearing 'em and we don't speak French, they might think we're spies and shoot us on the spot.' Leo folded the jacket and put it back on the pile. 'Take off the jacket, Harry.'

'You really need to lighten up,' Harry slurred as he made his way through another bottle. 'Always letting your imagination get carried away with you.'

'We're on duty; someone's bound to notice you're pissed. Let's keep moving.' Leo took the bottle from him.

'Still gutless as ever, aren't you?' Harry tried to grab the bottle back.

'Stealing from the French isn't brave, Harry. It's stupid. Put the jacket and the booze back and let's go,' Leo urged.

'Shit! No way!' Harry froze. Leo followed his transfixed gaze. On a sack of tapioca, raised on its ample haunches, was a huge rat. Part of its ear was missing.

'I'm done for.' Harry raised the bottle, gulped long, then pulled one arm out of the jacket. The rat twitched its whiskers, which seemed to make its teeth look even larger. Its tail hung from the sack like entrails. Leo found himself taking a step back, unable to reassure Harry at all.

Alfred, George and Bull stumbled through the door, sending the rat scurrying.

'What's going on here? I'll have you up on charges for this.' Alfred waved his rifle around the room. 'Pilfering from the French and being drunk on duty might keep you in shackles for the rest of the war. It's a shame they don't hang useless thieves like you two.'

Harry recovered himself and took another swig. 'I dunno, I wonder what they'd think of two blokes plotting to kill a general.'

Bull grabbed Alfred as he raised his rifle. George squawked and took off out of the cellar.

'What's that, Harry?' Bull threw the rifle aside.

'Nothin', just somethin' I heard around the traps. Might just be another furphy, hey Alf,' Harry said congenially. Rumours were always rife in the trenches, but this wasn't a rumour. He raised the bottle to Alf.

'I don't know what you're talking about, Fuller. I'm going, we are meant to be getting in position soon, you know.' Alf twisted out of Bull's grasp, snatched back his rifle, headed to the door, and held the battered doorknob before he turned back. 'You're not the only one who's heard a furphy. I've heard that your girl is Rose Shipley.'

'Yeah, so what of it?' Harry said as he swayed.

Leo's jaw tingled like he was going to vomit. Where was Alf going with this?

'*So*, I heard another furphy about that. Your old mate here has been kissing your girl behind your back.' Alfred closed the door. They could hear him chuckling as he crunched away.

221

Leo sucked his breath in hard. Damn it.

'Is that true?' Harry slurred.

Leo gave a slow nod.

'This cellar is full of stinking rats.' Harry glared at him and threw the empty bottle so hard it smashed against a crate.

'Easy there, Harry. We don't need to tell Fritz where we are,' Bull said. He guided Harry to sit on a lumpy sack, away from Leo.

'I didn't mean for anything to happen.' Even to his own ears, he sounded pathetic.

Bull sat on a crate of wine between them.

'Sure, you didn't mean to kiss your best mate's girl.' Harry rolled off the sack and grabbed another bottle. 'So, what are you expecting me to just step aside and let you have her?' His face twisted as he struggled to pop it open.

'Yes, uh, no. I mean it's up to Rose, really. She wasn't very happy about you having a go at her for coming over here. Besides, it's not like you own her or anything—'

Harry's eyes sparked and he flung the bottle back into the crate with a clang

'Enough Harry. Every German within ten miles probably heard that,' Bull warned. 'Let's sort out your love lives later. Harry, you'd want to be careful saying anything about shooting at the general. It's your word against his and given your track record, I know who'll they believe. I'd keep me mouth shut tighter than a nun's legs if I were you.' Bull sounded worried.

'Don't worry. Alf's more gutless than Leo here, stealing a bloke's girl,' Harry stumbled then punched Leo fair on the nose. That was it! Time to have it out with him.

'Shut up. I didn't steal your girl. Maybe Rose can do better than a drunken, whoring scab,' Leo roared. He punched Harry in the eye, watched him tumble, and stormed out of the cellar. Leo charged down the dirt road until the burn of a streaking bullet grazed his cheek.

He dropped and commando crawled to the next cottage and sat against the rough walls taking in gulps of frosty air. That was close! He needed to pull his head in. His fingers uncurled and the tightness in his chest loosened. Harry shouldn't have heard it from the likes of Alf. Harry was right, he had no guts. He should have owned up earlier.

'Leo,' Bull whispered, 'Are you all right?'

'Yeah'

He shuffled up next to Leo.

'I'll tell you, that Harry's a bit of work but … well … he's taken it hard, started crying into his bottle when you left. Either way, he's in no state to jump off tonight. We need to see if we can get him back somehow.'

Typical! Leo's fists rounded again. Here they were with the Germans breaking through the line and them having to recapture the village with hardly any men or ammunition—and now this.

'Maybe we can just lock him in the cellar until it's over and hope Fritz doesn't hold on and keep the village,' Leo whispered.

'Might not be a bad idea if we can't get him back,' Bull agreed. 'Let's go get him.'

They scrambled across the road and made their way back only to find the cellar empty.

'Shit! Where in the hell is he?'

They scoured the dark streets, asking anyone they bumped into if they'd seen Harry. Nobody had.

'He's probably passed out in a yard somewhere. I don't know how we'll ever find him in the dark,' Bull said.

'We can't look much longer, we've got to—'

The sound of splintering wood and shouts filled the still night air.

'Fritz has got him!' Bull said.

Throwing caution aside, Leo bolted towards the commotion. Shadows of other men joined him.

'You bastard, I'll get you for this!'

It was Harry, but where was he and who was he yelling at? A putrid smell filled the air. Leo told the others to get down while he lit a match. Bull leaped back as he realised he had nearly fallen through some rotted wood on top of a crumbling ancient well.

'Who's that?' Harry called from its depths. Harry hadn't been so lucky. He had fallen through.

'It's me, Leo.'

He stood gingerly on the wood and held another match over the top of the well. Hell's bloody bells! Harry was struggling to stay afloat in the slimy filth, his heavy French coat weighing him down.

'Try and get your coat off,' Leo urged while motioning to the others to clear the timber so he could get a better look.

'I can't, this bloody Frog suit is glued to me.'

Harry's head dropped below the scum's surface. Leo grabbed Bull's arm.

'Quick! Grab my legs,' Leo commanded. Oh shit, oh shit, oh shit …

Harry re-emerged, gasping for air. Leo was lowered down while Jack kept up the light.

'Grab hold, Harry!' their fingers were nearly touching, 'Lower, I need to get lower.'

The men tried to form a human ladder but the walls of the well began to crumble.

'Careful, or we'll lose the lot of you,' Bull warned.

'Hold on, nearly there,' Leo grunted. Harry tried to reach up but was sinking further. He pulled back his hand when a section of the well wall showered them.

'You're my best—' he sank into the slime, leaving a cluster of bubbles.

'Nooooo!' Leo felt around the oily water as clumps of stone plopped into the cesspool. Harry! Oh God, no.

Some rifle shots rang through the air. Their light had been spotted. Jack gave the order to heave Leo up. Leo held his head, not caring about the filth oozing down his face.

'Come on, we've got to get out of here,' Bull urged him.

'We can't just leave him in there. Give me another go,' Leo pleaded.

'We won't be able to get him out and we will probably get shot trying,' Bull said softly.

'He's my best mate. We can't just leave him,' Leo's voice cracked.

'Okay, one last go.'

Leo was lowered down again. Lower and lower. His fingers groped the filthy muck. Nothing. He took a deep breath. He moved deeper to the left, gagging on the fumes. There! He grabbed something. It was Harry's arm.

With a desperate lunge that almost caused Jack to drop him in it too, Leo yanked Harry's head up and gripped under his arms.

'Found him! Pull us up.'

With some effort, they were hauled up. Everyone collapsed on the cool ground, puffing.

'I'm real sorry.' Bull's warm arm wrapped around Leo's shoulders. 'I think he's done in. He's not …'

One of the blokes was clearing his mouth. He then pressed down on his chest. Harry was so still. Leo looked away.

'So stupid ... stupid way to die ... down a bloody well. Not shot up, hung on the wire or bombed ... not even Fritz taking him prisoner ... drowned in a bloody well. If I hadn't—' Leo gabbled.

'Don't start that, Leo, you'll go mad. It was an accident, mate. No one's fault.'

It was. He should have been there. Salty tears dribbled into his mouth. If only he hadn't followed Rose around London like a lovesick puppy. If only they hadn't kissed. If only he hadn't argued and charged off like a wounded bull, he'd have been there. If ... if ... if ... icy fingers clenched his heart.

Then he heard it. A cough.

'I don't believe it, he's okay. He'll be bloody sick after swallowing that muck, but he's alive.'

Bull's words filled his hollow gut. Harry was alive.

'Harry, chum, are you still kicking?' Leo cradled Harry's head. Bullets started whizzing and the other men scattered.

'I feel like I fell down a well,' he croaked.

Leo chuckled.

Bull gave Harry's shoulder a squeeze as Harry pulled himself to a seated position.

'We'd better get moving. I don't think you'll be fit for a while, Harry. I'll go find a medic for you. Go take cover back in the cellar, 'Bull said. He slung his gun over his shoulder and crept into the shadows.

Leo helped Harry back to the musty cellar, lit a candle and changed him into one of the clean French uniforms. They sat on some sacks of tapioca.

Apart from throwing up on the way there, Harry hadn't uttered a sound.

'Are you sure you're okay?' Leo asked, handing him his canteen.

Harry nodded. 'I'll live.' He wiped a rag over his dirty face, his eyes glinting in the soft glow of the candle.

Leo rolled his aching shoulders and stretched his back. 'That's good.'

Harry sighed. 'Thanks for, you know—'

Leo smiled. 'That's what mates are for, ay?'

Harry didn't smile back.

He stared at the stacks of uniforms. 'You might have saved me life, but I'm not so sure you're a mate anymore. As for Rose, I'm not giving up that easy.'

Chapter Forty-Eight

10 April 1918
Ana Jana Siding, Hazebrouck

'Sister Shipley, would you please attend that man over there? The Frenchman,' Major Kennick pointed. Rose was supposed to be on a tea break but couldn't resist helping in the dressing room. The convoy of wounded had come in at 7.30 that night and even though it was close to midnight, it showed no sign of stopping. The Hazebrouck and Bailleul areas were being heavily bombarded and Rose knew all three clearing stations lined along Ana Jana Siding were beginning to overflow with men.

'*Bonsoir*,' Rose began. She held her lantern closer to the man who was now trying to sit up. 'Harry? Where's your tag? Why are you in French uniform?'

'Is that really you, Rose?' He peered at her then pinched his arm. 'I am alive. I dunno where my tag is but I've been shot in the arm here.' Rose checked him over and made a tag. GSW. She crinkled her nose.

'I'll be right,' Harry said with a dimpled grin.

'No, it's not that. I mean, it's awful you've been shot, but I know you'll be fine. It's that, even for here, you're a bit on the nose.'

Harry's grin widened even further. 'Smell like a Froggie, don't I? I tell you, you don't ever want to take over their trenches. See, I heard about—' His smile faded.

Rose touched his good arm. 'What?'

He looked away. 'I heard about you and Leo.' His eyes told her everything.

'I meant to write and tell you, but Leo thought it would be better—'

Harry still wouldn't look at her. 'Alf told me. Leo didn't have the guts. I was wearing the Froggy suit, ended up down a well and Leo got

226

me out. I was told to head back to a CCS as a walking wounded due to the muck I swallowed.'

Rose moved closer to hear him. 'I was on my way when some new Froggy recruits got a bit excited that I didn't speak French. The idiots thought I was a spy and locked me up for a few days. Some German could speak English and set them straight.'

'How did you get shot?' Rose asked as she sat him up and removed the smelly overcoat.

'You'd have thought I would've dumped the coat, but I didn't have anything else, and it was cold enough to freeze a witch's ... ah ... it was cold. The same bloomin' recruits thought I'd escaped and took a shot until the *capitaine* pulled them up. I didn't like the Frenchies much, but like 'em even less now.' Harry finally looked at her. 'I'd forgotten how beautiful you are.'

Rose felt the heat rise. Embarrassment, not passion.

'So, what's his problem?' Major Rennick asked.

'Unrequited love,' Harry said with a grimace.

'Now, now, Private.' He checked Harry's tag. 'Do you want to have a go? I'll never get through this lot without some help.'

'What? Get the bullet out?' Rose asked. Her fingers tingled. Some minor surgery experience.

Harry paled. 'Sir, if it's all the same, I'd rather wait for you.'

Major Rennick chuckled as he walked away. 'You're in good hands, Private, whereas mine are rather full.'

Harry looked at the chaos around him and nodded.

Rose unfolded her chatelaine, the wallet that she wore around her waist, and searched through her instruments. No, of course there would be no scalpel among the forceps, scissors and thermometers. It would need to be sterilised anyway. She asked an orderly to go and fetch her one. Harry lay quiet until she was handed a scalpel.

'You're not going to cut into me, are you?' Harry started to tremble.

'For goodness sake, Harry. Stay still and let me work. You don't want that bullet in there any longer than necessary. We're taking in hundreds of blokes tonight, so I don't have time for any nonsense.' Rose jabbed him with a needle. 'Some morphia should help.'

'So, I haven't had any letters from you for a while,' Harry muttered as she worked.

'Nor have I from you. I did think I saw you back in December at Trois Arbres though,' she said casually as she dug around for the bullet. She motioned for the orderly to hold the lamp closer.

Harry winced. 'Ow. I can still feel that. I guess I deserve it. It's you I love, Rose.'

Rose handed him the bullet. 'I doubt that, Harry. I don't think you really understand what love is. I know you're not the serious type, so that's fine. Still the VD crew. What would your mother think?'

Harry's eyes darkened. 'How would I know? She dumped me on the church steps when I was a baby.'

Rose gulped. She touched his hand, then not knowing what to say, slipped back into nurse mode. 'Make sure you keep that bandage as clean as you can until you get to the 10th.'

Harry turned the bullet around in his fingers. 'You're wrong, Rose. I can be serious, and I'll prove it to you one day.'

'The evac tent is over there. Get some tea and a biscuit, it could be a bit of a wait.' She looked at his haggard face. 'I am terribly sorry about things between us but please don't punish Leo for it. He—'

'No, Rose. I don't want to hear about Leo. *Au revoir, ma belle*'

Guilt and relief washed over her. Harry would be fine. He'd move on and forget all about her.

'Sister Shipley, you're due in theatre. Thank you for your help tonight.' Rose groaned at Major Rennick's words. Lieutenant Colonel Quick would be angry if she didn't get there on the double. If only her limbs would cooperate with the urgency of her mind. She made her way to the co-joined Swiss cottage tents and willed her eyes to stay open.

'Thought the war'd be over by the time you got here,' Lieutenant Colonel Quick muttered as Rose entered.

'I was helping out in the dressing room.' She quickly checked the instruments were ready.

It was relentless. The bloodied heaps with horrific injuries kept coming. After three of the longest days of her life, they were ordered to pack up and move again, then it was another four gruelling days at Blendecques.

Major Rennick was relieved to have her return to the dressing room tent. 'Thank God, would you get to removing some of these bullets?'

She checked the tag of the nearest man. 'GOK'. What was a 'God Only Knows' doing in the dressing room? He should have been sent to the resus tent or maybe, by the look of his injuries, to the moribund tent. His head was sliced like a melon. The taste of her recent coffee rose to the back of her throat. Caffeine was no match for the weariness that seeped into her bones.

'Love, don't look at me like that.' Rose's heart leapt at his words. This man should not be talking. Rose took his hand.

'I'm a lucky bastard. Got a Blighty, that's all. Go help me digger, Tom, over there. He's got three young boys back home,' he said with a wheeze.

Rose squeezed his hand and went to his friend. A broken femur, multiple gunshot wounds, but nothing that should kill him. She looked up to tell his mate. She nodded that Tom was going to be fine. The soldier's bright blue eyes brightened he grinned, then his eyes faded into stillness.

Rose froze and held her chest. God, she wanted to sob forever. Or was that a scream?

'Sister? Are you—' Major Rennick asked softly.

'Tom here has a fractured femur and multiple gunshot wounds. I'll get him moved to pre-op as soon as possible.' She checked his forehead. There was no 'AT' written there. 'He also needs his anti-tetanus shot.'

Major Rennick nodded. 'I'll take it from here. Why don't you take a minute and get some fresh air?'

Rose all but sprinted outside. She leaned against the tent and watched the chaos around her. Trucks pulling in, wounded being unloaded, a train pulling out, bombs booming everywhere. It felt like she was the only thing standing still among the melee of destruction. It felt like she would never be able to move again.

Chapter Forty-Nine

12 April 1918
En route to 10th Stationary Hospital, Saint Omer

The London double-decker bus bumped over the edge of a shell hole, banging Rose's sleeping head against a window. She rubbed her scarred forehead then glanced out of the rain-streaked window at the last glow of light on a miserable day. They were still crawling among the throngs of French refugees fleeing west.

After being told to pack up Ana Jana Siding and move again within three days, Rose felt a bit like a refugee herself. They were on their way back to the 10th until their camp was set up again. Rose stretched and thought of Elise. She had no desire to see her again. Good grief, Rose had pointed a finger at the poor girl. She leaned a burning cheek against the cool glass of the window. Maybe Elise would forgive her.

A donkey brayed at the bus as it rumbled past and Rose looked more closely. Among the motley collection of the French refugees with their wagons, cows and horses, and the wounded soldiers, there was a woman bending over. No one stopped with her, they just trudged around her and kept going. The woman's shawl dropped from her shoulders and Rose could see she was clutching a heavily pregnant belly.

Rose stumbled her way up to the driver. 'There's a pregnant woman in trouble back there, we need to stop.'

The driver kept his eye on the crowded road. 'Not likely, we'll get mobbed.'

'What's the problem?' Sister Keyes asked as she rose from her seat.

Rose pointed back to the struggling woman. 'I think she's in labour.'

'Stop the bus, Private,' Sister Keyes ordered.

They sloshed through the mud to the woman who was now kneeling.

'*Bonsoir, Madame,*' Rose greeted her and then explained they would like to take her on the bus. The pale woman nodded gratefully, leaned on their arms then sank into one of the bus seats with a groan. The driver rolled his eyes and got them moving again.

A couple of the nurses with midwifery training came forward.

'Sister Shipley, your French is the best. You stay and translate for us.' Sister Keyes looked quite concerned as the woman gave a guttural moan.

Rose held the woman's hand as Sister Spencer nodded her head. 'I know that sound anywhere. She's awfully close. Get some lamps going.'

'Oh goodness, let's stop the bus and—' Sister Keyes waved her arms about. 'Girls, put some coats in the aisle and let's lay her down.'

'*Mon nom est Rose, comment t'appelles-tu?*' Rose asked once the contraction had subsided.

'Felicity.' Rose explained to Felicity that her baby was well on its way and they needed her to lie down so that Sister Spencer could examine her. Felicity kept her eyes on Rose the whole time. Even though Rose reassured her that things would be fine, Felicity looked like an abandoned fawn. Her face creased in pain and she moaned quietly.

'Let's get her on her knees, let gravity do some work,' Sister Spencer said. She rubbed Felicity's back until the contraction ended then hooked her arm under one of her arms while Rose grabbed the other, and they hoisted her up.

'She better not make a mess of my bus,' the driver muttered, earning more than a few dirty looks.

Rose stroked Felicity's tangled hair and started to softly sing a French lullaby that seemed to sooth Felicity's frantic breathing.

'Tell her to push from deep in her belly.' Sister Spencer worked under the folds of Felicity's skirts, preserving as much of her dignity as she could. 'And again … here we go.'

Felicity's deep moan blended into a soft mewling sound and Sister Spencer triumphantly held up a blood-jellied baby. Sister Keyes immediately wrapped it, cord and all, into her woollen scarf.

'Oh, it's a boy. You've had a baby boy.' Rose could barely speak for the tears. '*Vous avez eu un petit garçon.*'

Rose was handed the baby while they worked on delivering the placenta. He lay gazing silently at her in the lamp light. Rose felt a powerful tug in her centre as she touched his tiny fingers.

As soon as she was able, she handed the baby to Felicity, who looked dumbstruck then besotted. *'Je ne nommerai pas lui, Pierre, après son père qui est mort dans cette guerre terrible. Je vous remercie beaucoup de m'avoir aidé.'*

Rose smiled. 'He is going to be named Pierre after his father, who has died in this war. She wanted to thank you all for your help.'

The nurses stayed huddled around their new charges as they inched their way to Saint Omer and finally handed them onto the nuns running a civilian hospital nearby. Rose wiped away a straggling tear and, watched them go. Yet her arms felt peculiar. Empty. A longing she had buried deep bobbed up like a cork in wine.

As they trooped inside the hospital doors, she tried to push the feeling away. To be a doctor, some things would have to wait … or be sacrificed altogether.

'Rose!' Elise rushed up and embraced her.

'I'm so sorry I yelled at you.' Rose hugged Elise hard.

'It's fine, I reflected on what you said and you were right. My gossiping can get out of hand. I should tell you about Adel—' Her brow furrowed as her hand came out of her pocket and she handed Rose a telegram. 'Never mind that now. Your father has been trying to reach you. Failing that, he telegrammed me to let you know your mother is doing very poorly. He says she is no longer safe at Callan Park. He has hired a nurse until you get home.'

Rose stared at Elise. 'Home?'

'Yes, Rose. He needs you to come home. You will go, won't you?'

Rose saw the judgement on Elise's face as she wavered. 'Of course, I will. My family needs me.'

Elise nodded and took her arm. 'I know this is an awful shock. Let's get you a cup of cocoa.'

Rose followed her to the mess hall like a shell-shocked soldier. Yes, of course she would go straight home to nurse her mother. What choice did she have?

Chapter Fifty

April 1918
Boulogne, France

Rose breathed in the exquisite scent of the tiny bottle of French *parfum* she had bought her mother. Unlike the floral scent of the gift that Billy had given her long ago, this one smelt like cinnamon and musk, like one her mother had worn on special occasions. When Rose had gone to boarding school, her mother had dabbed some on a handkerchief for her. Rose had never washed it yet.

She put her mother's bottle aside and dabbed her wrists with her own perfume, relieved to smell something other than the lavender water she used as a disinfectant. She coiled her freshly washed hair up into a chignon and slipped into civilian clothes. Nothing took her further away from the front than a luxurious bath.

Wind rattled at her window, but she was almost glad for the wild weather. It had delayed her journey across the English Channel. The little French hotel in Boulogne was a blessing, but the extra time to ponder wasn't.

Her father knew of her delay and she knew her mother had not just deteriorated in health. He had finally told her that Mama had tried to take her own life by attempting to drown herself at Bondi Beach. He still didn't know how she had escaped or remained missing for so long. Rose tried to search for the feeling she had when she had read of it. There still wasn't one. She felt numb.

She had lost her mother years ago. Still, she had always hoped her mother would find her way back to them—even if she still blamed Rose. Rose could handle that now.

Rose folded her night gown and placed it on a fresh uniform. Sister Keyes had given her extended leave rather than letting her resign. Rose was grateful for Connie's support but knew that she had to face it. Her career beyond nursing her mother was now over. She gave a heavy sigh and made her way outside in search of some dinner. As she walked the uneven stone, her shoe caught and she tumbled into the man in front of her. He turned just as she was about to land in an undignified heap and caught her elbow.

'*Merci*,' Rose said as she straightened.

'Rose! How lovely to see you?'

Rose grinned. 'Always there to stop me making a fool of myself, Major Richmond.'

'Charles will do fine since you are not in uniform.' His smile dimmed as she lost hers. 'What's wrong?'

Rose glanced at some soldiers strolling by and Charles suggested that they move back into the quiet of a tiny café. Once they were seated and had ordered, he asked her again.

'I'm to return home to nurse my mother. She … ah … took a turn and my father feels they are unable to give her the attention she truly needs.' Rose gave the ache in her belly a slight rub. 'How is your father?'

'I am sorry to hear that, you've the makings of a great nurse … and doctor.' He gulped down some coffee. 'My father died just after I made it back.'

Rose fought the urge to embrace him as he bit his lip. 'I am so sorry to hear that.'

'It's the strangest feeling … to be an orphan.' He shrugged. 'I know I'm not a child but …'

'It still feels like you are.' Rose followed his gaze out the window to the ocean in the distance.

'I can handle the large waves of grief. I've learnt to just let them swallow me and I go with it. It's the smaller ones that lap at your feet. You know, a smell that reminds you of them, the way someone might walk by, or an expression they used. That's what catches me off guard.' He drained his cup and looked at her. 'Enough of that maudlin talk.'

Rose was overwhelmed by his candour. Perhaps it was because he was a war doctor, but the fact that he did not shy away from discussing his grief, Rose felt bolder to share her own.

'I know what you mean. I feel as though my mother is a ghost. I lost the woman who read stories, made madeleines with me and taught me to embroider. Mind, she'd be horrified to know that that I'd always wanted to use that skill to sew people up, rather than make pretty linen for my bridal trousseau.' Rose gave a tiny snort. She fiddled with the napkin. 'I miss her music, her laugh. I don't know how I'm going to nurse what she's become.'

Charles had such compassion in his eyes. How she wished she had ever seen that in her father's. 'It will be difficult, but I know you'll find what you need to do it. You are very resilient and capable. Sometimes we are given tests and we must make sense of them.'

Rose nodded, mulling over what he had said. Having talked about her mother with Leo and now Charles allowed her to finally see that she had been grieving for years. This test must be for a reason. Was she going to be a better doctor for it?

Charles gave a slight cough and Rose's attention snapped back. He touched her hand. 'Please write and let me know how you get on; I've appreciated your letters and must apologise for only sending a couple back once my father deteriorated.' He checked his fob watch. 'I'd better get my transport back. Take heart, Rose. It will sort itself out.'

'I hope so.' Rose tried not to sink with the heaviness now engulfing her. She ordered then toyed with her toast and eggs. There must be a reason this had happened. Was it a punishment she must endure for her carelessness with Edward? Was it to have more compassion and understanding for those with mental illness? She nodded to herself. Yes, that must be it. Rose lifted her head. Well, she would go home and give her mother the tender care she deserved and her father the assistance he needed. She would prove herself to be a capable and efficient nurse but even more a kind and loving daughter. No more running.

She headed back to her hotel and checked for messages at the reception desk.

She was handed two telegrams. One was from her Aunt Jeanne.

I AM TERRIBLY SORRY FOR YOUR LOSS
VISIT ME IN PARIS BEFORE YOU RETURN HOME

Rose frowned. Loss? She tore open the next telegram. It was from her father.

YOUR MOTHER HAS DIED
NO NEED TO RETURN
'*Mademoiselle, Mademoiselle…*' The alarmed voice of the receptionist faded into darkness.

***

Rose followed the concierge's direction and climbed the three flights of stairs then rang the bell, relieved to have finally found her aunt's Paris apartment. Aunt Jeanne pushed past the maid and enveloped her into a maternal hug. '*Mon Dieu, vous regardez tellement comme ma sœur.* Oh, do you speak French?'

Rose nodded 'Yes, of course.'

Her aunt handed her bag to the maid and lead her into a sun-drenched room, where a beautifully laid table was waiting for them. Rose's boots clonked on the Parquet floor, even though she tried to tread more softly.

'So, you had no trouble finding the apartment?' Aunt Jeanne asked.

'Just a little. It's like a village within a village here.' The lower Marais area was a blend of cobbled alleys, courtyards and medieval walls. Rose found it strange that a country-style hamlet could be hidden right in the centre of a city, but that was Paris. She hadn't known what to expect.

Aunt Jeanne nodded as she poured some tea. Rose compared her to her mother. They both had the same glossy, black hair and brown doe eyes, but Aunt Jeanne's nose was sharper than her mother's button nose and her expression much livelier. Or had she just forgotten her mother's same energetic bustle?

For the first half an hour Rose answered her aunt's many questions that skimmed the surface of her life. She offered her another macaroon.

'They were your mother's favourite,' Jeanne sighed. 'Let me tell you a little about my sister. Christiane was much like a delicate flower. Admired, fawned over and beautiful to look at, but she had no roots.'

'No roots?' Rose wasn't sure what her aunt meant at all. Was she jealous of her sister?

'I don't mean she had no family or depth, but her hold on things in life was fragile. If things did not go her way, she withdrew, curled up in a ball, or she pretended whatever it was just wasn't so.' Jeanne shrugged her shoulders. 'She took everything to heart. Music was her saving grace. Did she play often?'

Rose thought of the dusty piano at home. Her maman had played such beautiful music … until Edward had died. 'Until my brother died.'

Jeanne clicked her tongue. 'She should have known to keep playing. I wrote to her telling her so. I should have come when she asked.'

Rose heard the weight of guilt in the words. 'It was my fault. They left me in charge of Edward. I'd disobeyed father and gone into his surgery. I was determined to show him I could be a doctor too. Eddie followed me and got hold of a scalpel. He cut himself and I couldn't save him. Mama was distraught. Like a soldier with shell shock. She fell into melancholy … and never came back. I had hoped one day she would for—'

'Forgive you?' They both had tears dripping into their cold tea. Jeanne put her cup down and waved the maid away. 'Rose, darling. It was a tragic accident, and it seems that Christiane was unable to deal with it. I have my regrets, you have yours, but it is not her forgiveness we should beg. You must forgive yourself.'

Rose wasn't sure how to forgive herself, but for a woman who had been all but a stranger merely an hour ago, Rose felt a strong bond growing. Was this what having a real family felt like?

Chapter Fifty-One

28 April 1918
Villers-Bretonneux

Every time Leo leaned against the hastily dug trench wall, it gave way a little more. He spotted a German helmet in the distance, aimed and fired. The grey figure toppled onto the ground. Nothing stirred in Leo's heart.

It was supposed to be dark, but the Germans were doing their usual light-up-the-night routine with their flares. He would soon be crawling around in no man's land with the 13th to provide cover for the 4th field engineers. They'd been given the job of burning down two aeroplane hangars that the Germans were fond of massing unseen in. Leo knew it wasn't like going over the top for a big stunt, but it was still dangerous. So why didn't he give a rat's?

He didn't like this odd, empty feeling. Did it mean his time was up? He'd watched men … sturdy, brave men … give letters and watches and such to a mate with a grim knowing. Often, they'd been right. Knocked within minutes.

He rubbed his forehead. Maybe he still wasn't over Hebuterne yet? They'd been stuck holding the town for nineteen days without relief. By the time it had come in the form of the 13th Battalion English Rifle Brigade, he hadn't been able to walk half a mile, let alone the four to the bivouacs at Coigneux. He'd dropped by the roadside and slept with his head on a rock. He wasn't the only one. Bull told him it had taken him over eight hours to get there.

Maybe it was finding cellar after cellar full of gassed Tommies or Germans once they'd arrived in Villers-Bretonneux. They'd arrived after the big battle to recapture the town had been won, but holding it was still going to be hard and Leo didn't know if he had the strength left to care.

'Still thinking about Rose? Shame you didn't get to see her before she had to leave,' Bull said in between shots.

Leo could have slapped his head. Of course! He was feeling glum that Rose was going home. It wasn't anything to do with some premonition of death.

'Yeah,' was all he could mumble.

The order to stop sniping and go over the top rippled through. No whistles and warrior calls tonight, just silent creeping then freezing under the light of a flare until you found a good position to lie down and keep watch.

After ignoring the flash of rifle fire as he picked his way across the level field, Leo settled in a position close to the first hangar. It was only about fifty yards from the trench. The cold dampness of the earth soon seeped into his belly and ran along his body, setting his teeth chattering. Bloody hell, he hoped those engineers would get the hangar lit so they could get back soon.

In the distance, he could see Corporal Blaw tipping up one of the petrol tins onto some tinder. By the light of yet another flare, he could see him dousing the material that covered the steel ribs making up the hangar with petrol. Shouldn't be long. No doubt all hell would break loose once the Germans realised what they were up to.

Bull was a few paces back, lying in a shell hole. Leo could just see his head poking over the lip every now and then. Leo took his fingers away from his rifle trigger and blew some air on their numb tips. What was taking those bloomin' engineers so long? Neither hangar was alight.

Chilled to the core, he decided to inch forward and find out what was going on.

'What's the problem? It's freezing lying about in the dirt,' Leo whispered.

'I dunno. This bloody stuff won't light. Must be some kind of inflammable material. Think we are wasting our time.' Leo could hear his frustration.

'Give us a go.' Leo lifted the tin and poured petrol on his handkerchief. He lit a match but as Blaw said, even that wouldn't light. 'Well, my hanky's not inflammable.'

He sniffed the petrol tin, then his hanky. 'You bloody idiots, you've brought the water tins up instead.'

'Shit!' and many other Aussie oaths spilt from the engineers. Given that water was also stored in petrol tins, Leo could understand how easy it was to make such a mistake.

'What's going on? It's as cold as belly-blue hell out here,' Bull grumbled.

'They've brought A's water up here instead of the petrol,' Leo said.

'Are you f—'

Before Bull could mutter another sound, a machine gun within the hangar had sputtered into life, flinging bullets towards them. Bull clutched his arm and dropped to the ground. He was still.

Leo was in a tunnel with one goal—kill the bastards that had mowed down his last mate.

The groans and sobs of the wounded filled the crisp night air between the machine gun bursts. Very lights were popping off so often it was like being caught in a frenzy of photographer's camera flashes. It made it too easy for the gunners to spot them. Rotten mongrels.

Bullets pinged, shadowy men ran around him, but he made his around the hangar to the end where he could hear the clank of the fabric strip of rounds being fed. He waited for the short burst to stop. There were two four-man teams working two guns. When one gun stopped to be cooled with water, the other was supposed to take over, but Leo could hear them cursing and realised the gun was jammed. Time to move in.

His coiled muscles sprang quicker than a cobra strike. One German turned towards him and Leo gave him a perfect throat jab. The thrust up and into the German's spinal cord killed him quickly without a cry. With a slight sucking sound, Leo withdrew his bayonet and stuck it straight into his shocked comrade. One team was dead before the ones trying to fix their jammed gun had even noticed. Leo rushed at the next team with a roar.

Two of the men ran in terror as he jammed the bayonet in. He thrust so deep into the soft flesh of a gunner's gut until he slumped on the end of the now firing gun, upending it and sending bullets through the material above. Leo turned on the other, but he'd bolted. Some *kamerad.*

The desperate pleas of wounded Aussie man stuck out in no man's land echoed around him. One was crying for his mother in a plaintive bleat like that of a lost lamb. The gunner squirmed and uttered a soft moan. Leo yanked his bayonet free and plunged it back into him again and again.

'He's dead, mate. He won't be killing any more boys tonight,' a hand gripped Leo's arm from making another thrust forward.

Bull? Wasn't he ...?

'They couldn't knock old Bull out. Only a scrape.'

'Oh God ... I thought you were ... oh,' Leo stammered.

'Keep it together, Leo. Let's get back to the trench.' Bull clapped him on the back.

Later, Leo huddled miserably with the others with his gas mask on as the Germans hurled every shell they had at them. The air screamed and thudded with sizzling shards of metal and heavy cow pats of earth. Whole tree trunks spiralled to the heavens while antiquated French cottages were pulverised.

A thick curtain of gas enclosed them, filling Leo's throat. He longed to tear his mask off and gulp fresh air but even without the acrid haze of gas, the trenches had the pungent smell of cordite and overflowing latrines. He held his gut, willing it not to empty into his mask.

Hordes of Germans could be coming just behind that curtain at any moment. Leo's mind flooded with a blurry image of the slumped gunner.

If Leo's ma knew what he'd done in this war, she'd be sure her son's soul would end up frying in hell. That wasn't doing his duty. He'd wanted those gunners dead. It had felt good killing them. Seems he was no better than Alfred after all.

Chapter Fifty-Two

30 June 1918
Paris, France

L eo ignored the rowdy soldiers buzzing around him on the Amiens-Paris express and reread Rose's letter.

> *May 1918*
> *Dearest Leo,*
>
> *I hope this letter finds you well (and at all). I am spending some time with my Aunt Jeanne in Paris. She has been a wonderful comfort to me. I last wrote you that my mother was ill, and I was returning home. My mother has since died, and my father requested that I stay here. It seems that my mother's grief was too much to bear.*
>
> *I don't know how to feel. Is it wrong to be relieved that she may have found some peace at last? Or is that wishful thinking and because of the way she chose to die she is burning in hell? I don't think anyone who has suffered so much here on earth would end up in hell, surely not.*
>
> *My aunt is a strong woman but even she is getting a bit nervous about the news of Germans making their way closer and closer to Paris. She has sent her maid to her family down south and is considering whether to escape to the country house in Aix-en-Provence or stay here.*
>
> *I have my own decisions to make. Sister Keyes is happy to take me back in the 2nd ACCS (things have been frightfully busy so I feel guilty but she says to take some time in Paris and decide by the end of June) but I wonder if I should return to my father.*

Does him telling me to stay here mean he no longer wants to see me? Does he blame me for my mother's death? If only I had stayed to nurse her like he asked.

I'm not sure how I feel about returning to the Front. Have I made any difference whatsoever? Can I handle any more of the boys' suffering? My Aunt believes I should continue, become a doctor. She says I have my mother's beauty, my father's determination, and my own courage. I don't know who I am at all.

That's enough of that. I am hoping to see some of Paris while I am here, just in case the Germans do break through. Who knows what they might do to the Louvre, the Eiffel Tower, or the Arc de Triumph. Aunt Jeanne has told me about a wonderful tea house, Laduree, where the hot chocolates are divine. It sounds like a place I may have to visit more than once!

I think of you often. I hope you aren't having too hard a time of it. I will write to tell you what I decide. Take care.

Love, your Rose.

He had gotten leave and was on his way to Paris to surprise her. As the train rocked and swayed, he let his thoughts drift in wafty daydream.

Rose's skin was bathed in the golden glow of firelight. China and glasses clinked as the family gathered to celebrate another Sydney hotel taking up Dymond & Son's fine, quality wine. They cheered when his pa announced an export deal to …

Leo held a chubby toddler son on his hip and pointed to a dark-haired baby girl. 'Meet your new sister.' Rose ruffled the little boy's hair but held Leo's gaze with those deep purple eyes.

They walked together through the vineyard. The afternoon sun sparkled on the rain drops still dripping from the grapevine leaves. Her slender fingers entwined with his. Her soft lips reached for his.

The motion of the train had stopped. The soldiers were whooping as they grabbed their gear. Leo shook off his sleepy daydream state and joined the throng. They left the train, and the Aussies were rounded up to go to their compulsory VD lecture before being let loose on Paris. Leo wondered why they bothered when most of the soldiers would ignore it all anyway. The train had been abuzz with enthusiastic tales of men already fantasising about an '*affair du Coeur*' with the first pretty Parisian girl they could get their hands on. Good luck to 'em. Leo only had one girl he wanted to have an affair of the heart with.

Finally, they all tumbled out of the Caserne de la Pépinière barracks like school children released for summer holidays. Leo's whole body tingled.

Soldiers were flicking through their guidebook, 'Paris in Ten Days' around him but he wasn't interested in cramming in all the wonderful sights. He had to find that tea saloon called *Laduree*. If she wasn't there … no, she just had to be there. He cursed that she had forgotten to give her aunt's address.

He strode down Boulevard Malesherbes. She just had to be there.

His pace eventually slowed, and he allowed a little of Paris in. The wide boulevard was bustling with all means of transport. The fresh taupe apartments in the modern Haussmann style soothed his eye with their classic beauty and uniformity.

They were saved from blandness by ornate wrought iron railings and balconies dotted with red splashes of geraniums. Leo paused to take a deep breath and the tension drained from his body. It seemed that Paris could wash away almost anything.

As he mingled with the crowds, people smiled and greeted him with a hearty '*Bonjour, Monsieur*'. Even their eyes were smiling.

While the Parisian women were in war-sombre greys and charcoals, they spruced up a hat with a vivid red feather or flower. The longer he walked, the less it seemed that Paris was touched by the war at all. Yes. He had made the right decision coming here.

The corridor of silvery plane trees opened to Place de la Madeleine and he finally spotted Rue Royale. Before long, he stood before the mint green and gold of number sixteen. Ladurée. He paused. The bittersweet aroma of melted chocolate beckoned him in. Somehow, he managed to convey in his soldier French to the waif-like waitress that he was hoping to surprise a friend.

She guided him to a small table tucked into the back of the salon. Now he just hoped Rose would show up soon or he would have to haunt Ladurée every day of his two weeks leave.

Ladurée was the most opulent place he had ever set eyes on. Dark panelled walls, wainscoting and gilt accents framed the frescoes. Blimey! Even the roof had oil paintings of plump cherubs and maidens in flowing pastel robes. After he had recovered from the price, he allowed himself to bring the *chocolat chaud a l'acienne* to his lips. The hot chocolate tasted like bitter fudge and was as rich as the chandelier that glittered above him. This would have Bull groaning in ecstasy. How they managed to find the ingredients for the hot chocolate he didn't know, but it was worth the expense.

Small groups of women and a sprinkling of soldiers chatted around him. A table of young women were glancing his way and giggling. One winked at him. Leo found himself getting a bit hot under the collar until he became very absorbed with a painting on the wall. This caused more giggling and they returned to their conversation. He chanced a peek. The three women moved their dainty fingers expressively as they chatted.

Sparkling long-lashed eyes danced above aquiline noses and dimpled cheeks. Rosebud lips bubbled with musical words. These Parisian women were magnetic. Yep, the lecturers this morning were just flapping their gums. What red-blooded Aussie soldier could resist them?

Leo missed Rose so much his gut ached. He had to find her and tell her that while he understood how much nursing meant to her, she meant more to him. He loved her and was going to ask her … wait, was that her?

He'd caught a flash of scarlet among some British and Australian soldiers that were seated a few tables in front of him. Aussie nurses were here too. Was Rose among them? The rich chocolate stuck in his throat. There she was. Rose was gasping at the salon's beauty. His Rose. She was back in uniform. Did that mean she had chosen to stay?

Then she turned. Her eyes widened in delight and she squealed, rushing towards him.

Hey! His view was suddenly blocked by one of the soldiers. He looked familiar. Leo stood and tried to get around the tiny round table. What? Rose was embracing the soldier.

'Harry! What on Earth are you doing here?' Harry kissed her right on the mouth. In front of the whole café. Leo sank back into the chair with a thud. Noooooo! Time warped and shifted like an awkward silent movie. Harry wrapped himself around Rose and kissed her even harder.

'I told you I would show you how serious I am about you one day,' Harry said. He kneeled. Rose grabbed his arm and tried to help him up. Holy … sweet …bloo—. This was a bloody nightmare. Leo knew what was coming but his limbs and mouth were frozen.

'I'm fine, I'm fine. I don't need a hand up,' Harry reassured her. He put his hat on a table, took her hand and gazed up at her. Rose frowned as a couple of nurses gasped.

'Rose, I was hoping you'd do me the honour of being my wife. What do you say?'

The other nurses squealed. 'Oh, how romantic …'

Leo jammed his hat down on his head and slunk past them. He rushed through the Place de la Concorde and charged up the Avenue des Champs-Élysées. The faint perfume of lime trees mingled with a whiff of horse manure. He could smell but his vision was blurred to it all.

He'd left it too late.

***

Napoleon's stern gaze looked over the top of Leo's head. Flowing Grecian robes gave him a Roman emperor's air. Leo moved across the front of the massive limestone *Arc de Triomphe's* arch to examine the scene on the next stone relief. A sword-bearing angel was leading the charge to battle. Was the angel urging them to have courage and forge ahead or was it looking back in anguish? Its pained open-mouthed expression may have mirrored his own face when he saw Rose and Harry kiss.

Leo had calmed down after an hour and gone back to Ladurée, but Rose and Harry were gone. They'd all left. He'd scoured the area around the café but came up with nothing. Paris was such a large city that he despaired he'd find her in the four days left. He wasn't going to let Harry just get away with it. Maybe he'd read things with Rose wrong. Did Rose love him at all?

He'd wandered around until he came upon the *Arc de Triomphe de l'Étoile*. Maybe Rose would still be keen on seeing the sights. Unless she was distracted by Harry. He gulped the hot air, but it bought him little relief. Waves of grief tumbled and dumped their weight over him.

Leo clutched his guidebook and read, desperately trying to swim against the undertow. His guidebook told him these were just a few of the six and a half million that perished under Napoleon's rule. To honour his great victories in battles such as the Battle of Austerlitz and Friedland, Napoleon had dotted Paris with huge monuments. This one was massive.

He stared up at the sculptured flowers of the portico and scanned the row upon row of names inscribed on the pillars of the Jardon, Werle, Béchard, Thomières, Lacoste, Henry, Baste, Repin ... all were underscored ... all had died in battle. These carefully carved letters were names. Names of men. Men with fragile human bodies that were destroyed by other men. No more would these men take up a plough and farm the land, caress a woman's hair or hold a child upon a knee. Now they were just chiselled symbols to be gazed upon a hundred years later. Just a name on a wall.

Anger bubbled up from Leo's gut. What a waste. He wasn't after Napoleonic glory, medals of honour or even having his name stuck on some wall. He hadn't saved his family; he'd probably lost the vineyard and Rose and his dreams of the future. The wave crashed and he closed his eyes. Bereft.

'Are you alright there, Dig?'

Kind, crinkled eyes regarded him under a fresh khaki slouch hat.

'Yeah.'

'Are you sure?'

Leo could only raise a tight smile. 'Do you reckon that's all we'll end up being?'

'What do you mean?' the man's blue eyes clouded in confusion.

'Just some name on a wall. No kids, grandkids to remember us. Just some soldier of the Great War.'

'Jesus mate, that's a bit bloody morbid. I hope we'll be telling our grandkids tales of how we were heroes who stopped the Kaiser in his tracks.'

Leo felt a flush of embarrassment. He did sound morbid, but melancholy had settled deep into the marrow of his bones.

'We've got the Yanks and their tanks onboard now, so I reckon this thing has got to be done soon. Listen, name's Jimmy McDowd, but everyone calls me Macca. I reckon you ought to join me and the boys for a cuppa at Miss B's.'

He nodded at a few other blokes with 45th Battalion patches on their sleeves. Leo had come to Paris with some of the 13th, but he'd noticed that he didn't really take the time to get to know many of them anymore. It didn't seem worth it when often the bloke he'd just had a beer or shared a letter with ended up blown to smithereens or hung on the wire. But this was different. He was in Paris.

'Sounds good, thanks.'

'That's the spirit. Now, are you going to tell me what's really got you all down in the dumps?'

Macca sounded just like his dad.

'Just a bit of girl trouble.'

'Ah. Listen chum, you only live once and you're in the perfect place to find a remedy for that. You might as well enjoy Paree while you're here.'

Leo followed them across the square of Place Vendôme. The six of them stopped to have a closer look at the spiralling bas-relief bronze plates supposedly taken from cannons stolen by Napoleon. They were now moulded scenes depicting his victory at the battle of Austerlitz set on a massive column with Napoleon once again in his Roman toga propped at the top.

'Do you reckon Napoleon would have enjoyed making something out of German tanks?' one of them asked.

'Dunno. I'll say one thing though. Looks like he thought he had a big one to me,' Macca stated. They were still laughing as they entered the Hôtel d'Évreux.

Leo hesitated. 'Are you sure this isn't an officer's club?'

'Pretty swish, isn't it?' Macca replied with a grin as he plonked himself onto a plush chaise longue.

'My oath.'

Leo cautiously checked he hadn't trekked dirt on to the Parquet floor. For the second time that day, he was enjoying a hot chocolate under an ornate chandelier in a room fit for a king. It didn't have dancing cherubs painted on the ceilings like Ladurée, but the wood panelling, embossed wallpaper, gilded mouldings, and white marble fireplace created an atmosphere just as stylish. Who would have thought a bloke from the bush would find himself in a place like this?

Maybe Macca was right. He was alive, even if he did have a broken heart. When was he ever going to be in Paris again? If the Germans got through, who knew what would happen to the grand city of lights?

Leo's brief bubble of lightness popped. He didn't care about being in Paris, what the Germans were doing or even if he never had a vineyard. He only wanted to see Rose. He would scour every monument and attraction that could be on Rose's to-do list.

Chapter Fifty-Three

30 June 1918
Paris

'For goodness sake, Harry! Get up and let me go.' Rose struggled to release her hand from his grip. 'I'm sure I just saw Leo; I must go after him.'

Harry stood but held tight to her hand.

'What are you doing? Let me go.' Harry stood staring at her. 'No, I won't marry you,' she hissed.

The smiles of the nurses and other café patrons who were watching faded, and they awkwardly returned to their meals, discreetly glancing their way now and then.

'There's no need to worry, I'm sure that wasn't Leo. I said I was serious about you. What more could you want than to marry?' Harry sounded sincere and slightly angry. Rose bit her lip. He'd never understand.

'I don't want to marry anyone. I thought you knew that. I went out with you a few times and we've swapped a couple of letters. You barely know me.' Harry dropped her hand, and she ran outside. She scoured the sidewalks but no soldier looked like Leo. She tapped her foot. She was definite. It had been Leo. Right there in that café. Here in Paris.

Harry stood beside her. 'It was Leo,' he admitted. 'You really do love him, don't you?'

'Yes, I do. I may not want to marry but I do love him. How did you both find me?' Rose asked, moving out of the way of a couple of elegantly dressed French woman going into the café.

'I ... ah ... I read your last letter to him and when he got leave to come to Paris, I knew he was coming to find you so decided to pip him at the post.' He looked down at his boots.

'I can't believe you would do that!' Rose turned and walked away. Her cheeks burned at the thought of what she had shared in that letter.

'Rose, wait! I'm sorry.' He caught up to her and puffed alongside.

When he refused to leave her side, she turned on him. 'I don't want to marry you. I don't know what's happened to you, but you've been a terrible friend to Leo, who saved you from drowning in a well and you repay him by trying to steal his girl.'

'He stole you first,' Harry retorted.

Rose almost grabbed the parasol of a woman strolling past to poke Harry with. 'I am not a toy to be quarrelled over. My heart is with Leo,' she snapped.

Rose charged on, only looking back once. He was standing where she had left him, looking like a dejected puppy. Rose shook off any pity. He had left Leo wandering Paris thinking that she loved Harry. She prayed Leo hadn't jumped on the first train out of there ... or off the first bridge he found.

Chapter Fifty-Four

1 July 1918
Paris, France

The red quartzite sarcophagus rested on the solid green granite base. It was massive and despite being surrounded by stunning figures in marble drapes, to Leo it seemed a bit lonely.

'I wonder what Napoleon would have made of this war,' Leo whispered to Macca.

'I dunno but given how many big battles we've been in, he would have spent the next hundred years building stuff to celebrate how great he was,' Macca said loudly, ignoring the signs for silence in the tomb. Macca scratched his head and looked up. Above the crypt was a giant dome covered in beautiful paintings.

'I know one thing; we won't see anything like this back in Aus. This place is beaut. All those weapons, suits of armour and maps and stuff all about war. I wonder what they'll stick in here for this one,' Macca said.

Would their uniforms and rifles and other stuff end up on display in some museum like the Chinese war costumes they'd just looked at in the Musée de l'Armée at Les Invalides? How weird would that be?

Macca tapped his fingers on the marble balustrade.

'I think I've seen enough for now. Some of the boys were going to head over to 'Les Belles Poules' or 'As de Coeur'. Those girls will help you forget all about Rose.'

Leo couldn't be swayed.

'You've looked everywhere and she's with that bloke, Harry. You might never get to see Paris again. I heard the girls are gorgeous and only wear stockings and a scarf … did I mention *only* stockings and a scarf?' Macca said with a cheesy grin.

Leo grinned. No girls at 'The Beautiful Tarts' or ''Ace of Hearts' would have a patch on Rose. 'Not for me, I don't really want that kind of Parisian souvenir.'

Macca nodded. 'Yeah, not really my cup of tea either. Maybe we can promenade down the Chomps Deleezy and find one of the joy girls to take to the Omnia for a movie. Hey, are you going to show us those pics you got developed? Got one of Rose?'

Leo touched his paybook. Bull had taken some photos of Rose at the CCS for him. He dug through and found one.

'Bloody hell, you didn't tell me she looked like that. No wonder you haven't given the Frenchies the time of day.' Macca whistled his appreciation. Leo closed his eyes.

'Sorry, Dig. How about I leave you to it for a bit?' Macca handed back the photograph, chucked him under the chin and left.

Leo walked out of the domed tomb, back along the corridor past the courtyard, over the cobblestones and exited through the decorative scrolls of the gate of honour. To his left, the Eiffel Tower loomed above the creamy buildings, but he continued towards the glass dome of the Grand Palais. Sunlight sparkled on the cobblestone streets, wet from a recent shower. The smoky scent of roasting chestnuts drifting from a street vendor set his stomach rumbling, but he was captivated by the massive columns at the entrance of the bridge, Pont Alexandre III. A winged horse reared its golden legs above him from its perch at the top of the stone column.

He stepped to a balcony at the side and gazed at the full span of the metal structure. Why had he bothered with Napoleon's tomb? Rose wouldn't go there. This bridge was more like something she would have on her list.

The bridge stretched across the Seine in a sweep of gold ribboned garlands and amazing Belle Époque candelabras. It was the most elegant bridge he'd ever seen. He walked along the bridge that was dotted with soldier tourists, some with French girls, and stopped by a candelabra with cherubs dancing at its base.

Hearing a girl laugh, Leo saw a dark-haired beauty swat a British soldier's arm. Leo's throat squeezed tight. This wasn't how he'd pictured being in Paris at all. He was supposed to be holding Rose's hand, marvelling at the sights and kissing her …

Leo gazed down at the smooth flowing river and took out a carved rose from his pocket. It was his present for Rose. Each heart-shaped petal could be detached. He'd got the idea after watching a little French girl pull petals from a daisy as she recited a rhyme: *Je t'aime ... un peu, beaucoup, passionnement, a la folie, pas tout.* Her mother had told Leo it was a traditional rhyme that said 'I love you' ... a bit, a lot, passionately, madly, not at all.

He pulled the smooth heart-shaped petal and read the words he'd carefully carved. *I love you not at all.* That would never be true. He would always love Rose. He would never be able to tell her. He threw the petal and watched it float down to the caramel coloured water then bob slowly away with the current of the river.

He took the next petal. He had to let Rose go. She didn't want him. If it was meant to be, they would have been together by now. *I love you a bit.* He'd always loved her more than a bit. He clutched the petal then uncurled his fingers.

'Leo!'

A streak of red, grey and white rushed towards him. Warms arms and a cloud of lavender and cinnamon enveloped him.

'I thought I'd never find you,' Rose said breathlessly. 'I know you saw me ... and Harry... I ...'

His heart drummed. Rose had found him, but she didn't owe him anything.

'You don't have to explain,' Leo said as he squeezed the wooden rose so hard it felt like a pinecone in his hand.

'I do have to explain. When Harry proposed to me, I set him straight that you are the man who has my heart.' She folded her fingers over his. 'What have you got there?'

'Uh, a present. For you, actually. I was waiting to give it to you, to surprise you.' He handed her the flower. 'But forget that for now. So, I have your heart?'

'It's beautiful. Oh, it has French words on it. Will you read it for me?' Rose's eyes were sparkling.

He took it from her. 'It says, "I love you a bit". Leo gave her the petal and laughed as her mouth puckered in disappointment. He took another petal.

'I love you a lot.'

She smiled and he fought against the urge to toss the remaining petals in the river and just kiss her.

She took another petal. 'And this one?'

'I love you—madly.'

'Oooh, I do love this present. Now the last petal. How do you really feel about me?' Her cheeks were flushed.

'I love you … passionately.'

Rose beamed. 'You do?'

'I do.'

'I love you too.'

He locked onto her violet eyes and knew he was home. Leo pulled her to him. Heat coursed through him and he wanted to kiss her so hard, devour her, but he let his lips graze hers ever so gently. She was so smooth and soft. His grip around her tightened and he ran his hand down her back as he kissed her more deeply.

She pressed closer and he heard the petals drop onto the bridge. She gave a little moan and her lips parted. His tongue probed tentatively. She met his tongue with her own and he could barely breathe. He wanted every part of her there and then.

His mouth moved to the nape of her neck and his hands cupped her bottom. He knew she could feel him harden and he shifted away. She grabbed his hips and moved her mouth to meet his. Molten liquid. He was disappearing …

'I love you so much. I want you so much,' Leo mumbled into her ear.

'Oh, God. Me too,' came her breathless reply.

'Ah, I see you've found each other all right then.'

Leo and Rose broke apart. Macca wiggled his eyebrows up and down.

'Yes. Thank you so much.'

'She's been looking for you the past few days. I bumped into her. I can see why you've been such a misery guts now but looks like it's all sorted.'

Leo's grin could probably have lit Paris. His cheeks ached. Rose nodded and she collected her petals up.

'Did you want to bring Rose back to Miss Butler's for some tea. She does the most amazing chocolate torte. Or will I leave you to it?' Macca asked. Rose's stomach growled and they all laughed.

'Sorry. I am a bit partial to chocolate.'

'C'mon on then, plenty of time for all that later.' Macca placed himself between them and took both of their arms. 'What plans did you have for Paris, Rose?' Macca asked.

'Oh, she'll have a list,' Leo said.

Rose laughed. 'Yes, I do have actually. I've still got to see Versailles, the Conciergerie, and Notre Dame and … stop laughing at me. What did you want to see, Leo?'

He stopped walking and gazed at her. 'I only came here to see you.'

Macca gagged. 'I don't know if I can handle much more of you two.' He walked on.

'Really?' Rose whispered.

'Really.' He gave her another lingering kiss.

His heart thudded with a familiar staccato beat. This time he wasn't in the trenches about to go over the top. His soldier's heart was beating for Rose.

Chapter Fifty-Five

2 and 3 July 1918
Le Village Saint-Paul, Paris

Leo wiggled his back against the ridge of the wrought iron chair and Rose chuckled.

'They're not particularly comfortable but they are pretty,' she said. She traced the iron lace of the matching garden table.

'No wonder I couldn't find where you were staying, but this place is bonza.' Leo gestured to the neat hedges and lawn of the private garden with its elegant statue of a naked woman as its centrepiece.

'Aunt Jeanne has been so supportive. She was the one that convinced me that returning home would be pointless. Why go and sit in an empty house while my father worked all day when I could be doing something far more useful? I'll miss her when I go back.' Rose sipped her drink but not before Leo noticed her chin quiver. He touched her hand. 'She likes you.'

'She doesn't look much like my ma, but she feels the same,' Leo answered. Just the thought of his ma brought a swell of grief. 'I never got to tell you how sorry I was to hear about your ma.'

Rose looked away and he worried that he should have left things well alone.

'Thank you. I can't help thinking about how she did it … going into the ocean like that…' Rose's lips tightened as a couple of tears trickled down her cheeks.

Leo held her hand tighter.

She sniffed slightly. 'I hope she's with Edward.'

Leo nodded.

'So, are you going to ask me?' Rose raised an eyebrow as she drank a lemon iced tea.

Leo bit his lip and tapped his glass. Ask her what?

Rose grinned. 'Okay, I'll tell you what happened after Harry's proposal.'

Leo sucked in a breath. The worst moment of his life. His fingers gripped the glass.

'Don't look so worried. When I saw Harry down on his knee and heard him asking me to marry him, all I could think was I don't want to get married and certainly not to someone who doesn't love me.' Rose's eyes were as dark as a summer plum. 'Harry didn't take it very well, but I think he realised I couldn't help how I felt.'

Leo held his breath. His heart see-sawed. She didn't love Harry. That was good news. But she didn't want to get married. That was bad news.

Rose wrapped her fingers around his. 'That was when it hit me for sure. The only person I love is you.'

He was on the upswing again. Leo kissed her fingers and she sighed.

'Soooo. Of course, I love you, but you don't want to get married.' Leo tried not to sound like a whiny child.

A soft wind rippled the vine attached to the ancient garden wall behind Rose. She remained silent and he listened to the leaves rustle.

Rose withdrew her hand and scratched her arm. She removed her scarlet cape, hanging it on the back of her chair.

'It's tiresome having to wear uniform while on leave, don't you think? I did enjoy being a civilian for a while, especially when there are so many beautiful dresses in Paris,' Rose skirted. Leo wasn't going to let her off so easy.

'Rose?'

Rose blew a puff of air. 'I'm not sure I want to get married. My mother was lucky to escape the drudgery of housework but doing charity work and sitting in sewing circles ... losing babies. It just seems so pointless compared to nursing over here.'

Leo hadn't thought much about whether his mother enjoyed her life as a wife and mother. She seemed to, especially when it came to helping at the church. What did he have to offer Rose? He slumped against the chair and let the metal dig against the small of his back.

'I guess it doesn't seem that appealing when you put it like that,' Leo muttered.

Rose twirled a tendril of hair around and around her finger and her face glowed red.

'It's really nothing against my mother or other women but I'm not sure that's for me. I just wish I didn't have to choose. I would like nothing more to be sitting by the fire with you, sharing the news and a kiss.' Rose blushed even deeper. 'But I would like to also be able to continue my nursing. I still want to become a doctor.'

She flicked a leaf off the table and sighed. 'Even if I could do both, perhaps I wouldn't be able to do either very well.'

'You wouldn't be doing everything on your own, my ma and Dot would pitch in and we have a heap of people willing to lend a hand. I'd reckon we'd manage. I've heard of some nurses who get married and keep it under their hat,' Leo said eagerly. 'I'd like you to be a doctor. I'd wait.'

Rose looked up at the wrought iron verandah, where Leo noticed her aunt standing in front of the French doors, and gave a tiny wave. 'I couldn't ask you to wait.'

Leo took her other hand as well. 'I would anyway.'

Instead of being happy, he seemed to have made her even sadder.

'Uh, Leo. You're squeezing my fingers off.'

Rose dissolved into chuckles and Leo laughed when she snorted, which only made her snort louder.

'Stop it,' she gasped, swatting his arm.

'I haven't heard you do that before.'

Rose wiped her eyes. 'Oh, my mother would be horrified. She spent years training that out me. Said I sounded like a common farm girl.'

Leo's face turned as stony as the mansion's ornate facade. So that was the real reason. Sitting here, among her opulent French ancestry, it seemed beyond ridiculous that Rose would become exactly that. Rose could never be a common farm girl. The war would end, she'd return home and either obey her father and settle into her pre-destined life as a gentrified wife or rebel and continue her nursing. She might love him, but she wouldn't marry him.

'I've said something terrible, haven't I? I sounded like such a toff then, I'm awfully sorry. I don't mean that being a farmer is—'Leo put his hand up. 'Forget it, Rose.'

Her eyes began to water but Leo stayed a solid rock. Birds twittered around them and the sun heated their iced tea so the glasses beaded and ran like the sweat down his brow, but this little garden wasn't a secret paradise of Parisian love like he'd first hoped when he sat down.

Tears slid down Rose's cheeks. 'Forget what, Leo? Us?'

Anger surged with pride. 'Yes, I think so. I love you and want a future together but now I see that I have no place in yours.'

Rose gripped his hand. 'I love you too. I don't want to get married right now but if I did, it would be to you. Please ask me, I'm sure you'll know the right time to. Don't give up on me, I don't want to lose you.'

Rose's voice caught but her tears flowed freely.

Leo couldn't bear it. Soft as a sun-warmed grape he was. Bugger it, he would have to take what she offered and worry about the future later. Leo moved his chair next to hers and drew her into his arms until her sobs softened. She let go and blew her nose until it was red.

'Between snorting and being snotty, I'm a real prize, aren't I?'

Leo stroked her blotchy cheeks. 'Yes. No matter what, I think you are.' He bent his head down and touched her salty lips.

Their lips locked and their tongues danced. Leo pulled her tighter. He could feel the blood pumping through his temples and his groin. He moved his lips to her ear lobe and nibbled. Her breath was coming in short gasps. He slid his hand from her back and felt the curve of her breast. Oh Lord, if they continued like this, he was going to burst like a summer cloud.

The gravel crunched behind them and they broke apart. Aunt Jeanne held a fresh pitcher of iced tea. 'I think it is getting too warm to sit in the garden any longer, yes? Perhaps another glass of tea?'

Leo quickly released Rose and she blushed as she pulled herself upright. '*Merci*. So, what shall we visit tomorrow?' She looked at Leo, trying to keep a straight face. 'How about Notre Dame?'

Leo swallowed down a bubble of naughty schoolboy laughter. 'Uh. *Oui*, that sounds *tres bon*.' Aunt Jeanne just tutted and served the tea.

The next day, as they approached the western facade of Notre Dame, Leo stood back to appreciate the Gothic cathedral that he had heard so much about.

At ground level, there were three arched portals with beautifully carved figures in concentric arches as if you needed to peel back layers before entering the church. Above these entrances, grand statues of kings watched those who entered below.

On the next level, a large rose window. The facade was topped by two truncated towers that Leo thought gave a strange unfinished air to the cathedral, as if they were missing spire fingers trying to touch God, being left with stubby thumbs instead.

Rose tugged at his arm. They walked past the statues and entered the vast cavern of the candlelit cathedral.

He felt instantly small, dwarfed by the rows of massive round pillars supporting the enormous cross-ribbed, vaulted ceiling. The row of columns and arches drew his eye to where a rainbow of stained glass should have been above the nave. Instead of the three huge rose windows giving a kaleidoscope of colour to the transept, the precious stained glass had been removed. After Germany's big guns had fired on Paris, the windows were now a plain yellow glass for the duration of the war.

It didn't seem to matter. The cathedral was still stunning. A floaty awe ... his soul was pulling him away from the world ... deeper into himself ... peace washed over him.

When he looked at Rose standing next to him, he felt the calm energy encompass her too and they merged. Everything melted away. The people, the cathedral, his body. Only light was left. Only love.

'What are you doing, Leo? Are you well?'

The cool stone of the floor on his back penetrated his uniform.

'I'm great.' He grabbed the hand Rose offered but he did not stand. He moved to one knee. She gasped. Staring deeply into her glistening eyes, he could barely get the words out.

'I love you more than life itself. I couldn't bear to lose you. Rose, will you marry me?'

Tears trickled down her cheeks and she could only nod. She dropped down to him and squeezed him tightly. French soldiers started clapping and a passing clergyman gave them a frown, but a smile tugged at the corner of his lips.

Rose released her hold and she could finally speak. 'I know I told you I didn't want to get married but ... I'd love nothing more than to marry you, Leo. Yes, yes I will marry you.'

She said *YES!* Sweet Mary and Jesus. She said yes. He had no idea how he had managed to get her to agree to marry him.

Leo's chest radiated with heat as they embraced again. His knees were beginning to ache from the pitted stone floor, so he pulled Rose upright and twirled her around. He was getting married to the most beautiful, clever, brave, sweet, loving ...

His heart was in full bloom.

Chapter Fifty-Six

Rose watched the stars ripple in the pond as she trailed her fingers in the water. The pond returned to glass and she looked up from the reflection to the diamond twinkles above them. It had to be after ten. She still found it strange that the sun set so late in France.

They hadn't said a word in the last hour, just continued strolling aimlessly about the expansive Jardin du Luxembourg. The gardens were mostly deserted save the odd couple exchanging kisses. Ghostly statues of women watched over them.

'Did you know that one is Saint Genevieve, who saved Paris from the attack of Attila and his Huns back in 451 AD?' Rose paused at the statue's pedestal. 'Sorry, I sound like a guidebook, but I wish I had more time here. I really wanted to see the Halls of Mirrors at Versailles.' Rose stroked the stone. 'I wonder if she's protecting Paris right now.'

'I hope so. I wish we had more time too. I've been trying to forget we must get back into it. I'd rather this night go on forever.' Leo guided her away from the large octagonal pond to the shadows on the fringe of a grove of lime trees. He slid her black velvet hat off, releasing her hair. Her throat jammed.

One last night ... where did those last few days go? The war would soon swallow them again. They had agreed to wait at least until after the war to get married. He wanted her to go back and study to become a doctor, but Rose wasn't sure that mattered anymore. After talking to Aunt Jeanne long until the morning hours, she had come up with another idea that might work.

Dressed in her new raspberry tulle dress with silver lace and ribbon, she could almost forget she was a nurse and picture herself on his arm going to a show at the Tivoli in Sydney. After the war.

'I don't know how I'm going to bear it without you,' Rose choked back tears.

She rubbed a painful ache in her belly. Leo held her as she dissolved into sobs.

'I'm sorry I'm being such a baby.'

He cut her off with a gentle kiss.

'I'll miss you too. I hate not knowing when I'll see you next or when this damn war will ever end. I just want to marry you and get on with our lives.'

Rose wiped her face. 'Me too,' she said with a hiccup. 'I've been thinking that. I would still like to continue my nursing but when we get back, I'd like to be a midwife. I think it would be wonderful to welcome some little souls into the world after watching so many depart.'

Leo stroked her hand. 'I think you'd make a fantastic midwife. I hope for once the saying, "It'll be over by Christmas" is true this year. It seems such a long way off.' Leo brushed her tears from her cheeks. 'We'll be so busy and tired, time will fly. We'll write and … oh, God, I just don't know what I'll do without you.'

Rose squeezed him tight then kissed him hard. Salty tears mingled with the faint taste of chocolate. Her lips locked with his and they folded down onto the privacy of the cool grass, legs entwined. He stroked her skin and she soaked in his musky scent. When would she get to kiss him again?

As he slid his hands along her arms, they prickled with goose bumps. His hand skimmed along the swell of her breast and she ached for him. Should she stop, slap him? No, instead her mouth opened, and her tongue danced with his.

He grazed her nipple through the thin fabric and circled it with his thumb until the tingle made her moan and wriggle away. Then her hands made their way under his shirt to his chest and he shivered as she made delicate strokes across his stomach.

His breath was hot and ragged as he unbuttoned a few buttons and slid his hand under her chemise. He cupped her breast and slid a hand up her thigh until his fingers found moist heat. Her hands froze and she gasped as he stroked, no longer able to kiss him.

'Oh my … Leo … I don't know if I can wait until after the war … to be married.'

Rose shuddered and moved her hand towards his belt.

'I don't know if I can either.'

Chapter Fifty-Seven

18 September 1918
Le Verguier, France

One minute to go. Clenching his jaw, Leo checked his rifle yet again and shifted the heavy weight of his rain-soaked pack. *Boom!* His body jolted and his senses sharpened. His heart hammered in time with the barrage, barely a pause between beats. The whistle blew and Leo melted into the mist and smoke. The thick early morning fog swirled as he charged into a gully that flashed with enemy shells. Like so many long-term soldiers, he seemed to know how to dodge whizzing bullets and plopping shells, but he shivered in the cold clamminess. Where was his section?

Voices seemed to call from everywhere, but he couldn't get a fix on where they were. Was he still heading in the right direction towards the first objective? He felt the slope of the ground. The bombs seemed more distant now. He squinted. There was a hedge and a few farm buildings up ahead. The mist was melting into an overcast day.

Leo sidled along the hedge before bolting across to the cottage. The rough walls were cold under his fingers. He opened a broken shutter and climbed through. The farmhouse was a simple affair with whitewashed walls, stone floors and rafters on the ceiling. The inhabitants had packed all they could, leaving only a few wooden tables and chairs. Leo wished he could light a fire in the large fireplace.

He crept up the simple wooden stairs to a tiny bedroom. Silence. He threw his pack down. The walls were left their natural mottle of slate and nutmeg stone. There was nothing left in the room but a wooden dresser, the wooden frame of a bed with no mattress and an old rocking chair.

Maybe he could wait here until the fog lifted and then get his bearings. Leo settled into the chair, the rhythmic sway almost soothing his guilt. Well, he could hardly wander around like a lost sheep, now could he?

He felt around in his pockets for the couple of squares of chocolate he had saved and came across a half-carved kookaburra he'd started for Dot. He figured she could put it next to the one he'd already given her and feel closer to him. He ached to be there with her. To smell the eucalyptus, taste the lemon pudding, touch the grapevine leaves, feel the warm kiss of Aussie sun on his cheek. But most of all see his family's faces again. He stopped rocking and wiped his face.

Crack! Hell! Was that coming from inside the cottage?

Leo's breath came in bursts as he eyed the oak door. He grabbed his rifle and crept towards it.

'*Wir fanden diese ein Außen, er verlor.*'

Leo's heart pumped up another notch. Shit! Germans were in the cottage and they'd grabbed an Aussie. Leo's gut formed French winter ice. That could have been him.

'Here, stop going through my stuff. Have this. We are going to sit tight once we get to the brown line here and then in an hour or so we'll storm the red line here. That's what you want, isn't it?'

Bugger. He'd recognise that high pitched whine anywhere. It was Alfred. The idiot had taken his orders into the field and was blabbing everything. Some sergeant he turned out to be. Becoming a POW was obviously not in his grand plan of rising to lieutenant or getting his precious medal. Was he hoping they'd let him go for cooperating?

'Come on, let me go,' Alfred whined.

'*Er ist eine Schande. Keiner von den anderen Offizieren tat dies. Geh und hol Karl.*'

Leo translated their rapid-fire German in his head. 'He's a disgrace. None of the other officers did this.'

Leo kept his ear to the door and prayed they wouldn't come upstairs. Their gruff voices made the German sound so harsh. He listened carefully.

'There are more of us than them. They won't break through this outpost to the line.'

'These Australians are like bezerkers, nothing stops them.'

Were the Germans concerned this stunt might work? If they could crack the outpost, they'd finally get through to the infamous Hindenburg Line and then ...

'I've given you what you need, now let me go,' Alfred demanded. He was trying to sound indignant, but Leo heard the shaky thread of fear.

'You stay quiet.' A soldier told Alfred in English and then rumbled on in German. 'Addie's giving up leave to find his dog. He's mad. Here comes *Oberleutnant* Herrmann, he can deal with this *Dummkopf.*' The soldier's tone had shifted from lazy conversational to military in a few words. Was it that they respected this Lieutenant Herrmann, or did they fear him?

A loud squeak grated on Leo's ears.

'*Was! Wie hast du ihn gefunden? Dies ist der Hund, der mein Bruder getötet.*'

Leo's ragged breath stopped. Had he heard that right? The soldier who must be the lieutenant had sounded both astounded and angry. His words became a German/English cocktail in Leo's mind. 'What? How did you find him? This is the bastard that killed my brother.'

Alfred was toast. Leo chewed his lip.

'What should we do with him?' a soldier asked.

'Torture and kill him.' Lieutenant Herrmann did not hesitate.

'Take him to the barn.'

'What are you doing? Where are you taking me?' Alfred squeaked.

Leo heard their boots click on the stone, a door open and slam shut, then gravel crunching outside. He should leave, run while he had the chance.

Herrmann's flat tone saying, 'Torture and kill him' reverberated around Leo's brain and his gut sank. Could he live with himself knowing he'd left one of his own behind ... to die like that? But it was Alfred, he's given away secret orders and he was a piece of—.

Damn it. He couldn't do it. He couldn't leave Alfred to be tortured.

Leo sucked in a breath and shifted silently down the stairs. He clambered back out of the window, checked and darted over to the barn. All the shutters and doors were open, so Leo chanced a peek through a side door. The Germans and Alfred were all facing away towards the farm cottage so Leo slipped in and hid behind a tractor and plough.

He couldn't tell if the rumble in the distance was guns or thunder, but he hoped it would mask the jagged breath that was coming so fast his head was spinning. He rested his hand on the rusty rim of the tractor wheel and tried not to choke on the petrol fumes. He needed to calm down, get his head straight.

'You don't remember me, do you?' A broad-shouldered German asked in perfect English as he shoved Alfred and circled him. Two other burly soldiers stood guard. Leo held his gasp. Leo recognised that dark expression of hate. This man had sworn revenge and now he was going to get it.

'No,' Alfred answered. He tugged at his collar.

'Perhaps you remember my brother. He was just a boy. He had glasses, green eyes. No?'

Leo was right. It *was* the brother of the POW that Alfred had murdered. Maybe Alf deserved what was coming.

Herrmann slashed Alfred's pockets with a bayonet. 'You seemed to enjoy searching him … "ratting him" as you call it.'

Alfred's face paled.

'Ah, perhaps you do remember. You were rather careless with your bayonet.' He slashed Alfred's arm. Alfred screamed and it echoed in Leo's head long after Alfred's mouth closed. Lieutenant Herrmann pointed his bayonet tip towards Alfred's belly. The pungent smell of urine mingled with aged wood and musty earth. Leo pulled his head back and leaned against the steel wheel. It stank of manure.

Leo had often imagined humiliating and hurting Alf. Imagined enjoying it. But this just left him feeling wretched. A crack and an anguished cry. The Germans laughed. Leo looked and saw Alfred holding his gushing nose.

'Just kill me.' Blood sprayed from his lips as he spoke.

'We will. When I am ready.'

'Ooof!' Alfred crumpled to the ground. He was no match for those boots. Snap. A rib?

Leo couldn't watch. Or listen. Frozen again, just like when Harry had attacked that poor girl and he'd done nothing. Doing nothing to help that girl continued to haunt him. Mind, that girl had deserved his help. Did Alfred?

The muscles in his neck squeezed like a vice. What should he do? What *could* he do?

An image of his mother's fingers holding tight to her crucifix came to him. She'd raised him to be true to his heart and war couldn't change that. Alfred might not be his mate, but no one deserved to be tortured. He set his jaw and gripped the cold metal of his rifle. With a dog-growling rumble, the sky released its load and Leo heard the plink of drops hitting the tractor from a leak in the roof. With any luck, the noise would mask him fiddling with his gun.

As one of them aimed another boot, Leo released his shot. They all froze and stared at the leg now oozing blood. One fired a shot towards the tractor as Leo reloaded. Shit! Shit! Shit! He returned fire and watched another soldier do a contorted dance of pain as he clutched his leg and hopped from the shed. Herrmann gave a furtive glance at the tractor and followed the wounded out into the sheets of rain.

Leo charged over, grabbed Alfred and dragged his moaning body behind some crates, dressing his wounded arm as best he could.

'Alfred. Alf.' He slapped Alfred's pale face.

'What the—' Alfred's eyes lit up then narrowed. 'It's you.'

'Yes. I'm here to help. Are there more of them are in there?'

'A dozen or so.'

'Damn,' Leo uttered. Alfred wasn't up to walking yet. 'They'll be back any minute. Hide under this while I try and think of what the hell we do next.' He threw a horse blanket over Alfred.

Alfred pulled the blanket from his face. 'You should go.'

What? Alfred was telling him to go?

'No use both of us getting killed. Go on, before they come back.'

Leo gave Alfred's arm a soft punch and he winced.

'Sorry, forgot that was your bad arm. No, I'm staying.' He threw the blanket back over Alfred, shifted position behind a pile of machinery, and reloaded his rifle.

The tinkle of chains alerted him that someone was already in the barn. Blood thundered through his ears. They'd find him soon.

Cautious steps and scrapes eventually gave way to bangs as things were tossed around. Leo flinched at every bang.

'Where are they? Did they run?' the Germans asked each other.

A barrel crashed into the pile, collapsing his cover. Leo rose and shot at the first man aiming at him.

'My arm!' the soldier screamed.

The ping of bullets hitting metal followed him as he made again for the tractor. He slid under it and reloaded, cursing his fumbling fingers. He squeezed off another shot into the nearest boot. If he could just get out the door.

The ground moved beneath him.

Herrmann released his feet and yanked him up. His eyes widened and his mouth twisted into a sadistic smile.

'God is with us, *Kamerads*. This is the other one. He caused the fight.'

'Found him.'

They had Alfred again.

Leo's stomach dropped. It had all been for nothing.

They were both doomed.

Chapter Fifty-Eight

'Otto, go and get everyone. There's no reason the others should miss out on all the fun,' Herrmann ordered. He wiped his wet face and shook his jacket before turning to scrutinise Leo.

'Search him.' Rough hands dug into his pockets.

'If I remember correctly, you didn't seem to like this man much. Why would you risk your life for him?' Lieutenant Herrmann asked in clipped English.

'My mother always taught me to *die andere Wange*. He's a *Kamerad* after all.'

'This man is no one's *Kamerad*. I'm afraid I do not believe I can turn the other cheek in this case. I prefer to subscribe to an eye for an eye. Why do you speak German?' Herrmann flung Leo's things to the ground.

'My parents are German,' Leo answered. Herrman raised an eyebrow and completed his search of Leo's last pocket. A half-carved kookaburra and Dot's last letter joined the stash in the dirt.

A clatter of boots announced the arrival of more Germans. They took in the frozen scene and stood quietly.

'This man revealed his orders and has shown he is a coward and a disgrace. That, I may have forgiven, and kept him prisoner, but he did not offer that to my brother. He captured and killed him. What do you think we should do with him?' Herrmann asked, his bayonet trained on Alfred's heart. Alfred gulped and his lips trembled. Leo felt his own lips waver.

'I'd slice him into tiny pieces and feed him to the rats,' a German answered. Leo's eyes popped but he kept silent.

Herrmann turned and waved towards Leo. 'What a great idea! I'm not sure what to do with this one. He was trying to help my brother and has shown courage in defending a man he obviously detests. A better man than I am.'

The group murmured and Leo felt the stone walls shrink. He could barely breathe.

Herrmann turned on his heel. 'You are lucky today. I am much more interested in this man. I will let you go.' Karl nodded to the others and then put his face inches from Leo's. 'Just this once.'

Leo's shoulders slumped in relief.

The lieutenant indicated for the Goliath to step forward. He took Alfred's arm and shoved him to the burly man. 'You can have him. When you are done, shove the rifle up—''No!' The word was out before Leo could stop it.

Karl gave him a cold stare and stopped him gathering up his belongings. His paybook, kookaburra, rabbit's foot, Rose's handkerchiefs were to be left behind.

'It is time for you to go before I change my mind.'

Alfred gave him a desperate yet hopeful look. Leo grimaced in apology.

'Why do *you* get to leave? *What* did you tell them? You traitorous bastard!' Alfred's face was purple. Goliath let go of his arm and belted him across the head. Alfred swayed and dropped to the ground.

'Go!'Herrmann pushed Leo out of the barn.

Leo stumbled into the rain, a free man. He vomited into the hedge. He had to hurry and get help.

***

An hour later and he was still wandering around. Where was his platoon? Where was anyone? He had to get a rifle.

The rain had eased, and Leo squinted into the swirls of smoke and dense fog lit only by the flickering glow of exploding shells. He stumbled and when his hands touched the mud, he felt another clammy hand. He must be in no man's land. That would mean a rifle had to be here somewhere. Bulky grey forms parted the mist and charged straight at him. Germans. His gulping breath caught in his throat and his heart lurched.

The tables had turned and Alfred and George had rifles aimed at the Germans who had captured Alfred. The ground trembled with the thud of heavy boots. German POWs dodged past him with hands raised above their heads. How in the hell had they captured them?

Thwack! A whizzing bullet found his yielding flesh. Molten heat seared his stomach and Leo crumpled into the sticky morass. He felt the tremor of shock.

George gasped when he saw Leo bleeding into the mud.

'It's just murder out here, isn't it?' Alfred chuckled.

A spasm of pain shot through him and Leo could only utter a groan in reply.

'You shot him! Have you gone bloody mad?' George began to pull his field dressing out. Alfred gripped his arm.

'He's a traitor. I don't know what he plotted with this lot, but they let him go. So, I'm just going to leave him for dead like he left me.'

The POWs squelched nervously in the mud. Herrmann shrugged his shoulders at Leo.

George looked ill. 'I don't want any of this, Alf.'

Leo flopped about in the mud, unable to release himself from its tenacious grip. Alfred gave George a warning poke with his bayonet and nudged Leo's sinking boot. 'Looks like you won't be getting Rose after all.'

A shell shrieked beyond them and landed with a shudder.

'Time to go. Or maybe they'd like to join their new *Kamerad.*' He poked a blue-eyed soldier. The soldier lifted his chin. Another shell shrieked by. Alfred held his hand up. 'Let's move. So long, Leopold.' Alfred gave him a mock salute before urging the POWs on.

Leo heard them squelch away and he sank into the mud.

He could hear another wounded digger in the field start to croon.

Somewhere a soul is drifting,
Further and further apart,
Somewhere my love lies dreaming,
Somewhere a broken heart.

Was he about to break Rose's heart? Pain spiked through him and his neck tingled. He had to fix this and get to Rose. Something was wrong … really wrong.

'Alf! What are you doing?'

Leo lifted his leaden head and once his swimming vision cleared, he saw in the distance that George's arms were raised. Alfred's rifle was pointed at his head. Surely, he wouldn't.

Leo spotted a rifle poking up from the mud at his feet. How had he missed that earlier? Holding his belly, Leo slithered and elbowed his way around until his fingers latched onto the barrel. His breath caught in a wash of nauseous pain. Herrmann's eyes locked with his as Leo raised the rifle and took aim.

Chapter Fifty-Nine

The scent of lavender was overpowering. Rose's beautiful smile hovered over him and then she faded into the gloom.

'Here he is,' Harry said.

A bolt of pain jolted him awake. The stretcher bearer had thin, wiry arms that gathered him up.

'You'll be okay, mate.' He had the soothing tone of a tending mother. They loaded him onto a sticky stretcher and Leo noticed the almost imperceptible nod the stretcher bearer gave Harry. Harry's eyes softened and watered, his Adam's apple bobbing. They lifted him and started jostling forward. Leo felt like someone was trying to brand him like a cow on the tender flesh of his gut, but everywhere else was cold.

'Harry? Alf shot—.' The pain was so sharp Leo was lost for breath.

'I know, chum, settle down,' Harry said as he looked down on him from his end of the stretcher.

Leo groaned and closed his eyes. He felt empty. His eyes snapped open.

'I need to see Rose.'

Harry frowned and plodded on.

'It's important. Take me to the 2nd CCS,' Leo choked out. He had to see her.

'Sorry, we can't,' the stretcher bearer said over his shoulder. 'It's been bombed. They're on the move, but they will be along this way. We'll get you to the 12th.'

Harry wouldn't look at him. 'I'll see if I can get word to her.'

Finally, they loaded him into a lorry and Leo looked around. It was full of bodies. Not a good sign.

'Sorry about this, they ran out room.' Harry got in and the lorry roared into life.

A bump tossed him against hard metal and he gritted his teeth against the pain. It dislodged a blanket from the face of the man across from him. The waxen features were distorted but there was no mistaking that face. It was Alfred.

'Yep, he's dead, chum. He got his,' Harry told him. The fog cleared in Leo's brain and he tried to ignore the waves of arctic ice numbing his body.

'I was following Alf and George with those POWs. They were having a barney over Alfred taking a pot shot at you. The rotten beggar was going to take George and the POWs out too, so I shot him first. At least, I think I did. There were shots coming from all directions. Bull caught up and we decided to let the POWs go so we could get you sorted.'

Harry squeezed Leo's hand.

It didn't matter anymore. Nothing mattered. Just Rose.

'I need to find Rose … can you let her know?'

'Sure, said I would. Listen, I'm sorry about all of that. You two belong together so you'd better get well so I can be your best man.' Harry's eyes glistened.

'You already are.'

The lorry bumped and lurched through a pothole. Leo sucked in his breath and closed his eyes and didn't open them again until men unloaded him among the wounded. Harry sprinted off. Leo tried to sit up. It was no use; he was stuck to the stretcher, held fast by his own blood.

He gazed up at the iridescent streaks of cloud and watched them glow golden then deepen into melon and tangerine. A skylark let out a series of chirps and trills somewhere close by as it farewelled another day. Then, when it flew into the sky, Leo could see it circling for a moment, then it soared above him. At the front, it seemed you only needed to look up to be reminded of the beauty still left in the world.

Leo closed his heavy eyes and laid his hand on his heart that was beating slower and slower. His breath was fast and shallow. So, this was what death was like …

An astringent scent … lavender … filled his nostrils. A soft hand gripped his and floaty warmth tingled through his icy body. He opened his eyes one last time.

'Rose. You're here.'
She kissed him tenderly on his muddy cheek.
'Of course, I am. *Je t'aime pour toujours.*'
'I love you forever too.'

***

'Noooooooo,' someone was moaning.
A guttural moan.
That went on and on.
Please be quiet.

Everything was foggy.
It was her moaning.
Something stabbed her heart.
Was she dying?

Leo had been shot.
She'd held Leo's hand.
He told her he loved her …

Her heart shuddered, then her brain snapped into gear.
She would use every ounce of her to save this man.

Epilogue

The vineyard glittered with raindrops in the wash of a sun shower. Rose closed her arms around Leo's back, and he dropped his pick, turning into her embrace.

'What brings you down here?' he asked as he nuzzled her neck.

She laughed and pushed him away. 'Dot dropped in to tell me Adelaide is ready to pop.'

He grinned. 'I'll go and keep Bull company. Might tell him to give it a break before he adds to the footy team. Do you reckon it might be a girl this time?'

Rose shrugged. 'I have no idea. No matter how many expecting mothers I attend to, I am absolutely hopeless at getting that right.'

He stroked her belly. 'Make sure you take it easy; you look about ready to pop yourself.'

Rose swatted his arm. 'I've got plenty of time yet.'

She took his hand, and they made their way back to their cosy homestead. As Leo paused to look back on the vineyard, she stroked his fingers. She knew that sometimes he was caught by a flash. The neat, uniform rows reminded him of the crosses he had planted in France graveyards. The hardest one to leave had been Harry's. Those last months had been hard. Both had volunteered to stay behind and mop up.

Looking for, and digging up, corpses to be laid to rest in newly formed cemeteries had perhaps taken more of a toll on him than the adrenalin sapping battles.

'I forgot to tell you, Father wrote and asked me to thank you. He is finding his time with Dr Springthorpe most rewarding. He never would have thought to investigate treating shell-shocked men if it hadn't been for you. He plans to be back in time for the birth of his grandchild.' Rose collected up her midwife bag, which Leo took from her.

'Remind him to take a break from work and go and see the sights of London while he's there. The Tower of London can be full of all kinds of treasures.'

Rose kissed him then climbed onto the buggy. She gazed out over the sunlit plains. There they were, trotting along like any ordinary couple. And they were—ordinary people who had answered the call with courage to do extraordinary things. Her hand rested on her belly. She hoped her baby would be blessed with a peaceful life, but if not, then have the lion heart of his or her parents to meet whatever challenges lay ahead.

Acknowledgements

Writing a novel is a labour of love that needs many a midwife to birth it into the world.

There have been many who have offered their skill, support, and encouragement along the way.

Arna Radovich and Itu Taito have been my biggest fellow writer cheerleaders right from the start, sharing their wisdom, kind words and came along for the bumpy emotional journey. I would have given up if they had not been there to prod me along. They ploughed through many a draft of this novel, listened to my moaning and groaning, and cheered me up when my skill did not match my vision. Arna is always sharing the opportunities available and encouraging me to get out of my comfort zone. I would not have entered competitions or done live readings without her generous support.

Other writers had added their encouragement, and I am grateful to them (many from Fiona McIntosh's Masterclass group). Thanks go to Beth Amos for reading my terrible drafts and offering her thoughts and suggestions, along with a dose of support. To Angela Long for writerly support, including weekends away at her place and Emma Blackett-Notley who did not like historical fiction, but read mine anyway.

Cathie Tasker and Sarah Armstrong, both mentored me through my early years and this manuscript, giving me the confidence to move forward with my writing as well as invaluable advice/feedback. Julie Guthrie gave the draft its final polish with lightning speed. Fiona McIntosh has been a guide and believer in my writing. I love her energy, enthusiasm, and her selfless giving to the aspiring authors of Australia.

My daughter, Brooke once complained that this novel was demanding as much attention from me as having a toddler. My writing journey began along with the start of her adolescence, so while at first, she resented the time and energy I gave to writing, she was always a huge supporter. I was never more thrilled than her enjoying my writing and being proud of me. To my son, Zac, for not rolling his eyes when I started another family history story related to war and being proud of my creativity.

To my husband, Darren, who has watched yet another weird all-consuming passion of mine go for years and take much time and money to develop. Thank you for your patience.

Thanks to Mum and Dad for instilling a love of reading in me. To you, Mum, for listening to me babble on and for supporting me with such generosity when you thought it was needed. I really appreciate it.

To the rest of my family and friends (yes, Kathy- I did not forget you), it takes a tribe of people to listen to you (and not make fun of you) when you share a dream. Thanks for listening. To Wendy, for reading them all (now you have to start my fan club).

To you, the reader. Thank you for taking the time to read *The Heart of War*.

Jen x

If you'd like more information, or to say hi, reach out via www.jenkingsford.com.